INTRIGUE

Seek thrills. Solve crimes. Justice served.

Crash Landing
Janice Kay Johnson

Cold Murder In Kolton Lake
R. Barri Flowers

T0363010

MILLS & BOON

CRASH LANDING
© 2024 by Janice Kay Johnson
Philippine Copyright 2024
Australian Copyright 2024
New Zealand Copyright 2024

First Published 2024
First Australian Paperback Edition 2024
ISBN 978 1 867 90555 0

COLD MURDER IN KOLTON LAKE
© 2024 by R. Barri Flowers
Philippine Copyright 2024
Australian Copyright 2024
New Zealand Copyright 2024

First Published 2024
First Australian Paperback Edition 2024
ISBN 978 1 867 90555 0

MIX
Paper | Supporting
responsible forestry
FSC® C001695

Published by
Harlequin Mills & Boon
An imprint of Harlequin Enterprises (Australia) Pty Limited
(ABN 47 001 180 918), a subsidiary of HarperCollins
Publishers Australia Pty Limited
(ABN 36 009 913 517)
Level 19, 201 Elizabeth Street
SYDNEY NSW 2000 AUSTRALIA

Cover art used by arrangement with Harlequin Books S.A.. All rights reserved.

Printed and bound in Australia by McPherson's Printing Group

Crash Landing

Janice Kay Johnson

MILLS & BOON

An author of more than ninety books for children and adults with more than seventy-five for Harlequin, **Janice Kay Johnson** writes about love and family and pens books of gripping romantic suspense. A *USA TODAY* bestselling author and an eight-time finalist for the Romance Writers of America RITA® Award, she won a RITA® Award in 2008. A former librarian, Janice raised two daughters in a small town north of Seattle, Washington.

Visit the Author Profile page
at millsandboon.com.au.

DEDICATION

For Pat aka Alexis Morgan,
an amazing friend and plotting partner

CAST OF CHARACTERS

Gwen Allen—A paramedic with a helicopter rescue service, Gwen isn't supposed to be on the flight that goes so terribly wrong. But how much worse would it all have been if she had listened to her doubts and refused to board?

Rafe Salazar—A DEA agent who has been undercover with a drug cartel for over a year, Rafe is badly wounded when the location of his safe house is betrayed. Snatched out of the hospital, he might survive only thanks to the paramedic he wants to trust.

Bruce Kimball—Also a DEA agent, Kimball has begun to have second thoughts about his future. One big payoff could change everything.

Bill Thomson—A former military helicopter pilot, Bill is a new hire with the rescue service. He doesn't quite understand all the rules yet, or see why making a small exception could lead to deadly consequences.

Ron Zabrowsky—Salazar's supervisor in the DEA is stunned by what almost has to be an internal betrayal, and then having his injured agent—whose testimony is critical to bring down a drug trafficking organization—simply disappear off the face of the earth.

Chapter One

Gwen Allen inhaled the powerful smell of hot jet fuel as she walked across the tarmac toward one of the two helicopters parked near the long, low building that served as the base for EMS Flight, the helicopter rescue service she worked for. Her small rolling suitcase bumped along with her, and her enormous tote bag weighed heavily on her shoulder.

Her home base with EMS Flight was just outside Seattle, but she'd spent a week visiting a good friend from college in Yakima, Washington, on the dry side of the Cascade mountains. The very dry side. Heat radiated off the paved surface and it felt as if it were baking any exposed skin to leather. Within her fire-retardant Nomex suit, she was even hotter. She'd enjoyed a few days of sunshine—Seattle was having an unusually cool July—but she wouldn't want to live and work in this climate. Imagine how blistering August and September would be! Still, she was glad she'd been able to borrow the suit and a helmet from the locker of a nurse who was taking maternity leave.

Eyes on the two Bell helicopters painted with the familiar red and green stripes against an overall white, Gwen felt like skipping. A week ago, she'd gotten lucky enough to hitch a ride over with a coworker driving to Spokane, almost to the Idaho border, but she'd planned to either buy an airline ticket or hop a Greyhound bus for her return. Wonder of wonders, a guy in base dispatch had called yesterday to let her know they were transferring a helicopter to her base on a temporary basis to replace one that would be out for much-needed maintenance. Someone had mentioned she was in Yakima and planning to travel back at about the right time. Did she want a ride? She'd be alone with the pilot, no patient to monitor.

Of course, she could have afforded to pay for the trip home, but this way, she could tuck a few more dollars into her dream fund.

Only, to her puzzlement, an ambulance had just pulled up behind the Bell 419 helicopter she thought was supposed to be her ride, and as she watched, EMTs from the ambulance unloaded a patient packaged on a backboard and transferred him or her to the helicopter.

Nobody at all stood by the second helicopter.

Probably that pilot had already done his pre-flight and retreated back into the building, and she was heading for the wrong one.

She took out her phone to check the time. They were supposed to lift off five minutes from now.

She'd been a paramedic with EMS Flight for two years now after working on an ambulance and in the emergency department at Swedish Hospital in Seattle. She'd studied hard for the certifications required. She loved her job and the adrenaline boost with every rescue. The thing was, among her coworkers, she liked order and the certainty she could absolutely rely on them.

If that was her helicopter, the pilot had probably taken a last-minute restroom run, something she'd just done, too. In prep for the flight to Seattle, she'd restricted her fluid intake, too. She was fussing. Not like they were in any hurry.

The patient was now on board the helicopter right in front of her, the door closed. The rotors weren't turning yet, so she presumed the man in the Nomex suit sewn with the company patch was the pilot. The other guy wore chinos and a denim shirt open over a T-shirt. Who was *he*? Friend or family of the patient?

She'd almost reached them when they noticed her. The second guy moved fast to intercept her. His body language was weirdly aggressive enough that she had the sense he was blocking her.

"What are you doing out here?" he demanded.

"Is this the helicopter going to Seattle?"

"Who are you?" he asked impatiently.

By most women's standards, he was handsome. Sandy brown hair, square jaw, tall, nice shoulders. Gwen did not like the cold, verging-on-hostile way he was eyeing her.

"A paramedic with EMS Flight," she said shortly. She tapped the logo patch on her shoulder that said EMS followed by a bird in flight. "Who are *you*?"

Instead of answering, he turned just enough to wave the pilot over. "Bill?"

This man, somewhere around forty years old, was friendly looking, thin, with military-short hair, which didn't surprise her. Many of the pilots were ex-military. Knowing the training and experience they brought with them inspired a level of trust in the nurses, EMTs and paramedics who relied on their expertise.

She held out her hand. "Gwen Allen, a paramedic with EMS Flight, but out of Seattle."

"Oh, ah. We were told the nurse scheduled to fly with us couldn't make it. We were just talking about what to do."

"You're the pilot?"

"Yes. Sorry. Bill Thomson."

"Then...this isn't the helicopter being transferred to Seattle?"

"Yeah, it is," he said readily. "That's our end goal, but we, uh, kind of got hijacked." He nodded toward Mr. Unpleasant. "Law enforcement. I'm new with EMS Flight, but I'm told we try to help out whenever any LEA asks for help."

That was true, but law enforcement agencies typically called when they had a severely injured victim that needed quick transport with expert care. They didn't "hijack" a flight.

"So," she said, still trying to understand, "you don't have a nurse or paramedic, but you do have a patient?"

"That's right."

"We don't need a medical attendant," Mr. Unfriendly said. "We're transporting a man who had surgery some hours ago. He's stable. I'm assured there's no reason to expect a problem. I'm an agent with the Drug Enforcement Administration, and we want him moved to Seattle, get him checked out so he can be transferred to where he belongs."

The distaste and heightened hostility in his voice made it seem as if this patient was, if not dangerous, someone whose crimes were contemptible. A recent arrest, presumably.

Bill's phone rang, then hers. She glanced at

the number. Dispatch. She let the call go to voice mail, but saw that Bill had half turned away and was talking on his phone, his gaze staying on her. He gave her a nod.

She concentrated on the circumstances. This wouldn't be the first time the patient her team had rushed to pick up was someone who'd be placed under arrest—if he survived grave wounds. She'd given her all to save the life of many a street criminal.

"What kind of surgery?" she asked.

"He took two bullets."

She waited. No more information was apparently forthcoming.

"If I'm going to handle his or her care on this flight, I'll need to know more."

"His. But I told you. We don't—"

"You do," she interrupted, making sure there was no give in her voice. "The company does not allow a helicopter carrying a patient to take off without trained medical personnel on board." She shifted her gaze, raising her eyebrows. Fortunately, Bill had ended his call. "Isn't that right, Bill?"

"That's what I was just telling Agent Kimball," he agreed with a sidelong glance at his companion. "That was dispatch on the phone," he added. "I've only been with the company a month, though, and have never run into a situation like this. Er, Agent Kimball plans to fly with us."

"Salazar needs to remain under supervision by a law enforcement agent," Kimball said. "If he breaks free, you couldn't handle him."

"Okay," she said. "Where are you taking him?"

"The university hospital in Seattle."

The teaching hospital in Seattle was definitely where you wanted to go if you had any unusual problems. But if this guy had come out of surgery in good enough shape that his surgeon had anticipated no problems and okayed a long and uncomfortable helicopter flight, why send him there?

For someone who liked to be prepared, she had a lot of qualms: Was there even a trauma bag on board? If so, who had packed it? Before they lifted off from the ground, she could hustle to do some of her preflight checks, but there were half a dozen tasks she always completed at the start of her shift so there were no later surprises. She started running through potential issues in her mind. Had the levels of oxygen in the tanks been checked? Unexpectedly running out *was* a major crisis. Plugs and inverter functioning? Were they stocked on batteries for handheld devices? This would be an unusually long flight. EKG patches…

She cut herself off. The pilot had seen the patient, so she wasn't relying a hundred percent on Agent Kimball saying the guy was in peachy keen condition. The EMTs on the ambulance must not have been concerned, or they'd have waited to do an in-person handover.

And, hey, she'd not only get a free ride home, the company would now have to pay her for her services. That made her feel a little more cheerful. No reason to think there'd be any issues.

Famous last words, a voice whispered in her head. She ignored it.

"Fine," she said. "Then let's get on our way."

There was a short silence that felt…odd. Gwen didn't know how to read it. Neither man looked at each other, yet she had the weird sense that they were conferring, anyway. Maybe she *didn't* want to get on this helicopter, especially without having done her own preflight check.

Except…there was a patient who needed her. Besides, working with people who were new hires or pains in the butt wasn't out of the ordinary, and cops she dealt with at accident or crisis sites were given to being dictatorial with the medical team, wanting to give orders when that was no longer their place. The fact that she found DEA agent Kimball annoying was no reason to refuse to do her job *and* get a free— no, paid!—ride home.

"Works for me." Bill sounded agreeable, and

his wink at her was reassuring, hinting that he, too, found Kimball difficult.

"Fine," Kimball grumbled. "What's one more?"

Normally, if she were heading a team, she'd ride up front next to the pilot, in part to watch for potential hazards in the air and at a landing site. Of course, in that case, there would also be a nurse or EMT at the side of the patient.

Even as they walked the short distance to board the helicopter, she made up her mind: she was staying in back with the man who definitely needed monitoring and might need intercession. Agent Kimball could sit up front, where she mostly wouldn't be able to see a face that radiated impatience and irritation as much as the vast paved tarmac did heat.

Maybe, it occurred to her, he'd been relegated to what he considered to be scut work and resented it. After all, how challenging was accompanying a semiconscious, restrained man? She could give him a break.

RAFE HAD NO idea what was happening to him. He had a vague notion that he was in recovery at the hospital, except for some reason, he'd been trussed up like a Christmas tree ready to be stuffed in the rear hatch of a car to be sure branches weren't broken.

He opened his eyes and felt a surge of panic.

Why couldn't he see anything? He hadn't been blinded, had he? He tried to lift a hand to his face, but a tight restraint kept him from raising his arm. A minute ago, whatever he was lying on had tilted upright enough that he'd tried to grab for purchase, but then it leveled off.

The reason he should be—would have sworn he *was*—in the hospital flashed in jerky movements as if filmed with a handheld camera that often wasn't pointing the way it should be.

Knock on the front door; Eaton muting the TV and going to the door to look through the peephole. Stanton was there, too. Rafe saw him stiffen and unsnap his holster. They weren't expecting anyone. But Eaton immediately relaxed and unlocked and then started to open the door.

"Hey." Clearly, he knew the visitor. "What are you doing here?"

A burst of gunfire. Stanton yelling, "Run," as bullets sprayed the living room. Rafe leaped to his feet, bounced off the wall in the hall and spun into a bedroom. Smashed a chair through the window and dove out, a lilac bush scratching him as he fell. One arm useless. He rolled, seeing a man framed by the window he'd just thrown himself out of. More gunfire. Bullets struck his torso, and his body repeatedly jerked. Nothing hurt yet, but it would. Why had he been so complacent, he wasn't carrying this evening? Were his bodyguards down? Must be.

Voices raised, sirens. He couldn't see anyone through the jagged-edged windowpane now. Couldn't help closing his eyes.

It was all vivid but chaotic.

Didn't help him understand where he was now or why.

Then everything around him began to vibrate.

THE TWO MEN seemed to be engaged in a low-voiced intense conversation from the minute they took their seats in front. But Bill did turn his attention to business because the engines fired up.

After stowing her suitcase out of the way, Gwen scanned the cabin as she hurried through some of what should have been preflight checks, and her gaze caught on the surprising sight of what appeared to be a fully loaded backpack with a sleeping bag tied on. She tugged to be sure it was adequately wedged in so it wouldn't become a missile if the flight turned out to be turbulent. *Is it Bill's?* she wondered idly, then put it out of her mind.

She leaned over the patient to make a quick evaluation of his condition before she flipped through his chart. To look at his dressings, she'd have to pull back blankets, but that meant first undoing straps that kept him immobilized. That could wait. He wasn't on oxygen, but she considered putting him on it. Better to be preventative than to react to trouble. What surprised her was that thick foam plugs had been inserted in his ears, and a black mask covered his eyes. She hoped somebody had explained what they were doing before depriving him of two major senses. There were reasons why it was sometimes a good idea, but... He might freak if he'd still been in a hazy postanesthetic state and now surfaced to find himself blind and deaf.

She glanced at the manila envelope with a sticker on the front identifying him as one Rafael Salazar. Hair very dark, maybe black, disheveled and spiky from whatever he'd been through. Skin darker than hers that stretched over sharp cheekbones. Dark stubble on a strong jaw. Probably a good-looking guy. It was hard to be sure under the circumstances and didn't matter, anyway.

Besides...criminal, she reminded herself, even as instinct had her smoothing his hair back from his forehead.

She made herself take her own seat and belted herself in. Borrowed helmet—check. Somewhere in her bag were her own earplugs, but she didn't always wear them, and that could wait.

Normally, part of her job was handling four radio frequencies, although today not quite as many would be required. The pilot had several, too. Right now, she had to wait for the intercom to come on to talk to him.

"Gwen?" Bill's voice came in her ears. "Barring any problem, I'll need you to let me handle radio communications once we've lifted off. Agent Kimball is insistent that we stay off the air as much as possible. The agency would just as soon no one knows who we're transporting or where he's being taken. Or even that we have a federal agent on board."

Her forehead crinkled. It wasn't as if she'd have chatted on the radio about her patient, and they were still required to connect with local controllers along the way in part to make sure there were no midair collisions. This flight had been scheduled to be routine. Why would anyone, hearing them confirm altitude, direction or ETA—destination, for that matter—suspect for a moment that they carried a federal agent and his prisoner? Did Agent Kimball think they'd be shot out of the sky if the wrong people learned who was aboard?

Ridiculous.

As for the radio, a former military pilot would probably be accustomed to handling complex communications, or he wouldn't sound so casual about it.

Still, the unusual request ratcheted up Gwen's unease. Company policy was that if any member of the team felt strongly that the flight wouldn't be safe—usually because of expected severe weather—and refused to go, the mission was canceled, and the helicopter stayed grounded. Period. In these circumstances, Gwen could demand an okay from someone higher up the chain of authority.

Feeling vaguely unsettled didn't justify that step, she decided. Honestly, if Agent Kimball had been friendly and more open with her, she wouldn't be as uneasy as she was.

"Sure, Bill," she said. "Let me know if you need me to jump on."

"Will do." He still sounded cheerful. The pilots she knew best were happiest in the air or maneuvering to land at a tricky site.

She double-checked her seat belt and the patient's restraints, then felt the helicopter lift off. She remembered her terror on her first flights when she looked at the radio console, with a zillion buttons and switches. Like most newbies, she'd made mistakes. Today...she could switch most of them off. Why listen if she was supposed to keep her mouth shut?

Over the noise of the engines, she couldn't

even hear Bill confirm departure with base dispatch, but she could see him at an oblique angle. He was talking into his mic, seeming relaxed.

As the ground below them receded, she felt some of her usual excitement. No, they weren't racing to the scene of an auto accident where cops were even now employing the Jaws of Life to pry someone out of a dangerously compressed space, or aiming to pick up a mountain climber who'd fallen and suffered unknown injuries, or collecting a kid who'd been shot while playing with a gun.

Her gaze rested again on the man who lay within hand's reach—the man who *had* been shot twice. By the cops trying to arrest him? Clearly, she was never going to know.

Oxygen? she asked herself again. It wouldn't hurt anything, and even if it wasn't otherwise needed, it combated nausea and motion sickness.

Studying him, she was troubled to see movement, as if he were fighting against the restraints. No matter what, he had to remain secured in case of unexpected turbulence, but she could talk to him.

She could see part of the back of Kimball's head and one ear, but he couldn't get a good look at what she was doing. So she leaned forward, eased the foam plug from the patient's ear and spoke as close to it as possible. As it was, she had to raise her voice to have any chance of being heard.

"How are you doing? I'm Gwen, taking care of you during a helicopter ride, in case you wondered why your whole body is vibrating."

His head turned, just the slightest amount. Her lips brushed his ear.

She stole another look at Kimball, then pushed the mask up to Rafael Salazar's forehead. His eyes opened briefly. He squeezed them shut, then opened them again and stared blankly upward. Finally, he managed to focus on her face.

Those eyes were a rich brown—*dark chocolate*, she thought. He hadn't regained complete clarity postsurgery but was close to it.

He stared for so long that she repeated her introduction and explanation of where they were. "Do you understand?" she asked.

He swallowed, worked his mouth and finally spoke a single word. "Yes." Pause. "Where?"

She spoke slowly, and only after another glance to be sure Kimball couldn't see her or, presumably, hear her, given the noise made by the engines. "I understand we're transporting you to Harborview Hospital in Seattle to make sure the surgery you underwent in Yakima is all you need."

"Surgery?"

"I'm told you were shot twice. Do you remember?"

"Yeah." Another swallow. "Yes."

"Good." She smiled instead of apologizing for her choice of words. Unlikely *he* thought being shot twice was good. "Let me know if you become nauseated, hurt too much, feel anything unexpected. Okay?"

"Gwen?" A voice came through her earpieces. Bill, she realized.

"Yes?"

"Everything okay?" he asked.

"Yep."

"Agent Kimball would prefer you don't make any attempt to communicate with the patient. He says Salazar is a dangerous man."

"Mr. Salazar seemed distressed, so I took out an earplug long enough to explain where he is and reassure him. That seemed to help."

The second voice didn't surprise her. "Unless he has a medical crisis, I'm asking you to keep your distance."

She felt steam building up. That was an order, not a request.

"Whatever you want to think, I don't work for you, Agent Kimball. The patient is in my charge until I hand him off to another medical professional."

She cut off his sputtering, at least temporarily, and met Salazar's eyes again. Something had changed. That gaze was sharp and alarmed, if she was reading it right. What had she said?

She opened her mouth…and he gave his head the tiniest shake, all the restraints permitted. But she understood: he didn't want her to continue challenging Kimball or to ask what might be the wrong questions.

Chapter Two

Had he heard her right? Agent *Kimball*? Rafe's brain tried to grind itself into motion despite the rust clogging it. What would Kimball be doing here? Rafe barely knew the man and didn't much like him. Unless he'd been transferred recently, he belonged in Chicago.

Must have heard this woman wrong, Rafe decided. Gwen… Allen? Something like that. She was taking care of him. Nurse? She didn't wear scrubs. Instead, her jumpsuit looked like what a navy pilot might wear. Rafe guessed it was made out of fire-retardant fabric, which made sense if they really were in a helicopter. Now that he could exam his surroundings, albeit in a limited way, he decided that's exactly where he was. A radio console with a forest of lights, switches and what have you, barely visible out of the corner of his eye, and a window taller than it was wide that let him see bright blue sky.

He'd thought the haze in his head was clearing, but if so, it was being replaced by a different kind of confusion. At the hospital, Zabrowsky's face had hovered over his for a few minutes. Rafe's supervising special agent must have been allowed into recovery in lieu of a next of kin. Rafe thought he'd mumbled a few questions that weren't answered, but he was quite sure nothing was said about shipping him across the state.

Was he more seriously wounded than the nurse in recovery had said? Possible, but where was Zabrowsky? How was a federal agent who should be in Chicago involved in the latest mess?

Which had started because Eaton had known whoever knocked on that door. The same someone who'd burst in firing a semiautomatic weapon, who'd chased Rafe into the bedroom and tried to gun him down. Unless the person who'd come by had been followed and had also been a victim?

None of this made sense. Rafe would give a lot to have been clearer in his head when Zabrowsky came to talk to him.

He studied the woman who was presumably a nurse or EMT. She appeared to be inspecting him with equal interest.

Her smooth hair, the color of maple syrup, was pulled back from her face and disappeared

under a flight helmet. Eyes the rare gray of
a dove's feathers, not so much penetrating as
gentle. Fine-boned hands, slender build. He
guessed tall but couldn't be sure. Her face drew
him.

Would *she* answer any of his questions? He
decided to try.

"Do you know how badly I'm hurt?"

Given the racket in here, she was probably
lip-reading. She answered by bending again so
that her mouth tickled his ear.

"Two gunshot wounds. If you'll wait a minute, I can read your chart."

"Yes."

He pondered her some more as she removed
paperwork from a manila envelope and concentrated on every page. She didn't wear much if
any makeup, he decided, although that might
be the case only on the job. If she was a nurse,
she might have to deal with squirting blood and
the like, good reason not to bother with foundation or mascara. She didn't need it.

She shifted a little, setting aside a page,
and he saw the patch on the upper arm of her
Nomex suit. The letters EMS were part of a
bird in flight. He guessed they were a rescue
organization, the kind that plucked wounded
or sick people from remote or difficult positions when ground transportation to a hospital

would be too slow. He'd…encountered people from other such organizations before. Made him think of military medics. Same skill set, same personality type.

At last she raised her head, appeared to sneak a peek toward the front of the helicopter then leaned toward him.

"You took a bullet to your upper arm. That one will require physical therapy and conceivably additional surgery, because of the complexity of the rotator cuff where muscles and nerves are bundled together."

He tried for a nod but failed because his head, along with the rest of his body, was strapped down.

"Second bullet struck your thigh but missed the bone. You lost a lot of blood, though. You also have a cracked sternum and two broken ribs. I can't tell how those injuries came to be."

He could have enlightened her but chose not to. He might have been careless enough to leave his weapon in his bedroom, but he'd routinely worn a Kevlar vest, however relaxed he and his guards had become after over a month in the small ranch house in a working-class neighborhood in Yakima. Sounded like he'd be dead if he hadn't bothered with the vest.

He didn't remember noticing whether Eaton and Stanton had worn theirs. The air-conditioning only partially combated the summer heat, meaning vests weren't comfortable.

Why Yakima? Rafe wondered for probably the hundredth time. He'd barely heard of the town before getting deposited there. It had been settled on a river that joined the broad Columbia River not far downstream. These days, it was wine country, from what he understood, irrigated vineyards having supplanted other kinds of agriculture in the surrounding landscape. Wine grapes thrived in the hot, dry climate. That was the sum total of his knowledge of the town where he'd been prepared to stay for up to a year.

Gwen had flipped a couple more pages and now looked perturbed. Again, she leaned forward. "It sounds like you came through surgery with flying colors. Not sure what kind of follow-up they expect for you at Harborview, but it's a top-notch hospital, so you could have a worse destination."

Rafe only caught parts of what she said, given the engine noise. She seemed to be talking partly to herself, her puzzlement apparent.

He was becoming more aware of how much he hurt. Shouldn't he be in a hospital bed with a handy button within reach that he could push to boost the level of painkiller?

A memory niggled at him. He'd dated an ER

nurse, Nina Caldero, who said she'd worked helicopter rescue in Washington State for a few years. He thought this was the outfit she'd mentioned, which meant EMS Flight was reputable. A sense of wrongness still had Rafe's skin prickling, but he couldn't imagine Gwen or a pilot with the company cooperating in anything nefarious.

Maybe because he'd been on edge for so long—over a year now—it had become second nature to expect trouble. Literally tied down, there wasn't a damn thing he could do about it if his twitchy feeling was on target and everything was about to blow up in his face. Again. He might as well give in. The vibration and racket penetrating even the earplugs made his eyelids heavy. Maybe this would all make more sense if he slept for an hour or so.

Gwen must have thought the same or believed he'd already fallen asleep because he felt her touch as she replaced the plug in his ear. He was grateful she didn't cover his eyes again.

WATCHING THE MAN who slept beside her, Gwen began to feel a little drowsy herself. Flights weren't usually anywhere near this long. From takeoff, she'd have normally been mentally running over what equipment she'd need when they landed, what she could expect. Everyone on board would share the tension; they had a job to do, and it could go sideways in a heartbeat.

Today, she could have kicked back and admired the view from the window if it weren't for Rafael Salazar and his guard. She had a feeling Kimball wouldn't like knowing she'd talked to Salazar and began speculating even harder about why he was being taken to the hospital in Seattle. She felt sure the surgeons who'd operated on him in Yakima were competent.

She pulled a book from her tote and read for a while but found it hard to concentrate given that she also glanced up often to check on her patient. During one of those checks, some extra sense made her look out the window. Wisps of white appeared—and behind them was a sight any Washingtonian would know instantly: Mount Rainier, an active volcano that was the highest mountain in the lower forty-eight states. Black rock and glaciers forming a steep slope that plunged into the dark green of northwestern forests felt almost close enough to touch.

In other words, terrifyingly close.

Gwen snapped shut a mouth that had dropped open. As huge as the mountain was, she'd have expected a distant view of it as they crossed the

Cascade Range toward Seattle. There was no reason whatsoever they should be this close.

She used the mic to talk to Bill.

"Did you get lost?"

He chuckled. "No, Kimball wanted to see the mountain, and I didn't see any harm. We're not that far off course. Heck of a view, isn't it?"

"I'd like it better if it weren't for the clouds."

Whiteout could be a problem at higher elevations of a mountain that was over fourteen thousand feet and rose almost from sea level, unlike the Rocky Mountains. It seemed to Gwen that Bill was flirting with trouble. Micro weather events were the norm here. The National Park Service had their own resources for rescues on the mountain, including the giant Chinook helicopters from the army base, Fort Lewis, that could fly as high as the summit, which meant EMS Flight had never had reason to be in the vicinity.

Did Bill have any experience with the conditions he might meet here?

It's July, she reminded herself. Not exactly summer in the park, as it was elsewhere; snow would still be covering some trails, flowers just appearing in the meadows. She'd hiked one stretch of the Wonderland Trail that circled Mount Rainier. Eventually, she hoped to complete all of it, albeit one section at a time.

The engines sounded steady. She kept watching out the window, seeing less and less mountain, more and more clouds.

The helicopter gave an odd shudder.

Bill's voice in her ears. "Just a gust. I'm dropping in elevation."

Gwen had lost any hint of drowsiness. She sat tensely, expecting...she didn't know. The other shoe to drop in a day that was already peculiar.

"The fire light has come on," Bill suddenly snapped, a new sharpness in his voice.

She'd done the associated drills a hundred times. Her role right now was to look outside for smoke and identify where it was coming from. She all but did contortions to try to see where the trouble was, but the cloud cover had deepened, making it harder to pick out darker smoke.

"Nothing," she said. "Nothing."

"Damn it." Yes, there was mild tension in the pilot's voice, but mostly he sounded calm. A helicopter pilot with the experience he must have had to be hired by EMS Flight would remain calm and employ his every skill to, at worst, land the bird safely. "Going down," he added, confirming her suspicion. "Looking for a clear LZ."

LZ was the landing zone. Usually they'd be worrying about power wires, traffic and the competency of whatever firefighter, cop or ambulance crew had deemed a particular spot safe. Here, it would be too-steep slopes, enormous trees, tumbled boulders and lakes. Gwen wished intensely that she'd taken the seat beside Bill, where she could be of real help. That was a big part of her role, watching for unexpected trouble. What were the odds a DEA agent knew what a helicopter could handle and what would send it into a cataclysmic crash?

Instinctively, she tested the patient's restraints, then her own belt. She at least wore a helmet and a fire-retardant jumpsuit; Salazar was unlikely to have anything but scrubs on beneath the blankets that wrapped him. At least scrubs were cotton, better than fabrics that could melt into the skin.

If there was a fire, none of them were likely to survive. Even emergency medical helicopters staffed by experienced teams occasionally went down. Weather, rugged terrain, mechanical failure or a pilot's mistake could contribute. Right now, she couldn't see anything out the window except the lowering cloud cover, and the rocks and ice too close to her window.

The tail of the helicopter with the smaller rotor whipped subtly side to side.

The unusual movement had awakened the patient, whose dark eyes looked past her to a window, then fixed on her face. She sat close enough to him to remove both earplugs.

"Problem?"

"We should be fine," she shouted into his ear, "but we may have to set down. A warning light came on."

Still meeting Salazar's gaze, she sat back. "Bill?"

"We're dropping below the clouds. I think I see a potential LZ. Pretty lake. We can go fishing while we're here."

She could match his insouciance. "Just what I'd like to do today."

She heard an odd noise—somehow choked. Bill? *Please don't let him be having a heart attack, or—*

Abruptly, there was a hard thud after which they rocked, and suddenly she had the sense they were zigzagging. She automatically checked to be sure the oxygen was turned off, but of course it hadn't been on in the first place. Her patient didn't need it.

Bill had to be struggling to maintain control. What had really gone wrong? She wanted to talk to him but knew better than to distract him. Gwen focused on the view; she could see a glint of water, trees, a rocky buttress. No ideal place to set down.

And then they spun around entirely. Her fingers dug into the seat, as if she could hold herself in place. There was yelling, a screech of metal, and she knew they were down, bumping over rough ground. Her body was snapped forward, then back, and she knew vaguely that the top of the helicopter had been sheared off.

They came to a complete stop. The radio must have been damaged, because for a moment, the silence was absolute.

HER HANDS SHOOK as she unsnapped her seat belt and yelled to the front, "Bill? Kimball? Are you hurt?"

"I'm okay," the agent called back. "Pilot's unconscious."

"Get back here and help me unload the patient."

"What?" He must have unfastened his belt, too, because he'd twisted enough to look at her. "Why?"

"Fire. Jet fuel is incredibly volatile."

He let loose with some obscenities but, because the helicopter had become a convertible, was able to stand and step between seats. "We should get Bill first."

"No. Patient first. That's our protocol. He's completely helpless."

"You want *me* to help *him* first."

In the close quarters, she elbowed him out of

the way so she could free the backboard. "Yes! Let's move. Get him to a distance."

"I don't see any fire."

"I smell fuel. Try not to do anything that might incite a spark."

He went still for a moment, then his body language abruptly took on the urgency that she shared. Within moments, they'd heaved the backboard with a large man out an unapproved and usually nonexistent way. Once they were on the ground, she broke into a trot despite the weight she bore, and he did the same. Gwen didn't let herself stop until they were a good hundred yards from a helicopter that might blow sky high at any time. She was actually grateful for Kimball's strength, until he dropped his end without bothering to bend all the way. The sudden descent even to soft loam had to be painful for an already injured man.

Gwen finally turned to look at what had been a shiny, beautifully maintained helicopter and couldn't hold back a gasp.

The rotors at the rear were half drilled into the soil, half deep in a gash cut in a huge old tree. The main rotors were...gone. The cabin consisted of shards of metal that still formed a cup shape.

Kimball swore again beside her, sounding as shocked as she was.

She started at a trot back for the helicopter, calling urgently over her shoulder, "I'll grab what supplies I can. You wouldn't know what to get. Check on Bill. If he's alive, we'll have to pull him out even if we risk damaging his neck and spine."

If they had time, the chopper carried another backboard and a C-collar.

Time was something she was very afraid they didn't have.

Kimball looked reluctant, and she didn't blame him, but he was running beside her.

She lost sight of him when she clambered back inside the broken helicopter. The smell was almost overpowering, but she still didn't see any flicker of flame.

Hurry, she thought. Trauma bag first, her own tote that held some snack bars and other useful bits. Suitcase...no, the backpack. It had fallen and was wedged into an awkward spot, but the sleeping bag was something they might need if rescue didn't come quickly. Had Bill gotten off an emergency call?

Hurry.

Drugs. Only by long habit did she find her keys quickly and was able to fumble open the cabinet and narc box for pain relievers and syringes. Thank God EMS didn't require two people and two keys to get this open. Small bottles and more plastic syringes fell to her feet. She stuffed what was in her hand into the trauma bag. They had to get out of here... Her eye fell on a white plastic bag that was the kind the hospital used for a patient's personal effects. Salazar would need more clothing if they were here long.

There was nothing soft in the bag. Alarmingly, her fingers recognized the shape of a handgun. How could that be if he had been arrested?

She looped the strings over her arm, hefted the pack over her back and clambered back out, careful of the jagged metal. Not a good time to cut her own flesh open.

The moment her feet were on the ground, she broke into a run. She felt as if she were moving through sludge and bent under more pounds than she could possibly be carrying. Was she breathing in a whiff of smoke? Oh, God—hurry, hurry.

Kimball was already beside Salazar. Her first thought was to be mad. He could have tried to help her. But then her heart sank. He'd have called for her, surely, if Bill was alive but unconscious.

She fell to her knees beside the two men.

"Bill?" she wheezed.

"Dead. I think his neck was broken."

The man on the backboard yelled out, "Fire!"

"What?"

She turned her head to see the first flicker of flame. "We're too late to—"

With a hideous *whump*, a firestorm erupted.

A funeral pyre, she thought in horror.

Chapter Three

The blast of heat reached them in seconds.

As transfixed as the others, she managed to say, "Back. Let's get farther away."

Kimball reached as if automatically for the backpack.

"Patient first."

He frowned. "I can carry it at the same time."

"It's heavy. Let's move Salazar first. At worst, the bags will be hit by flying..." She petered out. Not coal. Bits of superheated metal? It didn't matter.

Once again, Kimball hoisted one end of the backboard and let her direct where they went. Water shone through the trees. She steered them that way. It seemed...safer, given the inferno behind them. They set down Salazar, and both ran back for the limited stuff she'd been able to pull out.

The uneasiness she'd felt all day made her kneel on the ground with her back to Kimball so she could slide the white hospital bag into her tote. Of course, he wore a weapon in a holster, but she could imagine how he'd react to learn that another gun was just kind of lying around.

In fact, she made sure he didn't see her remove the big black handgun from the bag and push it under the clothes she'd changed out of earlier.

Then she grabbed her two bags and stood. Both hurried back the way they'd come to escape the searing heat. She already felt as if she had a sunburn.

Once they reached the still bound patient, aka captive, Gwen sank to the ground. Kimball set down the pack and knelt beside it, twisted at the waist so he could look back the way they'd come.

"Will the fire spread?" he asked tersely.

Breathless, she said, "I think the couple of trees that are closest will burn. At this altitude, mid-July is more like spring than summer. I hope the vegetation hasn't dried enough to allow the fire to spread. That's...why I wanted to get farther away, though." She could only be grateful that Bill had found a relatively open place to set down.

A pang of grief struck her as she remembered his friendly face.

"You're right. I see a patch of snow," Kimball said in surprise.

"Yes. Um...worse comes to worst, we can immerse ourselves in the lake."

He gave her a sardonic look, for which she didn't blame him. How could they possibly stay under long enough if a full-blown forest fire roared along the shore?

They both watched as fire first crawled then leaped up the tree that had been impaled by the rotor. The crackles and hisses gave her chills. Burning branches plummeted to the ground. Within minutes, however, the flames fell back, having reached barely halfway up the massive trunk.

"Thank God," she murmured.

Kimball let out an audible breath. "Amen."

Seeing the possessive hand he kept on the pack, she nodded at it. "That yours?"

His gaze flicked to her patient, who had probably been watching the fire as well as he could, given his limited range of motion, but who was now watching them. Salazar hadn't said a single word to the DEA agent, she realized, but Kimball hadn't spoken a word to him, either. No matter how adversarial their relationship, that seemed...strange.

In response to her question, Kimball said gruffly, "Yeah. I was planning a short vacation once I delivered Salazar." He actually gave a twisted smile. "Ironically enough, I planned to backpack here in the park. I've never been to the Pacific Northwest before."

What was he going to do, take on the Wonderland Trail? Who knew they'd have an interest in common? She became suddenly and acutely aware of the aches and pains she'd acquired during that rough landing. *Focus*, she told herself.

"Do you have your cell phone? We should both check to see if we have service."

He went very still. "If?"

Had it never occurred to him that they might be entirely isolated in the middle of a wilderness? The pack did look awfully new. Maybe heading into the backcountry was a new hobby for him. Or maybe his hiking had been in regions where tall mountains didn't block phone and even radio service.

Gwen decided to be polite, informing him that cell phones didn't work in much of the park. "I wish I thought Bill had been able to let authorities know we were going down."

"He did." Now he sounded calm, albeit condescending. "Of course he did."

She'd heard chaos, maybe voices, but nothing she could pin down as responding radio traffic.

"Okay," she said slowly, wondering why she

doubted his word. There was surely no question he was the law enforcement agent he'd introduced himself as; Bill and the dispatcher at base would have checked his badge, maybe even made calls to verify his credentials. "Then I guess we just settle in and wait."

She still dug to the bottom of her tote to find her phone. Something flashed in Kimball's eyes at the sight of it. Annoyance that she would still bother checking?

Didn't matter; she had no bars. Maybe a flicker when she turned slightly... No. She'd imagined it.

"This isn't the most comfortable spot," she said. "Let me scout around a little."

Kimball didn't offer to do it for her, but in fairness to him, she hadn't mentioned her suspicion that she had cracked a couple of ribs during the rough fall to earth. Maybe if she had, he'd be more chivalrous. Probably he was afraid Salazar would suddenly throw off the restraints and, despite being recently postsurgery, spring up to take her hostage for his escape.

Right now, her pain felt...distant. Unimportant. She recognized the effect of adrenaline and shock.

Thinking she saw what might be a small open meadow through a nearby cluster of evergreens, she walked toward it. She realized she'd wrapped one arm protectively over her torso, and she was bent forward slightly like an old lady. Rescue couldn't come soon enough for her. She'd just stepped into the trees when she glanced back at the continuing hiss and crackle of the dying fire and heated metal, and instead saw Kimball straddling Rafael Salazar, his hands seemingly around his neck.

She shouted and ran back, her breath wheezing. By the time she reached the two men, Kimball knelt at one side of his prisoner and said, "Thank God! I think he was having a seizure! I was trying to get something in his mouth for him to bite on."

A thick chunk of bark fell from his hand, making his claim credible. But she also saw red prints on both sides of Salazar's neck.

She, too, fell to her knees and laid a hand on her patient's chest. "Mr. Salazar? Are you okay?"

His hands clenched into tight fists at his side. His deep voice had become impossibly gritty. "Now...that you're...here."

Was that a plea she saw in those dark eyes? Did he want her to stay beside him, as if she were his only protection?

"I think we should free him from the backboard," she said. "There's no indication he had a neck or back injury. It would help if he could walk when—"

"No," Kimball said flatly. "I need to keep him under as much restraint as possible." He glanced at the sky streaked with dark smoke. "I expect help will arrive in no time."

His note of smugness disturbed her, contributing to the tingle she recognized as fear. This…wasn't right.

She looked worriedly back at Salazar, seeing his jaw muscles flex. She knew, *knew*, that he wanted to tell her something.

"Well, I for one would like to stretch out on the grass instead of a rocky shore," she said, as lightly as she could manage. "Why don't *you* go check out that meadow beyond the trees? I'm better qualified to be here if Salazar seizes again. It wouldn't take you three minutes."

"Not happening."

Kimball's eyes were brown, too, she realized, but much lighter. Maybe hazel. She couldn't decide.

He knew a lot more about Rafael Salazar than she did—maybe the guy had committed heinous acts as a cartel enforcer, say—but if so, why hadn't he spoken quietly to her so she understood his wariness. As it was, she might not fully understand why she distrusted Agent Kimball, but she did.

It seemed smart not to confront him, so she shrugged. "Oh, fine. If you'll turn your back, I think I'll change clothes."

"Why?" He surveyed her. "What's wrong with that getup?"

"The fabric is designed to protect against fire, not from the cold, and it feels chilly here to me. It'll get colder as the sun lowers." Actually, the sun was high in the sky right now, but it sounded like a good excuse.

"I suppose so." Apparently, Kimball hadn't noticed the bite in the air. She hadn't, either, until she needed to make a production of re-thinking her wardrobe.

She'd apparently been convincing, because he didn't pay any attention while she poked around in her overstuffed tote and dug out a small pile of clothes: a pair of jeans, a T-shirt and the thin fleece jacket she hadn't anticipated needing until they landed in Seattle.

Maybe he really was a gentleman, because he did raise his eyebrow and then ostentatiously turned his back to her. She didn't wait to see if Salazar turned his gaze away, too. Whatever he saw, she felt confident he'd keep to himself.

Still, with two strange men so near, she got dressed in stages as she peeled off the Nomex suit, glad to finally button her jeans and pull on the jacket over the only long-sleeve T-shirt she'd packed. She hoped neither man noticed when she bent over the bag as she laid the now neatly folded flight suit on top of her other possessions in the tote—and eased out the handgun, checked that it was loaded and tucked it into her waistband.

It wasn't comfortable to realize that at this point, she couldn't trust either man. What if no one came for them, and they needed to lean on each other to trek out of what might well be a part of the park lacking roads or trails? She didn't like Kimball, but it was entirely possible that Salazar was playing her with the goal of convincing her to free him.

She had to pretend to explore without taking her eyes off the two of them for more than a minute at a time.

WHEN HE SAW her walking away again, Rafe would have sworn viciously if he didn't have his mouth clamped shut. He'd felt a moment of hope when he saw Gwen handling his gun so competently, then hiding it on her person. Now it appeared that Kimball had convinced her to see him as a threat.

Rafe had no more had a seizure than he had the flu. The fingers wrapped around his throat would have crushed it in short order. The agency rarely had defectors, but Bruce Kimball had to be dirty. And if that was the case, Rafe knew exactly who was paying him.

Out of the corner of his eye, Rafe saw that the woman had disappeared in the trees that weren't more than twenty feet away. The moment she did, Kimball rose abruptly to his feet, looming above him. His teeth showed in a near snarl. "You've been luckier than you deserve so far, but luck always runs out."

"And you're going to see to it." Rafe would have given anything to be able to wrench a single hand free in case Kimball decided to make this up close and personal again.

No such luck. He pulled his gun and aimed it at Rafe's face.

"I'd feel bad if I liked you, but nobody likes glory hogs. Did you really think you were going to bring down the Espinosa family? Sorry, Salazar. They're smarter and more ruthless than you are."

"And you don't feel a single qualm about helping deliver fentanyl to American households in lethal quantities."

A nerve twitched in his cheek. "Maybe I do, but the Espinosas caught me in a bad moment, and now they expect my help when they need it. A man's got to make choices."

Rafe didn't bother asking what Kimball had been doing in that "bad moment." Why bother?

Rafe knew he'd be dead any minute. His almost legendary luck had indeed run out. In one of those strange twists, what bothered him most was the certainty that Kimball intended to kill Gwen Allen, too. What else could he do? Unless he had some slick explanation up his sleeve?

Would she be smart enough to at least pretend to accept that excuse for having to shoot and kill a fully restrained man?

Kimball cast a glance toward the trees. Rafe couldn't even roll into that scumbag's legs in hopes of knocking him off balance thanks to the damn backboard and more secure fastenings than a prison guard could have managed.

"What are you doing?" Gwen called sharply.

Rafe's heart stopped at the same moment Kimball jerked and half turned toward her.

Rafe could barely see her stepping into sight. Chin up, hands at her sides, challenging a federal agent trained to kill under necessity. *Damn it, what was she thinking?*

He yelled, "Run!"

Kimball kicked him and turned his gun toward her.

"You're going to shoot me?" she asked, as if in disbelief.

"Yeah. Too bad." He shrugged. "You weren't supposed to be here, but you had to push."

Kimball was so damn arrogant that his stance

was utterly relaxed. Why not? He expected his audience to be dead in the next minute or two. Rafe had never hated anyone so much before.

Kimball steadied the gun as if he had all the time in the world.

A shot rang out. Rafe waited for death to smash into his head, but instead he heard a second shot, then another, the *crack, crack, crack* obscene in this magnificent country.

Bruce Kimball took a step forward, tripped over Rafe and crashed to the ground as if a logger had felled a magnificent old-growth Douglas fir that made the earth shake when it died.

Stunned, Rafe saw Gwen running forward, a pistol gripped in both hands in firing position.

SHE'D WATCHED ENOUGH cop shows to know it was smart to kick Kimball's weapon a distance away. Then her eyes met Rafe's. "He didn't shoot you?" she asked breathlessly.

"Didn't have a chance."

"Oh, God." Her voice trembled as she looked back at the fallen man. "Do you think…? Is he dead?"

"Yeah," Rafe said hoarsely. "I saw his face when he went down. But…you better check."

Her teeth chattered as she edged closer, leaned over, the gun still in her right hand, and laid two fingers on Kimball's neck.

Then she stumbled back and collapsed onto her butt. "I killed him. I killed a man."

"He didn't give you any choice," Rafe said as gently as he could. "It was you or him."

"You, too," she whispered.

"Definitely me."

Given that she was a person accustomed to making quick decisions in critical situations, she felt weirdly...blank. "What do I do now?"

"Put the gun down," he suggested.

"Oh. Oh, yes." She fumbled to set it on the ground. "Is, um, this yours?"

"I assume so. My boss defied hospital rules and gave it back to me when I was in recovery at the hospital."

She hadn't taken her eyes off the dead man. She was going to see that face, waking and dreaming, for a long time. It wasn't that she hadn't failed to save patients; she'd seen plenty of dead men, women and even children at accident and even disaster sites. But this was different.

I shot and killed a man.

A shudder ran through her.

"Gwen?" Rafe's voice pulled her back to the moment. "We need to move. Can you free me?" he asked.

Still feeling dazed, she looked at him. "I don't understand any of this."

"I...have a good idea. He just filled in a few of the blanks."

"Will you tell me?"

A bald eagle soared far above. With the vast wingspan and bright white head, it was unmistakable. They were common in the Pacific Northwest but always magnificent. She fixated on it, soaring free, because...she didn't want to focus on what had happened.

His voice and words pulled her back. "Yeah," he said. "If it's any consolation, he might have regretted having to kill you."

"Consolation?" she said incredulously. "He didn't sound all that regretful to me. In his worldview, it's my fault that I'm here." She shook her head. "He didn't want me on board. What I don't understand is why Bill—he was the pilot—had apparently agreed to the flight with an injured man and no medical personnel on board. I wanted to think he didn't know what he was doing."

"I'm guessing he didn't, not entirely."

"But...he must have agreed to this...detour." She waved a hand toward the mountain she could no longer see but knew still towered behind rock buttresses and thick evergreen trees.

"Figured pocketing a little money wasn't so bad. Nobody hurt by it."

Her laugh hurt. She curled forward into a tight ball, arms wrapped around her knees.

"He didn't get you, did he?" Rafe sounded alarmed. "I don't see any blood—"

"No. No. I think I suffered some damage during the crash. Like a cracked rib or two."

Which hurt like hell.

She rested her head on her crossed arms and studied him before asking baldly, "Can I trust you?"

Chapter Four

Was she really so naive, she didn't realize how effortlessly he could lie to her? Rafe wondered. It was one of his specialties.

But here and now...he wouldn't. His natural protective side had kicked in anyway, but above and beyond that, this woman had saved his life at least twice already. He owed her. He'd do anything to get her out of this mess alive and well. "You've gotten involved in something worse than you know. Yes, you can trust me. I'm a DEA agent. I don't have my badge or wallet on me—"

"I...think I might have them." She pushed herself to her feet and circled wide around the body to reach that bulging tote bag. After rooting around in it, she produced a white plastic bag with a string closure that he recalled from previous hospitalizations. All that she removed from it was a wallet and a simple billfold. She opened that and had to be looking at his badge.

Finally she lifted her head again. "Now I *really* don't understand."

Even frantic to be released from the restraints, he understood her doubts. "I've been undercover for the past year. I'd gathered enough information to justify warrants and a cascade of arrests. I was put in a safe house in Yakima to wait for the trial, which could be a year or more away. I expected nothing but excruciating boredom. Somehow, we were betrayed. One of my guards knew the man he opened the door for. I didn't see him. I'm guessing he and the second agent who was there for security are dead. I don't know, except if either had survived, they'd have ID'd the shooter. I crashed out a window, heard sirens as I lost consciousness. The cracked sternum and broken ribs? That's what happens when you're wearing a Kevlar vest and are shot. You survive, but you aren't always happy about it."

"Oh, no," she whispered.

"Next thing I knew, I was in recovery after surgery at the hospital. Like I said, my boss gave me back my gun, badge and wallet, but they must have cut my clothes off. He said some things I didn't comprehend. After that, I was on the helicopter."

"Were you working with Agent Kimball? Or...*was* he an agent?"

"Unfortunately, yes, but based in Chicago. We were in the same office a few years back—

Miami, I think—but I've never worked directly with him. I got a real bad feeling when I heard you say his name."

"You think he's the one your guard recognized."

"Makes sense."

He knew she was having trouble taking all these details in, but he worried about how much time this complicated explanation had eaten up.

"We need to get moving." He had an itch he never ignored, but he hadn't gotten through to her yet. "We're not safe sticking close to the helicopter. I think the pilot was supposed to land somewhere near here, drop Kimball and me off, and fly back. Not sure how he'd have explained that—"

She shook her head. "He was supposed to be flying an empty helicopter to Seattle to be loaned to the base I work out of. We're a lot busier than the team in Yakima, and we have a helicopter that needs serious maintenance. He could have dropped it off as planned, nobody the wiser."

Understanding dawned. "Until you got in the mix."

She explained jumping at the chance for a free ride to Seattle. "Except...there you were."

"I hate to hurry this, but I can't help wondering whether he was expecting a pickup."

"He might have planned to shoot you and then hike out. He did bring the backpack."

"Maybe, but his extracurricular employer might have wanted to see proof that the problem I represented was actually handled."

"We are really exposed." The whites of her eyes showed as her head turned. "We can't be exactly where Bill intended to set down. I mean, this isn't an ideal landing zone, but…"

Rafe followed her gaze to the dark smoke painting an obvious signal in the now mostly blue sky.

He couldn't tell if he'd convinced her at last or if pure instinct had her scooting toward him, her hands reaching for fastenings. Even the anticipation of being freed was almost more than he could stand. This involuntary immobility felt like being buried alive would, or maybe being mummified if you hadn't died yet. Rafe wasn't sure he'd ever be able to lie on his back again, bed covers tucked snugly around him, without feeling the kind of phantom pains amputees did in the missing limb.

Just being able to turn his head was an exquisite relief. To move his shoulders. As she worked her way down, to lift his arms, which promptly cramped.

When he lunged to a sitting position, Gwen fell back, fear on her face.

GWEN SCUTTLED BACK a few feet on the cold ground.

Salazar lifted a hand. "I didn't mean to scare you! I'm sorry. I was just…desperate to move."

She saw only sincerity on his face. The face, she realized even through her fear, that was model handsome, complete with hollows beneath high, sharp cheekbones, a straight, bold nose and a strong jaw darkened by the beginnings of beard growth. It was too bad her willingness to believe and trust was at a low ebb.

Uh-huh, an inner voice commented. *Didn't you already* make *a decision?*

When she turned her head, her gaze fixing unerringly on the man lying face down on the gravelly lakeshore. Dead. Because *she'd* shot and killed him.

Her stomach turned queasily.

What if she'd made a terrible mistake?

He'd admitted he intended to kill her. *You weren't supposed to be here, but you had to push.*

Even so, all she knew was that she'd gotten in the middle of something ugly and maybe convoluted. There might not be a bad guy and a good guy. What if *both* guys were bad?

But Rafael Salazar was still her patient. He'd done or said nothing to rouse her suspicions. She certainly couldn't leave him here to wait for a helicopter sent to pick up Agent Kimball, who had definitely intended to kill him.

She let out a breath and wondered how long she'd been holding it. She felt light-headed. "No, I'm sorry. After everything that's happened, I guess I scare easily."

To her dismay, his smile made him even more handsome. "Understandable. Uh… I think I can get the rest of these straps."

"No, I'll do it." She scooted closer again, then made quick work of freeing him. As he swiveled so that his lower legs lay stretched over the ground, she asked, "How do you feel?"

"Like I've been shot a few times, but I think I can walk."

After what she'd read in his chart, she thought he'd do well to shuffle. Even that would have been impossible if the bullet had struck a little higher and damaged his hip.

Before she could open her mouth, he said, "Except…" He waved at his feet, covered only by hospital socks.

"Oh, no! There weren't any shoes or boots in that bag. At least one of them might have gotten soaked in blood."

He grimaced. "That's…likely. I hate to ask you to rob from the dead, but will you bring me one of Kimball's boots to see if it would fit me?"

Cold—dead?—fingers tripped down her spine, but *practical* probably topped her list of personal qualities. She could do this. She half crawled the short distance, constantly aware of the heat from the helicopter, and studied the boots while trying not to see the rest of the body. No ties, like her hiking boots. These were what were usually called tactical boots. Good sole but flexible, and easy to slide in and out of. She'd seen plenty of cops wearing them. She pulled both off and carried them to Salazar, who said, "These can't be too far off my size."

After shoving his foot into the first, he said, "They're a little too big. If he has extra socks in that pack, the boots should be fine. Some borrowed clothes would be good, too."

Yes, if they had to go on the run in the high mountain wilderness, he'd do better if he wasn't wearing only thin scrubs. She gave thought to whoever had brought his gun and wallet. He couldn't have picked up a change of clothes while he was at it?

She realized she was straining for the distant sound of helicopter rotors. "We should hurry. We can get better organized once we're tucked away."

"You're right." He shoved his other foot in the boot and slowly, torturously got to his feet.

Gwen rose with him and discovered her arms

were out to catch him if he fell. Astonishingly, he didn't, although he swayed initially. She'd guessed he was tall, but at six foot two or three, minimum, he towered over her.

"What do we need to take?" he asked in a rougher voice.

Still half expecting him to go down, she stayed close as she scanned their few possessions.

"Pack, this bag—let me see if I can tie it onto the pack." She suited action to words, securing the trauma bag so she wouldn't have to carry it separately. She looked around. "My tote, your gun—" Which she no longer held, she realized with a tiny burst of panic. No, there it was. She'd set it down after Salazar told her to.

"Kimball's gun, too." He sounded all cop now, no human emotions allowed. "I hope he has clothes in the pack, because I don't think we dare take time to strip him."

"Yes. Okay." Even out of the corner of her eye, she saw that both of Kimball's shirts were bloody. She hurried to pick up both guns, tucking one back in her waistband, putting the other at the top of the tote before she positioned the handles over a shoulder and then hefted the pack onto her back. The weight was reassuring, suggesting that it held both clothes and food.

Unless it was really full of bomb makings or who knew what?

Nice thought.

When Salazar reached out as if he intended to take the tote from her, she stepped away. "Do you go by Rafael?"

"Usually Rafe. I can carry—"

"No, you can't. In fact, you'd better lean on me."

She saw the internal war play out in his dark eyes, but finally he dipped his head.

"I'll keep a hand on your shoulder until I can be sure I'm steady on my feet."

"Good." Gwen didn't even ask which way he thought they ought to go. The sun was too high in the sky to provide any idea of east, west, north or south. A ridge steeper than she thought they could handle rose beyond the lake. Running parallel to it, another ridge, both rocky and treed, put them in...not quite a valley. It wasn't wide enough for that. It was a V. She could see why Bill had seen this as the only option for an LZ.

She wasn't enthusiastic about passing the helicopter because of the heat, and she didn't want to look at the blackened remnants that included a man's body. That left the opposite direction.

She stopped in the act of turning. Even sickened, she had to say this. "What if we put Kimball's body in the helicopter? Or...or right beside it? Would that fool someone into thinking everyone had died in the crash?"

"They probably don't know about you." The man beside her sounded unnervingly thoughtful, but after a moment he shook his head. "I don't think we could pull it off. Not with the gunshot wounds. Anyway, the metal is too hot for us to get near, and even if we were able to put the backboard in, there should be blackened bones. Fire doesn't entirely burn up a body, you know."

She sort of did, since she had a box filled with what was left of her grandmother at home. Even a crematorium, which was *trying* to burn what was left of a human body, couldn't completely succeed.

Grateful that Rafe hadn't jumped on her macabre idea, she felt weak for a minute but hoped he didn't notice.

Still careful not to look at the body sprawled only a few feet away, she led Rafe past it in retracing her earlier path. They needed to find somewhere to hide soon, preferably near enough they could see if a rescue helicopter appeared, and to give Rafe a chance to get into warmer clothes, if there were any, and for her to give him a pain shot.

Once she was back on the job, she was going to have some explaining to do about the quantity of narcotics she'd appropriated without a plan or a coworker to sign off on them. Rules were strict where handling them was concerned.

They were almost to the first line of trees. She looked up to see only grim determination on Rafe's face—and stiff, careful placement of each foot that told her how much pain he had to be suppressing.

Once they reached the trees, Gwen allowed herself a glance over her shoulder. She could no longer see the remains of the helicopter well from here, only the body and the backboard as well as...some litter, she guessed, not sure what it was. She hoped they hadn't left anything important lying around.

If nobody showed up in the next hour or two, she could maybe go back and look more carefully. Also, to strip the man she'd shot of any clothes that didn't have bullet holes in them and weren't stained with blood.

That would be a very last resort, she reassured herself, and felt comforted by the thick cover the copse of feathery evergreen trees provided.

HE'D DO THIS because he had to, Rafe thought grimly, but at the moment, he had no idea how. When Gwen had freed him from the restraints, he'd had a burst of euphoria that made him unrealistically optimistic. Now, agony struck with every step, and the pain when he tried to take in a deep breath didn't help. He became aware that he wouldn't have been able to breathe deeply, anyway. His torso was wrapped tightly. Cracked sternum, he reminded himself. Broken ribs. Without the wrap, he'd probably fall to his knees screaming.

He took the next step, only then realizing how tightly he was gripping Gwen's shoulder. As slender as she was, she hadn't so much as flinched, but he was probably bruising her. He loosened his fingers.

"Sorry."

"Hold on as hard as you have to. It'll be worse if you go down."

In so many ways. He squeezed his eyes shut for a minute, picturing what it would feel like to crash to the rocky, uneven ground.

He moved his right leg forward. That was slightly easier, which meant… Left leg. He hoped that was a grunt rather than a groan that came out of his mouth.

"I'm taking us up this side of the ridge, where it isn't too steep," she said, the stress in her voice telling him she knew what he was going through. "I'm hoping it'll seem…unlikely."

This grunt was meant to be agreement. She seemed to take it as such, because the next bit was a struggle. She wedged herself under his good arm, at points getting behind him and pushing.

Rafe's eyes burned from sweat. The too-large boots rubbed and would eventually cause blisters if they kept moving, but he didn't think he'd be able to keep going very long at all.

Yet somehow he did. The strong woman beside him led and supported and sometimes bore almost all his weight, which had to be sixty, eighty pounds more than her finer-boned frame carried. *Conditioning*, he told himself. She must frequently lift one end of a backboard that carried someone a lot larger than him and carry it a distance to the helicopter. He'd be dead if it weren't for her. Again.

Eventually she said, "Let's take a break," and she guided him to a boulder that had a reasonably flat top. Bending to sit was almost worse than walking, but once his butt was supported, he let his head fall forward, closed his eyes and did nothing but breathe through his pain.

She watched him anxiously—he knew she was—but didn't say a word. No perky "You're doing great!" Or "Not that much farther!" which would have been a lie.

What she finally did say was, "I'm going to give you a shot of narcotics."

Real narcotics? Had he misheard?

She went on, "I should have done it sooner, but I have to calculate dose and—"

They hadn't dared sit around.

With a definite groan, he straightened his upper body. "You thought to grab pain meds from a helicopter that was going to blow up any second."

"Last thing I did," she admitted as she rooted in her voluminous tote. "In the helicopter, I intended to ask you about your pain level when I saw the mountain and realized we were so far off course. And... I guess I knew subliminally that we weren't going to be rescued in the next half hour. If you had to move at all, you'd need the good stuff."

He raised his eyebrows.

"Morphine." She asked for his weight and calculated a dose. As he watched, she progressed to drawing a clear liquid from a bottle into a syringe.

Rafe didn't say anything, not wanting to distract her.

"I'm thinking... I won't give you as much as you might get in one dose if you were lounging in a hospital bed. I don't dare take the chance of knocking you out. So you're going to keep hurting." She made a moue of distress.

"But able to stay on my feet. That's a good

decision. Besides—" he eyed the syringe "—I don't want to get addicted."

"No. I have Tylenol in my bag, but that wouldn't help you much for at least a few days."

He only nodded. "Do you want my hip?"

"Well...yes."

He fumbled with the string around the waist, pulled the thin pants down and turned sideways, rolling onto his opposite hip.

The jab came without any warning. The relief that almost immediately rolled through him had him groaning again, his muscles going slack.

"Better?"

"You're an angel of mercy."

She chuckled as she tugged the pants back up but let him tie them at the waist. He felt good enough at this first glorious moment, he wouldn't have minded her fingers playing down there.

Damn. Was he grinning like a fool?

She capped the syringe and replaced it and the bottle in her tote bag. "I think we'd better have a snack. I have some water that's probably warm. We'll undoubtedly come across streams where we can refill the bottle."

What she put in his hand was a Payday candy bar. He ripped it open and took a bite. Salted peanuts and caramel. Did life get any better?

She had chosen an Almond Joy, and both ate

in contented silence, taking sips in turn from her water bottle.

Rafe drew in a deep breath without the hit of pain. The air was so clean; it tasted and smelled of evergreens and something more ephemeral. There were sounds: the rustle of branches high above in a faint breeze, what might be the ripple of water, a birdcall answered by another, but the immensity of the sky and the stunning beauty of the vista around them had the impact of an ancient cathedral.

"I've never been to the Northwest." He grimaced. "Except Yakima, and I barely looked out a window."

"Eastern Washington is spectacular in its own way. The Columbia River Gorge, with crumbling red basalt rim rocks, is magnificent. But the Cascade Range has the most beautiful country in the US, at least."

"I can't argue," he said, taking pleasure in the moment.

Until she stirred. "We haven't come that far. I think we should keep moving, if you're up to it."

What could he say but "Yeah" and let her help him to his feet?

Chapter Five

Before they started out, Gwen did her best to orient herself by pinpointing the base of the column of smoke. It was dismaying to see what a short distance she and Rafe had covered. Not surprising when his every stride had been torturously slow.

Unfortunately, they hadn't crash-landed among old-growth forest, where centuries-old woodland giants would have hidden them well. Plus, that would have given her a better idea of where they were. The trees here were on the small side and seemed to grow in clumps that left quite a bit of open rocky ground and small meadows bright with wildflowers in between. She'd hoped that, in climbing, they'd find something like an overhang that would at least shield them from above.

"How are you?" she asked.

On his feet, Rafe rolled his good shoulder in self-assessment and said, "Better."

Unfortunately, Gwen's rib cage was not feeling better. Maybe she should have given herself some narcotic relief, too, but that would have fuzzed her thinking and would also, as a decision, be hard to defend when she sat down with her supervisor. If worse came to worst—well, she'd think about it then.

Turning her head, she spotted what appeared to be a cliff with tumbled boulders beneath it. That could be a dead end—or give them a place to hide. So she steered Rafe that way.

Apparently, this was her day for denial, because she kept blocking thoughts about everything from her initial decision to get on that cursed helicopter despite her sensible doubts to the crash, the explosion, the—nope. Especially not going there.

Look where you're putting your feet, she instructed herself. *Keep an eye on Rafe's tense face and be aware of his body language. Listen for the distinctive sound of another helicopter. Stay in the moment.*

Everything else could wait for later, including her inconvenient sexual awareness.

Twice she had to detour around crunchy-topped, gleaming white snow fields to be sure they didn't have a clear line of footprints. If he noticed the long ways around, it wasn't apparent.

He was able to reach with one hand for branches

to pull himself up a few feet, taking some of his weight off her shoulders. That was an improvement. Still, she had a feeling his thoughts weren't trying to scatter like a covey of quails the way hers were, but rather were grimly focused on the next moment. Maybe on-the-job experience had taught him an intense focus. Either way, she'd bet he was thinking about nothing but the next step.

Except then he spoke up in a gritty voice, surprising her.

"Do you know where we are in the park? I assume we *are* in the national park?"

"I think we're still in the park. We were awfully close to the mountain not that long before things went wrong. As for where…only sort of. I mean, the glimpse I had was out the left window, which would put us on the east side, except we could have been curving around the north side, depending on where Bill and Kimball had agreed to set down. Also, I have no idea how much time passed or how far we traveled after Bill claimed the alarm had gone off. And, well, the sun isn't any help yet."

"Hard to set a route, then."

Matter-of-fact, but with a growly undertone that spoke of pain.

"Unfortunately, yes. Depending on where we came down, we could be near a heavily used trail or even an entrance to the park." She hated to say this. "We could also be miles from help."

"Kimball wouldn't have wanted anyone to see the helicopter set down."

Yes, he was right. Had he and Bill plotted an especially remote part of the park?

Except…logic said if Kimball had intended to walk away with that pack on his back, he'd have planned for the original LZ to be within a reasonable distance of a trail. She didn't point that out. Speculation wouldn't get them very far.

Rafe didn't say any more for a long time. She didn't blame him, given that they were scrambling more than walking at the moment.

During a brief break to catch their breath, she decided a little optimism might help. "Once we look through the pack and see what resources we have, we might be better able to make an educated choice for our next move."

Surely this grunt wasn't meant to dismiss her near perkiness but was just the best he could do at the moment.

It felt as if they'd been on their way for an hour or more, but she suspected the time was a lot shorter than that. She saw what she'd been looking for, though—a boulder leaning against another that created something close to a shallow cave beneath. Soil and small pebbles made a nearly flat spot.

"This way," she said.

She nudged. He changed his path. When they arrived and she stopped him with a hand on his arm, he stared straight ahead like a robot that had been shut down.

Gwen dropped the tote and lowered the backpack to the ground, wishing it wasn't bright red, then touched Rafe's arm. "Let's sit down."

She could tell what an effort it took him to turn his head and assess their surroundings, but he nodded finally and said, "Good."

He didn't argue when she knelt, put his hand on her shoulder and said, "Slow and easy."

The last part of his descent was more of a fall, but he landed safely on his butt, leaned his head against the gritty rock to one side and exhaled a breath slowly.

Studying him worriedly, she touched his forehead. Was it too warm, or was her hand cold? She pressed it to her own cheek and couldn't tell. Knowing wouldn't help since the best she could do if he had a fever was Tylenol.

Well, she could look under his dressings for signs of infection, but she had no antibiotics to give him and, at the moment, didn't even have any more water for him to swallow a pill.

"Still no helicopter," he said hoarsely. "Maybe you were right."

"About the hiking-out thing?"

"Yeah."

Gwen told him her earlier thoughts.

"Too close to a trail, he'd have risked witnesses," he commented.

She nodded. "No matter what, I may have chosen the wrong direction."

"No." His big hand caught hers. "Smart."

"Okay." She closed her eyes and tipped her head sideways to rest on his shoulder. Her body felt compressed, even her bones scrunched. She'd carried too much weight, but now they could rest. There was no reason they couldn't stay here for a while. Maybe even overnight. They both might feel better tomorrow.

She gave herself what had to be five minutes before she straightened.

"Cross your fingers. Let's find you something better to wear."

He did cross his fingers, and she pulled a laugh out of somewhere.

She unfastened Velcro and explored. Rafe was bent over the pack as eagerly as she was.

RAFE WAS INCREDIBLY grateful when they found a couple changes of clothes in the pack, as well as three pairs of socks. He removed the boots and showed Gwen the red places on his feet close to forming blisters.

"Try two pairs of socks when we move on," she decided. "I wish we had some moleskin, but if you're still uncomfortable, I can figure out something else to cut up to protect those places."

Even one pair of socks warmed his feet. The fact that she knelt in front of him to put them on felt...good.

Apparently, Kimball really had intended to backpack, whether here at Rainier or elsewhere, because the pack disgorged a small stove with an extra fuel canister, a number of freeze-dried meals, purifying tablets for water, bags of dried fruit and nuts, and energy bars.

"This will keep us for a while," Gwen said with satisfaction. "I have some energy bars in my bag—I never go anywhere without any—and more candy bars."

"Sweet tooth?"

Her smile lit her face. "I'm not shy about admitting it. You?"

"I'd say no, except that Payday really hit the spot."

She chuckled, dug some more and laid out a miscellany of things: a lighter and matches, a folding knife with additional tools, a tarp and cord that could be used to rig a cover in case of rain, a compact pair of binoculars and a couple of magazines for Kimball's handgun.

"Did he know guns are banned in the park?"

Rafe raised an eyebrow at her, and she blanched. Frowning, he laid his hand on her arm. "I didn't mean it like that."

Suddenly, she started to shake. "I never thought I'd kill anybody."

She'd been so tough, he'd forgotten how disturbing today's events must have been for her. "You shot him in self-defense." He hoped his voice conveyed comfort. "Do you regret that choice?"

"No. No. It's just—" face pinched, Gwen hugged herself "—I couldn't let him kill us, but... I chose my profession to save lives," she said finally.

"I can see that." Damn. He wanted to put his arm around her but wasn't sure how she'd take that. "Gwen, look at me."

She did. In fact, she searched his eyes in a way that shook him, as if she saw deep into his darkest memories, the ones that turned up in an occasional nightmare.

"You did save my life," he reminded her. "Remember that. Isn't that your job?"

Her forehead creased as she visibly tried to reconcile the two concepts. "I just...never thought..."

"Why did you become a paramedic?"

"I became a nurse and then wanted to do more. I've always… I guess you could say I enjoy adrenaline. I mean, I don't do extreme sports or anything like that—"

"I'm relieved to hear it," he said dryly.

"But my rotation in the ER made other kinds of nursing seem dull. I got certified as an EMT and worked on an ambulance for a while, went back to the ER, then studied to become a paramedic."

"You still haven't said why. Were either of your parents in the medical field?"

She went so still that he suspected she'd quit breathing. He'd unwittingly touched on a sore place. Was this something she didn't talk about?

"Rafe," she said suddenly, her hand shooting out to grip his forearm hard. "Do you hear that?"

He did. Only his attention on her had kept him from noticing the distant sound of a plane flying low or a helicopter.

They both knew which it would be.

"Gun," he said, and she dug quickly in her tote and produced Kimball's Glock, the same model as his. Not surprising, since agents were encouraged to carry one of a couple of Glocks. Even with the pain in his shoulder, Rafe did a quick check to be sure it was ready to fire.

She produced the binoculars, too. Smart thinking. "Maybe…maybe somebody spotted the smoke, and it'll be a rescue helicopter."

She was whispering for no logical reason, but he understood why.

He took the binoculars, lifting them to his eyes and adjusting them until the vicinity of the crash, visible from here only by the smoke, snapped into sharp focus.

"There," Gwen said.

He saw it, too.

What emergency flight helicopters he'd seen were clearly marked. Big numbers on the tail, logo of the organization operating it on the side, paint job white or a bright color. The goal was to be visible. This one was black with a white stripe. Law enforcement? But even when it got close enough and he could examine it carefully, he saw no logo, and the FAA required numbers on the tail were present but small enough he couldn't quite make them out.

He handed the binoculars to Gwen and let her study it. She worked in the area and must see helicopters belonging to any number of emergency responders, sightseers, and search and rescue groups.

She shook her head. "It has to be private."

They watched it drop low and circle the crash site. Even from this distance, the noise was near deafening. It appeared to settle on the ground for what had to be five minutes. Undoubtedly, someone had gotten out to identify the dead man and try to figure out what had happened. Then it rose again, tipping to one side to curve into the beginning of a circle as if it were turning back the way it had come. Except it flew in a complete circle, then another, each enlarged.

"Search grid," he murmured. "They know at least one person is missing."

Her fingers bit into his arm.

"Let's pull back under cover as much as we can manage," he added, grateful when she didn't argue. In fact, she used her head and pushed the too-bright red pack to the very back of their V-shaped hideout, poking her flower-print tote bag after it. Finally, he and she shuffled backward until they were crouched, Rafe holding the gun in his right hand but propping that arm up with his stronger left hand.

The helicopter got louder. It passed frighteningly close to them. Rafe didn't try to use the binoculars, afraid a flash of light off a lens would give away their location. It didn't slow, though, only continued in another wide circle, this time passing above and behind them.

Finally, they could no longer see it or, after a few more minutes, hear it.

Gwen whimpered. "That was—"

"Scary as hell," he agreed.

She'd been the one shaking earlier, but he felt a tremor in his own hands now. In one way, he'd expected this. In another, he hadn't understood how difficult escape would be with him in such bad shape and with them having absolutely no idea which direction to go to find even an occasionally traveled trail. And there had to be *some* roads in the park, too, didn't there?

"Do you...think it'll come back?"

Rafe mulled over how to answer. Clearly, the enforcement arm of the traffickers had landed, seen the dead DEA agent they'd suborned and been forced to assume that Rafe had overpowered Kimball, shot him and gone on the run. They had no way to know he had help. They might wonder if he'd been injured as badly in the first place as they had been led to believe.

Problem with that was, they'd set up a pretty elaborate operation with only one goal: killing Rafe, the federal agent who'd fooled them well enough to gather information on their operations to bring down significant parts of their organization. Their goal was to keep him from ever testifying. A judge and jury needed him there in front of them to verify and elaborate on the evidence he'd collected. What the men who'd been given the job of getting rid of him had found was the body of their dirty agent.

The scene suggested Rafe was still alive and therefore a threat to some higher-ups in the cartel.

How could they go back to the bosses and admit he'd gotten away? That kind of major screwup wouldn't be accepted with any understanding.

"I wish you'd never gotten involved in this," Rafe told Gwen honestly, "but I wouldn't have a chance without you."

"So, that's a yes," she said slowly.

He had to think back to her original question and nodded. "My best guess is that they hadn't come prepared to drop any men to hunt for me. I think the pilot has gone back to pick up some armed trackers."

"I thought we could spend the night here." She sounded sad.

Seeing her exhaustion and stress and shock, Rafe wished he could spare her. "We're too near the crash site," he said bluntly. "We need to get as far away as we can before they come back."

She wrinkled her nose at him, straightened her shoulders and said with determination, "Then let's not waste any time."

He couldn't possibly have gotten any luckier in a partner, Rafe thought again, then hoped she didn't see his wince.

Rafe wasn't much for introspection. He

planned, he stayed fit in preparation for whatever would be thrown at him, he relied on his lightning-fast reaction time and, yeah, he knew one of his strengths was the subconscious calculations that he called gut feelings.

He compartmentalized, too, as most people in his line of work probably did. Had to shut bad experiences, tragedy, ugly scenes away. For the first time, it struck him that the consequence might be self-centeredness. He thought of himself as a compassionate man; he'd give his life for that of an innocent, no hesitation. But day to day...he calculated in terms of how events and people would help or hinder *him* on the job.

That's what he'd just done. Gwen Allen was a gutsy woman who improved his chances of escaping this disaster and making it to court to bring down a lot of bad guys.

But what would the fallout be for *her*—assuming both of them in fact survived? Keeping her alive had been a high priority for him, but was that enough?

Chapter Six

Gwen had set aside a map of Mount Rainier National Park found among Kimball's belongings. After laying out a change of clothes for Rafe, she said, "Let me know if you need me," and then turned her back to give him privacy to strip and get dressed. Over her shoulder, she added, "Oh! Or if you see any blood on your dressings."

While he was changing only a few feet away, she completely unfolded the map to scrutinize it. No, she wasn't delusional enough to think Kimball would have marked a big red X at the rendezvous point, although people did do things like that, didn't they? After all, he had no reason to believe anyone but him would get their hands on the map.

It wasn't completely pristine; there was enough wear and tear that she could tell the map had been opened a few times, and whoever had done it—Kimball—had struggled to refold it correctly so that it didn't tear or end up a wadded mess.

Rustles and scrapes came from behind her. Rafe's arm brushed against her. Gwen winced at some pained sounds, even as she pictured his powerful body unclothed. She'd seen enough of his muscles to know there had to be a lot more of them. She wanted to slap herself for even thinking like that. He was still her patient! She'd taken care of well-built guys before and not felt even an instant of attraction.

She let out a breath. Surely he'd let her help pull the shirt over his injured arm and shoulder.

Quit thinking about him seminaked, she ordered herself, bending to search the map.

Unfortunately, there were no helpful ink or pencil circles, Xs or margin notes to grab her attention. What was spread in front of her was just a topographical map published by National Geographic identical to one she owned, beautifully detailed, but not giving her a clue where their helicopter had come down. If only she had caught a better glimpse of the mountain before the clouds closed in!

She frowned. Since they'd gone on the run, she should have paid more attention to the foliage, the trees in particular. Pines were more common on the dryer east side, for example. Thinking about it now, she didn't remember noticing one, although her attention had been split too many ways.

She could identify different elevation zones because some species or types of trees lived only at lower elevations while others only appeared higher up. At the moment, she didn't believe they were at the subalpine elevation of 4,500 feet above sea level or higher, but they might not be much below that. In fact...

"Where are you from?" she asked Rafe.

There was a startled silence behind her. "We're going to exchange background info right now?"

She rolled her eyes. "No, I'm thinking about elevation. I've been puffing and panting more than usual, thinking my exercise regime doesn't cut it, but it's occurred to me that we might be at a high enough elevation that it would be normal for us to find it harder to breathe. Unless you're from somewhere like Denver..."

"No. I grew up in Southern California, and with the DEA, I've been transferred several times, but Miami, Houston and San Diego are essentially at sea level. Probably Chicago, too. Damn. This means there's another reason we're moving so damned slow."

"Afraid so."

Too bad their current elevation didn't help in identifying their location.

She leaned over the map again. The distinctively parallel ridges rising to each side of that narrow valley had worried her. She shouldn't generalize from them—her view had been pretty limited—but there were a number of places in the park where the land folded that way. A lot of those areas tended to be devoid of roads or trails because the terrain was so difficult.

Rafe said grittily, "I could use a hand."

He'd managed to pull on the heavy-duty cargo pants but had gotten stuck halfway taking off the surgical scrub top.

"Oh, no!"

He was so tangled that she grabbed the pocket knife and cut it off him. It wasn't anything he'd want to wear again, anyway. Of course a wide, white wrap supported his ribs. Somehow, she hadn't been picturing it. Rafe had a beautifully muscular chest with warm copper-brown skin and a dark dusting of hair, and powerful arms and broad shoulders. It was even better than she'd imagined. She wanted to touch him, but the lack of fresh blood on the dressing around his upper arm and over his shoulder meant she didn't have an excuse.

Considering they were on the run for their lives and he was seriously injured, what was she *thinking*?

"Um, let's see." She picked up the T-shirt like she'd never seen one before, finally deciding to slip it over the arm on his bad side, then maneuver to get his head and other arm in it.

She gently pulled it down, reluctant to hide that lovely male body, but reached for the Polartec fleece quarter-zip.

Only when he was fully dressed did she let herself meet his eyes. If there was a knowing glint in them, she wasn't acknowledging it.

"Boots," she declared, and helped him put them on.

He stamped each foot, then sighed. "Anything on the map?"

"Sad to say, no X marks the spot."

He leaned closer, and she pointed out some remote areas with the kind of ridges—or were they really mountains?—that might fit. There was a large area west of the Chinook Scenic Byway, for example, in which no roads or trails were displayed. From there, it wouldn't be that many miles to the highway—if they could get there at all. And they'd have to head east instead of the generally westward route she'd chosen. Those folds were more than ridges, she saw; they were definitely mountains over six thousand feet in elevation, many named.

The Chenius Mountain area, too, was devoid of trails. But really, by its very nature, the land surrounding a volcano this size consisted of pleats of land formed in some cases by glaciers, or at least the runoff of melting ice and snow. In other words, she had no more idea where they were than she'd had before she opened the map.

Rafe's dark gaze rested on her as she folded the map and put it away. She wasn't sure she wanted to know what he was thinking. Surely they'd eventually come upon a view of the mountain that would offer her guidance, but that was no help right now.

Look for the fastest path, she told herself, the one that would let them open up some distance, but still have thick groves of trees or rocky ground that might offer an overhang or the like to hide them. They'd have to avoid being in the open as much as they could, she realized; flower-strewn meadows made for more pleasant walking but were dangerous for them. Searchers might be on foot, but when the helicopter reappeared, it could hunt them from the air again, too.

"I guess right now, we just need to cover as much ground as we can while never being far from someplace we can duck to get out of sight."

"I agree," he said. "Except it would be ideal if we had a sight line when that helicopter comes back."

More reason to go up rather than scrambling along the side of the ridge. She could only hope it didn't get too steep.

Somehow he shoved himself to his feet, his good shoulder braced against the side of a boulder to give him support.

Relieved he hadn't asked for another shot of morphine, Gwen loaded herself down again even as she realized she had no idea how to determine intervals between shots. She didn't wear a watch, although she might rethink that after this adventure.

One more thing she'd have to guess at.

Those dark eyes raked her. "Do you have any idea how much I hate seeing you loaded down like a pack animal while I'm strolling along empty-handed?"

"*I* don't have two gunshot wounds," she pointed out tartly. "I carry this much weight when I'm backpacking, which I do for *fun*, and regularly for short periods on the job."

He grunted, his favorite sound.

She laughed at him and saw the beginnings of a reluctant, sexy grin.

"I think…this way." She pointed.

MAYBE HALF AN hour along, Rafe's feet balked. Since the rest of him was in agreement, he managed to grind out, "Break."

"What?" Gwen turned, saw the expression on his face and looked around. "If it's not too rotten, we can sit on that fallen tree."

He plodded that far, sinking down with enormous relief. She followed suit and moaned.

After a minute, he became aware she was watching him sidelong.

"Something on your mind?" he asked.

"I keep remembering. You know?"

He did, but that was part of the difference between them. He sought answers that might be of use; she might be stuck on the two deaths they'd walked away from. He had no idea whether he should discourage that or encourage her to talk it out.

He settled for making an inquiring sound.

"Back in the helicopter," she said in a rush, "I heard something strange just before it started spinning. What if we crashed because Kimball knocked Bill unconscious or even killed him *before* we landed?"

Although Rafe hadn't thought about it, that seemed entirely possible to him. At some point Kimball would have realized that Gwen's inclusion meant Bill couldn't live, either.

"What would make him think *he* could land a helicopter?" she begged.

He hated seeing the turmoil in those beautiful eyes. "DEA agents aren't like Navy SEALs," he explained, "who claim to be able to operate anything from a submarine to a NASA rocket." The couple of SEALs he'd met had been full of themselves. "But depending on what kind of investigations we've been involved in, we develop skills. I'm good with boats." He'd even piloted an illegal submersible. "We do have helicopter pilots. Kimball might have been one."

"If so, he chose a terrible time to take over."

"He was plenty arrogant. That isn't necessarily what happened, though."

After an interval, she said quietly, "Poor Bill."

"He chose a slippery slope."

Gwen didn't say anything. A minute later, without another word, they rose and set out again.

As they walked, he heard birdcalls and an odd shrill whistle he couldn't identify but felt sure wasn't human, saw the flick of a squirrel tail. Even he recognized the *rat-a-tat-tat* as a woodpecker.

Their next stop was made when crossing a small creek carrying snowmelt down to the lakes and rivers at a lower elevation. Just above them, a small waterfall dropped no more than five feet. The water sparkled as it danced and tumbled over moss-covered rocks, ferns clustered to each side. Thirsty as they were, Gwen recommended against drinking it without treatment. They filled her bottle and the empty one from the pack and dropped in the purifier tablets Kimball had thoughtfully provided for safe drinking. According to her, there were several nasty pathogens in what appeared to be pristine high mountain water.

Rafe slipped when stepping over the rock-strewn stream, twisted his ankle but found that Kimball's boots were more or less waterproof. Good thing, because he'd have hated to squelch as well as struggle for his footing over a rough side slope. He took a few cautious steps before deciding he hadn't done any significant damage.

He'd about hit his limit again, but he kept his jaws clamped together so he couldn't admit it when he heard something that made the hair on the back of his neck rise.

"Oh, no," Gwen breathed.

Good thing helicopters were such noisy machines. He and Gwen had enough advance warning to plunge into a stretch of woodland that wasn't as thick as he'd have liked but should serve to hide them.

Once he'd knelt and she crouched amidst some rare understory vegetation with purple berries, further shielded by low, almost feathery branches of an evergreen, he calculated it might have been an hour and a half to two hours since the helicopter left.

Sure enough, the damn thing started by flying over the same territory it had earlier and then expanding what wasn't quite a systematic grid but was close. On its last pass, it nearly went right overhead again.

But finally, it turned back and presumably set down, although Rafe could no longer see the thing.

Damn it, he *needed* to see what he and Gwen were up against, so instead of staying put, he pushed to his feet again. "I'm going to try to find a viewpoint."

"Wait! I'll come, too."

He wanted to say no, but right now, she was stronger than he was, so he waited until she'd shrugged off the pack. They were too far away to worry about being heard but had to be careful not to pop out too precipitously into the open.

All he could tell for the next few minutes was that the helicopter was still there, although the pilot never shut down the engines. Rafe must have subconsciously kept in mind where the crash site was, because this time, he led the way until he saw a rock promontory ahead. It took some effort to lower himself to his belly and crawl forward. Gwen stayed behind him.

He'd put the binoculars around his neck earlier. If too many tall trees blocked their view, they were screwed, but Gwen's strategy of gaining elevation was the best they could have done.

He reached the edge of the rocky outcrop, braced himself with the elbow on his good side and raised the binoculars. There was the smoke, a dark trail diminished now but still obvious. Maybe no longer visible from any great distance. Yeah, he could see the whirling blades on the helicopter...and movement beside it. Two men—no, there was another pair. All wearing green camouflage and equipped with hefty packs.

No rifles to be seen, but he supposed they wanted to look like your average backpackers if they happened upon any climbers or hikers.

Even so, he hoped no park ranger met up with them and asked too many questions. He doubted they'd bothered with backcountry permits.

One man lifted a hand, and the helicopter rose again, banked and returned the direction it had come.

Rafe wondered if Bruce Kimball's body was now in the belly of the helicopter. Had to be. If legitimate search and rescue should find the crash site, questions about a dead man with bullet wounds could prove awkward.

Rafe watched the foursome until his eyes burned, then squirmed backward. He looked at Gwen.

"Four men," he said, "wearing camouflage and carrying dark green packs. They're being discreet but no doubt have some firepower tucked away."

Her eyes closed for a moment, and then she retreated all the way to where she'd left their pack. He followed, rising to his feet at the end.

The only positive he could think of was that the two of them were also armed, and she'd taken out Bruce Kimball with a deadly accurate shot. Later, he'd have to ask Gwen how and why she'd learned to shoot like that, especially given her dedication to saving lives rather than taking them.

On the negative side, the two of them currently moved at the speed of a banana slug. They also weren't dressed to blend. He doubted either of them had paid attention to whether they were trampling vegetation when they set out. For all he knew, they'd all but laid down an airport runway.

"Let's move while we can," he suggested.

Once she'd hefted the damn pack on her back, Rafe bit off another groan as he pushed himself to his feet again. His body instantly revolted, muscles cramping into white-hot knots of agony. For a minute, he had to bend over at the hips, hands braced on his thighs, and do nothing but wait and try to breathe. Gwen hovered beside him, anxious. She reached for him, hesitated then took her hand back, obviously knowing there was nothing she could do.

Except give him more morphine, but he refused to ask for it. He had to push those intervals out as long as he could. For starters, he didn't know how much of the stuff she had. He didn't want to become too dependent, either, and he especially didn't want a drug scrambling his brain. Things were likely to get worse before they got better.

"I'm okay," he said roughly, straightening.

With an uneasy glimpse back the way they'd come, she started out again, bowed beneath the weight of the big pack. He shuffled after her.

THE PRIMAL INSTINCT that had steered Gwen toward higher ground despite the harder going kept flaring. She wanted to *see* behind and below them. They might initially have laid a trail a Scout could follow, which meant now sticking to rocky ground as much as possible would be smart.

Divorcing herself from her aching body, she brooded. This whole thing kept escalating. Four men were prepared to spend however much time was necessary to hunt down her and Rafe.

She'd thought that the moment when she realized Kimball was trying to strangle Rafe was the worst—until he'd turned his gun on her and she'd had to make such a horrible choice. Now she understood this might never end.

The whole elaborate scheme had been meant to make Rafe vanish from the face of the earth. That wouldn't have been hard to do in a wilderness where a tossed body would have been down to bones in no time, and those probably dragged off by animal activity.

She was the one who'd been the monkey wrench in the works. Next time…

Rafe would be dead if it weren't for me, she thought. *Although Bill would be alive.*

Only she no longer believed that. Could Kimball really have let Bill fly on to Seattle as planned and trusted he'd stay mum about his part in all this?

Gwen had to wonder what Rafe's boss at the DEA was doing right now, too. Even if he'd flown back to the office, wherever that was, he'd have learned at some point that Rafe was no longer convalescing in the hospital, that in fact he was missing.

Figuring out where he'd gone initially should, on the face of it, be a no-brainer. The hospital wouldn't have handed over a patient to just anybody. Kimball must have flashed credentials at the hospital as well as at the air rescue base. An ambulance crew had transported Rafe to the airfield and loaded him into the helicopter. Plenty of people knew what had happened to Rafe, up to the point when the helicopter took off.

Except, Kimball almost had to have used a badge with a fake name. He sure wouldn't have wanted to be on record. If that was so, why did Bill have his real name? She puzzled over that one, until she thought, *What if Bill recognized him?* Military helicopter pilot, DEA agent— they might have encountered each other at some time in the past.

If that was the case, Bill wouldn't have survived to fly the helicopter to Seattle no matter what.

Well, the helicopter never did arrive in Seattle. A search should have been instigated on both ends. Unfortunately, the initial focus would have been the expected route, not the scenic detour Bill had been paid off to take.

Whatever the scenario, she saw an inevitable outcome.

If Kimball had used a false name earlier, as that seemed logical—could he have stolen some other agent's badge?—that would confuse any attempt to find out who was involved in kidnapping Rafe.

"Let's take another break," she said.

His expression didn't change, but he nodded. Once they were seated, she handed him the water bottle and then dug in her tote for the bottle of Tylenol. When she gave him several pills, he swallowed them without question—for what good they'd do.

When her turn came to drink, she took some Tylenol, too.

"Do you think they'll split up?" she asked after a minute.

"Makes sense." He paused. "Maybe search in pairs."

What if they were able to stay in touch with SATCOM radios, too?

"You said you saw your boss at the hospital," she said abruptly.

He gave her a surprisingly sharp look from those brown eyes, given his exhaustion and pain. "Yes."

"Well, do you trust him?"

His silence lasted long enough to make her uneasy.

"Yeah. He's never given me reason not to." The slowness of his response told her this wasn't the first time he'd wondered. "He did give me back my weapon."

"In recovery at the hospital. That's…surely not usual."

"No. I was too out of it to think it through, but now I wonder…"

She wondered, too. About a lot. "If we had

internet access we might be able to find out whether your bodyguards died."

"Unless the whole incident was buried."

"Why would authorities—" *Oh, heck*, she could think of reasons. The city of Yakima may never have known that a federal law enforcement agency had set up a safe house there. They wouldn't have appreciated not being informed, especially after a gun battle erupted in a peaceful neighborhood. Or... "If one of the other men is alive..."

"I think that's unlikely, but I can hope."

She watched as a bird—a bright blue Steller's jay—sidled along a branch, head tilting one way and then the other as *he* watched her. After a moment, she said wryly, "I can't decide if I wish I'd bought a ticket on that Greyhound bus or am glad I didn't."

Rafe's hand caught hers. "You know my vote."

The warmth and strength of his grip was more comforting than it ought to be. She clasped his hand in return, and neither moved for a long time.

Chapter Seven

"Can you go on?" Gwen asked.

A flash of anger showed in Rafe's eyes. "I should be asking you that. You're having to do all the work."

Feeling a little grumpy herself, she retorted, "Here we go again. Is this because I'm a woman?"

"No!" He glared at her. "It's because you're half my weight."

"That's an exaggeration."

"And you're injured, too."

She sighed. "I don't think my ribs are broken, or they'd hurt more than they do." Which was bad enough, but she wasn't telling him that. "They're maybe cracked or just bruised. Later, I'll have you help me wrap them."

His jaw tightened still more.

"Have you forgotten that you were *shot* multiple times last night? That you had surgery *early this morning*? Were still woozy enough not to know what was happening to you when you got tied hand, foot and the rest of your body and then were kidnapped from the hospital? And, hey, a few hours later, *we fell out of the sky*?" She was practically shouting.

He stared for a minute longer, then let his head sink forward.

Gwen took a chance and patted his broad back. "I understand."

Lifting his head, he growled, "You had to do that?"

"Express sympathy?"

"You should have just slapped me and marched away. Let me catch up if I could."

She studied him. "Is it really so bad to lean on someone else a little?"

"Sometimes I work with partners. Needing to trust someone else isn't the same as feeling useless. Useless gets you killed in my profession."

Uneasiness had begun creeping over her. "Can we walk and argue at the same time?"

"Did you hear something?"

"No. Just…"

"Yeah." He pushed himself up. "Put the damn tote bag over my good shoulder." His eyes narrowed to slits when she hesitated.

As exhausted as she was, not carrying the surprisingly heavy and awkward bag would be an enormous relief. Once they stopped for the night, she should go through it. There might be things she could ditch. She did as he asked, then shrugged into the pack and forced herself to straighten.

"We don't have to argue," he said, as this time they fell into step together.

"No. Just…" He'd hate this, but she wanted to say it, anyway. If only once. "What you've succeeded in doing, essentially rising from a hospital bed postsurgery, is next to miraculous. You know that, don't you? And…if I were out here alone, I'd be a lot more scared than I am."

No, she'd probably still be sitting shell-shocked and sniveling beside the body of the man she shot and killed. Because of Rafe, she'd had to pull herself together and remember who she was: a strong, capable woman who wasn't going to let some drug-trafficking scum kill her *or* her patient.

HE'D APOLOGIZED FOR his momentary breakdown and then spent what was probably the next half hour trying to figure out what had triggered it.

It was true he hated being helpless. Most people probably did, and anyone who served in the military or law enforcement more than most. Not being at the top of your game equated to vulnerability. And, yes, that was certainly true right now. If he hadn't been so seriously wounded, *he'd* be carrying the pack, and he and

Gwen would be moving a lot faster. That she had to travel at the speed of a patient shuffling up and down the hospital corridor gripping an IV pole was his fault.

Hell, it was his fault she'd gotten mixed up in this in the first place.

Except that wasn't so. It was Bruce Kimball's. If he hadn't sold his soul to the devil, there never would have been an attack on the safe house. Rafe would still be resigned to the months of tedium to come. Gwen would have made her way to Seattle, and Rafe would never have met her. Bill the pilot wouldn't have been tempted, and he'd be alive.

And above and beyond all that, if an organization of morally bankrupt human beings weren't determined to profit by providing an incredibly dangerous substance to relative innocents, none of this would have happened.

A powerful, intensely addictive opioid, fentanyl could be produced cheaply and mixed into recreational drugs, in some cases increasing the high but too often killing the user, who wasn't even aware that an unknown, deadly substance was in their favorite products from the local dealer, or the pills labeled as painkillers or antianxiety meds or even muscle relaxants bought off the internet. If the quantity of fentanyl was too high, people died quickly. It was as simple as that. Fentanyl was currently considered to be the leading cause of death for Americans aged eighteen to forty-nine. It had zoomed to the top of the Drug Enforcement Administration's priorities.

The cartel Rafe had inserted himself into was based in Mexico, but the organization had tentacles spread throughout their chief market, the US.

Rafe had never hated the people he was investigating as much as he had the Espinosa family and their underlings. People smuggling cocaine knew it was illegal, that it was addictive, but it didn't have as much possibility of killing someone when they took their first snort. Every single person involved in manufacturing and trafficking fentanyl knew the risks that even one hit could kill. They didn't care.

By the end, Rafe had been desperate to answer every question he could, collect proof that would send the maximum number of these creeps to prison for long periods. He wanted to be done, to breathe clean air again, to allow himself to sleep deeply without a knife and gun under his pillow.

The idea of a year of stultifying boredom hadn't excited him, but that was the price he'd known he would have to pay. Settled into the safe house, at least initially, he'd been glad for some downtime.

Who knew this was the closest he'd get to a vacation? Struck by the irony, he lifted his gaze from his feet to take in the grandeur surrounding him, puffs of cloud crossing the brilliantly blue sky and the small yellow flowers growing from gritty soil between rocks. Then he absorbed the sight of the woman in front of him, her fat caramel-colored braid swaying over her slim back and her endless legs and a perfectly shaped rear that made his fingers twitch.

I'm damn lucky, he realized—which didn't shut down his fear that this gutsy woman might end up dying beside him.

He almost walked into her. Had she seen or heard something?

"The sun is dropping," she said. "At least the sun confirms we're northeast of Rainier. Probably in the park, but I can't be positive. There's a protected wilderness outside the park boundary. Anyway, we should look for someplace to stop for the night."

He tipped his head again. Yes, the sun was lower than it had been, but the sky was bright. This didn't look like sunset to him.

"If we can keep going even for another hour…"

She shook her head. "Night falls fast in the

mountains. Then the temperature plummets just as fast, even at this time of year. Besides, we both need a serious rest. I keep stumbling and my knees want to crumple and—"

He squeezed her upper arm. "You're right. I've gotten so all I do is stare at my feet to be sure I don't misstep. A grizzly could come roaring at us, and I wouldn't notice."

Her smile brought life back to her face. "No grizzlies in this part of the state."

He grimaced in return. "One small blessing."

Transfixed by her laugh—by her *ability* to laugh—he had to be staring. Her eyes widened, and she backed up a step or two.

"Well, let's, um, check out those trees over there."

"Good idea," he managed to say, and tore his gaze from her.

As exhausted as she was, the sound of falling water wove into her consciousness like orchestra music appropriate to the beauty around them. Gwen clambered above a small patch of snow, Rafe right behind her, the noise growing in volume until alarm belatedly riveted her attention.

Twenty feet farther on, they came abruptly in sight of the furious foaming white of a stream bigger than any they'd yet seen tumbling down a stair step of cliffs. Given the force of the waterfall, even from this distance, the mist wet her face and clung to her eyelashes. Surrounding rocks gleamed with moisture and bright green moss that would make them treacherous.

They wouldn't be crossing here.

Gwen groaned and turned, bumping into Rafe. He stared expressionlessly at the falls. "Pretty."

"I *hate* to backtrack." And that was putting it mildly. She was close to spent and guessed he'd passed that point a couple of hours ago.

Rafe grabbed her arm. "Look."

He didn't sound alarmed, but she still turned her head quickly. *Oh.* A deer accompanied by fawn drank from the stream. They hadn't noticed yet that they weren't alone.

At Gwen's first movement, the deer raised her head, and within moments, both had leaped into the trees.

She and Rafe retreated far enough that the rocks beneath their feet weren't slick, and the roar of the falls wasn't battering their ears.

She'd been taking in their surroundings, desperate for an alternative to making their way downstream far enough for a crossing to be feasible. "If you think you can get up there—" she pointed "—we'd be out of sight."

He looked. His mouth tightened, but he nodded. "Let's do it."

This was…well, a rock climber would have dismissed it as a mere scramble, but for two injured people as tired as they were, it felt more like scaling a straight-up-and-down cliff. A few handholds felt damp from spray blown this far. Her thigh muscles screamed. Once, her foot slipped out of the crack she'd thought secure, and the weight of the pack pulled her backward. Rafe leaned into her, using one strong hand and his bulk to keep her safe until her pulse settled down and she had overcome the rush of adrenaline to try again.

The stiff lower branches of small firs whipped her face but were also strong enough when she seized them to pull herself up.

All the while, a sixth sense she hadn't known she possessed kept her aware of the man behind her. She could *feel* his determination and the sheer will that kept him going. A few muttered curse words escaped him, and a few pained sounds that weren't uttered voluntarily.

I should have had him go ahead of me, she thought, but if she'd done that, she would have fallen far enough that she could have been seriously injured.

More seriously.

If *he* fell…

Gwen blocked that horrifying fear, instead worrying that they'd get up there and find no place adequate to set up even a minimal camp. No, she wouldn't second-guess herself now; from down below, she'd been sure she saw a ledge.

She groped for her next handhold until she satisfied herself that the rock outcrop wouldn't crumble. She heaved herself up another couple of feet. Six inches. A foot. She *had* to be almost there.

And then, suddenly, she was. She was able to crawl forward, brushing aside the dense, low branches of small evergreens. Above her, a bird took indignant flight. All she saw was a flash of yellow. Her pack snagged; she wriggled to free herself. *Keep going, keep going.*

She flopped face down, not sure she could move again. Unless Rafe— No, he stretched out beside her, eyes closed, pale lines of strain on his face.

Neither of them moved for a couple of minutes. Then she sighed, rolled and squirmed to get her arm out of one of the straps of the pack. A hand reached up to help.

"Thanks," she said. Once she was liberated from the pack, she managed to sit up and look around. A rock overhang seemed to promise protection from a helicopter flyover...if they could get to it. More clouds had been gathering, too, the threat of rain another thing she'd refused to let herself dwell on. Neither she nor Rafe had rain gear—or parkas if they should grow chilled once they were wet. This might be the perfect burrow.

She crawled forward, dragging the pack behind her, not caring about the beating her hands were taking. Yes, the ground was reasonably flat right in front of the overhang. They could compress some minor vegetation and be shielded behind the cluster of dark green trees.

"Perfect," she said, and stayed where she was on her hands and knees, swaying.

RAFE DIDN'T THINK he'd hurt like this when he was taking the bullets in the first place. Ten more feet, and he might not have made it.

He wasn't alone. Gwen had hit a wall, too, he saw.

"Hey," he said, "let me give you a hand."

His crawl was like a three-legged race since he knew he'd regret putting any weight on the damaged upper arm. Still, he got far enough to kneel beside her and wrap his good arm around her waist.

"Let yourself go," he murmured.

She collapsed in his hold, but only for a moment. Then she twisted and plopped down on her butt. "Thank you. I was about ready to do a face-plant."

"That actually sounds good."

Resilient enough to laugh, she continued to amaze him.

"I should have given you another shot of morphine at one of our last stops. Why didn't you ask?"

He wasn't about to admit how close he'd come to begging. "Figured the further we could spread them out, the better."

"Actually, that's not really true. Staying on top of the pain helps with recovery."

"I also didn't want to mask any pain that would tell me I was doing more damage," he told her.

"Oh. That makes sense." Apparently making this her first priority, she found what she needed and drew up whatever quantity of the drug she'd calculated for his size. He shifted, unfastened his pants and shoved them down far enough for her to administer the shot in his butt cheek.

And, oh, damn, that felt good. It didn't make him a new man, but it gave him back some of his natural confidence that he could overcome just about any obstacle.

Once she'd capped the used needle and slipped it into a baggy, she said, "We can set up camp here for the night."

Rafe frowned at her as she reached for the

pack again. "You look to me like you need to sit for a minute first."

"I guess there's no hurry. Wait!" She dug almost frantically in her tote, finally coming up with her phone.

Good thought. He all but hung over her shoulder.

No bars. She turned in a circle, lifted it over her head and finally said bitterly, "Things never work when you need them to."

Their lives might depend on them eventually regaining cell phone service, but he didn't have to say a word. She knew.

Less animated, she dropped the phone back into her tote and began searching again. "Let's have a snack before we start setting up."

Rafe couldn't remember how long it had been since they stopped long enough to each eat an energy bar. A single bar hadn't had enough calories for anyone working as hard as they had been, and especially not for someone his size. He pictured a juicy steak and baked potato heaped with sour cream and immediately regretted it when his stomach whined.

After digging deep in the bag, she produced another couple of candy bars. He suspected they'd be running low on those soon—these might even be the last—but he didn't ask. He took one, tore the wrapping and sank his teeth into it—he hadn't even looked to see what it was. It tasted damn good. That's all that mattered. Forget the steak.

"I hope we didn't break branches getting up here," he said after swallowing the last bite.

When she looked at him, he had an unsettling remembrance of thinking how soft the gray of her eyes was. Gentle, comforting. That wasn't true anymore. Maybe not surprising after what they'd gone through, they had darkened, almost seemed haunted. He tried to tell himself he was seeing a reflection of his own feelings about a brutally hard day but suspected that wasn't entirely true.

"Tarp," she said, as if to nudge herself, and opened the pack.

The additional crawling around was manageable for him now after the relief of the painkiller, and he liked the idea of something approaching comfort—and being able to stay put until morning. So he helped set up the tent, push the pad and the single sleeping bag inside it—something to think about later—and tie the green tarp over the too-bright red tent that might as well be a beacon should a helicopter fly right over them.

She set the stove aside and spread out the packets of freeze-dried meals. "Ten."

Rafe gazed at them. "Do you suppose he'd have enjoyed backpacking?"

"Maybe he did it all the time. Still…" She wrinkled her nose. "Weird plan."

"It was, but sure as hell his home office has him down as being on vacation. Heading into the backcountry gave him an excuse to have no cell phone service. In the original plan, the helicopter and my body would have just vanished. No reason to connect him, just one more hiker emerging from the park as far as possible from the crash site."

"Except that he'd flashed his credentials at the hospital and airfield."

"Those couldn't have been his."

"Bill knew his real name." She told him her speculation about the pair meeting in the past and said, "If that was so, it must have come as a shock to Kimball."

"That's one way to put it," Rafe said dryly.

"Do you suppose once he hiked to a trailhead, he was going to call someone for a lift?"

Instinct had Rafe shaking his head. "I doubt it. I'll bet he'd have put out his thumb. Some vacationers or other backpackers would have picked him up. A night at a hotel at SeaTac, and he could have flown out."

She sniffed. "*I* wouldn't have picked him up. Or I'd have kicked him out of my car ten miles down the road. Unless he managed a personality upgrade."

Rafe grinned. "Well, he wouldn't be threatening to shoot whoever gave him a ride."

"I don't know." She looked contemplative. "He jumped straight to hostile the minute he set eyes on me. He didn't even know who I was, and he was bristling. It was like his default. You know?" She shook her head. "I'd have been less suspicious if he'd dialed it back a little and tried a semipleasant 'Hey, this area is restricted. Are you looking for somebody?'"

Rafe cast his mind back, trying to remember why he'd instinctively disliked a fellow agent he'd never had much to do with. It wasn't the first time someone rubbed him wrong, of course. The snap judgments he made about people were presumably based on a subconscious conclusion rather than conscious reasoning. Because he and Kimball hadn't been assigned to work together, he'd had no reason to dwell on that twinge of dislike.

Now, though, he said, "I think that's what I responded to, also. Put a bunch of federal agents together for the first time, and there's often some posturing. Who's the alpha here? But we don't fight to determine it. We work together, smooth out any rough spots, determine strengths and weaknesses, and depend on each other. Kimball had a bad attitude. I saw him bump another guy's shoulder hard in passing when really he was the one who should have stepped aside. I didn't like the way he looked at a particular female agent, either."

"So, your dislike was more rational than you knew."

"I guess so." The corner of his mouth quirked. "On the job, I sometimes have to go with my gut. There are times I need to walk back my opinion, but not often."

She sighed. "This time, you were right on target."

"Except being arrogant doesn't translate to being willing to violate the very principles you're supposed to be defending."

"No." She slipped on a fleece jacket and zipped it. "Do you think it would be safe to take a quick nap before we make dinner?"

"I don't think anyone can sneak up on us here. We'll have to get cozy, though."

Her gaze shied from his. "Not like we have a lot of choice."

Was she still holding on to any doubt that he was who he claimed to be? He said carefully, "I'm afraid not."

The smile she offered him was more complicated than it appeared on the surface but was still so beautiful he quit breathing.

"I'd be delighted," she told him.

What?

Oh, getting cozy. Somehow, he doubted either of them would stay conscious long enough for the proximity to get awkward.

She let him make his awkward way into the tent first before following him. She wadded up extra clothing for pillows, and then they settled down side by side on top of the sleeping bag. Despite the talk of cuddling, their bodies barely brushed each other. He didn't like the distance between them. He wanted to roll onto his side and gather her into his arms, but he knew better. Any more intimacy than absolutely necessary had to be her decision.

Scaring her was the absolute last thing he wanted to do.

Chapter Eight

Gwen lay completely still until she was sure Rafe had fallen asleep. As his breathing deepened, genuine relaxation replaced what she'd recognized as pretend calm. A nerve in his cheek jerked a couple of times; his fingers twitched. He had to be dreaming.

Only then did she give herself permission to roll onto her side facing away from him, close her eyes and surrender to her own tiredness.

As it turned out, for all its aches and pains, her body was ready to let go, but her brain kept working. She didn't understand why she had been so determined not to be the first to fall asleep.

The answer just leaped into her mind: *I'd have been too vulnerable. Was I afraid he might hurt me?* she wondered in shock, but that wasn't right. Mostly…she didn't really *know* him, she realized. They'd gone through an awful lot today, but none of it allowed much in the way of conversation. So it was true that, in many re-spects, Rafe Salazar remained a stranger.

Not entirely, though. Despite suffering from extreme pain, he'd reached out over and over to save her from falls, to support her.

Yes, she reminded herself, but just because Kimball turned out to be corrupt didn't mean Rafe wasn't conning her. He could really and truly have been under arrest; only whoever he and Kimball were both working for had deter-mined to shut him up before he could be com-pelled to speak to law enforcement. Snatch him before he was fully conscious and be sure he never had a chance to open his mouth. The drug trade was notoriously violent. Mistakes—like getting arrested—she knew could be punish-able by death.

Yet her instincts insisted that Rafe was one of the good guys. He could so easily have over-powered her, taken the pack, the food and the morphine, and gone on the run by himself.

Yes. Instead, he'd been...careful with her. Gentle. *She* mattered.

She had a sinking feeling that some of the tension came from her awareness of him as a man. And...maybe some reciprocal awareness on his part?

Face it, he was a beautiful man. She resisted the temptation to roll over to study him. She didn't have to; behind closed eyes, she saw him. Big, broad-shouldered, lean and muscled. With those cheekbones and penetrating dark eyes, he could have modeled, although she felt sure he would laugh at the idea.

So, okay, if she'd met him another way, she'd have been interested. As it was...

A flutter of panic explained some of her self-consciousness. It would be easy to fall for him, given their mutual dependence. If she was okay with a casual easy-come-easy-go relationship, that wouldn't be any big deal. But she never had been. Having the last guy she'd been involved with ditch her the way he did left scars on top of her natural caution. Anyway, if—when—she and Rafe came upon other people or were finally able to make a call and get rescued, they'd go their own ways. His life was really complicated, and from what he'd said, he didn't even work out of the Seattle office, assuming the DEA had one.

Better to be sensible now.

Smart conclusion.

And, face it, the mutual attraction thing could be entirely wishful thinking. He might be protecting her because he needed her to get him out of a wilderness he couldn't navigate on his own.

Fine, she thought.

Having figured out what made her skittish, she was armored now. With that settled, she sank into sleep with astonishing speed.

THE NEXT THING she knew, she woke up with a jolt. Had she heard something alarming? The helicopter, or—

A hand smoothed hair back from her forehead. Rafe, of course. *Oh, heavens!* Somehow she'd ended up with her head on his upper arm, his body spooning hers.

Subconscious? Weren't you listening?

Apparently not.

"Sorry," he murmured. "I need to get up."

He needed to— *Oh.* Now that she thought about it, she did, too.

Busy with her thoughts, she let Rafe maneuver out the unzipped opening, climb to his feet and head for a rock outcrop. Once he was mostly out of sight, she tensed her stomach muscles in preparation for standing up herself and grimaced. Now that she thought about it, *everything* hurt. Darn it. She stayed in decent physical shape! She did.

Apparently, her several-mile three-times-a-week jog really wasn't enough. And then there were her ribs.

Glad Rafe couldn't see her as she managed to scoot out of the tent and get up without a hint of grace, Gwen went the opposite direction from him. Her thighs were *really* unhappy with her when she squatted.

Surely, she'd feel better in the morning. She sighed and made her way back to their encampment.

Dusk deepened the sky to violet tinged with a darker purple that was almost…gray. Clouds, she realized. It was good he'd woken up. A threat of rain looked more realistic, which made her glad they'd set up the tent.

She returned to find Rafe studying the tent with what she read as disfavor. She knew why. "Do you suppose that's his favorite color?"

Rafe grunted. "I'm thinking he chose it to grab attention. If he was lucky, he'd be seen half a dozen times by other hikers who could testify that he was by himself, just a lone, innocent backpacker."

Thank heavens for the green tarp. She'd succeeded in stretching it out above and in front of the tent, tying cords to branches and, in one case, a rock, giving them some room to sit in front without getting wet if it rained. Without asking her, Rafe now took the jackknife from a pocket in the pack and set to cutting branches that he laid over the tarp and sides of the tent.

"Looks like a deer blind," he said, closing the knife. "A lot of work for one night, but worth it if that damn helicopter flies overhead come morning."

"I've been thinking about that," she said.

In the dimming light, she could no longer make out his face clearly but could tell he'd narrowed his eyes. "Am I going to like this?"

"I don't know." She hesitated. "It's just...this was a really hard day."

"I can't argue." He rolled his one good shoulder and, with obvious effort, lowered himself to the ground again.

"Well... I'm wondering if it might be a good idea to stay here tomorrow and not set out again until the following morning. Right now, we're staggering around blind. I suspect that given an extra twenty-four hours, you'd do a lot of healing."

"I might, but then they could get ahead of us. That's not a comfortable idea."

HE'D HATED TO remind her of a brutal truth but knew he had to. That might be a small shudder she tried to hide.

After a minute, she said quietly, "You're right."

End of conversation. Gwen fired up the stove, and they agreed on an entrée from the array of freeze-dried meals Kimball had chosen. She set aside two of the packets. The guy was—

had obviously been—a meat eater. Which made Rafe think.

"What kind of predators do we need to watch out for?" he asked.

"You mean, aside from the human ones?"

At her wry tone, he grimaced. "Just thought I should know about any other threats."

She stirred the concoction that smelled better than it looked. "The only two animals in the park that can be a danger to people are black bears, and usually only females with cubs near, and cougars, which we're unlikely to see. Once in a while, a cougar will attack a human, but it's not common. There are smaller predators, like bobcats, which are rare to spot, and, hey, there was an episode a few years back when a mountain goat over in the Olympic Mountains attacked a backpacker. Most often, when people are injured by wildlife in one of the parks, it's not the animal's fault. It's because the humans have forgotten all common sense, if they ever had any. People will go so far as to set their kid on the back of a bear so they can get an exciting photo."

"I've heard stories like that. I'd say they get what they have coming, except it's their children who might suffer."

"Yes. There's a reason the park service has worked so hard to keep bears away from both roads and campgrounds in the parks. Yellow-stone was most notorious for problems way back when. You wouldn't think you'd have to tell tourists that a moose is a really big animal with an impressive rack on his head, and you might want to give him space."

"Are there moose here at Rainier?"

"No, but there are elk and foxes, not to mention marmots and picas, as well as rabbits, deer mice and—" she pointed upward "—bats."

The darting motion against the dusk sky was familiar.

She dished up his share of the stew in a light-weight bowl and ate hers out of the pan. The ranger-type patter had cut down on the tension, at least on his side. This was the first time since Eaton opened the front door upon seeing a familiar face and gunfire raked the small rambler that Rafe had felt relaxed. He couldn't remember what time that happened. Yesterday, for sure. Twenty-four hours ago? He wouldn't have survived most of the ensuing day if not for Gwen. Watching surreptitiously, he decided she had relaxed, too. Tension was less apparent on her face. He'd say they had been lucky to find someplace as safe as this, but luck hadn't had anything to do with it. He could thank her for that, too.

"Coffee?" she asked. "We even have sugar and powdered creamer, if you take either."

He moved from side to side to scratch his back against the rough rock he leaned against. "All the pleasures of home. Coffee sounds good. Yes to both."

She chuckled. "You're not one of those tough guys who drinks his coffee black even if it tastes like battery acid?"

He let himself smile, too. "Not me."

She heated some water, washed the dinner dishes with soap and a sponge she'd found in the pack, then started over with water for the coffee. He should be helping, but one-handed, how useful would he be, anyway?

"You know how to handle a gun," he commented. "You're a good shot, too. How'd you learn?"

Watching the small pan as if her focused concentration would make the water boil faster, she said, "I...knew someone." She paused. "Oh, I guess it doesn't matter. A foster father. Kind of paranoid. You know, the kind who was sure the government would be coming for his guns. I guess he must not have expressed much of that thinking to social workers, or his foster care license might have been suspended, but anyway. He taught all of us kids how to handle a .22 rifle and both an old-fashioned Colt six-shooter and a semiautomatic. It was fun shooting cans off a fence rail. It probably goes without saying that I didn't hurry out to buy my own handgun once I was living alone. In fact, I haven't handled one since I was in that foster home. He really drilled us, though. I guess some things you don't forget."

"Like riding a bike." If a little more lethal.

She shrugged, then concentrated on pouring not-quite-boiling water into a metal cup and some other container she'd unearthed from the kitchen supplies. "I never thought I'd be thankful for the skill."

"No," he said gently. "Maybe once you're home, you should drop him a note." He added half a spoonful of creamer to the coffee, followed by part of a paper packet of sugar.

Her smile looked sad. "Maybe I should. I didn't make any effort to stay in touch, and I feel bad about that."

Rafe guessed that she'd as soon drop this whole subject, but it would probably be at least a couple of hours before they'd crawl into the tent again, this time for the night. They had to talk about something. She'd gotten him curious earlier anyway, when he'd asked what had motivated her to become a medical first responder. There'd been something in her expression…

Trying to sound easy, undemanding, he asked, "What happened to your parents?"

With a hint of belligerence, she retorted, "Why don't you tell me about *your* parents?"

"Fair enough." His background was more complicated than this answer would tell her, but he could answer the question without getting personal. "Believe it or not, they're both university professors. Philosophy for Dad—I learned early on to tune him out when he got off on his thing—and Mom is a linguist. Teaches several languages at the university level and is working on a grammar and vocabulary dictionary for an obscure African language on the verge of disappearing. This is following work on a Central American Indigenous language."

"Huh."

Rafe laughed. "They're smart people. Well-meaning parents, but heads in the clouds. Mom would be away for months at a time on one of her research trips. Dad has written several books. I could tell you the titles, but they wouldn't mean any more to you than they did to me."

"That...doesn't sound like an easy household to grow up in."

Not for the first time, Rafe had that feeling she was seeing deeper than he liked. She'd hit the nail on the head.

"Your turn," he said roughly.

She watched him for another minute or two, then nodded. "Dad died when I was a kid, too young to remember him. One of those heart things that no one predicts. He was in his twenties, playing in a pickup basketball game, and just collapsed. Gone."

But she hadn't aimed to be a cardiologist, he thought.

"Mom…" Gwen had a gift for stillness, but now she shifted in a way that gave away her discomfort. "She and I were in a car accident. Head-on, drunk driver. The car was pushed through a guardrail and over something like a thirty-foot drop. This makes me really obvious, doesn't it? Mom was killed right away. I was…in bad shape. I thought I was going to die, too. I guess emergency response was reasonably quick. It felt like forever, but it probably always does when you're trapped like I was. I was eleven and in the front seat, too. The car was crumpled, and they couldn't get mom *or* me out, which was bad because she was *right there* and so obviously dead, and my legs were broken and I was bleeding bad. They used crowbars and whatever else they could lay their hands on, because later, they told me they didn't think I'd have survived a long wait."

He swore softly.

"They were calm, even when they probably

weren't really, and caring. This guy got an IV line in me, gave me oxygen when he thought I needed it and stayed with me except when the others made him get out of the way. He just talked, even told a few jokes, and he held my hand."

She wasn't crying at the memory, just appeared pensive. "So. Like I said, I'm not subtle. I wanted to grow up to do what he did."

He should have expected something like this, but hadn't. He felt fierce anger and a tight knot of pain behind the different kind of pain in his breastbone, but knew he shouldn't let her know what a hit he'd taken on her behalf.

"So, did they give you the good stuff, too?"

Obviously startled, Gwen giggled. "Yes, they did. Whatever they put in that IV was amazing."

"Morphine?"

"Who knows?"

Rafe set down his cup. "Did you ever see that guy again?"

"Yes. He visited me a couple of times in the hospital and, way later, got permission for me to ride along in his ambulance a couple of times. I wished..." This shrug was a cloaking device.

"Wished?"

"He could have taken me as a foster kid. I knew better than to ask, and he didn't offer."

"If he was single, he probably wouldn't have been allowed to take in a girl."

"That's true." Her chin rose, and she wiped the memories and regrets from her expression. "There are a few candy bars left. Do you want one?"

"I don't think I can resist," he admitted. "The only thing is, we may not be able to share a tent if neither of us can brush our teeth."

Gwen laughed. "Who gets to stay out in the rain?"

He grinned. "I'm the patient. Gives me priority, right?"

"You wish." She laughed again. "We're really going to owe that creep Kimball, you know. As it happens, I noticed a handy-dandy little travel pack with toothpaste. And get this, it looks like it came with two toothbrushes! Sort of miniature ones, and maybe meant to be disposable, but they'll do us."

"Has he used either?" Rafe asked dubiously. He wouldn't mind sharing spit with some people, but Bruce Kimball wasn't one of those.

"I doubt it. Doesn't look like anything has been touched since he packed it."

The silence that fell after that felt surprisingly easy. They'd said quite a bit for two people who had known each other for only twelve hours or so. He was glad for the fleece as the temperature dropped. Night sounds he wouldn't have otherwise noticed were soothing in their own way: a few hoots that had to be from an owl, or two of them chatting, small squeaks and rustles, the very distant murmur that he guessed was the muted roar of the waterfall. Once, there was a sharp squeal, quickly cut off, and Rafe reminded himself that owls were hunters.

Finally, he said, "We have a plan for tomorrow?"

Gwen sighed. "I wish."

He waited, and after a minute she went on.

"If possible, I'd like to reach the top of this ridge. It would help a lot to get a glimpse of the mountain."

That made sense.

"My goal has been to reach a trail, both for easier walking and in hopes we'll encounter other people. But I've had second thoughts."

He'd vaguely had the same hope, but now that the subject was out in the open, he had concerns, too.

"Would the people after us hesitate to gun down a couple of backpackers that happen by?" she asked.

Rafe suspected she knew the answer as well as he did.

"I doubt it," he said harshly. "Also, if we can move faster on a trail, so can they."

"So...maybe we could sort of make our way a few hundred yards from the trail. If we're lucky, we might spot a ranger. I'm pretty sure most of them are armed these days, and I assume they carry a radio with some distance."

Rafe didn't wonder aloud what the odds were of happening on a park ranger, partly because her plan was as good as any.

And *that* was assuming they kept ahead of their pursuers long enough to stumble upon a trail.

Chapter Nine

There had been an odd sense of intimacy while they talked, Gwen couldn't help thinking. She'd told Rafe things she hadn't talked about in a very long time, if ever. None of her relationships with men had progressed to the point where she wanted to tell them about the eon she'd spent trapped in the crumpled metal of the car along with her dead mother. Doing so made her feel...vulnerable.

Damn it, there was that word again.

Especially since, now that she thought of it, *he* hadn't shared anything comparable in *his* background. His parents were college professors. So, why wasn't he an academic, too? If there'd been a hint, it must have to do with the suggestion that neither parent was all that present for their son— or for their other children, if he had siblings.

That car accident had been what a psychologist would call a defining experience for her, and she guessed he'd had one of his own. But really, he didn't owe her answers. The bigger question was why *she'd* felt compelled to tell him something so important about herself.

Something he might have found mildly interesting, Gwen reminded herself. It wasn't a deep, dark secret. And they didn't have a real relationship.

Well, not the kind she'd been thinking about, anyway.

After their last depressing exchange, silence settled again until she stirred.

"Let me give you another shot, just enough to give you a chance to sleep, and then we should get ready for bed. An early departure might be a good idea."

"I agree." Was he frowning? "I can do without the morphine."

"No, you can't. Keep on top of the pain, remember? The better you sleep, the more relaxed your muscles, the more healing will happen."

He muttered under his breath but didn't argue while she found the supplies in her tote bag. As she drew up an accurate dose, he held the flashlight, shading the beam with his hand to limit how far out it could be seen from. While he had it on, they put toothpaste on the brushes, and she wet a washcloth and grabbed the bar of soap from Kimball's well-stocked pack. She had to have sweated more today than she usually did in a week.

Rafe eyed the washcloth and said, "Do I get kicked out of the tent if I don't follow your example?"

She made a face at him. "You're a patient. I'm assuming you started the day spotlessly clean."

"I'll bet you did, too."

"We'll see how you feel tomorrow." She waved the syringe. "Drop those drawers."

She enjoyed hearing him laugh, suspecting that the brief sting was worth the rush of euphoria and relief. He pulled the trousers back up, rising to his feet as she collected her toiletry supplies and sought privacy to do some minimal scrubbing. He presumably stepped a few feet away from their small camp to use the facilities, but she didn't hear a thing. When she returned to the tent, he had half sat on a rock and was wrestling off the boots.

"Oh! I can help—"

"Got 'em." He pulled off the socks, too, seemed to glance at her, and removed his pants and the Polartec quarter-zip, leaving him wearing only a pair of stretch boxers he'd appropriated—although he hadn't looked happy about it—and a T-shirt.

He was right, Gwen realized. He had only a single change of clothes in the pack, and she was in even worse shape. If only she'd been able to grab her suitcase! As it was, she could wear the Nomex suit one day instead of her current clothes, but it wasn't ideal for scrambling through the woods and over rocky ridges, to put it mildly. Given their extremely limited wardrobes, they needed to mostly strip at night. She would definitely do that stripping in the pitch dark, preferably once he'd already gone into the tent.

As if he wouldn't be able to tell how little she was wearing the minute she slipped into that sleeping bag with him.

Rafe suggested he get in the sleeping bag first, which was logical. They'd laid it out so their heads would be close to the tent flap in case of trouble. He held the flashlight, a bare glimmer escaping the top of the sleeping bag. Enough to guide her. Gwen wanted to claim she wasn't sleepy yet, but it wasn't true, even after the nap. Anyway, what would she do? Despite the matches Kimball had packed, they hadn't dared light a fire she could sit beside.

Just do it.

She crouched, mostly lay down and squirmed like a snake until she was far enough in. Of course, she bumped and slid against him the whole way. She tried very hard to pretend the solid wall that gave off such welcoming heat wasn't a man she'd known only a day.

Rafe only said, "You can use me as a pillow," and then, "No rain yet."

"No." Where else could she put her head? She should have bundled up some of their limited clothing again to form a facsimile of a cushion, at least for him.

She lay rigid until she felt light-headed and became aware she'd been holding her breath.

"Don't be afraid of me," he murmured, his mouth brushing her hair.

"I...don't think I am," she said after a minute. "It's just... I'm not used to hopping into bed with a guy I don't know that well." And that was putting it mildly.

Humor in his voice, he said, "We've had quite a first date, though, wouldn't you say?"

The laugh was just what she needed. "It's definitely the most eventful I've ever been on."

He chuckled, too, and she felt his chest vibrate even though she wasn't touching it. Was she?

"Want me to tell some jokes?"

"Jokes?" Then she got it. "Like the paramedic. Thank you, but no. Unless you have a really great one."

He told her a bawdy one that had her laughing despite herself. After that, when he said, "Can we get more comfortable?" and eased his arm beneath her head to wrap her in an embrace, she was relaxed enough to allow it. Even rest her head where she could hear his heartbeat and have some wistful thoughts she wouldn't let herself put into words.

Too concrete for something that wasn't happening.

IT WOULD BE nice if they could have shut down and *stayed* shut down until the dawn light beckoned them with a promise of a less painful day, but the truth was, Rafe thought he and Gwen both slept pretty well for three or four hours, but after that, he, for one, hurt and couldn't stay still, she had a nightmare and flailed an arm at his face, and, unable to help waking each other up, they tried half a dozen positions that didn't remain comfortable for more than an hour.

He took pleasure in holding her close for a few minutes at a time, wishing he had the right to cup her breast or slide his hand over her lithe, subtly curvaceous body. Those moments were torturous in their own way and didn't last long.

By morning, his mood was testy, and his first glimpse of Gwen's face suggested she was as tired and grumpy as he was. He submitted to another shot, at which his muscles untangled as if he'd had a deep-tissue massage. *Thank God.*

"You sure you don't want one, too?" he asked,

nodding at the syringe she was dropping into a plastic bag seemingly made for the purpose.

She grimaced. "I wish."

A cup of coffee and a couple of handfuls of trail mix helped both of them.

"That wasn't as cozy as I hoped it would be," she said after a lengthy silence.

Rafe was startled into laughing and was glad to see the corners of her mouth twitch. "You're right. It was more like a high school wrestling match."

She giggled. "I don't think I've ever really slept with anyone."

That was interesting. He said, "I haven't often, and on those occasions, we shared at least a queen-size bed. Not the same thing."

"No." Gwen sighed. "It's infuriating when you want to toss and turn, but you're too trussed up to be able even to turn over."

He lifted an eyebrow. "And you wondered why I was so desperate for you to release me from that damn backboard."

"Oh. Yes." She actually looked apologetic. "I'm sorry."

Rafe smiled. "Don't be. We had a lot going on at the time."

"Yes." Her shoulders slumped. "I suppose we should pack up."

"Yeah," he said gruffly.

Without another word, she started on the cords holding up the tarp, then rolled it, the sleeping bag and pad, and broke down the tent. He was able to take the stove apart and pack up what little they'd left out.

He watched as she delved in her fat tote bag and started discarding things. He saw her hesitate before putting an electronic reader back, but she chose to abandon a swirled glass paperweight about the side of a baseball—a gift from her friend, she said, after glancing at him—along with a box of tampons he pretended not to notice, a bottle of hand lotion, a zip bag that he suspected held makeup and a bag with a couple of wrapped presents she'd been taking back to friends. She looked sad about those, but he didn't say anything, because she was right: the lighter their load, the faster they could move.

She ditched most of the contents of what she called a trauma bag. "If one of us gets hurt again…" she mumbled. "But what are the odds we'll need any of this stuff?" That included emergency airway supplies, something she called a pleural decompression kit, IV supplies and blood pressure cuffs. The bulk and weight saved was substantial. About all she held on to were packages of bandaging materials, which she shifted back into the pack.

While they were able to weed out a couple

of things from Kimball's pack, most of what it held was necessary. As in lifesaving. Rafe hesitated over an extra magazine for Kimball's semiautomatic, briefly bouncing it in his hand, but made the decision to keep it.

Lifesaving.

As he attached the tent, sleeping bag and pad to the pack, Gwen asked how he felt today.

If he'd been honest, he'd have said, *Worse than yesterday.* Wasn't that always the case with injuries and abused muscles? Of course, he shrugged and said, "Better."

Gwen rolled her eyes. "Good for you. *I'm* sore."

"Walk it off."

She stuck her tongue out at him, which he fully deserved. Walking wasn't in their immediate future. Scrambling, climbing, bushwhacking was more like it.

And so it proved. They went up instead of back down, Rafe glad she went first so she couldn't see his gritted teeth or hear his mumbled curses as his thigh and hip especially cramped and zinged with electrical impulses and occasionally felt as if a knife was stabbing him. And this was *after* a dose of morphine. He'd been injured enough times to know he could have forced himself to go on no matter what, but he didn't want to contemplate how bad this trek would have been without the medical aid.

The terrain was incredibly difficult, heavily forested yet steep and rocky. Most of the time, they couldn't see more than ten paces away, but at least they had the comfort of knowing no one else could see them, either.

They obviously scared what wildlife they spotted. Birds went silent long before the humans reached them, then took startled wing at the last moment, often in bright flashes seen out of the corner of his eye. Rafe continued to hear running water, whether the same stream or different ones, he didn't know.

They didn't talk. The effort of climbing coupled with their various disabilities and the muscle soreness left from yesterday's exertions meant that he, at least, had to concentrate to take each painful step. To use a branch to heave himself upward. Not that he'd have gone far if he did fall; he'd just slam into a tree trunk. The thought made him wince. If he took a solid blow on his thigh or already excruciating rib cage…

Don't think about it.

When he saw daylight ahead, he clenched his jaw, unwilling to groan with relief. He kept up a facade of strength with everyone. Hell, maybe even to himself. By the time he'd been a teenager, he'd perfected the swagger, the confidence, the incredulity if anyone was foolish enough to challenge *him*.

The tree line ended suddenly, exposing rough-textured gray granite. By the time they'd scrambled the rest of the way to what he prayed was the ridgetop, he'd scraped and nicked his hands in several places.

In the back of his mind was the realization that he might have left a blood trail to follow, but really, what were the odds their pursuers would climb so exactly behind them? And, no, as he straightened cautiously, he saw that neither hand bled copiously. Just smears.

Gwen grabbed his arm. "Look!"

He took in a stunning vista. Way the hell down from them were at least a couple of lakes. And when he turned his head slightly, there was the mountain, enormous almost past understanding. Flying by it didn't count as a view. A few clouds drifted around the gleaming summit. It occurred to him that they were quite a long way from Mount Rainier here, but seeing the landscape formed by its historic eruptions made him a little queasy.

"Wouldn't want to be here if Rainier suddenly decided to blow its top," he remarked.

"No." Gwen paused. "All the Northwest volcanoes are monitored for seismic activity. Scientists learned from the Mount Saint Helens's eruption and at least delude themselves they can give some warning."

"Uh-huh." He bet the most magnificent mountain he'd ever seen knew how to keep its secrets. "Can we sit?" he added.

"Oh! Yes, of course." She joined him in looking around, then pointed. "That looks good."

"Good" would have been a recliner made for a large man, one that allowed him to put his feet up, but his mouth twitched into a smile at the thought. Somebody was getting soft.

The rock was flat enough to let him plant his butt. Gwen sat close to him, keeping her arms at her sides as if she didn't want to brush him. That bothered him, given how snug that sleeping bag had been, but he had to respect her need to maintain some space.

Both allowed themselves a few quiet, contemplative minutes before she dug out the water bottle and bags of peanuts and raisins.

"It's...steep going forward," he said finally. "Yes."

More open than was safe, too, although following the ridge would be worse.

"Do you recognize where we are?"

"I think I might. Let me get the map out." She set down her bag of peanuts and dug deeper in the pack. "Oh, and my phone, too! Maybe we're high enough..."

She got nothing. They both stared at the black screen.

"You didn't turn it off so the battery wouldn't run down?"

She looked stricken. "It never occurred to me. I hardly ever do."

It took him a minute to ask calmly, "When did you last charge it?"

"Um…early evening before we left. And—" she shifted a little "—the battery isn't what it used to be."

"I should have said something." Why hadn't he? He upgraded phones often to have maximum battery life even more than the features touted in commercials.

"Why didn't your boss give you yours back?" she asked, sounding timid.

"I didn't have it on me when I was shot. In the chaos, who knows what happened to it? The shooter might even have grabbed it, thinking he could get in and see who I'd been talking to."

Gwen nodded. She didn't want to meet his eyes, he thought. He refused to let her feel as if she'd screwed up, not when she'd been his lifesaver in so many ways.

"You thought you'd be home in a few hours when you got on that helicopter," he pointed out. "Unless you usually turn it off when you're in the air, you had no reason to give it a thought."

"Not then," she argued. "But after—" *After I shot and killed a man*, was what she meant.

Her fingers curled around the phone so tightly her knuckles showed white. Rafe pried it out of her hand and took that hand in his.

"Remember how busy we were? I was with you when you checked for bars. I should have thought of it, as well. I'm the guy who does this for a living, after all."

She gave a watery-sounding chuckle, even though there wasn't a tear to be seen. "Better you than me."

"I sit behind a desk sometimes."

The chuckle became a laugh, and he realized he was smiling, too. Either the morphine was speaking or the ever-present pain, but he felt incredibly reluctant to move. *Yeehaw*, he thought, remembering his gung-ho self from a decade ago. *Maybe I'm too old for this.*

Something to think about later.

She did say, "We had a portable charger in the helicopter. We always do. Only..." No need to finish that sentence. She could only grab so much so fast.

After a minute, Gwen tipped her head sideways to rest it on his upper arm for a moment, whether in understanding, solidarity or apology, he didn't know. He turned his head enough to brush a kiss against her forehead.

Then they both retreated as if they'd never shared that moment and resumed crunching on their lunch.

Until he felt a subliminal tingle right before Gwen stiffened, hearing as he did the distant sound of a helicopter.

"Oh, no!"

Could be a park ranger helicopter or a search and rescue one, he tried to tell himself, but his mouth twisted. When had he last been that optimistic?

No. They had to get out of sight and fast.

Chapter Ten

Why, oh, why had they had let themselves stop out in the open without first identifying a way to get out of sight quickly? That had been Gwen's cardinal rule so far.

Frantically, she spun to look around. The drop forward off the ridge was too precipitous for them. They had to go one way or the other…or back the way they'd come to get under the cover of the forest.

"Back!" Rafe said, grabbing the pack and slinging it over his shoulder before she could protest.

Maybe she'd been carrying the pack too long, because she felt unbalanced enough that she stumbled almost immediately and went to her knees.

Rafe yanked her up. She clutched the tote bag and scuttled after him over the rough ground.

The distinctive roar of a helicopter grew nearer. Given her experience, it should be a good sound, even heartwarming. They were on their way to save lives. Or on the ground, hearing backup coming. Her current fear made clear how drastically her perspective had changed.

They held hands as they skidded over the back edge of the ridge. The trees seemed impossibly far away. The climb hadn't been *that* long, had it? How could they possibly make it before the shadow of the bird covered them?

Rafe pulled her sideways. Her ankle tried to give way, but he wouldn't let her fall. Through the salt of sweat dripping into her eyes, Gwen saw what he aimed for. Not an overhang as perfect as they'd found the first day, but a jumble of slabs that might provide cover.

She still couldn't see the approaching helicopter, but it could be upon them any second, and someone in it would be using high-powered binoculars to search for movement or colors that didn't fit.

They'd draped the tarp over the pack, but it was subtly too bright, and they weren't currently surrounded by greenery, anyway.

The next time she stumbled, it was because Rafe had bent over and was pulling her between broken slabs.

"Get down!" he ordered. "Go, go!"

There was a narrow passage barely open to the sky above. He shoved her ahead of him, then pushed the pack after her. Somehow, he had lowered himself to a crouch that had to be unbearably painful, and he had his gun in his hands. The hard look on his face scared her as much as the circumstances.

The roar had become deafening. She squeezed against gritty rock, feeling the print of it on her cheek, trying to make it absorb her.

The shadow did literally fall over them, giving her chills.

But, oh God, oh God, it was continuing on. The terrible sound receded.

Rafe lowered his hands so his weapon pointed at the ground in front of his feet. "It might circle back," he said tensely.

"I never saw it. Did you?"

"A glimpse." With dark humor, he added, "Good thing Kimball didn't extend his passion for red to this fleece top."

"I never studied the map," she said, trying to sound as calm as Rafe did. This wasn't an ideal place to lay it out.

"No hurry," he said.

She kept leaning, not sure she'd still be on her feet if it weren't for the rock. Except that she felt sure if she started to topple, Rafe would step in to support her. The very thought made her ashamed. He was in worse shape than she was. He was her *patient*.

Only they'd moved irrevocably past that, hadn't they?

He swiveled to look right at her, his eyes even darker than usual, penetrating. "You're not going to like this." His voice was gritty. "It occurs to me that nobody but Bill and Kimball knew about you. I'm...not going to tell you to take off on your own right away. You could get into trouble, and I'd never know."

"You need me."

He bent his head in agreement. "But if they see me but not you, I want you to hide. Run. Whatever you can do." His jaw muscles flexed. "Seeing you die for me—"

"I feel the same about you!" she cried.

"But they'd leave you behind, not knowing what you've seen. They will never leave me."

"Rafe." She was afraid it came out as a whimper. He leaned toward her...just before they both heard the hum growing in volume.

He said a few vicious words and squeezed his eyes closed.

Gwen tried even harder to become one with the rock.

IF THEY MIRACULOUSLY found a trail, he'd make her leave him, Rafe decided. Who would know she was anything but another hiker trying to complete the Wonderland Trail, which circled all the way around Mount Rainier? She'd go for it if he convinced her that she could safely find help and send them back for him.

Nice, selfless thought, except he hadn't seen any suggestion of a trail as he scanned the vista, and he was pretty sure Gwen hadn't, either. Thinking about how close she'd come to falling yesterday, he knew he couldn't send her on alone. She didn't deserve any of what had happened to her in the past day and a half, and he was determined to protect her from anything more.

Yeah, except exhaustion, stress and the fun of being hunted by killers. Of perpetually feeling eyes on their backs and looking down from above.

Maybe the feet-on-the-ground hunters had gone in entirely different directions. Given the vast wilderness, it was possible, even likely. Rafe just couldn't count on it.

The fact that the helicopter had flown up one side of the ridge and back on the other gave him a bad feeling. He thought he'd have heard the roar, however muted, if it had been flying the kind of pattern they'd seen before. Had it come so close today out of sheer logic or because one of the pursuers had set eyes on them or just spotted a few broken branches or scuffs in the loamy soil beneath the trees?

"Okay," he said finally. "I think we can assume the search has shifted to another area. Let's move while we can."

He was very aware of her swallow followed by her squaring her shoulders. Gutsy as always.

"You're right. First, though, if we can get in a slightly more open spot, I want to take a look at the map again."

Rafe nodded, grabbed the straps of the pack and pulled it behind him as he edged out of their temporary refuge. Gwen came right behind, carrying the tote bag he'd started to equate with Mary Poppins's bag. Gwen had stuffed some damn wonderful things in it.

The minute there was room, she spread the map and pointed at the trio of lakes she thought they were looking down on. No trail came near, of course, but he didn't see any good alternative but to drop down to them, then make a torturous way south toward what the map had labeled as the Northern Loop Trail.

He didn't bother commenting. Gwen folded the map and stowed it at the top of the pack before closing it.

"You still carrying the gun?" Rafe asked.

She nodded.

"Safety on?"

"Yes." She turned her back to him and lifted the layers of tops she wore. "You can check it if you want."

He wanted to. The idea of her taking a tumble and the damn gun going off and potentially putting a bullet in her was enough to give him nightmares.

The safety was still in the off position, which didn't entirely satisfy him, but what could he say? Conceivably, they might find themselves under fire and need to respond without delay.

She hefted the pack again, something else Rafe didn't like, but he slung the now lighter tote bag over his shoulder and let her go ahead.

The next hours were grueling. Tree cover was sporadic, rocks crumbling, drop-offs potential killers. The sun climbed high in the sky, then began to descend. Rafe hadn't seen anyplace flat enough to set up the tent or even where they could lie side by side. They had to go on. Scrambling downward put more stress on his quads than going up had. His thigh had passed sheer agony and had almost become numb. A couple of times, he thumped it with a fist to be sure he still had any feeling in it.

They took a few breaks, which weren't much help. Looking at Gwen disturbed him. She'd lost enough weight to be visible, which shouldn't be possible in a day and a half. Her cheekbones stood out more prominently, and her eyes had sunken deeper in her face. He wanted to believe he was imagining things, but couldn't quite do so. She studied him the way he did her, but he didn't ask if he looked as bad as she did.

His gaze rested on her feet in the athletic shoes. *Good tread*, he thought, not for the first time, but no protection for her ankles if one twisted.

He clung to the idea of setting up camp on the shore of one of those pretty, probably rarely visited lakes, although at the moment, he couldn't see any of them.

Disaster struck between one heartbeat and the next. Ahead of him, Gwen crept along a narrow ledge he wasn't looking forward to traversing. Gravel crunched beneath her feet. Usually as sure-footed as a mountain goat, she stumbled, swayed and fought to regain her footing.

He lunged forward even as the weight of the pack helped pull her sideways. With a cry, she fell.

RAFE COULDN'T SEE HER. Anguish riding him, he rushed forward faster than he should have and knelt to look over the edge. She sprawled, unmoving, maybe thirty feet down. She hadn't tumbled as far as she could have, but she'd probably bounced off rock outcroppings, and she'd landed on what looked like the remnants of a rock fall. Her head pointed uphill, as if she'd struggled to right herself until the end. He saw no apparent soil, except here and there a few scrubby trees had dug roots deep.

She wasn't dead. She couldn't be.

He looked around frantically, needing to get to her. It was too steep to go directly down unroped, but he saw a zigzag path that might work. It required all his discipline to walk carefully. He wanted to run; he wanted to slide down to reach her side.

Every time he looked, he hoped she'd moved. A groan would have been music to his ears. But there was nothing.

He didn't even want to *think* about how long this was taking. Ten minutes? Fifteen?

What can you do for her when you do get there? an inner voice seemed to mock. *She* was the medic.

Rafe gritted his teeth. When she regained consciousness, she could tell him what to do for her.

He had to be especially careful the last few feet, given the precipice waiting if a hand-or toehold failed. But finally he made it, dropped the tote and squatted next to her.

"Gwen!" he called hoarsely. "Damn it, Gwen, talk to me!"

He rested his fingers on her neck, for a moment not feeling anything. With his own heart beating so damn hard and his hand shaking, would he be able to? Relying on sheer will-power, he calmed himself.

"Gwen." Not so calm. His voice was as gravelly as the ground beneath her.

But he felt the flutter of her pulse. She was alive. He'd thank God, except she could have broken her neck or back, have suffered a head injury that had her in a coma. He didn't dare remove the pack yet, but he was able to extract the sleeping bag. No matter what, she'd be in shock and unable to hold on to her own body warmth. What's more, the sun's downward path was becoming noticeable.

He tucked the down sleeping bag around her, then stroked hair away from her forehead, his fingertips rough against her smooth skin. He delved into her hair, his touch as delicate as he could manage, searching for any lumps.

Yeah, there was a goose egg not far back from her right temple. Was he seeing swelling and discoloration starting on her temple and reaching down toward her eye, too?

"I need you to talk to me." He swallowed. "Tell me where you're hurt."

Nothing.

What if the helicopter returned now?

They'd be dead, that's what. Even so, he took the handgun from the small of his back and laid it on the ground within reach.

Focus.

He ran his hands down her legs, not finding any obvious breaks. Up her spine and to her neck, which scared him the most. Did she have a cervical collar in the supplies she'd brought? He didn't remember seeing anything like that.

At a soft moan, his gaze snapped to her face. Her lips had parted.

"That's it, sweetheart," he murmured. "I know you must hurt, but you have to talk to me."

She mumbled something.

He bent his head closer. "What?"

"Don't...wanna."

"I know," he said softly. "Do you know where you are? Who I am?"

Her lips unmistakably formed his name.

"That's right. You fell. I...can't tell how badly you're hurt, except that you lost consciousness."

She seemed to be trying to dampen her lips. "Head hurts."

"Yeah. You have a hell of a lump." He slipped his fingers into her hair again and touched it lightly. "You scared me." *You're still scaring me.*

Her lashes fluttered; her face scrunched, and her eyes opened to slits as if she couldn't handle full daylight.

All Rafe could do was stroke her cheek and wait.

"...seen?"

Seen? He abruptly realized what she meant. Yeah, they were exposed to anyone from above on the ridge or, as he feared most, if the helicopter made another pass over. There was nothing to be done about that yet.

"We're exposed," he admitted, "but first things first. Can you tell me where you hurt besides your head?"

Her shoulders moved. She flexed each leg hesitantly, one at a time.

"I'd like to get this pack off you, but I'm not sure you should move yet."

"It...saved me."

The hell it had.

"The weight pulled you off the ledge."

She rolled her head to see him better.

"Don't move!"

"Neck...feels...okay."

He growled a couple of words he should have kept to himself.

"Hit...rocks, but the pack...protected me." Her speech was clearer all the time. "It...snagged. So I didn't fall as far. As fast."

She'd fallen in two segments. That's what she was saying. A strap on the pack catching on a small tree growing out of a crack, or maybe a sharp outthrust rock, really had saved her life.

Rafe sank onto his butt as if the adrenaline that had kept him crouching beside her had been expelled. Until this moment, he hadn't realized the stress his position had put on his wounded thigh.

"Okay." He sounded worse rather than better. "Let me do the work taking it off."

She obeyed, staying mostly still as he gently worked the straps over her shoulders and down her arms. Finally setting the pack aside, he put his hands on her back, moving them up and down, kneading the muscles between her neck and shoulders. "Where does it hurt?"

"Everywhere," she said so quietly he hardly heard her, "but mostly my head. I...think I'm okay. Just...a little battered."

"You were unconscious."

"If I sit up, I can take some Tylenol."

"You need the good stuff more than I do now," Rafe said grimly.

"Not...a good idea after a concussion."

He wanted to argue but had read or heard that before.

"Let me help you."

When she moved, he took most of her weight. Once she lay on her back, they paused, but since she hadn't gasped in pain, he continued to support her as she sat up.

Keeping his arm behind her, he said, "You scared at least ten years off my lifespan."

Was that a faint laugh? "Me too."

They sat quietly for a minute, but the still bright sunlight and sense of exposure made his skin crawl.

He took out a bottle of water and found the Tylenol in her tote bag, shaking out a couple onto his palm and offering them to her.

Gwen swallowed them, sighed and said, "We're mostly at the bottom."

"You took a plummeting elevator."

"Not recommended."

"No." He hesitated. "I hate the idea of making you go on, but we have to get as far as the trees."

"I know. I can do it."

The words were strong, but what he saw on her face scared him in a different way. The swelling and discoloration were worsening, and her eyes, darker than they ought to be, seemed to have sunk deeper yet. Her skin wasn't a healthy shade, despite the tan.

But they couldn't stay here. The risk was too high. He had to push her when he hated the very idea. They had to get under cover. He'd carry her if he had to. He wanted to believe he could despite his injuries and silenced any doubting voice.

He urged a handful of dried fruit on her, since eating seemed to settle people in shock, and finally boosted her to her feet.

Her eyes dilated, then became glassy. He couldn't make her continue hiking. He might kill her. But after standing very still for a minute or two, she blinked hard a few times and straightened.

"I'll carry both bags." He made sure his voice had no give. "I want you to hold on to my arm."

She swallowed and finally dipped her undoubtedly throbbing head a tiny bit. Too soon, they set off, one slow step at a time, as Rafe wished he had an earbud that received intel from a teammate situated to be his extra eyes.

With him and Gwen both severely injured, the danger had just expanded exponentially.

Chapter Eleven

Reasonably alert at first, Gwen understood why Rafe guided her the way he did.

The slope remained quite steep, the footing either irregular over remnants of a volcanic flow or chutes filled with small rocks that slid from beneath the soles of her shoes. When he stopped and turned her almost back the way they'd come, letting her go long enough to move to the downside before gently propelling her forward again, she thought, *Switchback. Smart.*

No more elevator.

Awareness of what he intended along with realizing her body was one solid mass of bruises and strained muscles faded into nothing so concrete. Her head pounded as if a jackhammer was trying to break apart a road surface to clear it away before laying a new one. She wasn't quite sure how she stayed upright, then didn't care if she really was. Rafe's arm wrapped around her, and occasionally he lifted her with the strength of only that arm when he must have doubted whether she could pick up one foot or the other enough to step over an obstacle. Was she leaning on him?

Maybe.

Time blurred. She heard his deep, often gravelly voice but didn't even try to make out words. If she wanted anything in the world, it was to sink to the ground, but the iron bar of his arm kept her upright, and her feet kept moving without any conscious order from her.

They went on, and on. His voice grew more insistent, but she could concentrate on only the one thing. Her next step and the one after that.

When he wrapped her more fully in those strong arms to stop her, she didn't understand. She lifted dazed eyes to him.

"Talk to me."

Was that what he'd been saying all along?

"Sit?" she managed to say.

"We can do better than that. As soon as I get the pad and sleeping bag spread out, you can lie down. Here." Once again, he took command of her body until she found herself sitting on the loamy ground that she began to realize was a forest floor.

Never docile, she didn't know if she could so much as lift a hand. Rafe whipped out the pad and sleeping bag, spreading them right next to her, unlaced Gwen's athletic shoes and eased her over onto the softer layers and onto her back.

She moaned in relief, wriggling her toes, and stared straight upward. The trees rearing above were larger than any they'd yet seen. On many, the lowest branches were far above her head. A squirrel watched her with bright eyes before disappearing in a flash.

Gwen transferred her gaze to the man sitting beside her. *So beautiful*, she thought, despite the lines carved deeper into his cheeks and forehead. The worried way he watched her gave her the strength after all to lift a hand and let it flop onto his hard thigh, the only part of him she could reach.

"All right," she muttered.

"God." He bent his head, but he also seized hold of her hand and held on tight, almost painfully so.

She hoped he never let go.

GWEN DRIFTED OFF to sleep. Rafe didn't move for a long time, watching for every twitch and flicker of an eyelash, at first afraid she wasn't asleep at all, but unconscious. At last, she tried to turn onto her side, convincing him this was a natural sleep. He yanked clothes out of the pack indiscriminately, bundled them up and placed the makeshift pillow under her head.

Then he left her long enough to push his aching body into action to walk a perimeter to be sure no obvious dangers lurked, and that there wasn't anything convenient, like a cave, in case they had to bolt.

No such luck, but at least they couldn't be seen from above, neither from the helicopter nor someone searching with binoculars from the ridge above.

Once he'd returned to their small camp, he started setting up. He didn't want to do this in the fast-approaching darkness. It took him a lot longer than it would have Gwen to get the tent up, simple as it was, but he managed. The stove, he fumbled, but had it ready to heat two more meals from Kimball's stash once Gwen woke up.

His stomach rumbled enough that he did some snacking on nuts and dried fruit, but limited his intake. Who knew how much longer they'd have to stumble around in this primeval wilderness before they were able to contact anyone to call for rescue? They should start portioning out the food more carefully.

As Gwen continued to sleep, he took everything out of the pack and examined it, unfortunately not finding anything he hadn't already seen. He repacked more carefully, with an eye to squeezing in necessities from Gwen's tote bag. They'd have to discard more yet, but he wasn't going to root through her personal possessions without her, much less make that kind of decision.

She didn't stir until the sky had turned a deep purple.

The movement had him turning toward her. She scrunched her face up and mumbled, "Ugh."

Yeah, that about said it all. He couldn't help a silent laugh that cut off quickly as he waited to see how alert she'd be.

"Hey," he said, and she blinked bemusedly his way before starting to push herself up. He reached out to help her.

An owl hooted, and she swiveled her head to look around them. "How long have I been asleep?" She made another of those faces he'd think were cute if it weren't for the distortion caused by swelling. "How would you know?"

"I'm guessing four hours, given how close it is to full darkness. How do you feel?"

How she felt was that she needed privacy. He walked her to her chosen tree, stepped away, then gave her his arm when she reappeared, looking flustered.

After that, he encouraged her to eat a handful of the snack mix and swallow some water before taking more Tylenol.

"I guess if I said I feel fine, you'd know I was lying, huh?" she said unexpectedly.

"Yeah. You lost consciousness long enough to be a real worry."

"The headache is the biggest problem. Otherwise, I think mostly I have bruises."

"Like head to toe?"

"Not quite that bad."

He cocked an eyebrow at her to express his opinion of her upbeat evaluation of her own condition. She quit trying.

They agreed on another of the freeze-dried meals, and he fired up the stove. Since he hadn't seen any running water or heard a stream all afternoon, it was a good thing they'd filled a couple of bottles with water and treated it midday. He decided to dispense with any scrubbing except for his teeth, and would encourage her to do the same. A cup of coffee tonight and another in the morning would do more for both of them than a sponge bath.

Their surroundings dimmed rapidly. She turned on the flashlight a couple of times as he dished up the meal and then made the coffee, but otherwise they sat side by side on the sleeping bag, indulging in long silences but also talking in odd spurts.

Not about today or tomorrow. Gwen didn't bring up the subject of Bill or Bruce Kimball or the map. She told him a few stories from her working life: about delivering a baby in the helicopter, about transporting two men who'd been in a shoot-out and who kept trying to break the restraints to resume their conflict.

"Best friends, one of the wives said. And they were trying to kill each other. What could be worth that?"

Rafe's first thought was that one might have caught his wife in bed with the friend. There'd be two betrayals there, but he personally would consider his wife's the greater.

If he ever married...

After a suitable silence, Gwen asked softly, "Did you grow up with a best friend?"

"Yeah," Rafe said gruffly. The memories and the pain only occasionally jabbed at him. Mostly, they'd dulled.

She didn't ask a question or even turn her head, as if expecting him to elaborate. She'd let it drop if he didn't say anything, Rafe felt sure. She'd been open enough, though, that he felt a twinge of guilt. And really, what difference did it make if he bled a little for her?

"Mateo and I were friends from second grade on, after his mom moved with him and his little sister to live in my school district." Rafe wondered now and again what had become of Ileana but hadn't let himself try to find out. It probably wasn't anything good.

"My parents didn't pay much attention to what I was doing or where I was. Mateo's mom didn't, either, because she worked two jobs. He was supposed to be watching over his sister, but when she got old enough, he decided she could take care of herself."

Gwen was looking at him now. Rafe could feel her regard more than he could make out her features.

"By the time we were fourteen, fifteen, we'd gotten sucked into a gang. At first it was a lot of strutting, wearing the right kind of kick-butt boots and bandannas. Feeling tough. As we got older, closer to graduating, we were expected to do some things." He stared ahead at the trunks of trees he could barely make out. "I started to get cold feet. I think he did, too, but he wanted to belong more than I did. I was afraid I'd be killed if I tried to walk away. He stood with the gang. We had a fight. I'd always believed we'd have each other's backs forever."

Slim, cold fingers slipped into his hand, shaped into a near fist. He squeezed her hand harder than he probably should have.

"When I made noises about walking away, eight or ten of the guys took turns beating me.

I ended up in the hospital, lying to my parents about what had happened. At around the same time, our gang and another had been butting heads. I was still recuperating when a war erupted and Mateo was killed. He was found with drugs on him. I guess he got interrupted before he could deliver them."

"Was he using?" she asked softly.

He cleared his throat. "Yeah. By that time, he was. When I could, I went to see his mom. She knew I'd been part of it, and she screamed at me and then slammed the door in my face. I...waylaid Ileana after school one day, and she gave me a look I'll never forget." To this day, his throat clogged whenever he remembered.

Gwen's head tipped to rest momentarily against his upper arm. The generosity of her touch meant enough to make him uncomfortable. She could get to him. He wasn't sure he wanted that—or dared let himself soften to such an extent.

"My parents were sorry to hear about Mateo. It never occurred to them that I'd been taking the same road. As it was, I headed off to college, got summer jobs or internships that meant I was never home for more than a couple of a weeks at a time, and I dodged any chance of being seen by my former compatriots. Mom and Dad didn't understand my decision to go into law enforcement, and especially when I chose the DEA, but, uh…"

"That's what you intended from the minute you learned about your friend's death."

"Yeah." Hearing how rough his voice had become, he decided he'd said enough. In fact, he released her hand and rose to his feet.

"Time to get some sleep." If he sounded brusque, so be it. "How's your head feel?"

DESPITE THE FACT that she'd had a lengthy nap not that long ago, Gwen felt sure she could sleep again, no problem. She'd taken as much Tylenol as she dared, so there was no point complaining about the drilling still going on in her skull.

She and Rafe briefly discussed whether to set up the tent and agreed they didn't need it. Through the dense lace of the forest canopy, they could make out astonishingly bright stars against a velvety black sky.

Rafe said tersely, "Unless rain is a possibility, I'd prefer to be able to better hear and see what's approaching."

Thank you for the reminder.

Of course, she couldn't disagree. He was already easing into the sleeping bag when she suddenly said, "I didn't have a chance to give you your shot this afternoon. I can—"

"No. I did okay. My injuries aren't the kind

that require continuing on a painkiller as powerful as morphine."

She stood above him, not moving. "I know that, but you weren't in any shape to leap up and go on the run in the mountains, either!"

"I'm not sure I could have that first day," he admitted, his voice a deep rumble that made her think of the purr of a big cat.

Why did he sound gentle? Did he think she needed soothing? If she hadn't proved her competence by now—

"Are you coming?" Nice segue into impatient.

Her response was wordless and grouchy, which she felt a little bad about. Only…she was entitled! Most of her body still hurt. The pad beneath the sleeping bag was maybe half an inch thick. She was grateful for it—really, she was—but she was starting to crave a fat memory foam mattress.

Living long enough for luxuries to be any kind of possibility had to be their priority, she reminded herself. Rafe hadn't whined, and neither would she.

"Yeah," she said, and lowered herself to her hands and knees to begin the backward squirm to fit herself into the limited space left after his big body filled most of it.

The awkwardness seemed to be missing tonight, though. Maybe she just felt too miserable to care about anything like that. And maybe it was the way he helped her, hands careful, until she settled with a sigh, her back to his front so that he spooned her. He held out his arm to provide a perfect resting place for her head, and the heat he seemed to emit all the time was seductive enough that she had to make an effort to hold some small distance between them.

Once she fell asleep...well, she wouldn't know, and neither would he. At least, until morning, when they were bound to be intertwined like ivy climbing a solid brick building.

She took responsibility for pulling up the zipper, necessitating some more wriggling, then relaxed.

"G'night," Rafe murmured, his breath stirring her hair. Unless she was imagining things, he hugged her.

"Good night," she whispered, and closed her eyes, pondering how few times in her life she'd ever slept wrapped in a man's arms, and why this felt so different. So...comforting.

She tried to think about the ultimately tragic story he'd told about his childhood and his best friend, but didn't get any further than picturing a young, possibly lanky Rafe with a bandanna tied around his head, his black hair longer.

Maybe even brushing his shoulders? Tough guy, but not as much as he'd imagined.

What things had he been asked to do? How many had he persuaded himself to do before the values he'd been raised with had kicked in? Did he imagine that if he'd been with Mateo when the gang war broke out, he'd have been able to save his best friend?

Wasn't that what he'd been trying to do ever since?

Feeling fuzzy, Gwen sighed and let herself snuggle just the tiniest bit into the hard curve of Rafe's body. Then she slept.

RAFE HAD TO readjust Gwen a couple of times during the night. The first time, he woke up to discover his dream had prompted the erection he had pressed to her firm but still well-rounded behind. Or maybe it was the other way around. She made some grumbly noises but never really woke up as he eased himself to his back with her partially sprawled over his chest. It took some willpower to persuade his body to subside, given that he still had an armful of sexy, brave, compassionate woman. He must have managed, because he did fall asleep again, this time to a pale dawn and the discovery that Gwen had somehow squirmed her way entirely on top of him.

Her face was pressed into the crook between his neck and shoulder. Her toes flexed against his shins. With him able to feel every curve and dip between, his body had reacted with enthusiasm.

Rafe held himself very still, listening to her slow, even breathing. He didn't feel any need to move even though he'd been fully alert from the moment he opened his eyes. Why not enjoy the pleasure of a harmless arousal?

For all that he relaxed, his mind was always determined to puzzle over every hint of anyone's motivation, including his own. And what he realized was that, beyond the straightforward lust, he felt something more that he hardly recognized: contentment. A quiet sense of peace, as if all were right with his world.

His cynical side kicked in with no trouble. So much had gone wrong in the past three days, he couldn't count all the disasters on one hand. Maybe not even on two. Had she drugged him during the night, and he just hadn't noticed?

Rafe knew better, but he was disconcerted enough by the strange mood that he immediately tensed, shifted Gwen to the side and squirmed out of the sleeping bag.

Peace.

He'd half hoped she would keep sleeping but wasn't surprised after he'd gotten dressed to see that she had sat up and was pushing her tangled hair back from her face. Apparently, the elastic she'd used to keep it tamed in an increasingly disheveled braid had disappeared altogether. It might have looked sexy if not for the bruises on her face.

"It's early," she observed.

"Yeah, sorry to wake you." He'd been about to go use the facilities but paused. "How do you feel?"

Her eyes were clear, no longer dazed, the best sign he could have hoped for.

"Not bad." She grimaced. "My back hurts. And I still have a headache."

"You slept well."

"I guess I must have," she said in bemusement. "Unless I went sleepwalking."

Amused, he said, "Nope. I'd have noticed that."

She gave him a crooked smile that didn't succeed at being as upbeat as she may have meant it to be, given the deep lines between her brows and the furrows on her forehead.

After deciding priority one was bringing her Tylenol and water to wash it down, he did that much before disappearing for a few minutes.

He came back to find she'd washed down the pills but otherwise hadn't moved.

"We should make an early start. Just…give me a few minutes," Gwen said.

Not fooled, he squatted to her level and studied her more carefully. He didn't like this idea but had to offer it.

"We have enough food. What if we rest for the day?"

She fired back, "You mean, what if *I* rest for the day. We didn't sit around when you were in worse shape than I am."

"I didn't have a concussion," Rafe said bluntly. "You slept especially heavy last night. You picked at your food." He'd finished her portion last night. "Be honest. How does a big breakfast sound?"

She scrunched up her face, then winced. "Bacon and eggs?"

"What if I said yes?"

Her chin lifted. She wanted to tell him to bring it on, he could tell, but she finally sighed. "I'm queasy."

"That's what I thought." He frowned at her. "We're tucked away pretty well here."

"I don't remember much after I fell, but that side of the ridge was mostly rock. We had to have been in plain sight for at least a couple of hours, if not more. Especially as slow as I must have been once you picked me up and put me back together."

"That's...a worry," he agreed. He'd been preoccupied by her, too, and not as observant as he usually would be.

Staying put on the assumption they *hadn't* been seen was a gamble, but he also hated to put her at any more risk than she already was.

Chapter Twelve

"We have to keep moving." Gwen dug in stubbornly, but Rafe didn't argue too hard even though he also didn't appear happy. He had to know she was right; they didn't dare laze the day away, giving any pursuers time to catch up.

Or, as he'd pointed out once, even worse would be walking into an ambush because they'd allowed those cold-blooded creeps to get ahead of them.

After insisting he handle packing up, Rafe seemed to dawdle. Gwen defied him by drying the couple of dishes he'd already washed and dismantling the stove. She refused to admit to Rafe how lousy she really felt after the amazing stoicism he'd displayed the first day. She might have worried he could see right through her, except once he'd conceded the argument, he noticeably retreated. For a while, he seemed to pretend she wasn't there at all.

He did finally urge her to help consolidate

what was left in the tote bag with the contents of the pack. "I'd rather you didn't have to carry anything."

In the end, she looked in dismay at her discard pile.

"The rules are that if you carry it in, you carry it out."

"Our situation is extreme."

"Yes, but…" Seeing his impatience, she gave up, but she did insist on burying the bag to the best of their ability, considering their lack of a shovel.

She had a feeling Rafe cooperated only out of a reluctance to leave any trace of their presence behind.

Given that they had no compass, and she had no memory of which way they'd come, she had to depend on his sense of direction. Although, passing through a grove of large trees that they had to wind between made her wonder in a short while whether they might be going in a circle.

Pride kept her walking, with only one break in her composure. She had to lurch behind a tree to empty her stomach of the small amount of breakfast she'd managed to eat. Rafe's expression was so grim when she returned, she avoided meeting his eyes.

"I'm all right."

He didn't say a word.

Since he stepped back to let her go ahead this time, she felt his gaze boring into her back. Excellent incentive for keeping her shoulders squared and her throbbing head high.

They couldn't have been on their way an hour when he said, "Let's take a break."

Gwen didn't argue or even comment. She wondered if the Tylenol she'd taken earlier had been absorbed before she puked, but decided she didn't dare double up. Sitting down on a huge, ancient fallen tree, if only for a few minutes, was a massive relief.

Staring into the shadows of the forest, he said, "I'm depending on you to tell me when you need to stop. Even lie down and close your eyes for a while."

"I'm not sleepy."

"The more rest—"

She huffed out a breath. "I took a four-hour nap yesterday, then we went to bed as soon as the sun went down. I think it's safe to say I've had plenty of sleep!"

He scowled at her, which was the most expression she'd seen on his face since she woke up. She didn't think she'd behaved especially badly this morning. Was this fallout because he'd told her more last night about himself than he'd intended to? Or did *he* hurt more than he wanted to admit? Maybe now that *he* felt stronger, he would become impatient with their slow pace.

Heck, maybe he hadn't gotten any sleep at all, given that he couldn't so much as roll over with her wrapped around him like an invasive vine.

Would he tell her what was going on in his head if she asked?

A little brooding of her own coupled with the brief rest, and she decided there wasn't any reason not to discuss options.

"Maybe we should rethink the plan to stay together. What if *you* go on and leave me hunkered down here instead of the other way around?"

This scowl made him appear forbidding. "Don't be ridiculous! If anyone saw us yesterday, they now know about you. Do you really think I'd leave you?"

"How should I know? You're not being very... communicative."

"Maybe I think it's a good idea for us to try to be quiet."

Because she never shut up? Starting to get mad, Gwen opened her mouth but forgot what she'd intended to say when he abruptly cocked his head and lifted a hand in a stop gesture.

She didn't hear a thing, certainly not an approaching helicopter, but she froze, holding her breath.

With a suddenness she could never have predicted, Rafe tackled her backward over the log. At almost the same instant he fell on top of her, a distinctive *crack* rang in her ears, and bark splintered just above them.

RAFE FOUGHT TO free himself of the pack. Damn this soft ground! He'd never hear footsteps. He didn't even know whether a sound or hint of movement had triggered his alarm in the first place.

Face inches from hers, he murmured, "Once I return fire, throw yourself into those ferns. I think it's a well around the tree that would give you some protection."

Eyes wide and dark, she bobbed her head. He hoped like hell he hadn't hurt her by flattening her, but there'd been no choice.

He pushed himself up enough to half crawl forward, leaving her free to move. Once he'd opened some distance from her, he lifted his Glock and took a few blind shots. A startled sound came to his ears.

Behind him, Gwen squirmed away.

A flurry of shots tore into the rotting log they'd taken cover behind as well as a tree above his head. Bark flew, some peppering his face.

He flicked a glance back. Thank God Gwen had disappeared. He edged forward another few feet.

Would these bastards be wearing bulletproof vests? He'd guess they weren't. The things were hot and uncomfortable, and these kinds of enforcers were more likely to lift weights to achieve impressive muscles than run or hike to stay in shape.

A faint whisper of sound gave him a target even though the bright green camouflage blended too well. He fired even before he'd raised himself high enough to see the SOB not twenty-five feet away. Marking himself as a dead man walking, the bastard's eyes were narrowed on the cluster of ferns surrounding the giant cedar, but he had already started swinging toward Rafe.

Not fast enough. Rafe pulled the trigger with the instinct honed by endless hours at the range. Once, twice, three times.

The man shouted, fired wildly as he staggered and then crashed down with as much force as one of these trees would have if a saw severed it from its roots.

A flicker of movement almost gave Rafe time to dive for cover again, but the second man was already firing. A sting told Rafe he'd at least been grazed by a bullet as he dove sideways.

A series of shots coming from a different direction had him rolling to look behind him. If the four men had joined together—

But what he saw was Gwen, who'd popped into sight like a genie from a bottle and was firing with the same assurance she had when she brought down Kimball.

This second man's face went through the same stages as Kimball's had, too: astonishment, agony…and a vacancy Rafe had seen too many times in his career.

GWEN TRIED TO keep holding the gun steady but saw that her hands shook as if she had a raging fever. Her teeth chattered, too.

Out of the corner of her eye, she saw Rafe rise to his feet as lithely as if he'd never been hurt and rotate in a circle, his own weapon still held in front of him in firing position. He surveyed their surroundings with that hard expression she'd seen so rarely. She suspected that, despite the dim green-tinted light here in the dense forest, he saw more sharply than she ever had, too. Finally, he approached the man he'd shot, kicked his handgun away and stared down at him, then approached the man she'd shot and did the same.

Once she really looked at that body, she couldn't look away. Even from here, she saw the blood and a hole in his temple.

Slowly, her hands dropped. The next thing she knew, she was retching violently, nothing but thin bile coming up, but she couldn't seem to stop.

She'd killed again. How could she have done that?

How could she not?

Rafe prowled out of her sight. He was gone long enough that she assumed he was searching to be sure these two had no nearby backup. When he at last reappeared, he carried a camouflage print pack over one shoulder and a second one with his free hand.

He dropped them both and came to her, dropping to his knees in front of her. She hadn't realized she still held the gun in a tremulous grip until he gently relieved her of it.

"You're not hurt?" he said.

She shook her head, reminding her just how much her head ached. That didn't count.

"I... They followed us."

"Yeah." He cleared his throat. "Lucky we stopped. Otherwise, we'd have had no cover at all."

"No." They might have been gunned down from behind and died. Just like that. Just like... With her gaze compulsively drawn back to the face of the man she'd killed, she had dry heaves.

Rafe rubbed her back. When she raised her

head, he smoothed her hair back from her forehead with a completely steady hand, in con-
trast to hers. *He often did that*, she thought,
and imagined how wild and tangled her hair
must be by now.

"C'mon." He reached out a hand. "Let me
pull you up."

As he had guessed, the ferns had disguised
a hole around the tree trunk. She'd essentially
fallen into it and had fought to right herself fast
enough to be able to provide backup. As shaky
as she felt, she was grateful for the strength that
swung her up as if she weighed nothing.

She probably *had* lost weight, she thought,
her mind inexplicably drifting. *What a diet
plan*, she thought.

Rafe settled her on the log again so that her
back was to the dead men.

"Let's go through their packs quickly and
see whether there's anything that will help us.
Otherwise, later we can try to pinpoint where
we left them."

"Their guns?"

"We'll take those."

Because he thought they might still need
them? Or because he didn't want a backcountry hiker stumbling on them?

Did his motives matter?

She wasn't an awful lot of help, mostly watching as he transferred first a pair of wallets and then some food to their own pack.

"We could take a second sleeping bag," he offered, sounding oddly neutral, "although that would probably mean carrying a second pack, too."

"If you'd prefer that…"

"No. I thought you might."

She couldn't imagine nights not having the comfort of his arms around her. "No," she whispered.

His eyes caught hers for an unnerving moment. The creases in his forehead betrayed a perturbation she couldn't read. Did he think she might be cracking up?

Was she?

No.

She quit bothering to watch him sort. When he said, "Let's cover some distance before we stop for a bite to eat," she stood up before Rafe could help her. The idea of eating didn't entice her, but she'd have to try at some point, wouldn't she?

THOUGH THE PACK was now weighed down by four handguns—two full-size, two smaller backup weapons—as well as a few supplements to his wardrobe and to their diet, Rafe was barely conscious of it. He focused primarily on Gwen. Even as her drawn face and careful steps that were clumsy compared to her usual grace scared the hell out of him, he felt unfamiliar pride in her strength and the intense concentration that kept her moving forward despite what had to be a world of pain. Out of necessity he also listened for any sound coming from behind that wasn't natural. And, of course, for the hum of helicopter rotors.

He brooded about why he hadn't found a SAT radio. Why wouldn't they have carried one to stay in touch with the other pair and their base? Once the men on the ground spotted him and Gwen, you'd think they'd have called in backup. He'd located one cell phone, but it had been locked by fingerprint or some other method that made it as useless as Gwen's phone with the drained battery. Had it worked to reach whatever airbase the helicopter was flying out of?

It was also possible, he reflected, that none of these men was aware that cell phones didn't work in much of the park. Unless they'd hiked or climbed here, why would they? To most Americans, the idea that there were still wild parts of their own country where their precious mobile phones became useless baggage was unthinkable.

He'd noted on the map he and Gwen carried that they might be coming in reach of cell phone towers to the north, although plenty of mountainous terrain could still be interfering. Unless the helicopter showed up again in the near future, Rafe's intent was to get Gwen and himself to a trail where they might find hikers with working cell phones.

Between trees, he saw water glinting blue ahead. The lake nestled in a bowl in the land, but he suspected it was still at a significant elevation. The water was startlingly clear, the shores rocky.

Some serious work remained ahead of them to climb more ridges or to see if it was possible to follow one of the streams he remembered noting on the map that meandered to ultimately join the west fork of the White River. What Gwen had called the Northern Loop Trail crossed the west fork at one point.

Otherwise, the distance wasn't great to another pair of lakes to the south with a backcountry campground and even a park ranger patrol cabin marked on the map, but the scrambles over more ridges might be beyond Gwen's capability now. What Rafe knew was that they wouldn't make it today. This was as good a place to stop as any, although they needed to retreat back into the trees so as not to be seen from above.

Predictably, she said, "I can go on," but Rafe shook his head.

"One more day, we should make it to that patrol cabin. We don't have enough hours of daylight left today."

"I don't think there's always a ranger at those cabins."

His mouth tightened. "There's also a campground marked."

"The kind with something like three or four sites."

"I get that. But from that point, our odds improve of meeting someone with a working phone, or a charger you can use."

"Yes. You're right." She looked around with unsettling vagueness. "Here?"

"Looks good enough to me."

He wished he had any idea *which* lake they'd found, but it was pretty. One shore was wooded enough, somebody would have to stumble over them to find them—unless, like the dead men, they'd been tracking him and Gwen.

He shied away from thinking about the two corpses they'd left to the mercy of the wildlife. The glassy look in Gwen's eyes either meant she, too, was picturing them or that her concussion was deeper than he'd believed.

As soon as he lowered the pack to the ground, he extracted the sleeping bag and pad and spread them out. A glance at the sky found a scattering of clouds, but whether they suggested rain tonight, he couldn't tell. For now, he just wanted Gwen to lie down.

Once again, he helped lower her to a sitting position. She watched as he knelt, untied her shoes and tugged them off.

Her smile was unexpected. "I can't remember any man who wasn't a shoe salesman taking my shoes off."

He grinned. "If I put them back on in the morning, just to be sure they fit, you know…"

Gwen wrinkled her nose. "Cinderella, I am not."

Rafe wasn't so sure. She was beautiful enough to play the part, although he felt damn sure she wouldn't have ducked her head and obeyed the cruel stepmother no matter what she dished out. Under these circumstances, they'd gotten to know each other in a way a couple might not in a normal relationship, even over the course of months.

He frowned. *This isn't a romantic relationship.* He hadn't had one of those in years. Sex, yes. Letting himself feel hope for the future? No. And he didn't even know why he was thinking about this.

He let that slide, though he wasn't a man who usually let a lie to himself pass.

GWEN WOULD HAVE liked to find a comfortable slab of rock overhanging the lake and lie there watching for minnows. She didn't even try, for too many reasons, starting with the lack of a conveniently placed slab. Placing herself out in the open would have been foolish beyond belief, too. What she *really* wanted, she realized, was for them to be on a backpacking trip for fun instead of being the prey still hunted by a ruthless offshoot of a drug cartel.

She wanted to have saved a life instead of taking two.

Except…she had. Rafe's.

She caught him watching her, as she so often did, and wished his expression wasn't so often unreadable.

He swore suddenly.

Oh, no. She heard it, too—distant but undoubtedly approaching.

"They can't see us even if they fly right overhead!" she cried.

"If they get close, it's because they have a damn good idea where we are," said Rafe, rough voice shaped by familiar grimness.

"You think the four men on the ground stayed in communication? Which means the two we haven't met might know where we are?"

"I do."

Head cocked as she listened, Gwen said, "It's coming fast."

"I want to see it. Where did we stash the binoculars?" He flung a few things out of the pack before locating them.

"I should come, too."

Rafe barely hesitated before nodding. "Bring your gun."

A couple of minutes later, they found a thicket of what Gwen said were huckleberries growing from a rotting stump that showed signs of having burned from a lightning strike or forest fire at some point in the past. Right at the edge of the tree line, they were able to see a stretch of sky above the lake. He'd set his handgun within easy reach, and now lifted the binoculars to his eyes.

The helicopter snapped into sharp focus minutes later as it buzzed a lower elevation than it did yesterday. It had to be skimming barely over the treetops. A small herd of what Rafe recognized as elk burst from cover onto the lakeshore and ran in great bounds before disappearing again. The damn thing was flying straight enough toward them that his gut tightened.

Through the binoculars, he could just see a couple of men crouched in the open side door, rifles raised. Fury struck Rafe. Enough was enough. He was going to bring the whole organization down, if it was the last thing he ever did.

"Do you hear that?" Gwen murmured as if she were afraid they could be overheard.

"What the hell?"

A second later, a much larger helicopter appeared on a trajectory meant to cut off the first one. This second one was painted an army green and displayed what Rafe thought had to be government insignia. Was that a Chinook? Not impossible, considering how near the joint army/air force base of Lewis-McChord was.

The helicopter that was their nemesis abruptly lifted, gained altitude and circled back the way it had come, topping the ridge moments later to take it out of sight. The army helicopter changed path, too, swinging in a wide semicircle in apparent pursuit. Or just aiming to drive an unauthorized intruder past the national park boundaries?

In anguish, Gwen exclaimed, "If only we had a flare!"

"Took the words right out of my mouth," he growled.

Chapter Thirteen

After watching the army helicopter disappear over the treetops and ridge, Gwen had clung very briefly to the hope that it might reappear, might even have been assigned to search for her and Rafe.

Or at least for Rafe.

When twenty or thirty minutes passed and it hadn't returned, she gave up on what had been an unrealistic hope. How would the army have gotten involved?

Upon their return to their camp, Rafe asked that question.

Gwen shrugged. "I've read that they do call in the Chinook helicopters for rescues near the summit where the smaller ones can't go. If it had transferred an injured climber to an ambulance at Paradise or Sunrise or gone all the way to a hospital, there's no reason it would have been out this way, though. It might have been on some kind of training flight and didn't like the looks of an unmarked helicopter flying without clearance in the national park. Or..." Okay, she still had a grain of optimism. "Is there any chance the DEA could have reached out for help searching for the missing helicopter and you?"

Seated now on the sleeping bag beside her, he grimaced. "I doubt it, but...maybe. A search was surely mounted, but probably focused on the planned route."

"That's true, except...you'd think *some*body, somewhere would have seen that plume of smoke."

"If the crash site was located, I think we have to assume Kimball's body had already been removed. If that's so, I'm not sure what regular search and rescue personnel would have made of the burned helicopter. They'd have found the pilot and presumably contacted EMS Flight. They must have known you were on board. Are we sure they knew *I* was?"

She frowned at that. As sketchy as the whole thing was, she couldn't guarantee EMS did. Bill had claimed to be talking to dispatch, so she hadn't answered her phone. What if he'd lied?

And would the hospital who'd sent Rafe as a patient over for transport to Seattle have reason to connect him with a missing helicopter? Would the EMTs who'd loaded him have ever given that part of their job another thought? They'd certainly have had no way to suspect they were part of something secretive.

She told him what she'd been thinking.

"I've had most of the same thoughts, except I didn't realize your base didn't specifically send you to take care of me." He shrugged. "We'll know more once I can talk to Zabrowsky." Rafe's mouth quirked. "If he's able to snap his fingers and demand the army pick me up, I'll be impressed."

Gwen smiled. The never-ending headache and debilitating exhaustion had temporarily stolen her ability to laugh. Given a few hours of rest, she felt sure she'd regain her determination and maybe even optimism. Look how far they'd come! Relatively speaking, they didn't have all that far to go. And, would anyone dare send that helicopter out again after they'd received what at least constituted a warning? They'd have to be desperate.

Which, unfortunately, they seemed to be.

After some discussion about the increasingly gray sky, Rafe set up the tent and covered it with the tarp. He cooked dinner, too, which Gwen hadn't been sure she'd be able to eat. Her appetite was returning, though, which was good news. Maybe by morning, the headache would be gone, too. She made a face. Sad to say, she wasn't *that* optimistic.

When the evening became chilly as the gray of the sky deepened, Rafe urged a parka on Gwen that he'd appropriated from one of the dead men. She wasn't quite squeamish enough to refuse the cozy warmth. He seemed comfortable with a fleece quarter-zip, but it was heavier than hers. Plus, Rafe's natural thermostat had a higher setting than hers did.

They sipped coffee, letting the quiet sink in. An owl's soft hoot was followed by small shrieks as a nocturnal hunter—possibly the same owl— found prey. Rafe made her feel surprisingly safe by his mere presence, and that disturbed her. This was surely one of their last nights together. She had let herself become more…attached than she should. Than was safe, Gwen thought, deliberately echoing the word she'd used a minute ago in her head.

She'd never been a fan of sticking her head in the sand. Better to look straight on at reality. So she asked, in an I'm-just-wondering voice, "What will happen to you once this is over?"

This silence felt quite different. Rafe went still, with the coffee cup halfway to his mouth. Finally, he said, "Unfortunately, I suspect I'll be stashed again in some kind of safe house. I think I told you the trial will likely be at least a year away. Hell, maybe longer than that. After all this, the agency will want to up the protection."

"A dank fortress?"

He smiled faintly.

She asked, "How can you trust the same kind of arrangement after you were betrayed?"

"Not sure I do." He resumed movement, swallowing what appeared to be the rest of the coffee in his cup and then setting it down before he turned his head to look at her. He didn't have a lot of the tells most people did, the kind that would give away his real thoughts, and the oncoming darkness didn't help.

"So?" she asked softly. Whispered, really.

He shook his head. "I may have no choice. Even if I could get away with it, I can't walk away. I want to bring these scumbags down like you wouldn't believe. For the victims of the drug trade in general, for the guys who were gunned down guarding me, for that pilot who didn't know what he was getting into and now for *you*."

Her heart did something odd that made her briefly light-headed. No, she couldn't let herself believe for a minute that he was suggesting...what it sounded as if he was suggesting.

"You've saved me as often as I've saved you" was the best retort she could offer.

To her shock, he took her hand even as he said huskily, "This isn't all about our body count, or who has picked up whom the most times."

"You're stuck on the fact that you think I didn't deserve to get sucked into this."

"Partly," he agreed in the deep voice that gave her goose bumps. "Some of it is just because of who you are."

Gwen wanted desperately to ask what he meant by that. He seemed to be inviting the question, which scared her. They would part ways tomorrow or the next day. Soon. Assuming they *were* able to make a phone call to the DEA. Despite what a short time they'd had together, she could care too much about Rafe Salazar. Maybe she already did, but she had to nip it in the bud, or she'd suffer for letting herself fall for him.

"That's nice of you to say," she told him blithely. She was proud of herself for being able to sound so casual.

It worked, too, because after a moment, he released her hand and withdrew into himself.

Her newly chilled fingers curled into a painful fist at her side.

DAMN. IF HE wasn't in love with this woman, he was coming close. No, that was ridiculous. He'd never even kissed her. This was just the kind of intense bond that came into being when you shared a level of danger with someone else. He'd felt it working lengthy operations with fellow agents when they'd all developed complete trust. A few times, one of those agents had been female, so he couldn't blame these disturbing emotions entirely on the fact that Gwen was a woman.

Don't make this into something it isn't, he told himself, but he couldn't push back the crushing sense of dread he felt when thinking about saying goodbye to her.

Either she didn't share these emotions, or she was smart enough to know they couldn't go anywhere. He had to accept that.

It might have been easier if, half an hour later, they didn't have to squeeze into the same sleeping bag and almost effortlessly twine their bodies together as if they'd done this every night for weeks or months rather than mere days.

She didn't say a word after a mumbled "Good night." He didn't know if she felt the kiss he pressed to her head. What he did know was that she didn't surrender to sleep anywhere near as soon as her physical condition suggested she should have. Rafe loved the soft feel of her breasts pressed against his side and chest, her arm crooked over his belly and her hand splayed over his heart. Once she really conked out, she'd lift her leg and lay it across his, too. That she hadn't was one way he knew she was probably brooding the same way he was.

He sure as hell couldn't sleep until he felt her utter relaxation.

It came, eventually, after a soft sigh. He turned his head enough to kiss her forehead, having the wry thought that they'd both have slept sooner if they'd let themselves make love first.

Have sex. Love…was off the table.

The words, *for now*, drifted through his head just before he let himself relax into sleep, too.

As always, his sleep was restless. He'd tuned his radar to pick up any untoward sounds, and given how little time he had spent in the mountains in this part of the world, too many of those sounds triggered brief waking moments. Gwen squirming had the same effect on him, as did what he suspected were a couple of nightmares. Both times, she let out a gasp and stiffened. The second time, she cried out. Whether she actually heard his comforting words or felt him kneading whatever tight muscles he could reach, Rafe didn't know, but she gave no sign of waking up and relaxed back to sleep.

Would she keep having nightmares? Yeah, he'd bet on it. These days of sustained tension and fear provided plenty of material. They might have reawakened nightmares from after the car accident and her mother's death, too.

He had his own share of them. He'd come to think of them as a slideshow. A different one would haunt him every night. They tended to circle around until they replayed. Again and again.

Grimacing at the darkness, he knew damn well he'd added a couple new ones. Being tied securely to a backboard, unable to so much as lift an arm when that greedy sellout, Bruce Kimball, held a gun on him and then, worse, turned it on Gwen—that rose to the top. Watching her fall, unable to reach her... That had been bad, too.

The soft patter of rainfall on the tarp awakened him once, not heavy enough to be a real concern, although if it kept raining tomorrow—today?—the going would be miserable for two people not equipped with rain gear.

He did manage to drop off again, although by morning, he'd swear he'd been lucky to catch half an hour of shut-eye at a time throughout the entire night.

With the pearly light of dawn, he eased himself out of the sleeping bag without quite waking Gwen, who merely grumbled and clutched at him as if someone were stealing her favorite teddy bear.

He hastily dressed even as he looked around. The foliage was damp but no longer dripping, and what he could see of the sky made him think the clouds had cleared. Rafe grunted at the thought that they were lucky. He couldn't label much that had happened recently as lucky.

Except, of course, Gwen.

Growling under his breath, he opened some distance from their campsite to relieve himself, then returned to set up the stove again and put on water to heat for oatmeal and coffee.

RAFE'S MOOD DIDN'T appear to have improved today, although Gwen could hardly blame him. She wondered whether he could possibly have recovered from his gunshot wounds as miraculously as it appeared—or as he made an enormous effort to make it appear.

His face was drawn, hollows noticeable beneath sharp cheekbones. He kept scratching irritably at dark stubble on his jaw and neck that could now be called a beard. She made an effort to brush out the tangles in her hair—along with twigs, leaves and one small slug that she tossed away with a shudder—but the best she could do was pull it back out of her face and hope it didn't look as greasy and sweat-soaked as it had to be.

"What I'd give for a shower," she muttered,

not intending to be heard, but Rafe, who was strapping the tent and sleeping bag to the backpack, raised his eyebrows at her.

"I'd put living another day ahead of the shower, but both sound good."

She laughed, which made her realize she felt better today. *Better* being a relative term. His mouth quirked briefly in response.

Astonishingly enough, their route today headed downhill. Probably too steeply, so she'd run her fingertip along what looked to be their best path, although really, who knew? Even a topographical map only told you so much.

The zigzag lines of the Northern Loop Trail about where they hoped to join it made Rafe frown.

She said, "That's nothing compared to what we've already accomplished."

He bent to study the map again before saying, "You're right. This'll be a breeze."

She almost smiled again at the wryness in his tone.

Downhill was harder than uphill for aching thigh muscles and creaking joints. Grateful that the rainfall hadn't extended into the morning, Gwen pushed herself as hard as she could and felt guilty that Rafe still carried the pack.

Within an hour, her headache worsened and throbbed in time with every step. Scrambling along the side of a drop-off too steep to permit them to directly descend unroped kept her from being able to sink into the kind of lethargy she had yesterday.

Was it only yesterday that she'd fallen over the cliff? Her memory felt fuzzy enough, she wasn't sure.

Rafe issued curt orders to stop for a break every so often, usually when he spotted a fallen log or rock that allowed them to sit for a few minutes.

Halfway through the day, he suggested they get out the stove and heat water for one of the freeze-dried meals, of which they had plenty, and she could only say dully, "If you want to." None of the nuts or trail mix they had left appealed very much to her.

While he set up and prepared their meals, she refilled their water bottles at the creek they'd reached but hadn't yet figured out how to cross. She dropped purifying tablets in the bottles after returning. When she sat down and accepted a dish, she ate because he insisted on it.

She began to fear that when they actually came to the trail, she'd think it was a mirage.

Both ended up wet, and not just their boots and lower legs, when they scrambled over the rocky bed of the stream tumbling down the steep slope. From the map, she knew they'd had no choice but to cross it somewhere. At least here, it didn't quite qualify as a waterfall.

Midafternoon, when Gwen saw a lake a few hundred feet below them, she wanted to cry. That almost had to be Lake Ethel, didn't it? Which meant...

They'd made it.

Almost made it.

What if they reached the campsite and patrol cabin, and no one was there? She had no idea how long ago the map had been published. Maybe the patrol cabin had been abandoned, burned down—who knew?

What if...?

They'd keep walking, that's what. Once they reached the trail, it should be maintained and therefore mostly smooth, nothing like the country they'd traversed to this point.

Easy peasy, Mom would have said, because *her* mother had said it, too. Except, of course, for having to watch out for the ruthless men still hunting them.

The remaining descent to the lake and the short hike to the neighbouring Lake James, where the campsite was, wasn't as easy as she'd have liked it to be, but Rafe stopped her with a hand on her shoulder.

"I see a couple of backpackers."

"What?" Gwen whirled and made her-

self dizzy. She'd have gone down if he hadn't grabbed for her.

"Okay?"

"I…" She blinked a few times. "Just… shouldn't move so quickly."

He handed her the binoculars she hadn't seen him remove from the pack.

She didn't have to adjust them very much to spot the two hefty brightly covered packs carried by unidentifiable hikers. Unidentifiable, because the tops of their heads could barely be seen over the packs, and they were walking away—northeast, to be exact—taking the switchback descent depicted on the map.

Gwen couldn't see running after them, crying, "Stop! Do you have a phone?"

"Where they are," Rafe observed, "there'll be others."

"Like seeing a mosquito?" she asked politely.

He flashed a grin that weakened her already shaky knees. "Right. Except I'd have said an elk. People are herd animals."

That smile almost erased the lines of tiredness and pain she'd become accustomed to seeing on his lean face. She had to look away. Sky? Blue. One long white tail of vapor left by a jet probably rising from the Seattle airport. No helicopters.

"Let's go." Rafe urged her forward, and she complied.

Just finding the trail was astonishing. They turned right: southwest. She'd been right. The way was not level, but relatively speaking, this was like strolling on a sidewalk. She'd never again think of hiking on designated trails as roughing it.

The campsite was empty.

After a detour to the patrol cabin, ditto. They knocked on the door, opened it and peered in. It looked abandoned.

Rafe muttered something she suspected was stronger than the *damn, damn, damn* Gwen was thinking.

He rolled his head, making her realize that his shoulders, at least, must ache. "Wait here? Or go looking for other backpackers?"

"Go looking. At this time of year, there are bound to be other hikers on a trail talked up in every guidebook."

"You want a bite to eat first?"

"Uh-uh. I'm afraid if I sit down, I won't be able to get myself up again."

Honesty was not, in this case, the best policy. Worry carved grooves in his forehead. "That means you definitely *should* take a break or even stop for the night."

"We can do better than that if only we find

someone with a working phone," she reminded him. "Shower. Bed."

"Helicopter ride."

She had to think about that. Would she start feeling nervous on the job every time the copter lifted off the pad? Surviving a second crash would be pushing her luck. But Gwen had been flying for her job too long. She had…faith. The EMS Bell helicopter wouldn't have gone down as it did if Bill had been left in control.

"A dream come true," she told Rafe, who half smiled, half grimaced and waved a hand ahead.

"You first, Ms. I-Puked-in-Secret-Last-Night."

And she'd thought he hadn't noticed.

Chapter Fourteen

The first backpacker, a lone young guy, looked alarmed at the sight of them. Rafe didn't think they could possibly look *that* bad. He asked, "Do you have a phone?"

The guy shook his head hard and scuttled by them, walking sideways like a crab. "No phone, sorry. There's, ah, some other people back there." He gestured vaguely, then hurried away.

Rafe watched him break into a trot.

Gwen smiled weakly. "Apparently, we could be cast in a horror movie."

"Maybe we're zombies and don't know it."

He was awed that Gwen had found humor in having their hopes dashed. That flash of laughter was gone, though, and now she stood still with her eyes closed, doing nothing but waiting.

He really wanted to get her to a hospital.

Rafe took her hand and squeezed it. "Onward."

Her lashes fluttered and she met his eyes. "Sure."

He wished the trail was wide enough for them to walk abreast, but instead he nudged her ahead. Without a word or a complaint, she went.

He didn't love to discover they were once again climbing, but Gwen trudged on, Rafe sticking close behind in case she hit the wall.

It didn't happen. She was still on her feet, putting one in front of the other, when he heard voices. She did, too, her head coming up.

This time, they were met by a group of four, three men and a woman.

Instead of panic, he saw concern on the face of the guy in the lead.

"What happened to you two?"

Rafe moved up beside Gwen and wrapped an arm around her. She leaned into him slightly.

"We were on a helicopter that crashed in rough country a few days ago. The pilot was killed. We're the only survivors."

All four people stared at them in a kind of awe. "I read something about a medical helicopter disappearing," another of the men said.

"That was us," Rafe agreed. "Is there any chance you have a phone with enough bars to allow us to make a call?"

He, for one, held his breath waiting for the answer.

THE RINGS WERE one of the best things Rafe had ever heard. The snarled "Zabrowsky" might be number two.

"It's Rafe Salazar." He watched as the woman and one of the men convinced Gwen to sit down on a folding camp stool—who knew there was such a thing?—and sip water. The woman had produced a Butterfinger bar that she handed over.

"Salazar?" Rafe's boss sounded genuinely stunned. "Goddamn. I was afraid you were dead. You just…disappeared. If personnel at the hospital were right, you were on that damn helicopter that went down, except there was no trace of you when we did locate it."

Rafe turned his back on the group and lowered his voice. "I was still coming out of anesthesia—couldn't have been long after they let you in to see me—when I found myself being transported to an airfield and loaded onto a rescue helicopter. Supposedly, I was being taken to Seattle for better care at a major hospital. Really, Bruce Kimball had paid off the EMS pilot to rendezvous with someone else in Mount Rainier National Park."

"Kimball?"

"You know him?"

"Vaguely. Was he the one…?"

"Who shot up the safe house? I assume so.

I didn't get a good look, but I know Eaton let the shooter in because he recognized him. Uh, I don't suppose he or Stanton survived?"

The clipped no didn't surprise him.

"I'm on a borrowed phone. The paramedic who saved my life is with me. I'm still hurting, but she's in worse shape now. We'd love a pickup."

Rafe turned, consulted with everyone else and finally conceded that they would be best to go back to the campsite and cabin, where a helicopter could land.

Zabrowsky apparently pulled up a map on his computer and agreed he'd get a bird in the air as quickly as possible.

"Sit tight," he said, and Rafe gave a rough laugh. That sounded a lot better than any of the alternatives.

He handed the phone to the backpacker and said, "Thank you. Our ride will be along. I can't tell you how glad we were to see you."

Their new friends escorted them back to the campsite and insisted on waiting with them. He hesitated briefly, but most often there was safety of a sort in numbers, and even if that damn unmarked helicopter swept overhead, if Rafe and Gwen ducked their heads, they might appear to be part of the group.

All kinds of goodies appeared from the packs,

and he dug out the remaining freeze-dried meals. A hot late lunch and early dinner helped fill the time until Rafe heard the distant, ominous roar of an approaching helicopter—except this one came from the north.

Gwen had a shimmer of tears in her eyes, although she never let them fall. The relief was so profound that Rafe might have shed some tears himself if they'd been alone.

But under it all, a heavy weight had settled in his chest, somewhere under his breastbone. He didn't want to leave Gwen. Say a quick goodbye to her in a hospital ER, say, leaving her to be evaluated while he walked away.

But would he be given a choice?

IT TURNED OUT worse than Gwen had expected. Within seconds of the helicopter landing on the roof of the hospital, medical personnel ran to it. Her protests were ignored when someone wrapped a collar around her neck, she was eased onto a backboard and lifted onto a wheeled gurney. Talking to an older man who had walked out with the hospital employees, a man she presumed to be his boss, Rafe had his back to her when the team around her pushed her at the speed of a trot toward the entrance to the hospital.

Gwen opened her mouth to call to him...

but then closed it. Anguish squeezed her chest. She didn't want more thanks, and would a last, terrible look into his dark eyes really be better than this, a clean severing of their relationship?

No. He was probably glad to hand her off safely. She needed to be glad *he* had made it this far safely, too.

Given what a short time she'd known him, how could parting hurt this much?

All she could do was close her eyes and experience being the patient for the second time in her life. Like most medical professionals, she was terrible at it.

"I'm sure I did have a concussion," she repeated countless times. "But I'm feeling better. I'm not dizzy anymore." Which wasn't quite true, but she just wanted to go home. She identified how many fingers were being held up, stared into the blinding light shone into her eyes and endured the claustrophobia induced by an MRI.

Her doctor, an eager young resident who she recognized from EMS deliveries to this hospital, finally conceded.

"I'm tempted to insist you stay the night, but as long as you go straight home—and not on a bus—" He broke off again to level a stern look at her. "I trust there are no tall flights of stairs in your building."

She almost laughed. She and Rafe had scrambled up thousands of feet in elevation, then down and up again, and now a staircase was supposed to daunt her?

"Elevator," she said.

The doctor frowned at her. "All right. You need to see your own doctor soon. Immediately if your headache worsens, you become dizzy, pass out or you experience difficulty with your vision."

Gwen tuned him out while making sure her expression was pleasant and accepting.

Only as she sat in a wheelchair and allowed an orderly to push her toward the main entrance was she hit by the realization that she couldn't even call for an Uber or pay for a taxi or let herself into her apartment. There had to be a way to reclaim her possessions, specifically, her keys, wallet and phone.

"Wait!" she said.

Almost simultaneously, she heard her name being called from behind her.

"Ms. Allen? Glad I caught you."

It was the man she'd seen on the helipad with Rafe. Iron-gray hair cut short, and the furrows in his face had her placing him in his fifties.

"I'll take over," he announced, firmly edging the orderly aside. "I need to speak to Ms. Allen."

His force of personality won the brief tussle, and she found herself being wheeled back to the elevator.

Once the doors had closed behind them and the elevator was dropping to what had to be a basement level, he introduced himself as supervisory agent Ron Zabrowsky and said, "I'd appreciate it if we could talk for a minute. I know an interview is probably the last thing you want right now—"

"No, it's okay. Is… Has Rafe—Agent Salazar—been checked out by a doctor?"

"Yes, immediately. He's recovered extraordinarily well given his activities this past week. From what he's said, he wouldn't have gotten far without you."

"Strapped to the backboard, he couldn't fight back," she said.

"No."

Was she in trouble for having shot and killed a federal agent?

They exited the elevator at a level that appeared to be deserted. Gwen felt uneasy for the first time. What would this man do if she insisted on walking? Having him behind her, pushing her to an unknown destination, made the hair on the back of her neck prickle. What if *he* had been allied with Bruce Kimball? When she asked Rafe what he thought about his boss, he'd hesitated.

"Where are we going?" she asked.

"Right here." He stepped to the side to open a door, held it with his hip and pushed her inside.

The first thing she saw was the pack lying on a table, a pile of things that had been in it to one side. A doctor rose from a padded office chair, scaring Gwen even more for a fleeting moment.

Then she realized he was *not* a doctor. It was Rafe—tall, sexy and somehow intimidating in undoubtedly borrowed clean blue scrubs to replace his filthy, torn clothing. Why intimidating? She didn't know. It wasn't as if she ever backed down just because a man or woman had the letters MD on an identity badge. She continued to take in Rafe's appearance, from his gleaming hair to the tuft of equally black hair that showed in the V of the scrub top, which bared his powerful arms. Her gaze swept all the way to the familiar borrowed boots.

She blinked back tears. Had *he* insisted on having a chance to say goodbye?

Humor seemed like a better idea than diving into his arms and sobbing.

"You look better than I do."

A grin flickered as he came straight to her. "For some reason, they insisted on cleaning me up before they replaced my dressings." Then his jaw tightened. "I can't believe they're booting you out! You can't tell me you don't have a concussion!"

"No, I did have one, but I don't have any symptoms alarming enough for the doctor to keep me overnight. I was going to take a taxi home, except I suddenly remembered I can't because you have my stuff."

He grinned. "I was holding it hostage so you couldn't get away."

"Oh." She cast a glance over her shoulder to see that Rafe's boss had strolled to a conference table and settled himself close enough to watch them but gave them a measure of privacy.

She lowered her voice. "Do you know yet where you'll be sent?"

Zabrowsky cleared his throat, and she realized that privacy was illusory.

Rafe grimaced. "That's...not yet settled."

She turned a blistering stare on his boss. "It had better be more secure than the last safe house!"

Rafe's crooked smile calmed her. "I'm not liking the idea of any agency safe house right now."

Gwen sniffed. "I can see why, at least until you can be sure Kimball was the only DEA agent willing to sell out."

Both men winced.

"So?" If she sounded acid, she couldn't help

it. "Will you be put up in a hotel under a false identity until somebody comes up with a better solution?"

"You know I can't tell you," he said with the gentle timbre to his voice that always undid her.

Gwen tried to smile. "I know." He'd tried all along to hide how much pain he was in. Feeling vulnerable in any way might have been a new experience for him. Would he hate knowing she still felt protective of him?

She took a deep breath. Of course her idea would be shot down right away, but she decided to throw it out there, anyway. "You'd be welcome to come home with me while the investigation is underway. Who would expect that? Even though I was seen with you, does anyone know who I am?"

Rafe froze. She glanced uneasily at Zabrowsky to see a strange expression on his face.

"My apartment isn't super secure," she said tentatively, "but it's not bad. In theory, no one can get in or use the elevator without an electronic fob. If you stay out of sight…"

"I could be endangering you."

"We've kind of got a mutual aid society going already, don't we? I wouldn't mind having someone do the cooking until I'm feeling a little better."

"You won't be able to go back to work for a while," he said slowly.

Gwen sighed. "No. Even aside from the head injury, I'll be grounded until my ribs fully heal. I will need to let my superior know why I didn't show up to work Monday."

Zabrowsky joined them, half sitting on the conference table. "Surely he or she knows you were on the helicopter that disappeared."

"I'm actually not sure. Dispatch in Yakima offered me a ride along with the pilot to deliver an empty helicopter to Seattle. It's possible even that was kind of under the table. You know, a favor for a coworker. How much anyone higher up the chain knows about the unauthorized patient or Kimball as passenger—and whether I was on the helicopter or not—I won't know until I talk to them. And… I suppose you may want me to limit what I say?"

"We'll talk about that," Zabrowsky agreed.

She frowned. "You did look at the crash site."

"Eventually," he agreed. "I was still in Yakima when I heard some buzz about the medical helicopter that had gone missing, and then several days later, the fact that it had been found way off course, having gone down in the national park. Since supposedly there hadn't been passengers because it was merely being transferred between bases, I couldn't be positive it was connected to Rafe's disappearance. We'd already turned that town upside down and given it a hard shake."

She would bet he was popular with the Yakima PD.

"At the hospital, several people claimed a DEA agent, who'd showed his credentials, had cleared Rafe's transfer to the EMS base and thus to Seattle. Needless to say, the badge did not belong to Bruce Kimball. Somehow, he'd gotten his hands on a badge belonging to an agent who had just retired. So recently—" he grimaced "—it might have been verified if anyone had thought to call to make sure it was legit. As it was, nobody did."

Keeping her focus on the crash, Gwen questioned, "The, um, body was gone by the time search and rescue found the crash site?"

His eyebrows rose. "Agent Bruce Kimball's body?"

That man she'd shot and killed. "Yes."

"No sign of it. No backboard. No proof anyone but the pilot was on board. To the contrary. The surroundings had been completely cleaned up. From what I know secondhand, it was assumed the pilot had deviated from his flight plan for an unknown reason, had a medical crisis or got caught in some weather anomaly and went down before he could let anyone know he was in trouble."

"I think Kimball must have killed him. Did Rafe tell you that?"

Rafe laid a hand on her shoulder. "I did. I told him everything that happened and all our speculation." He lifted his gaze to Zabrowsky. "What do you think?"

The already deep furrows in Ron Zabrowsky's forehead became chasms. "About the idea of staying with Ms. Allen."

Rafe's fingers tightened on Gwen's shoulder. "Yeah."

She held her breath.

"I have reservations for obvious reasons, but... it might work as a very temporary measure. Discovering we had an internal betrayal—" He broke off.

She didn't ask herself whether this was a good idea or whether she was just setting herself up for real heartbreak. She only knew she wanted this. Days if not weeks more with Rafe. Time to talk when they weren't running for their lives.

If it became awkward, if they turned out to have nothing in common, then that might be just as well.

"Gwen." Rafe crouched in front of her wheelchair, his hands covering hers where they rested on the arms. His dark eyes were searching. "Are you sure?"

"Of course I'm sure." To her ears, she sounded a little shaky. She hoped he hadn't noticed.

He kept looking into her eyes for an unnerving length of time before he gave her hands a quick squeeze and rose to his feet.

"Ron?"

"It would solve some immediate problems. You can't go with her right away, though. We need her to be seen making her way home alone." Zabrowsky gave her an apologetic glance. "Not that it's likely anyone is watching, but we can't afford to be careless."

Rafe's jaw had tightened, but Gwen nodded. "No. That makes sense."

"Then let's plan how we can slip him in late tonight."

Her chest expanded as if with the first full breath she'd been able to take in longer than she could remember. This wasn't goodbye—not yet.

Chapter Fifteen

"The pull-out sofa is fine," Rafe said even though what he'd really like was to sleep with her in the queen-size bed he'd caught a glimpse of in the single bedroom during the brief tour she'd given him after his 2:00 a.m. arrival. "You must be beat."

"I slept for a few hours." A smile lit her face. "*After* the best shower I've ever taken. I'm bitter the hospital personnel didn't let me shower then and there. They know me! But no—they sent me home in *filthy* clothes with *gross* hair. I won't be surprised if someone didn't take a few photos to post or at least pass around. Or maybe to blackmail me with."

He'd have been outraged if he hadn't been able to tell she was kidding. Who'd dislike the courageous, kind, patient woman who'd saved his life repeatedly?

And damn. Not even her visible bruises could keep him from thinking about how beautiful she was.

To distract himself, he said, "Ah, I didn't think to ask whether you have friends, neighbors, whatever, who are used to dropping by."

Her surprise was evident. "Not really. I'm not big on parties, and this place isn't large enough for me to host one, anyway. Usually, I meet friends out somewhere. With my work schedule being so different, even my closest friends can't keep track. When people call, I'll meet them somewhere else, like your boss suggested. That's usual for me, anyway. No one will wonder."

"Good." He dropped the duffel bag in a corner of the small living room. He unzipped it and removed the small toiletry kit, a result of the quick shopping trip Zabrowsky had personally made this evening while leaving Rafe stashed in that windowless, locked room in the hospital basement. It was unsettling that Zabrowsky was so determined to keep Rafe's reappearance among the living a deep, dark secret. He didn't dare even trust an underling enough to send him on the errand. The pilot and copilot of the helicopter that picked him and Gwen up were under orders to keep their damn mouths shut. The quote was straight from Zabrowsky. Rafe knew from experience that consequences for an indiscretion would be extreme.

At the moment, Gwen looked as uncomfortable as he felt. Him moving in with her here didn't feel like an extension of their desperate trek through the wilds of the park. It wasn't that he'd never had a roommate. During undercover investigations, he'd slept plenty of times in close quarters with the men he had to fit in with. In his personal life, it had been years. Generally when he was involved with a woman, overnights weren't included. He liked his space and privacy.

Had liked them, until he'd discovered the pleasure of holding this woman, waking to find her wrapped around him.

That's what he wanted right now and wasn't going to get.

"You probably haven't had any sleep yet at all, have you?" she said quickly. "I'll get out of your way. If you're up before me in the morning, I've programmed the coffee maker. Otherwise, help yourself to anything you can find. There isn't much, but I'll put in a grocery order in the morning. You can add to the list."

"Thanks."

"Well, then…" She backed up, bumped into the edge of the kitchen island and forced a smile. "Good night."

He opened his mouth, but she'd retreated down the extremely short hall to her bathroom, leaving him alone. For all that he was beat, he wasn't so sure sleep would come easily tonight.

HE'D BEEN RIGHT. The pull-out mattress was fine, if nowhere near as comfortable as his bed in his apartment had been, or the one at the safe house, for that matter. It was incomparable luxury compared to the thin, too narrow foam pad he and Gwen had shared the past few nights, so he couldn't use it to excuse his restlessness.

He did drop off, wake up and sleep again. The third time he came awake, he saw a faint glow coming from the bedroom or bathroom. Rafe lay still and waited. The toilet didn't flush; the light didn't go out. Finally, he climbed out of bed and walked on silent feet toward the source of the light: a six-inch crack where she'd left her bedroom door open.

He glanced down at himself and decided he was decent enough in pajama pants and a T-shirt from a package of three that had been part of his new wardrobe. He wrapped lightly on the door with his knuckles.

A no-doubt startled silence was followed by, "Rafe? Come in."

He pushed open the door and stepped into her bedroom. Gwen sat up in bed, pillows piled behind her, a laptop on crossed legs beneath the covers. Gleaming strands of golden-brown hair had worked their way loose from her braid.

"I'm sorry. Did I wake you up?" she asked.

He shook his head and wandered closer. "Wasn't sleeping well."

"The sofa—"

"Is fine. Just...have a lot on my mind." *Especially you*, he didn't say.

She smiled weakly. "Me too. I guess I shouldn't have slept earlier. Um... I was reading what coverage appeared in the *Seattle Times* about the crash."

"Yeah, I did that earlier. It's scanty, and what's there has no resemblance to what really happened."

"No." She looked shy. "If you want to sit down..."

On the bed, she meant. There were no other options. A dresser, bedside stand and treadmill filled most available floor space. He sat near the foot.

"You having nightmares?" he asked.

"I...don't really know." The uncertainty looked genuine. "I keep jerking awake, so my dreams probably aren't all sunshine and roses." Her forehead creased as she studied him. "What about you? Or... I suppose you become inured."

"To some extent." He talked for a minute about the necessity of being able to separate the ugly things he saw and did on the job from the rest of his life. He didn't mention that the process wasn't nearly as tidy as it sounded. "Right now, I'm having trouble remembering what the rest of my life was like," he heard himself say.

Where did that come from?

Her eyes were warm. "You were undercover for a year, you said. That's…a long time."

He moved his shoulders uncomfortably. Talking about feelings, that was something he did even less often than he went home, which he no longer had. He'd stored his possessions before taking on the last investigation.

"Then over a month in the safe house," he reminded her.

She closed her laptop and set it aside without looking away from him. "You must have friends."

"Sure." Rafe grimaced. Did he? Given that his best friend from growing up was dead, the closest to longtime friends he had were from college, and they were spread across the country and contact consisted mostly of an occasional phone conversation. "In my job, friends come and go. We get transferred, disappear for varying lengths of time. We intend to stay in touch but rarely do. It's hard to make friends outside the agency when you can't talk about most of what you do."

"No, I suppose not." She kept studying him. "What do you do for, well, recreation?"

"I run, lift weights, play in baseball and basketball leagues our agency fields. Join a regular poker group, read, watch TV." He shrugged. "On my rare vacations, I enjoy diving."

Gwen wrinkled her nose. "Diving in the Puget Sound isn't the same experience as it would be in the Caribbean."

He laughed. "So I hear. You've tried it, then?"

"Yes. I wasn't enthused. I did snorkel once in Hawaii and loved that."

He interpreted that as her saying she'd be open to diving again in warm, clear waters in some imaginary future with him.

They kept talking, voices low, sharing bits and pieces of their lives from the trivial to the important. Given the nighttime quiet, the atmosphere felt intimate. Just the two of them. They'd had that a lot recently, but this was different. He couldn't quite put his finger on why.

"What time is it?" he asked at last.

"Hm? Oh." She reached for her phone, which was plugged in on the bedside stand. "Five thirty. You should go back to sleep."

"I was thinking a cup of coffee sounds good. I'll try to be quiet—"

Gwen shook her head. "I would have gotten up earlier if I hadn't been trying not to wake you. I'll probably need a nap later, but hey! I don't have anything better to do."

With a yawn, he stretched his arms over his head, aware of a pull in the injured arm but overall appreciating more mobility than he'd have expected so soon. "You're able to go out, at least." Zabrowsky wanted anybody watching to see her follow a normal routine on days when she wasn't working. "Now, me, I'm free to do nothing but lounge on the couch and stare mindlessly at the TV."

"You don't even have a laptop, do you?"

A fact that irritated him no end. "Nope. And I won't have one."

"Well, you're welcome to use mine. And… surely you were given a phone."

"I was, but Ron made it clear he didn't want me online to do more than read news updates."

"Oh. Well, um, I do have the treadmill."

Rafe laughed. "And I'll use it, but probably not for a few more days."

She scrunched her face up. "Me either. So… I think there are some waffles in the freezer."

Accepting the signal, he stood. "I'd better get dressed."

It was while getting dressed in the bathroom, anticipating more than he should the very kind of breakfast he often had when hurried, that Rafe had an epiphany. That conversation really had been different. Simple as that. He'd never let himself talk to anyone as he had to Gwen. The closest might have been when he started a relationship with a girl in college, but it wouldn't have even crossed his mind to tell her about Mateo, as an example.

No, he and Gwen had shared like two people who really wanted to know each other, from the fun parts to the deep, hurtful places. They weren't on the run anymore; they were in the comfort of her home. What they'd gone through with each other had answered many of the biggest questions, meaning he could be open in a way he had never been with a woman.

The very fact that he really did want to know about everything that had made Gwen Allen the woman she was, from the heartbreaking to the trivial, shook him to his foundation. There was no question that he'd be walking out of her life soon. He knew better than to fall for her, if that's what was happening.

He stared at himself in the mirror. *Hell.* Maybe it was too late.

GWYN'S EMPLOYERS WEREN'T thrilled to have to remove her from the roster for a minimum of a month. After Zabrowsky confirmed in some mysterious way that nobody beyond the dispatcher at EMS Flight had had the slightest idea she'd gotten on that helicopter—and the dispatcher had been exceedingly grateful to be ordered to forget that he knew anything about it—she'd required a new excuse for her disappearance and injuries.

Apparently, federal agents were encouraged to be creative. Now she and an unnamed friend had gone backpacking without taking sensible precautions, like charging their phones. They'd gotten lost, after which Gwen stumbled over a cliff. The friend had helped her hobble out of the wilderness. Gwen made herself grovel while clenching her teeth and being officially reprimanded. She didn't appreciate any of it. The only plus side was that she didn't have to explain helping herself to narcotics or what she'd done with the missing doses.

Rafe's annoyance that her courageous conduct had been rewarded so shabbily helped her get over being mad. She even resented the implication that she and an apparently brainless friend would have been so careless as to forget to pack a charger for their phones.

He'd wrapped an arm around her while she grumbled.

"I don't blame you for being irritated," he said sympathetically, "but the story doesn't hang together if you'd carried a charger. Claiming no cell service might make someone wonder if you hadn't been in Mount Rainier National Park, and that's the last thing we want."

"Yeah, yeah." She sighed, letting herself lean into him for a moment, but not too long. The heat she occasionally saw in his eyes let her know that surrendering to temptation could have long-term consequences she was trying to avoid.

Like making love with a man she'd never be able to forget and might forever use as a standard other men couldn't match.

In the next couple of days, she learned he was a good roommate in most respects. He never complained about the confinement, although she felt his tension as if he exuded an electrical charge. He tried to work it out doing exercises— she was awestruck by the number of sit-ups he could do—and he hadn't been kidding about using the treadmill. He ran what had to be ten miles or more a day on it. They'd be talking in the kitchen, and he'd suddenly jump up and say, "I need a run," and vanish to her bedroom.

Which meant, of course, that she couldn't go to her bedroom, because then she'd have to feast on the sight of him in low-slung sweatpants and a tank top that exposed an imposing amount of muscle as he ran. Fast and hard until sweat dripped, until the intensity on his face almost frightened her.

He did that *right next to her bed*.

She couldn't help thinking of another excellent way for him to burn off some of that stress. She wanted to burn off her own that way, too, except for this fear that making love with him would be *too* good.

By the third day, she felt better enough to start going out occasionally, even though she felt guilty because Rafe was one hundred percent confined. Since she'd been assigned the task of appearing as if she were back from her vacation a little battered but otherwise normal, except for the frustration of not being able to work, she had to show her face. She met friends from work for coffee, stopped by base to say hi and listened to them talk with shock about the crash and the pilot's death.

"I mean, I've never flown with him," a trauma nurse who was a frequent partner of Gwen's said, "but…"

She didn't have to finish. The dead man could have been any of the pilots they knew well and appreciated with every flight. *They* could be on the next flight that went down, claiming all lives aboard.

Of course, Gwen couldn't admit that she'd met Bill, never mind seen his charred remains. Puked after seeing that. Shot and killed the man who'd been responsible.

She claimed headaches to avoid getting to-gether with coworkers after that. Instead, she grocery-shopped and stopped at the pharmacy to keep up on birth control she hadn't needed in a very long time and didn't need right now, either, but it still seemed...smart. She bought a pair of expensive athletic shoes to replace the ones now tattered and stinky after the use she'd put them through. She picked up a news-paper daily at the box on the corner. Both she and Rafe read it voraciously.

And every time she left her apartment, she had the uncomfortable feeling that she was being watched. She never saw anyone seem-ing to pay attention to her, but she tried.

On the fifth day, Rafe received a phone call.

"Bodies?" he repeated, glanced at her and went to her bedroom. She heard the door close as she continued with dinner preparations.

When he reappeared, his expression was grim. "Zabrowsky says they found the bodies of the two men we shot." His jaw tightened.

Gwen guessed those bodies weren't in good shape by this time.

"They also found a SAT radio that might have flown out of a pocket when one of them went down. It was deep in some ferns and other underbrush."

Her hands, one holding a paring knife, stopped,

unmoving, above the cutting board and a half-chopped bell pepper. "A radio."

"That means they probably did report on us when they saw us descending the ridge. They know a woman was with me, likely even gave a description of you."

Her breathing had become choppy, and she looked down to see that her hands trembled. Carefully, she set down the knife. "They still don't know my name," she pointed out.

"It gets worse," Rafe continued. "The dispatcher who okayed you on that flight admits now to a phone call that came in three or four days after the helicopter went down. Somebody claiming to be a cousin wanted to be sure a woman made it onto a flight that was supposed to be going directly to Seattle. Since you hadn't been in touch, the caller claimed to be worried. He evidently confirmed you boarded the helicopter but can't remember whether he used your name when he agreed."

"Oh, God. You're not safe here. You need to leave."

"If they'd found you, we'd know."

"What?" She stared at him. "Somebody could be watching me."

"Somebody is."

"You're kidding."

"Why would I kid?" He sounded genuinely bewildered.

"Because I've had this creepy feeling that I'm being watched!" she cried. "I told myself I was imagining things, that it was just a leftover from when we knew we *were* being hunted, but now you're telling me...?" Conflicted emotions choked off everything else she wanted to say.

"I'm sorry." Rafe came to her, turned her slowly and pulled her against him, his arms wrapping her snugly. "I should have said something. With this kind of informal arrangement, Ron just about had to keep an eye on us. He and I agreed on a female agent we've both worked with before and believe in. Figured a woman would be less conspicuous."

Dark-haired, medium-height, friendly smile. Gwen had seen the same woman several times and just assumed she was new in the neighborhood. When she described her, Rafe nodded. "That's Carolyn."

Gwen debated between shoving him away and continuing to lean on his strong body. Outrage versus the usual temptation, which won. She punched him in the shoulder, anyway. The uninjured one, of course.

Finally, head resting on his shoulder, she said, "You're confident she'll spot anyone else following me or lurking around the building."

"That's the idea."

The answer wasn't as complete as she'd have liked, but how could he give her a guarantee? She'd agreed to a level of risk when she offered him sanctuary with her. *Live with it*, she told herself.

"Okay," she mumbled.

Being held might have been comfortable if she hadn't been so aware that they were in full body contact—her thighs and breasts pressed against his chest, her cheek on her shoulder. And, was he getting aroused? He didn't say anything, just stayed exceptionally still.

Gwen realized she was doing the same.

Abruptly, his arms dropped from around her, and he backed away. "If you don't need help with dinner, I'm going to use the treadmill."

"This is getting to you, isn't it?"

"This?" he echoed sharply.

"I mean—" Gwen gestured "—being trapped in such a small space. It must feel like a prison cell."

A rough sound escaped him. "It's not the space. You have to know that."

The hot light in his dark eyes transfixed her. "I...wondered," she whispered. "You...get to me, too, you know."

"I swore I'd keep my hands off you."

She knew suddenly how much better having

even a single memory of a night with him would be than nothing.

Warmth flushed her cheeks and she swallowed. "I wish you wouldn't."

One long stride, and his mouth closed over hers.

As if they'd done this a thousand times, they kissed deeply, intensely, tongues stroking and tangling. He gripped her butt to lift her higher while his other hand cupped her jaw. Gwen quit thinking, quit worrying and only felt. She slung her arm around his neck and rose on tiptoe. She wanted to touch him everywhere, but right now, the best she could do was to slide her free hand under his T-shirt and stroke the hard muscles in his back while her fingertips traced his vertebrae.

She wanted everything.

He nipped her lower lip and raised his head. "Gwen?" he asked hoarsely. "Are you sure?"

She wouldn't have sworn she could talk at all, but she managed. "I'm sure."

He said something gritty she couldn't make out, swept her high in his arms and carried her out of the kitchen and toward the bed where she'd felt so alone since he came home with her.

Chapter Sixteen

His hands were shaking. He'd never wanted a woman as much as he did this one, and it had been scaring the hell out of him. He'd have no choice but to leave her. Right now, though, he could give her everything he could.

Instead of throwing her down on the bed, he let her slide down his body until she was back on her feet. The friction with her curves felt so damn good, he wanted to do it again. Instead, he looked down at her face, so vulnerable, her cheeks pink, her eyes dazed, dreamy. She wanted this, too. He eased her shirt over her head, careful not to hurt her, and unclipped her bra, letting it fall. Then he stared, drinking in the sight of her long, pale torso and high, full breasts with delectable rosy nipples.

"I have to—" He lifted her again so he could lick and kiss and suck one of her breasts, then the other.

She whimpered and said something he thought might be "Not fair."

He did most of the stripping, but she helped. He was just trying to decide how he could bend over far enough with this erection to untie his shoes when she knelt at his feet. Rafe watched helplessly as she tugged off first one, then the other and finally his socks. Still on her knees, she squeezed his calves with strong hands before trailing them over his thighs and higher, until his back bowed in a combination of ecstasy and agony that forced him to take control again.

Once he had her on her back in bed, he stroked and tasted and kissed her until he was shaking again. Her legs spread, her knees tightened on his hips, and he had a horrifying realization. For the first time in his life, he wasn't sure he could stop, but he had to.

He pulled back. "I don't have a condom."

"I bought some a few days ago. Just in case. But I'm on birth control, anyway."

He had never dared trust a woman to that extent. This time…he did. Gwen wouldn't lie, but no one method of birth control was entirely safe, and he wouldn't be around. He couldn't take a chance.

"Where are they?"

"Drawer."

He fumbled, tore open a box with one hand,

ripped the small packet even faster and covered himself.

And then he buried himself inside her, never taking his eyes from hers.

She moved with him as if she knew what he needed—or as if she needed the same. With one keening cry, she came with shocking speed, tightening around him until he groaned out her name and spilled himself inside her. If he hadn't been wearing the condom— *Don't think it.*

Rafe came down heavily on her, barely able to make himself move and roll to one side. She rolled with him, her head finding the familiar resting place, their bodies fitting together as if they were one.

Both sated and stunned, Rafe wished he could absorb her. He'd be happy to stay just like that for the rest of his life.

And if anything had ever rattled him, it was that thought.

NEITHER SAID A word in the aftermath. They did finally have dinner, avoiding even a glance at the elephant in the room. Gwen worried aloud about the earlier phone call. Rafe reassured her when he didn't believe himself.

If those bastards had her name or had even learned she was a paramedic with EMS Flight who'd hitched a ride on the helicopter that carried him, they'd find her. She was right—he should insist that he be moved *now*, except that would leave her alone. Here, he had a chance of protecting her. How would he feel if he'd been settled in another damn rambler in Idaho or Minnesota or South Carolina only to be told Gwen was dead?

That…really wasn't a question. Rafe didn't think he could live with the knowledge she'd died for him. He had a bad feeling he was head over heels in love with her, although it was hard to be sure since he'd never experienced anything like this before.

He cleaned up after dinner while keeping an eye on her. She plopped down on the couch and turned on the TV, going to local news on a Seattle channel. Rafe didn't know if she'd always been a news junkie, but she certainly qualified now. What did she think the air-brushed newscasters could tell her that she didn't already know…or fear?

When he joined her, sinking down on the cushion right next to hers and laying his arm around her shoulders, she didn't even look at him. He hoped it was his imagination that she stiffened. Whatever topic the reporters currently covered had them laughing. He didn't pay any attention.

"Are you sorry?" he asked abruptly.

Gwen turned sharply to scrutinize him. "You mean, about…? Of course I'm not! I've been… attracted to you since you were still strapped down and I was told you were a criminal."

"Ah." He relaxed. "I thought you were beautiful from the minute you uncovered my eyes, too. An angel of mercy, despite the fact that I was desperate to see where I was."

She made a face at the humor in his voice. "I did a lot more important things for you than that."

Even that flicker of amusement left him. "Yeah, you did. You'll have nightmares about them for years."

"No. I didn't do anything that wasn't necessary. And I'm not like most people, you know. I see terrible things on the job. We might pick up an injured person from a five-car pileup on the freeway, but we also see all the people, adults and children who didn't survive long enough even to have a chance."

Rafe knew that but had let himself forget. He'd say her job was what made her tougher than average, quicker thinking, willing to face danger most people would shrink from—except that her determination to become a paramedic said something about who she'd been all along. If she had nightmares, they were probably still about being trapped in that car as a child with her mother's body inches away.

He drew her to him and kissed her, maybe roughly, he didn't know, just that he had to have her again right now. With a sound that was nearly a sob, Gwen flung herself at him and kissed him back with all the passion he felt. At one point, he became irritated enough at the canned voices coming from the TV to stab a button on the remote and shut the damn thing up. That was the closest to a conscious thought he had.

Otherwise, he struggled to get her clothes off and enough of his so that he could make love to her again. The bedroom was too far away. He laid her back on the couch, pushed into her and kept thrusting until her climax flung him into his own.

Then he got the rest of his clothes off and did it again.

It wasn't until an hour later, as she led him by one hand to bed, that he remembered he hadn't used a condom either time. Despite knowing she was on birth control, his carelessness would have panicked him normally. This time, he had a tantalizing vision of her swelling with his baby.

He made sure she couldn't see his face while he shut down a dream he couldn't allow himself. What he felt for her was too new. Those emotions were the equivalent of tiny green shoots emerging from the soil. Most new growth ended up frozen because of late cold snaps or fried in a midsummer drought or trampled under uncaring feet.

Rafe couldn't let himself forget that he wouldn't be around this fall or next spring or probably even next fall. Imagining that whatever he felt for Gwen, or her for him, would survive a year and a half absence was too much of a stretch to be believable.

The kindest thing he could do would be to make it clear to her that this thing between them wasn't going anywhere. Because it wasn't.

But he might have a few more days, a few more nights, and he couldn't make himself hurt her now—or miss the chance to have mind-blowing sex as often as possible.

Call him selfish, but he'd never lied to Gwen. She knew as well as he did that they were existing in a tiny slice of time that could be snatched away from them any minute.

For all the passion she showed him, she didn't ask for reassurance that he cared about her. Even as that was a relief, it bothered him. They made love twice more that night but never discussed it.

He remembered her saying something about

going out for a few casual errands the next day, but wrinkled her nose when he asked her plans and said, "Maybe tomorrow. Unless there's something you need, I'm happy here." Her smile teased and tempted. "It's not like we're bored."

"No." He hadn't been bored a minute since he'd set eyes on her. There'd been days when he'd felt like a big cat pacing the perimeter of his cage in search of a weakness, but boredom hadn't been the reason for that. Nope. It was all about Gwen.

Right now, all he wanted was to extend the days with her as long as possible.

Ron called that evening. "I can't find any hint that Bruce Kimball wasn't working alone, at least out of the Chicago office. I spoke to his supervising special agent, who admitted there have been some issues with him. Mostly personality clashes, attitude. He was close to being terminated. Knowing that might have motivated him to take a big paycheck, although you'd think he'd have been smart enough to know the odds weren't good a cartel would let him live once he'd served his purpose."

"No."

"Given what I've learned—and what I haven't learned—I'm going to have you moved to a new safe house. Expect to hear from me in the next day or two."

"Will do."

Ron ended the call. Feeling almost numb, Rafe sat on the edge of Gwen's bed. Tell her how soon he was going? Or wait until he had no choice?

His conscience twinging, all he could think was *Hell*.

SOMETHING CHANGED AFTER the phone call Rafe took in her bedroom that evening. When Gwen asked about it, he only shook his head, his expression impassive in that way he had when he was in special agent mode.

She couldn't help immediately speculating. Had he learned that other agents had been compromised, too, and was sick with disappointment or anger? Had the Espinosa family shifted practices or personnel in a way that would make Rafe's testimony less powerful to a jury? Or had the call been from someone else altogether, perhaps giving him personal news?

The reminder was timely. Despite their closeness, she didn't know much about his personal life. He enjoyed playing poker and baseball. His parents, he'd talked about. What happened with his friend Mateo, which she thought he'd offered up because she'd told him about the car accident that had killed her mother and changed the trajectory of Gwen's life. Otherwise, surely a man who looked like Rafe and had his charisma and wicked smile usually had a girlfriend. Probably not a live-in one currently, not after his year plus spent undercover, but there could still be someone for whom he cared deeply.

Gwen rolled her eyes. Way to feel sorry for herself. He kept warning her in his not-so-subtle way that what they enjoyed was temporary. In other words, he wasn't until-death-do-us-part in love with *her*.

Too bad she did love him. Her little secret.

The next morning, she asked if he needed anything when she went out.

Sitting at the table with a cup of coffee in front of him, he frowned. "Nothing I can't live without."

"To rephrase, is there anything you *want*?"

His grin came close to making her knees buckle, except…it didn't seem to reach his eyes. Disturbed, she still didn't protest when he tugged her forward, slipped a hand behind her neck and urged her to bend over enough for him to kiss her.

"You," he whispered. "I want you."

But apparently didn't need her.

She emerged from the kiss, smiled at him and said, "I may buy all kinds of goodies while I'm out. You'll be sorry."

"I'll live with it."

Gwen grabbed her handbag, dropped her phone in it, made sure she had her keys and said, "Bye."

Too bad there was nowhere she especially wanted to go or anyone she needed to see.

Behave normally, she'd been ordered. Now that the bruises on her face had faded from sight and the lump on her head was gone, her only remaining physical symptom was soreness from her bruised rib cage. Give her another week, and she'd probably be able to persuade a doctor to clear her to go back to work.

What then?

Rafe would be gone. She knew that with painful certainty, one she both forced herself to confront and pushed back at. Why torture herself?

She let herself out of the apartment, took the elevator down and strolled out. She hadn't gone a block when she caught a glimpse of an attractive dark-haired woman sitting at a bus stop apparently intent on her phone. Carolyn.

Carolyn didn't so much as glance toward Gwen, who ignored her, too. As far as she could tell, the agent didn't follow her, or if she did, she had a gift for subterfuge.

Gwen went to her favorite neighborhood grocery store, not huge and really expensive because of the superior quality of their produce and breads. This was the only place she ever bought cherry tomatoes because they'd be really ripe and tasty. Maybe she'd make a favorite recipe tonight with cherry tomatoes and dumplings.

She browsed, bought more than she needed and had enough to carry after she checked out to give her an excuse to skip any other errands.

Half a block from her building, just passing an alley, she saw something strange. A foot stuck out from behind a dumpster. Probably one of the houseless people who called this neighborhood home, she thought, although this was the middle of the day. And...the athletic shoe on the foot was bright white with a logo she recognized. Those shoes weren't cheap.

Carolyn had been wearing those shoes.

Gwen's step stalled. She should check, be sure it wasn't Carolyn or anyone else who needed help. But the leap of her pulse said, *You can't help.* She had to pretend not to notice, keep an eye around herself and hurry home while trying very hard not to *look* as if she were hurrying.

And...call Rafe?

She started to fumble in her bag, but she'd be home in a matter of minutes. In fact, the steps into the building were just ahead. She bounded up them, smiled vaguely at another tenant who had been coming out and held the door for her, and stole a look back the direction she'd come.

Two men had their gazes on her and were walking fast.

Gwen dashed in, pushed the button for the elevator and leaped in when it proved to be on the ground floor. The doors shut, giving her a momentary illusion of safety, but the elevator seemed to take forever to rise to her floor.

Once she was in her apartment, she and Rafe could hold anyone off, couldn't they? She should have called to warn him—maybe she still should?—but the elevator glided to a stop and the doors parted.

She ran and was fumbling to get her key in the lock when she heard the metal door at the head of the staircase slam open not twenty feet from her. Running footsteps thudded toward her as the apartment door gave way, and she screamed, "Rafe!"

HE FELT RESTLESS, but not in a way running mindlessly on the treadmill would help. In fact, had he stepped foot on it since the first time he and Gwen had made love?

He shook his head hard. He never liked it when Gwen went out by herself, for all practical purposes setting herself up as bait, although she didn't seem to realize that was what Ron had in mind.

Part of what Ron had in mind, anyway.

Today his uneasiness grew even though she hadn't been gone all that long. Nothing like when she'd met friends for coffee. For all he knew, she'd taken the bus to the university bookstore to browse and would be gone for a couple of hours. She hadn't said.

But half an hour after she went out the door, he began to pace. Every so often, he'd crack the blinds at the front of the small living room to let him see the street and some of the sidewalk. He'd try to make himself sit but was too antsy to be still for long, and the next thing he knew, he'd be up and walking again.

Ten feet that way, twenty-five if he went through the kitchen and down the very short hall, too. Then back. Peek through the blinds. Repeat.

Instead of leaving his gun sitting on an end table, he slipped it in his waistband at the back for quick access. Did Gwen carry Kimball's, which Ron had not asked her to return? Rafe realized he didn't know. Maybe just as well if it wasn't deep in that capacious handbag of hers. She'd proven herself a good shot, but even the best of police marksmen didn't dare open fire on a busy sidewalk with passing cars and buses. She didn't have their experience.

This time when he scanned the sidewalk, he saw two men walking fast in this direction. Nothing that would catch most people's attention—they could be hurrying to catch a bus or late getting back to their desks at work—but he didn't like the look of them. The thermometer was supposed to top ninety degrees today, hot by northwestern standards, but one wore a jacket and the other a denim overshirt.

He didn't see Gwen, but he'd swear their speed increased. Then they moved out of sight—as if they'd turned into this or a neighboring building.

He heard the elevator and tensed. Let it be Gwen. Feet that had to be running in the hall. Rafe had just reached the door when it opened and Gwen threw herself forward, yelling, "Rafe!"

Seconds later, a man brandishing a handgun shoved her in.

Rafe pulled his gun even as a bullet splintered the glass on a piece of framed art on the wall. He immediately noted from the thickness of their upper bodies that they wore Kevlar vests.

Gwen screamed and staggered, the second man having gripped her ponytail and using it to whip her to one side.

Rafe dove behind the easy chair as a bullet burned his arm. From behind the minimal cover, he fired without his usual icy calm. He wouldn't take a chance of hitting Gwen, but if he didn't take these two down, both he and Gwen would die.

The chair jumped from a fusillade of bullets. Only a decade and a half of practice and experience allowed him to aim carefully instead of firing wildly. He didn't like headshots, but throats...

The first attacker went down, gun skittering across the floor toward Rafe. The second man, a brawny blue-eyed blond, wrenched Gwen in front of him, her head pulled painfully back, and pressed the barrel of his handgun at her temple.

"Drop the gun! I'll kill her! You know I will."

Rafe calculated. If he dropped his Glock, would he have time to get his hands on the other gun that lay temptingly close to him? Would the piece of scum turn his sights on Rafe the minute he moved or shoot Gwen and throw her aside as if she were a distraction done serving his purpose?

"I'll put it down," he called. "Let her go."

The creep laughed. Gwen made a gurgling sound.

Rafe gathered himself, laid his Glock on the

floor and gently pushed it away. At the very moment he launched himself forward for the other weapon, the man holding Gwen started swinging his gun toward Rafe.

Chapter Seventeen

Gwen grabbed her assailant's arm and shoved it up.

Bullets flew over Rafe's nearly supine body. He snatched up the gun he'd gone for, raised it and risked a couple of shots at the arm and shoulder, away from Gwen.

Her captor reeled and kept shooting wildly as he went down, bringing Gwen with him. Rafe leaped forward to free her from the grip on her hair, except she hammered a fist down on the fool's wounded arm. He screamed, letting go of both her ponytail and his gun. Rafe took barely five seconds to flip him face down on the blood-slick oak floor.

"Call 911!" he ordered, drilling his knee into the man's back. "Check the other guy."

She sensibly did that first. "He's dead," she said, almost calmly, and a moment later, he heard her talking to a dispatcher.

Zabrowsky would not be happy about this

debacle, except his witness was alive, and there wouldn't have to be an explanation as to why an innocent local woman had been killed.

Rafe felt sick at how close it had been.

Gwen turned as she ended the call and said, "I have to go down and let them in."

"You're not hurt?" he asked hoarsely.

She was shaking but shook her head. "You are. You're bleeding."

"Nothing significant." How had he sounded so calm? After surveying her, he said, "You have blood on you, too. You have time to change shirts."

Without a word, she turned and disappeared into her bedroom. She returned looking almost pristine, except for the shock and stress on her face and a ponytail that was wildly askew.

Rafe had rarely felt a desire to kill unnecessarily, but right this minute, the relentless effort to hunt him and Gwen down, the ruthlessness of it, weighed on his shoulders, and he stared down at the profile of the first of their attackers, who'd survived.

"Nobody would know if I broke your neck," he said, almost conversationally.

The bastard was smart enough not to beg for mercy. Not that he'd be getting any. He would undoubtedly go away for a good long while.

"You're not worth it," Rafe said decidedly.

Within minutes, the apartment was overrun by emergency personnel. A medic treated Rafe, determining the bullet was a through and through, and although she bandaged his arm, she encouraged him to have a doctor look at it, too.

With a sense of unreality, he looked around. He'd seen dozens of similar scenes. No, that was an understatement. Bullet holes decorated the walls and had torn the chair Gwen most often sat in to shreds and broken pieces of wood. Everyone stepped around the broken glass from the framed art that now hung drunkenly on the wall. The contents in grocery bags she must have dropped were smashed flat. Something red leaked from one of them. He glanced up; yeah, there were even a few bullet holes in the ceiling. Thank God this was the top floor of the apartment building.

She stood in the kitchen out of the way, pressed to the lower cabinets, her expression stricken. Did she have insurance that would cover this mess? How would the landlord react? Would she be able to give an explanation resembling anything close to the real story about what happened?

No, of course not. Zabrowsky would work his wizardry, expect silence from the responding cops, and Gwen would be stuck as the victim of a vicious home invasion assault.

And Rafe? He was powerless and knew it.

FIRST, THE INJURED assailant was removed, and finally, after the appearance of a pair of detectives who asked questions Rafe and Gwen had already answered but did again, the body was zipped into a bag and also hauled away.

Sometime during the chaos, Rafe had disappeared long enough to make a phone call. She didn't like the expression on his face when he reappeared. She'd have called it desperation if she hadn't known better.

He wouldn't be allowed to stay here any longer; she did know that.

The door had no sooner shut behind the detectives, leaving her alone with Rafe, than he said, "Give me your bank account number. I'll make sure you're reimbursed, even if I have to do it myself."

As if they'd ever let him trot off to a bank or even access his own account from a safe house. But she nodded numbly, called up her own account on her phone and scribbled the numbers on a piece of paper that he pocketed.

"This is it, then?" she asked, holding on to her pride with both hands.

"I'm afraid so." He looked around. "You've paid a high price for getting sucked into my problems."

"I don't regret it." She didn't move. Her eyes might be burning, but she refused to let a tear fall until he was gone. "If somebody is coming soon, you'd better make sure you have everything together."

"Gwen…"

She tried to smile. "If you're going to tell me you're madly in love with me and will be back in a year or so—"

Of course, he was shaking his head before she got that far. "You know I can't say that. I won't forget you, but I'm looking at a minimum of a year, maybe as much as two years, before the trial is behind me. I might as well be going to prison in the meantime. You need to move on with your life. I can't promise anything."

That last sentence seemed to be torn from him, as if—No, she wouldn't delude herself.

"I'll be fine. Back to work before I know it."

To give herself something to do, she grabbed a black plastic bag from beneath the kitchen sink and started by sweeping up the glass. Rafe picked up shreds and broken pieces of her chair to add them to the bag.

They'd mostly straightened what was left in her small living room when a knock came on the door. Rafe looked through the peephole, a safety feature that was one of the reasons she'd rented this apartment—and had been so much help today—and let a man and woman in. If she'd seen them on the street, she'd have guessed they were FBI agents from their clothes and their sharply observant expressions. But nope, they were DEA instead. Apparently, feds all looked alike.

One kept an eye on Gwen as he asked Rafe, "You ready?"

"Yeah." He sounded hoarse, turned to face her.

She just shook her head. "We've said everything. You...take care, Rafe. Try to avoid any more bullet holes, okay?"

He almost smiled, then was gone.

Gwen locked the door behind them, and finally let herself collapse.

SHE DIDN'T GO back to EMS Flight. The higher-ups were jerks about her injury and need for weeks off, and then were shocked to hear she'd been the victim of a home invasion. Gwen didn't like the attitude and resigned. Medical helicopter rescue organizations all across the country were desperate for paramedics as well trained and experienced as she was. She wouldn't have any trouble finding a new job.

Once she did her best to repair her apartment and dealt with the landlord, she made the decision to move away from the area. Here, she caught glimpses of Rainier from city streets, and it dominated the skyline every time she went up in a helicopter. She loved Seattle and the Northwest, and she'd be leaving behind a lot of friends, but…she needed a change. To go someplace she wouldn't be constantly reminded of Rafe.

She tried to convince herself it wasn't him so much as the crash, followed by the traumatic days fleeing through incredibly rough country to escape armed pursuers—all culminating in the horrifying attack in her own apartment. But she knew better. It was all about him.

He hadn't even been in her life two full weeks, but she'd fallen in love with him. They'd… meshed, maybe in part because they'd both learned to guard themselves from the sight of desperate survivors of violence, accidental and otherwise. Of course, she arrived in the aftermath, while he might have been part of a whole bunch of shoot-outs, for all she knew. Or, worse, he'd had to see men or women tortured and been unable to do a thing to stop it because he'd been undercover and had to stay in the role if he was ever to bring down the monsters he investigated.

Maybe he wasn't capable of loving a woman, or maybe she just wasn't the right one; she didn't know. Only that she had to believe him when he told her to forget him and move on. Well, he hadn't said the "forget him" part, but he'd meant it.

She couldn't go back to her life as if nothing had happened. A complete change was what she needed.

Gwen applied for several jobs in parts of the country she thought she might like and finally accepted one with CALSTAR in Central California. She was able to live within visiting distance of San Francisco, a city with a flavor of its own that she quickly grew to love, but had a halfway affordable apartment in Stockton. She made friends, if not as close as the ones she'd left behind, had an alert on her phone for any news about the Espinosa family and read articles about the never-ending battle against drug trafficking in general, the profitability of fentanyl and connections to the Mexican cartels, and major DEA operations. Nothing ever popped up closely enough related to the operation Rafe had described, admittedly in skimpy detail, for her to believe it had to do with him.

Months later, when she let herself think about him, she imagined him trapped indoors all this time, able to do nothing but run on a treadmill, maybe lift weights, read, watch TV, chat with fellow agents who shuttled in and out to protect him. It had to be driving him mad. Of course, some of those agents were women—she thought about Carolyn, but nobody had ever told her whether Carolyn had lived or died—

so maybe he had a sexual partner. Or would he let himself, when the other agents who were around would know all about it?

Probably not.

She convinced herself it was good she didn't have a photo of him and couldn't find one online. Sooner or later, she'd forget what he looked like. Anyway, she'd mostly quit thinking about him, although the anniversary of him walking out of her life was hard. She was grateful that she had to work and that she was busy. Also that no one died that day, or she'd have had to feel guilty about being glad her services were needed.

I'll meet someone, she tried desperately to convince herself. She mixed with cops, firefighters, doctors and other emergency personnel. There had to be a man among them who'd measure up to Rafe Salazar and who would also be attracted to her. No, not just attracted—who would fall in love with her. Who wouldn't be able to sleep with her but then shrug and say, *Move on with your life.*

Except he'd also said, *I won't forget you.* And, *I can't promise you anything.* Both of which made her wonder if he had felt more for her than he'd admitted, if there was any chance at all—

Of course there wasn't.

The intercom blared to life, calling her unit to

Interstate 5 and a head-on collision with at least three fatalities and several critical survivors. Probably other helicopters would be needed, too.

RAFE HAD THOUGHT himself to be patient. Damn it, he'd *known* what he was getting into when he'd agreed to go deep undercover with one of the most notorious illegal drug manufacturing and trafficking organizations in North America. After the assault on the safe house and the death of two fellow agents—good guys—and then the ruthless disregard for Gwen's life as he was hunted, Rafe had been even more determined.

That was a year ago. A year during which he couldn't say he was actually living. *Existing* was a more accurate word. Updates on progress were rare. He got to wondering whether he'd been forgotten, whether warrants were being issued at all or whether no one wanted to admit to him that his testimony wouldn't be enough and he'd now thrown away *two years* of his life.

Except for the days—weeks—with Gwen. Those, he fixated on like a shipwrecked man might the broken piece of his boat that kept him afloat. It was downright pathetic.

He was stunned when things actually started to move, and he had to concentrate on reviewing material and reviving his memories of the hellish year he'd served as a useful underling while pretending to ignore assassinations taking place right in front of him and terrorization of whole towns where the cartel operated.

Turned out, getting excited didn't mean the first and biggest trial was actually starting. Arrests did finally take place, including a DEA operation that scooped up the head of the family who'd been in hiding, a man Rafe particularly despised. Rafe would be very glad to testify that he'd seen Papa Espinosa himself hold a gun to a Mexican police officer's temple and pull the trigger, after which he'd curled his lip and walked away while others hustled to toss the body into the back of an SUV and take it away.

Jury selection commenced and dragged on.

Fifteen months after he'd said goodbye to Gwen, Ron Zabrowsky brought him a couple of new suits and hustled him to a hotel in Houston, where he'd stay for the duration of the trial. It might drag on for weeks, and, yeah, there were at least two more in which his testimony would be required, but he saw the light at the end of the tunnel. And he knew that he'd come to the right decision for him.

The day the final trial ended, triumphantly or not, he was turning in his resignation.

GWEN WALKED AWAY from the helicopter carrying debris from their latest mission. Not the body—that waited for the morgue van. A sixty-four-year-old man had been nailed in a crosswalk by a speeding car that tossed him twenty feet or more to land on his head on the pavement. The driver didn't stop. An unusually observant teenager had noted at least part of the license plate number, which had the cops hopeful they'd be able to make an arrest in this particular hit-and-run. CALSTAR had been called because the incident had happened in a small town without a medical facility. An ambulance would have been too slow getting the victim to a trauma center.

But despite offering first-line trauma care themselves, he hadn't made it. From the moment she'd knelt at his side, she'd known he wouldn't live.

Thank God this was the end of her shift and she had a couple of days off coming to her. She felt as tired and discouraged as she had in a long time. A chill February wind tore hair from her braid and made her long for a hot shower.

"Call me shallow," her partner and friend who walked beside her said, "but that is one nice-looking man."

Gwen hardly noticed nice-looking men anymore, but she said, "Yeah? Where?" Her words dried up. That couldn't be—

The tall, dark and handsome man leaning against the door leading into their quarters straightened as he saw them approaching. Gwen quit walking. Didn't even notice that Nancy stopped, looked from one to the other and tactfully kept going.

"Rafe?" Gwen whispered.

He started toward her. "Yeah. It's me." He sounded as hoarse as he had when he said goodbye. "It's been a long time…"

"It has." She was surprised she could speak at all beyond his name. She didn't know what to feel.

"And I told you to forget me."

"No, that's one thing you didn't say. You said I should move on with my life." She gestured vaguely at the airfield and the bright red helicopter behind her. "I have."

"We hadn't known each other that long."

Her head bobbed.

He stopped right in front of her, head bent so he could look into her eyes with all the intensity she'd never forgotten. "If I'd said anything else, it wouldn't have been fair to you."

Wow. Suddenly, she wanted to scream at him. A year and a half of misery, and that was *fair*? But she also understood. His year and a half couldn't have been any better than hers, even if he hadn't been pining for her.

"I get it." Then she blinked, realizing. "The trial is over? Did you win?"

He grinned, doing impossible things to her heart. "Multiple trials. Once the head of the family was convicted of a dozen charges, including first-degree murder, his two sons, a cousin and five men who were also high-ranked went down like bowling pins."

"Then the entire cartel is done for?"

Now his smile twisted. "The leadership, but someone else will step into their place. And there are other cartels, other drug traffickers. It's a triumph, a warning to the rest of them, but we never achieve real victory in this fight."

"Oh, Rafe." Loaded down as she was with several bags, she could only reach out with one hand. "I'm sorry. Glad for you, too. I mean, you did more than anyone could have expected, but you sacrificed a lot for it, too."

He lifted one of the bags from her shoulder and gripped her hand. "I sacrificed any chance of a relationship with you."

She'd taken a step before what he said sunk in and she stopped again, swinging around to look at him. "That's what you were doing?"

"What would you call it?"

"I suppose I thought…"

"Thought?" he prodded, voice getting sharper. Oh, just say it. "That you were just as glad to have an excuse to leave without having some kind of big scene."

Now his eyebrows shot up. "You don't consider having your apartment shot up, the guy you were sleeping with shot and him getting hauled away by a couple of federal agents while leaving you holding the bag a *scene*?"

A laugh she'd never expected bubbled up in her. "Now that you mention it…"

He offered her a friendly grin that looked only slightly forced and said, "I'm told you're going off shift. Can we find someplace to talk?"

"Of course." She might as well be on a roller coaster, because suddenly tears blurred her vision. Despite the various bags and her being less than clean, she threw herself at him. "Oh, Rafe! I didn't think I'd ever see you again."

He pulled her close with his free arm. "God, Gwen. I missed you. If you're involved with someone, I understand, but—" He didn't finish, because she was sniveling against his shoulder.

She forced herself to lift her head. "I'm not. I…couldn't."

His dark eyes searched hers. "Even though you'd given up on me?"

"I guess I couldn't quite."

He bent and rested his forehead against hers, and for a moment, neither moved. Then he said gruffly, "Can we get out of here?"

Gwen wiped her tears on his denim shirt. "Absolutely."

Naturally, she took him home to an apartment that was barely bigger than the one she'd had in Seattle. He followed her in a shiny sedan she suspected was a rental, and was able to use a visitor slot in her parking garage.

The moment they got there, she begged off and took a quick shower. When she came out, he'd made coffee and offered her a cup.

Seeing something on her face, he said, "Bad day?"

"Until I saw you."

Sitting on a stool at the breakfast bar, he separated his legs and drew her to stand between them. "Tell me about it?"

Gwen did, seeing the understanding in his eyes. When she was done, she asked, "How long do you have? Zabrowsky doesn't have the nerve to call the time in a safe house a vacation, does he?"

Rafe laughed at that. "Even he's not that brazen." He hesitated. "After leaving the courthouse the last day, I quit my job. My schedule is entirely open."

Weirdly, she didn't feel the need to ask him why he'd done that. *Or maybe not so weirdly*, she thought, after what he'd said about the hopelessness of stopping the drug trafficking.

But he led her to the couch in her living room, and they sat as they had so many other times, her curled up next to him, and he talked. When he was done, he tipped his head so he could see her face.

"I guess I just have to ask." Without moving a muscle, he still appeared to be bracing himself. "Are you open to picking up where we left off in Seattle?"

She suddenly wasn't sure she could draw a breath. "That's what you want?"

"It's what I want." He hesitated, his expression becoming wary. "It happened fast, but I fell hard for you. I've never felt close to the same about any other woman."

Gwen wanted to burst into sobs, which was a completely counterintuitive response. After sucking in a breath—yes, she could still do it— she said, "Yes. Please. I fell for you, too. You had to have known."

He swallowed. "I hoped. *God.*" He pulled her onto his lap and kissed her. They didn't talk after that for a long while.

By the time they got dressed again and she called to order some Thai food to be delivered, she asked what he intended to do professionally and offered to move anywhere he could get a job.

"I can work anywhere," she said.

Rafe's smile crinkled the skin at the corners of his eyes. "I figured. I think I'll stay in law enforcement, but something local." He shrugged. "I could get on with San Francisco PD, but I think I'd like a smaller town."

It didn't take them long to agree that they'd take a good look around and do some serious thinking before they decided. And that in the meantime, taking up where they left off was exactly what they'd do. Only this time, fear had no claim over them.

The last thing she said on the verge of sleep was "I can't believe this."

As he pulled her into a wonderfully familiar embrace, he murmured in a low, deep voice, "I'm here for good."

* * * * *

Cold Murder In Kolton Lake

R. Barri Flowers

MILLS & BOON

R. Barri Flowers is an award-winning author of crime, thriller, mystery and romance fiction featuring three-dimensional protagonists, riveting plots, unexpected twists and turns, and heart-pounding climaxes. With an expertise in true crime, serial killers and characterizing dangerous offenders, he is perfectly suited for the Harlequin Intrigue line. Chemistry and conflict between the hero and heroine, attention to detail and incorporating the very latest advances in criminal investigations are the cornerstones of his romantic suspense fiction. Discover more on popular social networks and Wikipedia.

Visit the Author Profile page
at millsandboon.com.au.

DEDICATION

To H. Loraine, the cherished love of my life and very best friend, whose support has been unwavering through the many wonderful years together. To my dear mother, Marjah Aljean, who gave me the tools to pursue my passions in life, including writing fiction for publication; and for my loving sister, Jacquelyn, who helped me become the person I am today along the way. To the loyal fans of my romance, mystery, suspense and thriller fiction published over the years.
Lastly, a nod goes out to my wonderful editors, Allison Lyons and Denise Zaza, for the great opportunity to lend my literary voice and creative spirit to the successful Harlequin Intrigue line.

CAST OF CHARACTERS

Scott Lynley—An FBI special agent who reopens a cold case and solicits the victim's niece to help solve the case. Opening up a can of worms places the Chinese American beauty in danger and steels his resolve to protect as they grow closer.

Abby Zhang—An FBI victim specialist whose aunt, Veronica Liu, was murdered twenty years ago. Having discovered the body and still haunted by the unsolved crime, Abby is eager to work with the handsome cold case investigator in getting answers and opening her heart again.

Freda Myerson—The mayor of Kolton Lake who knew the victim and offers assistance in solving the case. But is she hiding something that could hinder the investigation?

Zach Gilliard—A mass shooting survivor who becomes fixated on Abby. But could his interest put her in peril and be linked to the cold case?

Selena Nunez—The detective who originally investigated the homicide and would like nothing better than to see the killer brought to justice.

Jeanne Singletary—Veronica's real estate business partner, who benefited professionally from her death, putting her under suspicion.

Oliver Dillman—A real estate agent who was once rejected by the victim. Did he seek payback through murder?

Prologue

Veronica Liu felt she was in a good place in her life. Her successful career as a real estate agent in Breckinridge County, Kentucky, was thriving. She had a great two-story residence right on the water in the town of Kolton Lake that she'd worked hard to be able to comfortably afford. Her up-and-down love life finally seemed to be going somewhere again, after being happily divorced for two years from a controlling man in Evan Liu. And perhaps most of all, she was delighted to be caring for her precocious but lovable twelve-year-old niece, Abby, whose Chinese American parents, Roslyn and Donald Zhang, died in a train accident when Abby was only six years old. Though she had no children of her own, Veronica considered Abby her daughter and planned to make it the real thing by formally adopting her.

Driving her white Mercedes-Benz AMG sedan down the yellowwood tree–lined Flagstone Lane that afternoon, Veronica pulled onto her property. She brought the car to a stop in the circular driveway. Her brown eyes gazed at the log cabin with loads of windows at every angle as she ran a hand through long black hair with blunt bangs. She knew this would all be Abby's someday. Or at least a place she could always come back to. In Veronica's mind, her late sister, Roslyn, would have done the same in caring for her daughter had their situations been reversed.

Veronica decided to make an apple pie, knowing it was Abby's favorite dessert. But first came dinner. Maybe leftovers to save time. When Veronica's cell phone rang, she lifted it from the pocket of her open-front blazer. She saw that it was an unidentified caller, who had disconnected. Wrong number? She was just about to get out of the car when she heard a noise. Turning toward the driver's-side window, Veronica saw the gun. It was aimed at her face. She had just enough time to meet the hard gaze of the familiar holder of the firearm before a shot went off.

It shattered the glass and struck Veronica point-blank. Everything went dark from that moment on. The instant death had deprived her of the opportunity to say goodbye to her niece. Or to identify her killer.

THE SHOOTER REACHED carefully through the shards of glass and checked the pulse of Veronica Liu in her neck, while ignoring her shattered face and splattered blood. When it became clear that she was dead, if not yet buried, the shooter took a moment or two to gloat, still holding the Colt Python .357 Magnum revolver before backing away from the vehicle as though it was about to explode. Giving the surroundings a sixty-degree look, there was no one in sight who would throw a crimp into the plan to escape the crime scene unscathed. Good. While there was no desire to kill anyone else, plans could always change if the situation warranted it.

When another glance indicated that the coast was clear, the shooter headed for the wooded area behind the victim's house and made for a clean getaway. The work was done and Veronica Liu would no longer be a problem. Certainly not one that couldn't be solved effectively, as had been the case.

The shooter got into a vehicle at a safe distance from the murder scene and drove off with no one the wiser and the target now a dead woman.

ABBY ZHANG WAS in the sixth grade at Kolton Lake Middle School. At twelve, six months away from turning thirteen, she was in the visual and performing arts club and on the problem-solving team. She wished her parents were still around to see her life today, but they weren't. But at least her aunt Veronica was there and always encouraging her to be the person she was meant to be. Abby took that to heart whenever she felt down, knowing her aunt was always looking out for her best interests.

When the school bus dropped Abby off about a block from her house, she waved goodbye to her friends and walked the rest of the way. Running a hand down her long black ponytail and holding her schoolbooks, she wondered what was for dinner tonight. Maybe they could go out for burgers and fries. As she neared the log cabin, Abby's big brown eyes took note of her aunt's car in the driveway. She was still inside the car, but didn't seem to be moving. Why?

Once Abby reached the vehicle, her heart raced when she saw the blood on her aunt's face. Or what was left of it. The girl screamed with shock, dropping the books. What happened? Who did this? Abby thought she caught a glimpse of someone disappearing into the woods. Even as she opened the car door and saw her aunt slump toward her, but otherwise showing no signs of life, Abby sensed what she dreaded to comprehend while wailing.

Her aunt Veronica Liu was dead.

Chapter One

FBI Special Agent Scott Lynley had a stack of case files spread across his L-shaped cherry desk. Specializing in cold case investigations, he'd been assigned to the Federal Bureau of Investigation's field office in Louisville, Kentucky. He hated the idea of homicides and missing persons under mysterious or suspicious circumstances going unsolved. Such as his last case. The decades-old strangulation death of Lexington resident Felicity Yamasaki lay dormant, with investigators unable to identify the suspect for years. Scott was able to discover a latent fingerprint and link it to a suspect, Blake Kitsch, who, when pressed, confessed to the murder in feeling a need to get it off his chest. The retired carpenter had been arrested and was now in the Fayette County Detention Center in Lexington.

At least the victim's surviving family was able to get some closure, Scott told himself, believing that was at least half the battle of his job. The other half was bringing the culprit to justice. He'd been at this with the Bureau for the last fifteen of his thirty-eight years of life, choosing to follow in the footsteps of his late parents, Taylor and Caroline Lynley, by having a career in criminal justice. His dad had been a chief of police with the Oklahoma City Police Department and his mom an Oklahoma County District Court criminal judge. After receiving his Bachelor of Arts in Criminal Justice from Southwestern Oklahoma State University, Scott had completed the new agent training session at the FBI Academy in Quantico, Virginia, and was off and running. His three younger siblings, Madison, Russell and adopted sister, Annette, had also found careers in law enforcement, with Russell becoming an FBI special agent too.

Scott had been divorced from his ex, Paula, for nearly a year now. He had hoped their marriage could have lasted as long as that of his parents, but it wasn't to be. Seemed as though the marriage couldn't survive the demands of their jobs and not spending enough time with each other. He hadn't dated anyone seriously since the divorce. Not that he was necessarily looking to get involved with someone. Or maybe he was, but the right person hadn't come along. Either way, for now he was content to concentrate on his work, jog for exercise in keeping his six-foot, two-inch frame in the best shape possible, or ride one of the horses on his ranch.

Stretching out a long arm, Scott haphazardly grabbed one of the folders and opened it to see the report on a twenty-year-old unsolved murder. Peering his gold-flecked gray eyes at it, he read about Veronica Liu, a thirty-one-year-old real estate agent who'd been shot and killed in her vehicle while parked in the driveway of her cabin in Kolton Lake, Kentucky, in Breckinridge County. A .38 Special cartridge case had been found at the scene. The round had been fired at point-blank range from a Colt Python .357 Magnum revolver that was never located. There was an unidentified DNA profile found inside Liu's vehicle, and a partial fingerprint detected on the outside of the car door, which may or may not have belonged to the perp, with no indication that this had been a robbery gone terribly bad.

A few suspects had been interviewed, but no arrests had been made and no clear motive established.

The victim had left behind a twelve-year-old niece, Abby Zhang, who'd reported seeing someone fleeing the scene, but had offered little to go on beyond that. Abby had been living with her aunt since she was six, when her parents, Roslyn and Donald Zhang, had died in a train derailment. *Talk about bad luck*, Scott told himself, no stranger to losing one's parents as his own had died in a car accident. But he'd been old enough at the time to be able to better process it.

With her aunt murdered, Abby Zhang had been sent to live with another relative. Scott wondered whatever became of the girl, who would be thirty-two today. Maybe he could talk with her. See if she could provide him with any useful information pertaining to the death of Veronica Liu. His thoughts were interrupted when Scott's superior, Diane Huggett, the assistant special agent in charge in the field office, entered his office. Tall, and in her midfifties, she had short blond hair with triangle layers, and was wearing one of her usual dark pantsuits and low heels.

Narrowing green eyes at him, she said, "Blake Kitsch killed himself."

Scott sat up in his well-worn, high-backed leather chair. "What?" He had been hoping to gather more information from the perp, including questioning him about a similar unsolved murder around the same time as the one Kitsch had confessed to.

"Looks like he was able to grab a pen from his attorney and stick it in his own neck, leading to a fatal outcome." Diane sighed. "The lawyer claimed that Kitsch admitted to killing another woman and just wanted this over and done with, before taking his action."

Scott scratched inside his thick short hair and asked interestedly, "Did Kitsch happen to name this other woman he says he killed?"

"It's still under investigation," she responded.

Scott frowned, fearful that Kitsch would take to the grave anything that might have closed another cold case. "At least Felicity Yamasaki can rest in peace that her killer was caught, no matter how long it took."

"Agreed." Diane glanced at his desk and the open folder. "What are you up to?"

"Looking into the murder twenty years ago of Veronica Liu," he answered matter-of-factly. "She was shot to death in her car, in the driveway of her cabin, and discovered that way by her twelve-year-old niece."

"Hmm..." The assistant special agent in charge was thoughtful. "Think you can solve this case?"

"I'd like to try." He had been given latitude to investigate cold cases that struck his fancy, only choosing to tackle those that left enough on the table to give him a fighting chance at cracking. More often than not, he'd been able to eventually solve them and help bring closure to the families and friends of the victims.

"Go for it." She gave her permission. "Every homicide needs accountability, no matter how long it takes."

"My sentiments exactly." He flashed a crooked grin.

"Whatever support we can spare will be available to assist you."

"Okay."

Diane smoothed a wrinkle in her linen jacket. "Keep me posted."

Scott nodded. "I will." He watched her walk out the door and then glanced again at the file on Veronica Liu. Who had killed her? And why? Might her niece, Abby, be able to give some clues? *I'd like to find out*, Scott told himself, as a good place to begin the investigation. He hoped she was cooperative, knowing that some secondary victims of violent crimes found it too painful to want to talk about. Even years later. Would that be the case here?

Opening up his laptop, Scott began an initial search for Abby Zhang, knowing that she could be anywhere or have a different surname now in marriage. There was also the possibility that she could be dead, for one reason or another. That last disturbing thought was put on hold when he spotted an article in the search engine, a few months old, about National Crime Victims' Rights Week, where an Abby Zhang was mentioned.

Clicking on it, Scott saw that the woman in question worked for the FBI as a victim specialist. Her job for the Bureau was to provide assistance and support for victims of crime. There was a photograph of her. Attractive and slender with long, dark hair and brown eyes, Abby Zhang looked to be in her early thirties, which would fit the age of Veronica Liu's niece today. The article indicated her deep commitment to aiding victims of crimes of violence.

That has to be her. Scott was amazed that the key witness to Veronica Liu's murder was actually an FBI employee. It certainly fit and was apropos, all things considered. With that in mind, he accessed the Bureau's site and confirmed that Abby Zhang was still employed as a victim specialist and working out of the Louisville field office's Owensboro resident agency.

Let's pay Ms. Zhang a visit, Scott mused after learning that she would be participating in an FBI human trafficking operation in Breckinridge County to rescue child victims and bring the traffickers to justice. He opened the top drawer of his desk, removed his Bureau-issued Glock 17 Gen5 MOS pistol from his leather shoulder holster and put it inside for safekeeping. He rose to his feet, wearing black loafers, and headed out for the two-hour drive.

NOT A DAY went by when FBI Victim Specialist Abby Zhang didn't think about the haunting loss of her aunt Veronica twenty years ago. The fact that her murder had gone unsolved was just as saddening to Abby. Seemed as though her aunt had simply become another statistic, buried beneath the piles of other homicide victims lost in the criminal justice system. Still, she had to believe that someday her aunt's killer would be identified and made to pay for taking a life Abby had been so dependent upon following the accidental death of her own parents.

Abby had been forced to go live with a distant relative, Kristin Shao, in the San Francisco Bay Area. Though it hadn't been an unpleasant experience, Abby had felt she was more of a burden due to obligation than a welcome addition to the family. It was only after she'd graduated from high school and went on to college that Abby realized her calling in life. She wanted to help other kids navigate through the difficulties all around during childhood tragedies.

Ten years ago, she'd followed up her Bachelor of Arts in Social Work with a Master of

Social Work from the University of Kentucky in Lexington, before taking a job with the FBI's Victim Assistance Program. Her specialty was child welfare after being primary or secondary victims of violent crime and/or sexual exploitation, but she was just as committed to making the transition from victim to survivor for all age groups.

Abby worked at the Bureau's satellite office in Owensboro, Kentucky, whose jurisdiction included Breckinridge County and Kolton Lake, where she'd spent part of her childhood and currently lived. At thirty-two, she was still single, having never found her soulmate and unwilling to settle for less. Why should she? Especially when she knew of others who had settled and were unhappy as a result. Till the right person came along, Abby was content with her work, along with favorite pastimes of jogging, swimming, and reading contemporary and historical novels.

Agents from the FBI's Crimes Against Children and Human Trafficking Program were currently in the midst of a human trafficking sting in Breckinridge County, with assistance from the Breckinridge County Sheriff's Office, Louisville Metro Police Department's Crimes Against Children Unit, and the Department of Homeland Security's Center for Countering

Human Trafficking. Abby was told that there were at least ten children believed to have been forced into prostitution and held captive by sexual exploiters and traffickers at a ranch home in an unincorporated community on Feldon Street.

Wearing an FBI jacket that seemed oversize on her slim body, Abby stood at a safe distance from the action, alongside Victim Services Coordinator Elise Martinez. She was a few years older, but looked younger with a cute two-tone pixie cut and curtain bangs, and blue eyes behind aviator-style glasses.

"How many of those poor children will need therapy for the rest of their lives?" Elise asked, wrinkling her small nose.

"Probably all of them," Abby answered truthfully, imagining what they had been put through by the pimps and johns. *No child should ever be sexually exploited or otherwise victimized by these creeps*, she thought. "But that doesn't mean they can't come out on the other side," she insisted, tucking an errant strand of curly sable hair behind her ear.

"I know. But still, it's hard." Elise had been the victim of sex trafficking and Abby felt for her, fully understanding her commitment to helping other victims.

"That's what we're here for, right?" she reminded the victim services coordinator. "To do whatever's needed to help them cope."

"Yeah." Elise pushed her glasses up. "Looks like it's about to go down. Let's hope everything goes according to plan."

Abby knew that the plan included an undercover agent giving the go-ahead to agents and other law enforcement to storm the house while minimizing any further trauma to the victims. "It will," she responded more confidently than she truly felt. Even a slight wrinkle in the operation could prove costly for those who needed to be rescued. *And that would be disastrous*, she told herself.

As the team closed in, armed with Glocks and Colt M4 carbines, they burst into the home and shots were fired. Abby held her breath till she saw the children being led out by the authorities. All were disheveled and clearly traumatized, but alive. They were turned over to Abby and Elise, as the traffickers were rounded up, handcuffed and placed under arrest, while facing multiple charges related to the imprisonment, prostituting and sexual exploitation of minors.

After initial checks for obvious health issues, questioning, and provision of food and water, the victims were handed over to EMS workers for further medical evaluation and treatment.

Families were notified, or arrangements otherwise made for a safe environment to place the trafficking victims.

Abby felt a sense of relief that the children had been safely rescued, even with a long road of recovery ahead of them. *I'll do everything in my power to help them get through this*, she mused.

After conferring briefly with Elise and law enforcement on the scene, Abby was about to head to her car when she was approached by a tall, solidly built, handsome man who screamed FBI agent, judging by the air of confidence he exuded. She guessed he was in his mid to late thirties. His gray eyes were intriguing on an oblong, smooth-shaven face with a long chin. Thick black hair was styled in a comb-over pomp, low fade cut with an edge up. He was wearing a maroon polo shirt, navy chino deck pants and black loafers.

"Are you Abby Zhang?" he asked in a deep but pleasant tone.

"Yes," Abby confirmed while sensing he already knew that. "Who are you?"

"FBI Special Agent Scott Lynley, Louisville field office." He flashed his identification to prove it.

"How can I help you, Agent Lynley?" Abby wondered if it pertained to the current or a previous investigation she had participated in as a victim specialist. She was used to follow-ups from the FBI on the victims, often in relation to the ongoing cases against the perpetrators. Was that what this was about?

"I'm a cold case investigator," he said, and seemed to give her a moment to process that. "I've reopened the case into the death of Veronica Liu."

Abby reacted to this unexpected news. "You... you have?" she stammered, almost at a loss for words.

"Yes," he said. "If I'm not mistaken, Ms. Liu was your aunt?"

When she caught her breath, Abby felt herself traveling back in time to twelve years of age when her life was so different until that one fateful afternoon. She looked him squarely in the eye and said straightforwardly, "You're definitely not mistaken, Agent Lynley."

He grinned crookedly. "In that case, we need to talk, Ms. Zhang."

All things considered—and there were many when it came to trying to comprehend why her aunt Veronica had had to die, with the authorities seemingly looking the other way for answers, and why the FBI had chosen to restart the investigation after all these years—Abby couldn't agree more.

Chapter Two

Scott couldn't help but be impressed by Abby Zhang. To say that the online photo didn't do her justice would be a gross understatement. He loved her complexion on a gorgeous oval-shaped face, with enchanting bold cappuccino eyes, upturned nose, Cupid's-bow mouth and a cute, dimpled chin. Her long raven hair had layered bangs and was pulled back in a wavy chignon. He put her height at about five feet six inches, with a slender frame. Inside an FBI jacket, she was wearing a white ribbed top, blue straight-leg pants and beige moc toe loafer flats.

"Can I buy you lunch?" he asked her, believing it would make for a more comfortable setting to talk than outside or in an office.

Abby gave him a curious smile. "Sure, why not?"

"Good." He flashed a grin back. "Pick any place you like to eat at."

"Okay. There's a casual restaurant two blocks away that I go to often."

"Great. We can take my car."

She nodded. "Lead the way."

A couple of minutes later, they were riding in Scott's official vehicle, a black Ford Explorer SUV.

"So, looks like the sex trafficking operation went off without a hitch," he commented.

"Thank goodness," Abby said. "Had things gone south and any of the children been caught in the crossfire…" She paused. "Anyway, they were put through enough by the traffickers."

"I agree." Scott glanced over at her in the passenger seat. He could see just how seriously she took her job. Not that he could blame her for wanting to protect children, given Abby's own childhood ordeal where there had been no one present to prevent her from having to face it head-on. "The victimizers will pay the price," he promised her. "People like them usually don't fare very well behind bars."

"So they say." Abby faced him thoughtfully. "What led you to taking a look at Aunt Veronica's murder after so many years?"

It was a good question and one Scott usually got from family members of cold case victims, often in disbelief that their loved ones had not been forgotten. He took his eyes off the road for a moment to glance at his good-looking passenger and responded candidly.

"I get a lot of cold cases passed my way, including those that would not normally be federal cases in and of themselves but found their way into our sphere at the request of local law enforcement seeking assistance. In spite of their best efforts at solving at the time of the crime, some investigators run into a brick wall and the cases are pushed to the back burners. As a cold case investigator, that's where I come in. Some of these are more difficult than others to believe I might be able to crack. In this instance, the nature of the crime and manner of your aunt's death made me feel it was worth a shot." He paused. "What drew me to want to take on the case, in particular, was you."

"Me?" Abby fluttered her curly lashes. "I don't follow."

"You were twelve years old when Veronica Liu was murdered," Scott told her. "Losing the closest thing you had to a parent in such a violent way, at that point in your life, had to be devastating."

"It was," she uttered painfully.

"Not knowing why it happened and why the killer was never apprehended, I felt you deserved answers. Or, at least, I wanted to give it my best shot to make that happen."

"Thank you." Abby's voice broke. "Honestly, it's never sat well with me, the mystery of my aunt's death. I know the police had theories at the time and tried to piece them together and identify her killer. But as the years passed and nothing happened, I'd pretty much decided it was just something I'd have to live with."

"Maybe not," Scott indicated, knowing that he could only be prolonging her frustration with more disappointing results. Or lack thereof. But it was certainly worth pursuing for both of them, and he intended to do just that. With her help.

He pulled into the parking lot of Gwen's Grill on Bogue Road. They went inside and got a table near the window.

After ordering the soup of the day and a Reuben sandwich, to go with black coffee, Scott decided to ease his way into talking about Veronica Liu's death, and what Abby could remember about it, by getting to know a bit more about Abby herself. "How long have you been a victim specialist with the Bureau?" he asked.

Abby, who'd ordered iced tea, a veggie burger and fresh fruit, replied, "Nearly a decade now."

"That's a good while. You obviously like what you're doing." Scott considered her work indispensable to FBI operations in dealing with crime victims and their needs in the aftermath of victimization.

"I love being able to provide assistance to

those most in need during times of crisis," she acknowledged. "After being put through the ringer, without a lifeline from someone who cares, many victims would be totally lost. Especially child victims."

"I hear you and couldn't agree more. The Bureau's victim-centered method to investigations is what makes it so successful, and you're obviously a big part of that in your work with victims." He sipped the hot coffee and found himself wondering about her personal life. Or, more specifically, her love life. She apparently wasn't married, as near as he was able to determine. That didn't mean she wasn't happily involved with someone. Unlike him.

"What about you?" Abby got his attention. "How long have you been an FBI agent?"

"Fifteen years and counting," Scott answered proudly. "I come from a law and law enforcement family, starting with my parents and including a younger brother, also with the Bureau." Was that more information than she wanted or needed to hear?

"Interesting." As Abby tasted the iced tea, she seemed to mean it by the tone of her voice. "Have you always worked cold cases?"

"For about the last decade," he told her, having started out in counterintelligence and moving into investigating white-collar crime before voluntarily being assigned to his current duties. "I felt it was important to try and give a voice to those who no longer had one. Cold case investigations gave me that opportunity."

Abby smiled softly. "I'm glad you zeroed in on my aunt Veronica's murder," she said. "I can't begin to express how grateful I'd be if her killer could somehow still be brought to justice."

It was something Scott had heard many times before from family members of murder victims. Only, in this instance, it seemed to hit him in a more profound way, coming from Veronica Liu's niece. This put even more pressure on him to try to make things right for her. But could he? Or would this cold case remain on ice, despite his best efforts?

AFTER THE FOOD ARRIVED, Abby braced herself for needing to relive that awful day twenty years ago when she'd discovered her aunt's body. But painful as it was, she would gladly go through it if this could somehow result in the good-looking FBI agent being successful in his attempt to close the cold case.

She picked up her veggie burger and, before taking a bite, said contemplatively, "I'll tell you everything I can remember about my aunt Veronica's death, Agent Lynley."

He spooned his minestrone soup and said equably, "First of all, call me Scott. We're both on the same team here, so no need for formal titles."

"Okay, Scott." She grinned. "Abby is always preferred to Ms. Zhang."

"Good." His own grin was slightly crooked. "So, if you can go back to the day your aunt died, you reported to the police seeing someone in the woods behind the cabin. Is that right?"

"Yes." She moved her fork around the fresh fruit in a bowl. "At least, I believe so." Abby took a breath. "I was mostly focused on Aunt Veronica, as I could see that she was in a bad way. But when I looked up, it seemed as though someone or something was moving rapidly through the woods. Honestly, it could have been an animal. I can't say for sure, one way or the other. Everything happened so fast. After checking on my aunt, by the time I looked again toward the woods, I saw nothing. Sorry."

"Don't be." Scott spoke in a gentle voice. "You were understandably in a state of shock at the time and your primary focus would have been on your aunt." He paused. "You came upon the crime scene when you got home from school in the afternoon, right?"

"Yes."

"And it was still daytime?"

"Yes," Abby answered, forking a slice of pineapple.

"How far would you say you were standing in the driveway from where this person or animal in the woods was moving?"

Abby had never been particularly good at measuring distances. Still, she was willing to hazard a guess. "Maybe fifty yards," she speculated. "Or less."

Scott seemed to calculate this in his head. "That's a hundred and fifty feet. Close enough during the day hours to differentiate between an animal and human, don't you think?"

"Yes," she agreed, under normal circumstances. But that wasn't the case. "Except that the woods behind the property were a bit dense and I only caught a glimpse by happenstance, without truly homing in on it," Abby defended herself, even if knowing he was only trying to do his job. "Not to mention, I was too overwrought with emotion to think about anything but my aunt's terrible condition."

"Fair enough." He took a bite out of his Reuben sandwich. "You just never mentioned the possibility that you could have seen an animal."

"My first instinct then…even second and third, for that matter," she pointed out candidly, "was that it was a human being. I only mentioned the animal as a possibility in retrospect, given the craziness of the moment at hand." Abby ate more fruit. "Can't say if the person was male or female, as they were too far away and moving too quickly. I wish I could be more forthcoming."

"You're doing fine," Scott offered her reassurance. He sipped his coffee. "Did you see anyone else on foot or in a vehicle once you were off the school bus?"

"Not that I can recall," she responded. "The cabin was kind of secluded, so I would have noticed had anyone or a car caught my eye."

"When you went inside the cabin, was there anything that seemed off? Like someone might have been lying in wait for your aunt to get home?" Before Abby could respond, Scott added, "I know in the police report there was no indication of a break-in or anything that was reported missing. But maybe you can remember something that you didn't then?"

Abby sat back on the wooden seat, straining her memory for anything unusual inside the cabin. Nothing clicked. "Everything seemed normal inside the cabin," she told him. "The door was even locked. I doubt that the killer went inside." She sighed. "It's much more likely that the person came from the woods..." *And left the same way*, she pondered plausibly.

"Makes sense," he agreed coolly.

Abby felt a chill when thinking that this was likely the shadowy figure she'd seen in the woods, fleeing after killing her aunt. If only she had come home a little sooner, she might have frightened the attacker off. Seen the person to report to the police. *Or become a victim myself*, Abby thought frighteningly.

Breaking her reverie, Scott asked, "Can you recall if your aunt mentioned anything about having enemies?"

Abby pursed her lips musingly. "This probably sounds cliché, but as I told the police back then, everyone seemed to like my aunt Veronica. She was the type of person others quickly warmed up to." Abby recognized that this obviously wasn't the case with her killer. But had the person been a stranger? Or someone her aunt had known?

"Sometimes having that kind of personality can work against you," the special agent surmised, "strange as that may sound."

"It doesn't sound strange," she told him. "I've come across such people in my line of work, ones who were friendly to a fault and attracted some crazies who wished them harm." Was that what had happened to her aunt?

Scott leaned forward. "Did you ever witness any altercations between your aunt and someone else?"

Abby had to think about it again. "Only my uncle Evan Liu," she said, running a finger around the rim of her glass. "Before they got divorced two years prior to Aunt Veronica's death, they argued a lot, seemingly about everything. And anything."

"Think he would've wanted to hurt her?" Scott asked bluntly.

"No. I certainly don't believe he killed her, if that's what you're asking." Abby drew a breath. "Even with their difficulties, I think Uncle Evan never stopped loving my aunt and would not have wanted to see her dead. Besides that, he was remarried when she was killed and had a strong alibi for the time in question." For Abby, talking about this was harder than she'd realized, but she knew it needed to be flushed out, if it could help in any way in the reopened investigation.

Scott angled his head and asked, "What do you remember about your aunt's love life?" He added, "The police report seemed to indicate that she was seeing one guy in particular at the time of her death."

Abby rested an arm on the table. "Aunt Veronica seemed to date a lot, as I recall, but didn't share much about the specifics of her love life with me. I didn't learn till after her death that she had apparently been serious about a

man she was dating, Mathew Yang, who, un-
beknownst to her, was married at the time."
Abby furrowed her brow. "Up until that point,
my impressions were that Aunt Veronica was
happily single, playing the game of romance
by her own rules. Guess somewhere along the
way, those rules were broken."

"Maybe your aunt was merely trying to protect you in her own way—" Scott tossed the notion out there "—by keeping a romance under
wraps until she felt it was the right time to di-
vulge it. If there would be such a time, in light
of what she would likely have learned about
Yang."

"I suppose you're right." Abby wondered if
his deception could have led to murder. The
fact that it was a cold case suggested it wasn't
so cut-and-dried. She gazed at Scott and found
herself wondering about his love life. Was he
married? A family man? He seemed like the
type of person who would not necessarily be
satisfied being single and alone. But what did
she know? Especially when her attempts at
romance had fallen flat. Maybe some people
weren't meant to live happily ever after. Was
he one of those too?

"That should be all for now," Scott told her
evenly, finishing off his second cup of coffee.

"Okay." Abby deduced from his words that

he intended to speak with her again. She found herself looking forward to it, which surprised her somewhat, as she didn't know him. But that could change.

When Scott drove them back to her car, Abby said, "I'm not sure how much I can offer in your investigation, but I certainly want to see justice served in my aunt's murder, at long last. As such, if you feel I can help in any way, let me know."

He hit her with that appealingly crooked grin again. "Count on it."

I will, Abby mused enthusiastically. She got out of his vehicle and into her own car, a red Subaru Solterra, and headed back to the FBI satellite office in Owensboro on Frederica Street.

That afternoon, Abby received an update on the condition of the rescued children, all of whom she was told were going to recover fully from their physical trauma and would be receiving extensive counseling to deal with the mental fallout from the captivity and sexual exploitation they'd endured. It only reinforced to Abby the urgency for the Bureau and local law enforcement to go after the human and sex traffickers, pimps and johns, and others who preyed upon children for profit and pleasure.

Then there were still the other child victims of crimes who were traumatized, either through direct or indirect victimization, when violence struck, and in sore need of specialists like herself to give comfort and hope. Abby now had a whole new reason for such in her own life. With Scott Lynley reopening the investigation into her aunt Veronica's murder, the possibility that it might finally be solved was a bridge Abby would gladly walk over in his company.

Chapter Three

Abby parked in the driveway of the two-story log cabin she'd inherited on Flagstone Lane from her aunt Veronica. She had heeded the advice from her aunt's friend and fellow real estate agent, Jeanne Singletary, to hang on to the valuable lakefront property, bordered by black walnut and yellowwood trees, for when she was ready to take possession of it. She did just that, moving into the residence five years ago, just as her aunt would have wanted.

Going inside, Abby took a sweeping glance at the spacious cabin with its vaulted ceiling, pine interior walls and floor-to-ceiling windows, which overlooked Lake Kolton, and had plantation shutters. She had chosen to remodel three years ago, putting her own spin on the residence. This included rustic engineered hardwood flooring, a stone fireplace and an eat-in L-shaped peninsula kitchen with a breakfast bar. She had replaced her aunt's more contemporary furnishings with log and handcrafted furniture, while adding some perennial house-plants such as silver vine and pink anthurium. A security system had also been installed for peace of mind.

Abby went up the straight staircase to the second floor, where there were two bedrooms, similarly outfitted, with the primary bedroom including an en suite, walk-in closet, and deck that overlooked a wooded area and the lake. Gazing at the woods through the window, she couldn't help but think about the conversation with Scott Lynley and the notion that those woods had provided a perfect escape route for a killer twenty years ago. And she may have seen the culprit. Or not.

Putting those uncomfortable thoughts on hold for now, Abby freshened up and let her hair down, retying it in a high ponytail. She was soon out the door and on her way to meet up with a friend, Beverly Welch, for a drink at the Yantun Club on Evemoore Drive. The two had bonded a year ago, after Beverly's husband, Julius, had been shot to death in a drive-by shooting and Abby had helped get her through it as a victim specialist. Though gang-related, the shooter had apparently targeted the wrong person, making the crime all the more tragic.

When Abby arrived, she found Beverly already seated at the table, waving her over. She worked her way through several other tables and was then greeted by her friend, who stood. African American and in her early thirties, Beverly was taller and just as slender, with a blond Afro worn in Bantu knots, and big brown eyes.

"Hey, girl," Beverly said spiritedly, giving her a little hug.

"Hey." Abby hugged her back.

"I took the liberty of ordering us both a Grey Goose Oaks Lily."

"Cool." Abby smiled at her, approving of the vodka cocktail that she liked.

They sat down and Beverly eyed her and asked, "So, what's going on? You sounded tense over the phone when you said you wanted to get together."

Abby sipped the drink thoughtfully. "My aunt Veronica's case is being reopened by the FBI. Or, one cold case agent, in particular," she told her.

"Seriously?" Beverly licked her lips.

"That was my reaction." Abby chuckled. "It's true."

"How did this come about?"

"Special Agent Scott Lynley took an interest in the case," she explained. "Seems as though he was touched by a little twelve-year-old girl being left to deal with something much bigger than her, after witnessing such a horrific scene."

Beverly gazed at her. "You?"

Abby nodded. "Yep."

"Wow." She tasted her drink. "How does it make you feel, having to dredge up old, painful memories?"

Abby pondered the question while tasting the drink. "Honestly, there are mixed feelings," she told her. "I hate having to go back there, when I was my most vulnerable and felt so helpless. But knowing my aunt died the way she did, and having no resolution, I want to know why she was killed and who was responsible for her death."

"Understood. You deserve some answers. I hope that the special agent can deliver them."

"So do I." Abby had learned long ago not to get her hopes up too high, only to be disappointed. But Scott seemed genuinely committed to the cause. For that, she had to believe he would be able to uncover what had been buried for two long decades.

"If he's successful, maybe you could send him my way," Beverly quipped. "Still waiting for some resolution in Julius's death."

"It's still an ongoing investigation," Abby pointed out, as far as she was aware. And currently a police matter.

"I know. But they seem to be dragging their feet, with no end in sight."

Abby felt her pain, considering the length of time she'd been waiting for her aunt's murder to be solved. "You just have to be patient," she told her gingerly. "I'm sure Julius's killer will be brought to justice." Was she really? Or would the gang win out and get off scot-free?

Beverly eyed her with skepticism. "You truly think so?"

"Yes." She kept her voice steady. "Most killers are eventually held accountable for their actions. No matter how long it takes."

Beverly gave a nod and Abby was sure she knew there was a double meaning to her declaration. It had been far too many years since her aunt Veronica had been laid to rest. But deep down inside, Abby had never given up on the belief that her killer would be brought to the surface, wherever currently submerged in hiding. No reason to back away from that now. Especially now that she had an ally in Scott Lynley in that regard.

The conversation shifted toward Beverly's ten-year-old son, Julius Jr., whom Beverly was doing her best to be both mother and father to at an age where he most needed parental guidance. It made Abby think about having children of her own someday and the joy it would bring into her life. As well as the potential heart-break were she to lose a child prematurely. Or to leave a child behind as the secondary victim of violence, much as had been the case in her own life.

She chose to remain on the positive side of bringing a child into this world. Now she just needed to meet, bond and fall in love with that special person of a like mind as a potential father to the child. For some reason, Special Agent Scott Lynley popped into her head.

Abby colored at the private thought while aware that it was way too premature, if at all, to think of the nice-looking FBI agent in romantic terms. Much less the father of her child. Wasn't it? Right now, it was much more important to want him to find her aunt Veronica's killer, whether alive or dead. And go from there.

DURING THE DRIVE back to Louisville, Scott had to admit that Abby Zhang had crossed his mind more than once. She had held up well in his questioning and provided him with some added perspective on her tragedy to work with. Apart from wanting to give her closure in the murder of her aunt Veronica Liu, the victim specialist seemed like someone he would enjoy getting to know better. She had left the door open in this respect, making herself accessible should he ever need to talk more about her aunt. So, no harm in taking advantage of the possibilities that could potentially present themselves, if Abby were also available, like him. If not, he would certainly be able to respect that and leave her alone.

Scott reached his ranch on Dry Ridge Road in good time, parking in the brick paver driveway. He had been living on the ten-acre, fenced property since purchasing it a decade ago, before prices had started to skyrocket in the city. The two-story, four-bedroom, Prairie-style house had been built at the turn of the twentieth century. In spite of various renovations over the decades, it had retained its architectural bones, which had attracted Scott to the place, reminding him on a small scale of the ranch he'd grown up on. This one came with a four-stall barn, where he kept two American Cream Draft horses and one Thoroughbred for leisure riding on the property's rolling hills and trails, amid tall, swamp white oak and southern magnolia trees.

He moved through the landscaped walkway and onto the long porch, supported by square columns, and went inside the house. It had an open concept with a great room, formal dining room and chef's-style kitchen, vinyl plank flooring and big windows throughout for natural lighting. The furnishings were a mixture of modern and vintage. Though the place suited him, and was his comfort zone, it still lacked the warmth of companionship. He'd had it once and lost it. Maybe he could get it back someday with the right person. Maybe not.

Scott went into the kitchen and grabbed a bottle of beer out of the Sub-Zero refrigerator. He opened it, took a sip and set it on the marble countertop. Taking out his cell phone, he called his brother, Russell, for a video chat. Being a fellow special agent who worked out of the FBI Houston field office, where his wife, Rosamund, was a Homeland Security Investigations special agent, Scott considered himself closest to Russell, among his younger siblings, though four years his junior.

After accepting the chat request, Russell's square face appeared on the small screen. Like him, Russell had their father's steel-gray eyes and prominent features. His jet-black hair was styled in a high and tight cut. He grinned. "Hey."

"Hello, Russ." Scott smiled at him. "Did I catch you at a bad time?"

"No. I've got a few minutes."

"Okay. So, what are you working on?"

"Just the run-of-the-mill bank robbery," Russell responded with a frown. "Happened yesterday in broad daylight in downtown Houston. A male and female pair, wearing hoodies and dark clothing while wielding semiautomatic handguns, made off with a few hundred dollars for their trouble."

"Not exactly a windfall for spending the next two decades behind bars," Scott quipped. "Have they been caught?"

"Not yet, but it shouldn't be long before we have them in custody." Russell looked at him. "What's the latest with you?"

Scott summarized the cold case investigation into the murder of Veronica Liu twenty years ago. He finished with, "I'm hoping that her niece, Abby Zhang, now thirty-two, and the only witness after the fact to emerge, can help to solve this case."

"Hmm…" Russell pinched the bridge of his nose. "Sounds like there's not much to go on at this point."

"That's often the case in age-old investigations," Scott pointed out. "Which is usually what makes them cold cases. But there is some unidentified DNA and latent print evidence that will need to be looked at again in a new light that may lead somewhere. Along with any original suspects who were passed over."

"Well, if anyone can crack a two-decades-old murder, it's you, Scott," Russell said flatly.

He grinned. "Thanks for the vote of confidence, little brother."

"Hey, just telling it as I see it," Russell insisted.

"As always, I'll dig as deep as necessary and see where it goes," Scott told him, tasting the beer.

They spoke a little longer before the call ended. Scott finished off the beer, changed into riding clothes, Western boots and a Stetson wool cowboy hat, and headed out to the barn for a ride on his Thoroughbred, Sammie. After saddling up and giving the sometimes-ornery horse some needed exercise, Scott couldn't help but wonder if Abby rode. If not, he would be happy to give her lessons one day, should she choose to accept.

THE FOLLOWING MORNING, Scott was up and at it for another day on the job. He wondered if he could come up with a good enough reason for a follow-up meeting with Abby. But first things first. He needed to speak with Art Reilly, the original FBI agent who'd worked the Veronica Liu case in conjunction with the local police department, and see what he could learn. Today, Reilly was the supervisory senior resident agent, heading the Louisville field office's Bowling Green resident agency.

Scott took the drive to Wilkinson Trace and

went inside the field office, where he was greeted by Art Reilly, who was muscular and in his mid-fifties, bald-headed and blue-eyed, with a horse-shoe mustache.

They shook hands as Scott said, "Thanks for meeting with me."

"Not a problem. Happy to do whatever I can to help in your investigation, Agent Lynley."

Scott gave him an appreciative nod. "Great."

"Why don't we step into my office?" Reilly told him and led the way inside. "Have a seat."

Scott sat on a soft-sided chair across from a double pedestal desk, which Reilly sat at. "So, what can you tell me about the original investigation into Veronica Liu's death?" he asked the supervisory senior agent in cutting to the chase.

Reilly pondered this for a beat and answered, "Well, after your call, I took a trip down memory lane to reacquaint myself with the case. As I recall, Ms. Liu was found slumped over in her car in her own driveway. Based on her positioning, it appeared as though she was caught completely off guard by her assailant and unable to react before being gunned down. My guess is that the unsub ran off into the wooded area behind the log cabin and probably made an escape in a waiting car in the clearing."

Scott rubbed his jawline. "Any thoughts on a motive?"

"There were a few, actually. Apparently, Liu had an active social and dating life, and a frenetic professional life. So, we considered that it could have been an act of jealous rage or revenge on the one hand. And on the other, a desire to eliminate her from the equation in the highly competitive real estate market in which she worked. Then, there was still the possibility that it was an attempted robbery and the robber panicked and took off without taking anything, other than the victim's life." Reilly sat back in his leather chair, his brow creased. "Unfortunately, we weren't able to pin it down, whichever way in terms of a suspect, that we could make stick. From there, the case went cold."

Scott thought about Abby finding her aunt's body. "Is it your sense that the killer may have been lying in wait for Veronica to arrive home? Or may have even lured her there?"

"It does stand to reason that the killer may have been hiding while waiting for Liu to show up," Reilly said matter-of-factly. "She did receive a call from an unidentified person just before the estimated time of death," he noted. "Could have simply been a wrong number. Or it may have been to draw her attention, giving the killer a further advantage in catching Liu off guard. The Kolton Lake PD took the lead in the investigation. You might want to speak with them for more details on the case and where things stand."

"I'll do that," Scott told him, having already planned to make that his next stop.

"If I come up with anything else that may be useful, I'll let you know."

"Appreciate that."

After getting up and shaking hands with the supervisory senior agent, Scott showed himself out. He wondered just how difficult it would be to crack the twenty-year-old case. Or was the devil within the details waiting to be unraveled?

Chapter Four

Abby got her day started by paying a visit to Jeanne Singletary, her aunt Veronica's best friend and former business partner, whom Abby had stayed in contact with through the years. As someone who had taken her aunt's death nearly as hard as herself, Abby wanted to tell her in person about Scott reopening the investigation.

After pulling her car up into the lot of Singletary Realty, Abby went inside. She spotted Jeanne, who was now the owner, seated at a laminate corner desk in front of a curtain wall. She was talking on her cell phone. In her mid-fifties, she was of medium height and slender build. Her short ash-blond hair was in a stacked bob cut and her blue eyes were covered with horn-rimmed glasses.

Abby wondered if she should have called ahead of time, but Jeanne waved her over. By the time she got to the desk, her late aunt's colleague had ended her phone chat. "Hello there, stranger." Jeanne spoke in a bubbly tone as she stood up in her designer lilac pantsuit and pumps and gave Abby a hug.

"Hi, Jeanne," Abby said, offering her a slight smile. "Sorry for just dropping in on you."

"Don't be silly. You're always welcome." She peered at Abby. "Is everything okay?" she asked, as if sensing the opposite.

Abby met her eyes. "The FBI has reopened the investigation into Aunt Veronica's murder."

Jeanne reacted in a stunned manner. "Really?"

"Yeah. A cold case special agent, Scott Lynley, has taken the case. He seems to think he can finally solve her death."

"Hmm…" Jeanne batted her lashes. "It's been twenty years, Abby. People come and go. Evidence disappears, which was apparently already lacking in the original investigation."

"I know," Abby conceded. "But if there's any chance at all of finding out who did this—"

"I'd like some answers too," Jeanne told her and took Abby's hands. "Veronica was my best friend and we started this real estate agency together. She would have loved to see how it's evolved over time to get to where it is today. I just don't want to see you get your hopes up again, only to be disappointed if this FBI agent doesn't deliver results you can take to the bank."

Abby squeezed her hands, realizing her concerns were coming from a good place. "I'm not twelve anymore," she said frankly. "I'll get through this either way. In the meantime, I can only keep my fingers crossed that Scott— Agent Lynley can unravel the twenty-year-old mystery."

"Me too." Jeanne met her eyes warmly.

"I suspect that Agent Lynley will want to talk to you at some point," Abby warned her, all things considered.

"Not sure I can add any more to what I told the police back then, but of course I'll be happy to answer any questions the FBI agent has. Thanks for the heads-up."

Abby nodded. When Jeanne's phone rang, it was the perfect time to say their goodbyes, with Abby promising to get together for dinner sooner than later.

SHE HAD JUST gotten to her nondescript, windowless office, and was at her workstation doing follow-up on the children they'd rescued from traffickers, when Elise Martinez came in and said, "Look what was just delivered!"

Abby smiled. She knew that Elise was currently in a serious relationship with a handsome firefighter, so sending her a bouquet of red roses was not surprising. "They're beautiful," she remarked.

"I was thinking the same thing." Elise moved closer. "The roses are for you."

"Me?" Abby widened her eyes. "From who?"

"You tell me. There's no card." Elise handed the flowers to her. "Secret admirer, perhaps?"

"Not so sure about that." Abby smelled the roses while considering whom they may have come from. Scott was the first thought to enter her head. Maybe it was a show of appreciation that she had been cooperative in his cold case investigation, even if that was a given in her own way of thinking. But why would he need to keep her in suspense? She also pondered that someone she had assisted as a victim specialist might have felt it was an anonymous way to express gratitude. She set the flowers on her desk. "Guess I'll just have to wait and see. Or maybe be left forever wondering."

"Hope not." Elise chuckled. "What fun would that be?"

"Not very," Abby had to admit. But right now, there were more important things on her plate. They began to talk about their latest undertaking, for which Abby brought up the movement of the victims. "From what I've gathered, they were shuffled around from house to house in an effort to stay one step ahead of the authorities," she noted.

"Didn't do the traffickers much good," Elise said. "Once the undercover agent was able to infiltrate their ranks and let the Bureau in on what the offenders were up to, they moved in and made the arrests."

"Thank goodness for that," Abby said. "I'd hate to think what might have happened if the victims had been relocated again, perhaps to another state, as so many others have had to endure, while their predators go about their business, hidden in plain view."

"I know." Elise pushed her glasses up. "Unfortunately, it's a never-ending cycle of child sexual exploitation and human trafficking in this country and elsewhere. I should know." Her brow furrowed thoughtfully. "Anyway, all we can do is be there for those rescued and see to it that they receive the best care available and let the system work in holding the perpetrators accountable."

"You're right." Abby knew full well that Elise, a survivor of sexual exploitation, was as committed to her job, as the victim services coordinator for the entire region under the jurisdiction of the FBI's Louisville field office, as she was. When her cell phone rang, Abby grabbed it out of the pocket of her linen pants and saw that it was Scott Lynley calling. "I should probably get this," she told Elise, resisting a smile in her eagerness to speak with him.

"Okay." Elise glanced at the roses and back. "Better put those in some water when you get the chance."

"I will." Abby waited until she'd left the office—having chosen to keep the cold case investigation to herself in the workplace till there was more to go on—before answering. "Hello."

"I'm about to go talk to Detective Selena Nunez, the original investigator who worked the Veronica Liu case for the Kolton Lake PD," Scott said. "She is still with the department. If you're game and have the time, I was wondering if you'd like to be there. Maybe hearing what she has to say might trigger memories. Or at least give you some greater perspective on where things stood when the case stalled."

"Yes, I would like to be there when you speak with the detective," Abby was quick to say. She recalled being interviewed by the detective twenty years ago, but had not seen or spoken to her since.

"I was hoping you'd say that." His voice was smooth and persuasive.

She agreed to meet him at the Kolton Lake PD in two hours, which gave Abby just enough time to do some work and anticipate seeing the FBI agent again.

SCOTT HAD JUST arrived at the Kolton Lake Police Department on Scoggins Street when he spotted Abby drive up. Admittedly, he'd wanted to see her as much for himself as to give her the opportunity to ask Detective Nunez anything Abby had wanted to ask as a twelve-year-old but had been unable to articulate at the time. *I'll try to keep my attraction to the attractive victim specialist in check for now*, he told himself, suspecting that might be a tall task as some things in life simply couldn't be helped.

He got out of his SUV and met her halfway in the parking lot. "Hey."

"Hi." She tucked a tendril of hair behind her ear, which Scott suspected was a nervous habit. The last thing he wanted to do was make her uncomfortable around him.

"Shall we go in?" he asked politely.

"Yes," she said. "Hopefully Detective Nunez can shed some light on the case that might help you in the investigation."

"That's the plan." On the way inside the building, Scott mentioned briefly his conversation with Supervisory Senior Resident Agent Art Reilly, who'd been involved in the original investigation for the Bureau. "Reilly has made himself available for further communication, while directing me to the lead investigator in the case."

"Hmm… I remember Agent Reilly," Abby stated thoughtfully as they entered the PD. "He seemed to be all business."

Scott laughed. "Some things never change."

"By the way," she asked casually, "you didn't, by chance, send me some roses, did you?"

"Uh, I'm afraid not." He gave her an unintended strange look. "Someone sent you roses?" A twinge of jealousy hit Scott while wishing he had been the lucky guy, whoever it was.

"Never mind," Abby uttered hastily, coloring as she walked ahead of him.

What was that all about? Scott wondered. Perhaps she would fill him in sometime on the details.

They went up to the second floor, where Selena Nunez stood from her cubicle desk when she saw them approaching. "Agent Lynley," she surmised.

"Yes," Scott acknowledged as they neared her.

"I'm Detective Nunez," Selena said, extending a small hand to shake his.

He did so and sized up the good-looking Latina. Midforties, slender and about five-eight, she had hazel eyes and brown hair in a textured lob. "Nice to meet you, Detective." Scott glanced at Abby. "This is FBI Victim Specialist

Abby Zhang." He noted for effect, "Veronica Liu's niece."

"Abby?" Selena arched a brow. "You're all grown up now."

Abby smiled softly. "Hello, Detective Nunez," she told her. "It's been a long time."

"Yes, it has." The detective shook her hand. After an awkward pause, she proffered a vinyl guest chair for one and grabbed a second from another desk for the other.

Once they were seated, Scott wasted no time in seeing what he could gather from her. "What can you tell us about the original investigation, Detective?" he asked evenly.

"Well, for starters, as I'm sure you read in the report, we were notified that a woman appeared to have been shot dead in a vehicle outside her home. She was identified as thirty-one-year-old Veronica Liu." Selena shifted uncomfortably in her desk chair. "I was assigned the case and went through the normal procedures of securing the scene, collecting evidence, interviewing witnesses and the like." Her brow creased. "In spite of chasing leads that turned into dead ends and having DNA and partial print evidence, unfortunately we were unable to establish motive or identify the killer. The FBI was brought in to assist and they, too, drew blanks, and the case went cold." Selena eyed Abby. "I wish I had been able to catch your aunt's killer. It still bothers me that I couldn't solve the case. I'm glad that Agent Lynley is reopening it to try and give you some closure."

"So am I." Abby glanced at him and back. "I'm sure you gave it your best shot, Detective Nunez, and I, too, wish things had turned out differently." She took a sharp breath. "I wish Aunt Veronica hadn't been murdered, and I'm sorry that I wasn't more helpful when you interviewed me."

"Don't be." Selena waved this off. "You were just twelve years old. I actually thought you did a good job in telling me everything you'd seen and done, including having the wherewithal to report the crime. Based on the estimated time of death and likelihood that the killer missed seeing you by perhaps mere minutes, it's a blessing that you're here today, alive and well."

Abby nodded meekly. "I feel the same way."

So did Scott, as he hated to even think about her having been taken out of the equation by her aunt's killer, depriving him of the opportunity to meet her and maybe solve the crime together. "Tell me about the suspects," he prompted the detective, having only had a cursory look at them in the file.

"I reacquainted myself with them," Selena said, and opened the folder on her desk. "There were really four suspects who stood out from the rest as possible murderers. Evan Liu, the victim's ex-husband, was obviously someone we took a hard look at. With no clear indication it was a stranger or random homicide, one that was intimate in nature was our primary focus. In spite of a bitter divorce, Liu's alibi held up.

"Mathew Yang was a businessman and had been dating Veronica at the time of her death, but apparently failed to inform her that he was married to someone else," Selena said. "He, too, was ruled out as the killer, along with his wife, Loretta Yang. Same was true for Katlyn Johansson, a bartender and exotic dancer whom Veronica had nearly come to blows with at the Tygers Club on Third Street the night before. And Bennie Romero, a meth addict who was seen wandering around the nearby wooded area shortly before the murder occurred. Other suspects either checked out or were low on the list due to circumstances and probability of guilt."

"Were there any similar-type murders at the time?" Scott asked curiously as the notion of a serial killer crossed his mind.

"Yeah, a few," she acknowledged. "But none that we believed could be linked to this case. In most instances, in fact, we were able to solve the crime." She frowned. "Sometimes we come up short."

Scott conceded this much, owing his current job as a cold case investigator to that reality. Still, it was hard to see a case fall between the cracks, leaving unsubs free to roam and possibly kill again. Whether or not Veronica Liu's killer had other dead victims remained to be seen. "Were you ever able to come up with anything else on the murder weapon?"

"Unfortunately, no." Selena ran a hand through her hair. "The ballistic evidence was submitted to the NIBIN," she said, which was short for the Bureau of Alcohol, Tobacco, Firearms and Explosives' National Integrated Ballistic Information Network, "and we failed to get a hit. I'm guessing that the shooter got rid of the Colt Python .357 Magnum revolver used in the crime, where no one could ever find it."

"Do you still believe that someone was targeting my aunt?" Abby posed the question directly to her. "Or could Aunt Veronica's murder be about something entirely different?"

Selena took a moment to consider the question before answering. "I definitely still believe this was a targeted attack," she said straightforwardly. "For lack of a better way to put this, someone wanted your aunt dead and made it happen. Who and exactly why remains a question mark." Selena gazed at Scott. "I'm happy to make all our files and evidence available to you for your investigation into the murder."

"Appreciate that." He gave her a nod, knowing that any stone that remained unturned just might hold the key to breaking the case. "If you come up with anything else relevant to solving the crime, Detective Nunez…"

"I'll be sure to contact you, Agent Lynley," Selena assured him clearly. "In the meantime, you might want to talk with two of Veronica Liu's friends who may be able to remember something they couldn't twenty years ago. Jeanne Singletary was her business partner and is still active as a local Realtor. Another person in Veronica's then inner circle was Freda Myerson—"

Abby practically blurted out, "As in Freda Myerson, the mayor of Kolton Lake?"

"That's the one," the detective responded. "At the time, she was Freda Neville. I'm sure that Mayor Myerson will be happy to cooperate in the investigation into her friend's death."

"I'll definitely pay her a visit," Scott said, and could tell that Abby was just as eager to speak with the mayor, too, who she apparently was unaware had known her aunt.

When they left the police department, Abby confirmed this. "I don't remember Aunt Veronica knowing a Freda Neville," she admitted.

"But, then again, I didn't know all her friends. Or apparently foes."

"What about her business partner, Jeanne Singletary?" He assumed that Abby knew in more than a passing glance whom her aunt had worked with.

"Yes, I knew—know—Jeanne," she told him. "We've kept in touch over the years since Aunt Veronica died. I actually went to see Jeanne this morning, knowing she would want to know that the investigation was being reopened." Abby looked at him. "I hope that was all right?"

"Of course." Scott grinned at her in concurrence. "As your aunt's friend and partner, she deserved to be kept abreast of what's happening."

"Okay." Abby smiled back at him.

"Why don't we go see Mayor Myerson, if you have the time?"

"I'd like that," she said, leaving no doubt that they were on the same page.

SELENA NUNEZ WENT back to her desk after seeing the FBI agent and Abby Zhang out. She again leafed through the case file for the murder of Veronica Liu. Selena had only been twenty-five and a second-year homicide detective for the Kolton Lake PD when handed the disturbing case. She'd had no idea at the time that it would go unsolved for the next two decades. In that time frame, she had gotten married, had three children and solved more than her fair share of murders, while moving up the detective ranks with the Homicide Unit.

But all that said, it still haunted Selena that she had been unable to bring Veronica Liu's killer to justice. And, as such, had failed to bring peace to some degree to that little girl. Now, Abby was a grown woman and, not too surprisingly, a victim specialist. Selena imagined it was her way to pay homage to the aunt she had lost. With the FBI reopening the case, maybe it could finally be solved once and for all. Or maybe, as with her own investigation, the leads would dry up and the murder would remain unsolved and the unsub would remain unidentified.

Selena sucked in a deep breath. Her gut told her that Agent Scott Lynley just might succeed where she had failed. Or, at least, it seemed as though he was all in on helping Abby get over the hump. If so, this would certainly be welcome news to Selena as well. After all, a win would still be a win. No matter how long it took to achieve success.

Selena grabbed the cell phone off her desk and gave Mayor Myerson a courtesy call to let her know she was about to have company.

Chapter Five

Abby was still pondering the notion that her aunt Veronica had been friends with Mayor Freda Myerson. *How did I not know this?* she wondered as she accompanied Scott for the short drive to the mayor's office on Walton Road. Although she hadn't been privy to everyone in her aunt's life, Abby felt she'd at least had a handle on those her aunt had been most chummy with. Apparently not.

"Don't know if we can get anything useful out of the mayor." Scott broke into Abby's thoughts. "But it's worth a shot as I try to lay the groundwork for reinterviewing suspects who are alive and nearby, for starters."

"I couldn't agree more," she told him from the passenger seat of his vehicle, while not getting her hopes up. "If nothing else, it would be nice to speak with someone my aunt Veronica was acquainted with, for memories' sake."

"I hear you." His voice was reflective and

made Abby want to know more about his background. And, for that matter, the status of his own family life today. She was starting to sense that he wasn't married after all. Or was that wishful thinking on her part? "So, what's up with the roses?" he asked abruptly, glancing at her.

"Roses?" She pretended she was dumbfounded with the question.

"You mentioned earlier about receiving roses. Have any idea who they came from, once I was knocked out of the picture?"

"Not really." Abby cocked a brow at his bluntness. "They just showed up at my office this morning with no card." She felt silly assuming they'd been sent by him.

"Really?" Scott jutted his chin. "Maybe someone you are or were dating?"

"Haven't dated anyone in a while," she told him, "if you must know." Or was that his way of asking if she was single? "I suspect the roses may have come from someone I helped as a victim specialist, but didn't want to make a big deal out of it by identifying themselves."

"Okay." He left it at that, as though satisfied.

"So, what about you?" Abby decided that she may as well get her own curiosity over with. "Are you single, married, dating someone, what?"

"I'd say 'what' probably is the best answer." Scott gave her a crooked grin with a glint in his eye. "I'm divorced, single and unattached."

"I see." She found herself relieved in hearing this. Or was excited more appropriate? "Guess we have that much in common," she said lightly, even as she wondered how someone had managed to let him get away.

"Yep," he concurred, grinning. "Looks that way."

Neither of them spoke the rest of the way, but it certainly gave Abby food for thought as she wondered what to do with the information. If anything.

When they arrived at the office, she brushed shoulders with Scott, sending an unexpected wave of electricity through Abby. Had he felt it too? Or had she convinced herself of something that wasn't truly there, other than in her head?

They were shown into the mayor's spacious office and she was standing there to greet them. "Freda Myerson," she said coolly by way of introduction.

"Special Agent Scott Lynley."

"Abby Zhang." She studied the attractive woman who'd known her aunt Veronica. In her early fifties, Freda was several inches taller and not quite as slender as Abby, but seemed just as fit, wearing a designer navy skirt suit and low heels. Her curly dark hair was medium length and parted squarely in the middle. Abby tried to picture the twenty-years-younger version, but drew a blank for recognition.

Scott stuck out his hand. "Thanks for seeing us on short notice, Mayor."

"Not a problem," she contended. "Detective Nunez told me you were on your way and what this was all about. I have a few minutes before a meeting I have to attend." Freda turned big blue-green eyes onto Abby. "I can see the resemblance between you and Veronica," she expressed, taking her hands. "I'm sorry I never got the chance to formally meet you twenty years ago, Abby."

"Me too." She met Freda's steady gaze, and in so doing, Abby could almost envision her as someone in attendance at her aunt Veronica's funeral. Had she not been so overwrought with emotion at the time, Abby might have remembered her.

Freda released her hands, smiled warmly and said, "Why don't we sit down?" She eyed a small area by a window that included three fabric lounge chairs surrounding an oval conference table.

Once they were seated, Scott said equably to her, "I understand that you and Veronica Liu were close."

"I wouldn't exactly say that we were close," Freda corrected him in a level tone. "Veronica sold me my first home, and we went out a couple of times for drinks, and maybe met once or twice in relation to the purchase. But that was about it."

He sat back pensively. "Detective Nunez seemed to believe that you were part of Veronica's inner circle," he said. "You're saying this wasn't true?"

Freda took a calming breath. "Not sure how the detective drew that conclusion," she argued. "Yes, I was friendly with both Veronica and Jeanne Singletary, her real estate partner, after establishing a good working relationship with them as a home buyer. I wasn't part of Veronica's inner circle, though, or vice versa. When I heard about what happened to her, of course I was broken up by it, like everyone else who knew her. Especially since I was aware that she was leaving behind a little girl." She eyed Abby sorrowfully. "I gave a statement to the police to that effect, outlining the nature of my association with Veronica. Never had any follow-up after that." She paused. "I did attend the funeral to pay my respects to Veronica," she uttered, thoughtful. "It never occurred to me at the time that her murder would go unsolved all these years."

Abby choked up at the heartfelt words, considering she was of the same mind. Even if the mayor hadn't been very close to her aunt Veronica, the fact that they'd known each other at all was a connection of sorts between the past and present. "Mayor Myerson, in the time you spent with my aunt, did she ever mention anything about someone who may have wanted to harm her?" Abby asked keenly.

Freda looked her in the eye and replied without preface. "Veronica never told me someone was after her, if in fact this was personal, as opposed to an attempted robbery or random attack. In our conversations, your aunt seemed very likable and not one to get on someone's bad side. Obviously, that did happen, for whatever reason, and I'm happy to see that the case has been reopened. Veronica left us—and you, Abby—way too soon. You both deserve some resolution to this." Freda looked at Scott. "As mayor of Kolton Lake, if there's anything you need to help facilitate cooperation with the police department, please let me know."

"I will," he promised.

"Good." Freda stood, indicating the chat was over. "Well, I have a meeting to go to. I'll walk you out." At the front door, she shook both their hands and said, "I'm sure your aunt would have been proud, Abby, to see that you've grown up to become a lovely young woman."

Abby blushed. "Thank you."

"I agree," Scott pitched in. "Abby also happens to work for the Bureau as a victim specialist."

"Really?" Freda bobbed her head. "All the more impressive."

"It's a good fit for me," Abby said as though she needed to explain her choice of profession to someone who had succeeded in her own right as the mayor of Kolton Lake.

"I'm sure it is."

Freda's sympathetic expression seemed to acknowledge the fragile line between being a victim and survivor, which Abby now considered herself. Albeit now one on a new mission. Or at least with a new ray of hope. That was to finally get to the bottom of Aunt Veronica's murder, with the help of Scott Lynley.

SCOTT WAS GLAD to see that he had the cooperation of Mayor Freda Myerson, should she be needed to run interference with the Kolton Lake PD. He doubted it would come to that, as Selena Nunez seemed more than supportive in assisting in any way she could on the cold case she'd originally investigated. That included the detective turning over forensic evidence taken from the crime scene, which he planned to have retested at the FBI Laboratory in Quantico, Virginia, for a possible match with a known offender. It would be up to him to continue to do some digging and see what he could unearth in the investigation.

Though he enjoyed spending official time with Abby, Scott reluctantly drove her back to her vehicle in the police department's parking lot. Clearly, she was enthusiastic about playing a role in cracking the mystery of Veronica Liu's death. But she had her own work with the Bureau and he needed to respect that without overstepping for his cold case. On the other hand, there was no reason why they couldn't continue to see each other on a more personal level, if she were willing.

He turned to Abby, who seemed to be lost in thought, perhaps feeling a bit let down that Freda Myerson was not as close to Veronica as advertised. Consequently, she'd been unable to fill in any of the blanks that Abby may have been seeking in learning more about her aunt from the mayor. "Would you like to grab a bite to eat this evening, once we're both off the clock?" Scott asked her tentatively, hoping she was game.

Abby looked up at him and smiled. "Yes, that would be nice."

"Great." He grinned back, thoughtful in remembering the veggie burger she'd ordered for lunch at the restaurant. "So, are you a vegetarian?" he asked curiously, if only for the record.

"No," she surprised him by saying. "If you're referring to the veggie burger, I think it's healthier and tastier than regular burgers, but otherwise, I wouldn't say I dine on a vegetarian diet."

"Just checking." Scott looked at the steering wheel. "Would have been fine either way."

"Nice to know." After a beat, Abby suggested, "We could have dinner at my place. As it's the same cabin my aunt Veronica lived in twenty years ago, it would give you an opportunity to check out the surroundings for some perspective in the investigation into her death."

That made sense to Scott on multiple levels, not the least of which being that they would get to dine in a cozier setting than a restaurant. Then there was the fact that he hadn't realized Abby was living in the same location as the scene of the crime. He imagined that was both a difficult and a practical way to move on as a grown woman herself now. Last, perhaps the setting could provide some clues as to the crime and getaway, even after all these years.

"You're on," he told her. "But I'll bring the wine. Or whatever your pleasure."

"Wine sounds good," she said. "Red or white?"

"White wine, it is." Scott stopped in front of

her car and they set a time for six o'clock, giving him some leeway for more interviews. "See you later," he said as Abby unbuckled her seat belt and opened the SUV door.

"All right." She got out. "'Bye, Scott."

"'Bye." He waited until Abby was inside her vehicle before driving off, already counting the hours till they met again.

ABBY ADMITTEDLY FELT giddy at the prospect of making dinner for Scott, while trying to decide on the meal. They said that the key to a man's heart was his stomach. She wasn't necessarily seeking his heart at this point. After all, it could have been closed off to newcomers—or at least held back—following the collapse of his marriage. But she did relish the opportunity to get to know the FBI agent on a more personal basis. And vice versa. She started the car, backed out of the slot, and drove out of the parking lot and onto the street, just in time to see Scott's SUV turn right on a main street. Abby imagined he would be poring over any evidence available. As well as speaking with anyone who had been interviewed originally, including Jeanne Singletary, while trying to connect the dots as cold case investigators needed to do if they were to succeed in their mission.

Abby's thoughts turned to Freda Myerson.

In spite of wishing the mayor had given them more to go on as a confidante of her aunt Veronica's, that hadn't been the case. This meant the lingering questions would continue to linger longer as the investigation unfolded. And Abby had to be prepared to face the reality that she might never get a complete picture of her aunt. Or the circumstances that had led to her murder.

While barely realizing how she had gotten there, Abby found herself at Kolton Lake Cemetery. It was where her aunt Veronica was buried. The reopening of the investigation had given new life to the possibility that her death could finally be solved. Leaving her car, Abby felt compelled to visit the gravesite of the woman who'd been like a mother to her for six years of Abby's preteen life.

Walking across grass wet from sprinklers, she made her way to the spot where Veronica Liu had been laid to rest. Abby touched the granite headstone, as if touching the spirit of her aunt. "Miss you, Aunt Veronica," she said out loud. "Wish you could see and talk to me now."

Abby said a silent prayer and extended this to her parents as well. Just as she was about to leave, Abby heard the squishing of footsteps behind her. She turned around and saw a tall man standing there.

"Did you get the roses?" he asked succinctly.

It took Abby a moment as she studied the man who was in his early forties and long-limbed, with light brown hair in a spiky cut. He was staring back at her with dark, foreboding eyes. Abby recognized him as Zach Gilliard, a survivor of a mass shooting at a shopping center in Grayson County last month, before the gunman killed himself. Zach had suffered only minor injuries but had been traumatized nevertheless by the incident the FBI had investigated as part of a joint task force. Within her duties, Abby had provided crisis intervention for Zach and other victims of the crime.

"You sent them?" Abby asked him with uneasiness.

"Yeah," Zach acknowledged. "Hope you liked them."

She stiffened. It wasn't uncommon for victims, or near victims, of traumatic incidents to become fixated somewhat on victim specialists. Still, seeing Zach at the cemetery, of all places, was a little creepy. Had he followed her there?

"They were nice," she placated him. "But you really shouldn't have."

"I wanted to give them to you," he insisted. "It was the least I could do when you were there for me after I saw my life flash before my eyes."

Abby looked at him with alarm. "What are

you doing here?" She hadn't necessarily seen him as a dangerous person. Or a stalker. Could she have misjudged the man?

Zach raised his hands as if in mock surrender. "Don't be afraid," he said. "I'm not going to hurt you. I was at the police department to donate some items and saw you there. Before I could speak with you, you'd gotten in your car and driven off. I thought you might be headed back to your office, where I was going to make sure you received the roses as my way of thanking you for helping me out. I didn't leave a note because I didn't want you to get the wrong impression. Anyway, when I saw you go into the cemetery, I figured it was as good a place as any to say what I needed to. Sorry if I scared you."

"It's fine," Abby told him, remaining wary. "Again, thanks for the roses, but I was just doing my job." Didn't he get that?

"I know and I appreciate it." He glanced at the headstone. "A relative?"

"Yes." She left it at that, having no wish to elaborate on something that was none of his business.

Seeming to pick up on that and her uncomfortableness, Zach said, "Well, I'll let you get back to paying your respects. See ya."

I don't think so, Abby thought, not seeing any reason why she would need to follow up with him as a victim specialist. "Goodbye, Zach," she told him simply.

She watched him walk away till out of sight and then turned back to her aunt Veronica's grave, where she spoke a few more words of sympathy, remembrance and regrets, before leaving.

Still a bit rattled from the unexpected presence of Zach Gilliard, Abby hurried to her car and locked the door once safely inside. She saw no sign of the unemployed warehouse worker, breathing a sigh of relief.

After starting the car, Abby drove from the cemetery. She checked the rearview mirror to see if she was being followed. There was no indication of such. She remained tense, nevertheless, until getting back to the safety of the FBI's Owensboro resident agency.

Chapter Six

Scott parked in the lot of Singletary Realty for a visit with Veronica Liu's business partner, Jeanne Singletary. The fact that she had kept in touch with Abby through the years was a good thing. Even better would be her ability to provide clues as to who might have killed Veronica.

He walked inside the real estate office and saw a slender twentysomething male with brunette hair in a topknot fade on the phone at one desk. Angling his eyes, Scott faced the owner, recognizing her from the picture on the front window of the office. She was seated at her desk and, when spotting him, stood and approached with a smile on her face.

"May I help you?"

"Special Agent Lynley." Scott flashed his identification. "Jeanne Singletary?" he asked rhetorically.

"That would be me." She stuck out her hand

and shook his. "Agent Lynley. You want to talk to me about Veronica," she said knowingly. "Abby told me you would come by."

"I'm aware that she visited you," Scott said. "I'd like to go over a few things in your original statement to the police and see if you might have missed anything pertinent in the investigation."

"Of course." Jeanne pushed her glasses up. "I'm happy to cooperate in any way I can. Why don't we go over to my desk?"

Scott followed her to a corner of the office that was all her own. She sat back at her desk and he took a seat across from her in a swivel guest chair. Before he could question her, Jeanne said, "Honestly, I was surprised to learn that the FBI was taking another look at the case. How did this come about, if I may ask?"

"You may," he told her. "We typically try to keep even the coldest cases in our viewfinder, hoping the day will come when we can still crack the case. I took an interest in this one, given that the death of Veronica Liu totally upended the life of her twelve-year-old niece. I felt that even twenty years later, Abby deserved some answers."

"I agree. She should learn why someone killed her aunt. If that's possible so many years later." Jeanne lifted a brow musingly. "Has new evidence surfaced?"

"I'm not at liberty to say." Scott went with the standard line when questioning parties pertinent to a criminal investigation. Not to say that he considered Jeanne Singletary a suspect, per se. She had been cleared by the original investigators, but the fact remained that she'd stood to gain the most financially by Veronica's death. And it appeared as though she was still riding that wave as the owner of the real estate agency. "Why don't you tell me what you remember about that time in Ms. Liu's life?"

"All right." Jeanne squared her shoulders. "Veronica was a hard worker and was just as hard in her play. She loved the rewards of success as measured against the risks of failure. We didn't always see eye to eye on every aspect of running a business. Much less our romantic ups and downs, but we always had each other's backs. I was very sorry to lose my dear friend."

Sounded sincere enough to Scott, but good actors could be convincing, were that the case. "You told the police that you didn't know of anyone who would have wanted Veronica dead. Do you still stand by that?"

"Yes," Jeanne uttered. "I mean, professionally speaking, we worked in the cutthroat business of real estate so, theoretically, someone could have wanted one less competitor. But if that was the case, I should have been killed too." She took a breath. "Yet here I am, alive and well."

"You make a good point," he allowed, if not one that hadn't already been accepted for years by investigators. This didn't mean it was rock-solid, though, with a fresh set of eyes. "What can you tell me about Ms. Liu's romantic life?"

"Veronica was ever the optimist when it came to romance," she indicated. "Problem was she never seemed to get it right when it came to picking men. But not for lack of trying. First there was her ex, Evan Liu, who barely gave Veronica room to breathe. She finally kicked him to the curb, but didn't have much better luck with the other men who came along. That included her last boyfriend, Mathew Yang. She thought he might be the one. Except for the fact that he was married to someone else."

"Did Veronica know about the wife?" Scott stared across the desk while wondering if Yang's wife had known about his having an affair and with whom.

"Not to my knowledge." Jeanne leaned to one side in her faux leather ergonomic chair. "I think that Veronica was even planning to spend a week with him in Hawaii, and maybe take Abby with them."

But that never came to pass, Scott told himself. Someone saw to that. He moved on. "Was there anyone you can recall that Ms. Liu had a problem with for whatever reason?"

Jeanne pondered this and responded, "As I told the police back then, one of our agents, Oliver Dillman, did hit on Veronica. She made it pretty clear that she wasn't interested."

"And how did he take it?"

"At first, he didn't seem to want to take no for an answer," she claimed. "But, eventually, he got the message." Jeanne frowned. "Unfortunately, after Veronica's death, Oliver tried to put the moves on another female agent. Enough was enough. I fired him."

Scott vaguely remembered seeing Dillman's name in the cold case file as a suspect who hadn't made the main suspects category. Maybe he merited a second look. "Do you know where Oliver is today?"

"As a matter of fact, I do." Her voice dropped an octave. "He's now an agent at Murlock Realty Group, a competing real estate office in Kolton Lake."

Scott made a note. "That should do it for now." He stood. "I won't take up any more of your time."

Veronica remained seated. "I hope for Abby's sake that you find what—or who—you're looking for, Agent Lynley."

"Thanks." He gave her a crooked smile. As another passing thought entered his head, Scott asked curiously, "I understand that you and Veronica were friends with Mayor Freda Myerson?"

Jeanne nodded musingly. "Yes, we knew Freda long before she became mayor, after selling her a nice town house. We weren't close or anything, but I do remember that she gave a fun house-warming party. After Veronica died, we lost touch."

"At least you can say you knew the mayor way back when," he said in a lighthearted manner.

"True." She gazed up at him. "I prefer not to live in the past though. Except, of course, for the fond memories I'll always have of Veronica."

He accepted that at face value. "I'm sure Abby feels the same."

ABBY HAD TOSSED back and forth whether to go with Char siu, which was a Chinese-style roasted pork, or baked chicken and mushrooms, as the main home-cooked dish. She decided on the former, having learned it from her aunt Veronica, along with peas, honey-glazed carrots and cornbread muffins. A homemade apple pie, her favorite dessert, would complete the meal. She hoped it would meet with Scott's approval, after being used to cooking only for herself in recent memory. At least it would give them an opportunity to see if the sparks she felt were there between them were real or not. She certainly wasn't getting her hopes up too much, having been there and done that with less than ideal results. Would this be any different? Or should it be, since their primary focus was on solving her aunt's murder? So why couldn't both be a possibility?

Abby calmed her nerves as she tended to the food and, when ready, left the kitchen to change clothes and wash her face. She wore little makeup and saw no reason to change that. Her hair was let loose and she brushed it across her shoulders. When she heard a car drive up, Abby peeked out the window and saw that it was Scott. She felt a tingle at the thought of kissing him, but allowed it to subside as she went outside to greet him.

Abby smiled as she watched him get out of the car. "Hey."

"Hey." Scott grinned and held out the bottle of white wine. "For you."

She took it from him. "Thanks."

He glanced about and commented soberly, "So, this is where it happened?"

"Yes." She had a feeling that he had looked at crime scene photos to correspond with the precise location. "Aunt Veronica was murdered precisely where you're standing."

He stepped away, as if it was hallowed ground. "Sorry."

"It's okay. That was twenty years ago," she reminded him. "So it's not nearly as unsettling to step or drive on the spot today." Never mind that the memories couldn't help but resurface by the very nature of his investigation.

"I suppose it wouldn't be." Scott gazed at the wooded area that Abby knew had filled out even more over the years. "The unsub had to have been familiar with this location and the best way to commit the crime and escape without merely getting into a car that could be seen and described by witnesses, along with the driver. Or anyone else inside the vehicle."

"I agree," Abby said, wondering if there could have been more than one person involved in the crime. And if her aunt had actually been targeted for reasons still unknown.

"Why don't you show me around inside?" Scott told her. "Then we can eat, whenever you're ready."

"Okay." She led him into the log cabin, wanting Scott to have a feel for the place that might somehow play on his mindset in trying to reconstruct the cold-blooded murder of her aunt Veronica and how the cold case might start to warm up.

SCOTT HADN'T NEEDED long to size up the landscape surrounding Abby's property. There was the lake on one side and the wooded area on another. He didn't imagine Veronica Liu's killer making his or her escape by boat, though not impossible. No, the greater likelihood was that the trees formed the perfect cover for a getaway. Whereas the street was the worst means for leaving the scene of a murder. Given the case had aged by two decades, with no killer in custody, that would seem to rule the possibility out.

While taking in the scent of food in the air and before touring the place, Scott turned his attention to the woman of the house. Abby was wearing a white V-necked top, gold Bermuda shorts, showing off shapely legs, and flats. He wondered if she knew how sexy she looked, enhanced by wearing her long hair down.

"Nice place," he told her at a glance, though knowing it came at a high price, after what she had lost.

"Thanks." Abby gave him a thoughtful look. "My aunt Veronica left it to me. It took me a long time to lay claim to it, but I decided she wouldn't have wanted me to sell simply as a means to block out what happened. For one, I couldn't even if I tried. Then there's the fact that I happen to love this location by the lake and wouldn't want to give it up for the wrong reason."

"I understand." Scott wondered if the right reason to sell would be if something—or someone—better came along that might make her rethink her position.

"I'll give you the grand tour before we eat," she told him.

"All right."

Scott followed her as Abby walked him around downstairs and then upstairs. He couldn't help but be impressed with the original architecture of the cabin, as well as the remodeling. At the same time, he found himself imagining Veronica Liu living there with the young Abby before everything had changed irrevocably for both of them. Someone out there needed to be held accountable for that.

Peeking inside the primary bedroom, Scott couldn't help but home in on the hickory log bed and pictured himself on it with Abby, cuddling and the rest. That flicker of desire inflated as she inadvertently touched him while moving on down the hall before lessening as they headed back downstairs.

He helped bring the food and drinks to the rustic reclaimed-wood dining table, then they sat across from one another in pine log chairs and began to eat.

"It's delicious," Scott said of the Char siu, which Abby had revealed had been passed on to her from her aunt.

Abby smiled. "Glad you like it."

I like you even more, he mused, imagining that this was something he could get used to. "I'm always up for new dishes," Scott said. "And old ones too."

"Good." She scooped up some peas, put them in her mouth and, after eating, said, "So, I had a rather odd encounter after we parted at the police station."

"Oh...?" He met her eyes. "Tell me about it."

"I went to visit Aunt Veronica's gravesite and a man showed up there without warning." She paused. "His name is Zach Gilliard. He survived the mass shooting last month in Grayson County."

"Yeah, it was a terrible incident," Scott acknowledged, frowning.

"Anyway, though Zach wasn't seriously hurt, he was understandably pretty shaken up by what happened. As a victim specialist, I was there to offer him and others support. Nothing more. Then, yesterday, I received those roses anonymously."

"They were from him?" Scott asked, wide-eyed while forking honey-glazed carrots.

"Yes." Abby tasted her wine. "He followed me to the cemetery from the police department, where Zach claimed he was only there to donate some items, and just wanted to acknowledge sending the flowers and thank me again for assisting him."

"You think he was stalking you?"

"I don't know," she admitted. "Maybe it was a harmless one-off. In my line of work, you do get some victims or near victims developing a fixation that is usually short-lived. Hopefully, that's the case here. If it was even that."

"It's easy enough to check out his story about donating goods to the Kolton Lake PD," Scott pointed out, and tasted the wine.

"I suppose."

"Of course, even if true, it could still have been a pretext for stalking." He had come across dangerous stalkers as an FBI agent and Scott knew they could never be taken lightly. Including those whose behavior could escalate from little more than a nuisance to deadly. "I'll give the police department a call," he told her. "And also do a criminal background check on Zach Gilliard, to be on the safe side."

Abby nodded. "Thank you."

"No problem." On the contrary, Scott didn't want to see any harm come to her from a stalker or anyone else. "If Gilliard threatens you in any way, let me know."

"I will." They ate in silence before she asked him, after biting into a cornbread muffin, "So, I take it you live in Louisville?"

"That's correct." He grinned. "I have a ten-acre ranch with a few horses."

"Seriously?" Her eyes widened with fascination. "How cool."

Scott laughed. "Well, this is the Bluegrass State." That, in his mind, went hand in hand with cowboys, pastures, horses and the like.

"True." She chuckled and sipped more wine. "Guess I pictured you as... I don't know, more of a house-in-a-residential-neighborhood-type city dweller."

"That's not too far off the mark." He gave another laugh. "I'm pretty close to all the city action. But I'm also a country boy, having grown up on a sprawling ranch in Oklahoma."

"Interesting." Abby regarded him for a long moment. "Where did you meet your ex-wife?"

The question took Scott by surprise, but he quickly recovered. "In Kentucky... Lexington," he answered, wondering where this was going.

She sat back. "What happened to cause the marriage to end, if you don't mind my asking?"

Even more direct. But he didn't fault her for it. Scott saw this as part of the process of getting to know someone, in spite of the regrets he had in seeing his marriage blow up. "I don't mind," he said sincerely, touching the wineglass but not drinking from it. "We were relatively young when we married and, unfortunately, seemed to lose our way as time progressed. Neither of us really knew how to get back there and decided it was best to call it quits."

Abby met his eyes steadily. "Ever wish you could have a redo? I mean, hindsight is twenty-twenty, as they say. A second chance to iron out the wrinkles maybe?"

Though amused with the clever probing as if to see if he could somehow end up back with his ex instead of a clear willingness to take a chance on someone else, Scott held her gaze and replied in earnest, "No. We had a good marriage for a time, but I have no desire to replay the stress and strain we put on ourselves. Nor will I allow past faults to frighten me from putting myself out there again. Especially when I now have a clean slate and can try to get it right with someone else."

"Hmm…" Her voice had a catch to it as she

finished off her wine. "Hope you like home-made apple pie?"

"I love apple pie," he told her, grinning.

"Me too."

Moments later in the kitchen, they were eating slices of pie, which Scott found just as scrumptious as the main course. In fact, admittedly, there wasn't anything he didn't like about Abby Zhang, with cooking right up there among her qualities. Along with the courage to get past a terrible crime that had forever altered her life. To say nothing about her looks and coolheadedness. So how had she managed to remain single?

He sliced into another piece of pie and asked interestedly, "When was your last relationship?" Had someone turned her off from dating? Or was she just very picky?

"A few months ago." Abby set her plate on the breakfast bar. "A banking executive, his name's Steven Leclerc, and he was way too full of himself for me."

"That's not a good thing in making a relationship work," Scott had to admit, putting his own plate down.

"Right? On top of that, he just wasn't what I was looking for in terms of having the right stuff for true boyfriend material."

"What might that stuff be?" Scott gave her a curious eye.

"Oh, nothing unreachable," she clarified. "Integrity, open-mindedness, no commitment phobias, and a willingness to meet me halfway and see where it can go."

"Sounds more than reasonable to me," he told her intently.

Abby gazed at him. "You think?"

"Yeah. You deserve at least that much from a partner." *So do I,* Scott thought.

"We all do," she stressed.

He looked at Abby's beautiful face and reached out to a corner of her mouth. "There's a little crumb there." He gladly removed it and flicked it onto her plate.

She blushed. "Thanks."

Scott felt this was the perfect moment to do what he had been wanting to do for some time. Were they on the same page? He lifted her chin up, tilted his own face and, while staring into Abby's eyes, slowly leaned forward till he was certain she had no objections, and gently kissed her lips. They were as soft as he could have imagined.

Better yet was when Abby deepened the kiss and Scott happily went with it, feeling her heartbeat. Or was it his own?

After a few minutes of kissing, Scott forced himself to pull back. "I should probably go," he told her reluctantly.

Abby touched her swollen mouth. "Okay."

Though he relished the thought of making love to her, Scott had decided it best to take things slow, so as not to blow what had the potential of becoming something special.

After she walked him out, he told her, "I'll let you know what I learn about Gilliard."

She nodded. "Okay."

"Thanks again for the dinner and dessert. They were great." He smiled. "Hopefully, you'll let me return the favor sometime."

Abby smiled back. "Whenever you like."

Scott took that to heart and immediately began to make tentative plans to play host to her for a meal as he climbed into his Ford Explorer and drove off.

Chapter Seven

On Friday morning, Scott was up bright and early to exercise his horse while still on a high from kissing Abby last evening. He saw that as a positive sign for what could become a regular thing for them and so much more. Having failed at this once before did not mean he couldn't correct his mistakes in the future, with the help of the right woman in his life. Maybe that would be Abby.

After half an hour of riding, Scott drove to work. Inside the field office, he gave his boss, Diane Huggett, a brief update on the cold case investigation, got limited feedback and headed to his office. Sitting at his desk, he got on the laptop and ran a criminal background check on Zach Gilliard. Aside from a couple of parking tickets and a minor drug offense from fifteen years ago, he was clean. At least officially. Though there was no record of stalking or harassment, it didn't mean there was no history there. Or, more specifically, that he hadn't chosen Abby to become his first stalking victim.

Scott grabbed his cell phone from the pocket of his pants and called Detective Selena Nunez. She answered after one ring and said, "Agent Lynley."

"Detective. I need a favor."

"Sure. How can I help you?"

"I need to know if a Zach Gilliard was at the police department yesterday afternoon, donating some items," Scott told her.

"Let me check the log on that," she responded. "Okay."

A minute later, Selena came back on the line. "Yeah, Gilliard did donate some used clothing and books in the afternoon for us to distribute to those in need," she confirmed. "Why do you ask?"

"I was looking into a possible stalking incident," Scott explained, leaving it at that.

"So, how are you doing on the cold case?"

"Still a work in progress," he admitted. "Following leads as they come."

"Well, keep at it," Selena urged. "No one would like to see this case solved more than myself. Short of Abby Zhang."

I'm just as keen on that, Scott thought. "Will do."

After disconnecting, he opened the Veronica

Liu file and found the info on Oliver Dillman. Not too much. Dillman, thirty-seven at the time and divorced, once questioned, had produced an alibi and had no longer been considered a suspect worth focusing on. Was that a mistake?

Scott took a deeper look at the primary suspects in the Liu homicide: Evan Liu, the ex-husband; Mathew Yang, the boyfriend; Katlyn Johansson, the possibly vindictive exotic dancer; and Bennie Romero, a wanderer with a meth-amphetamine addiction. Could one of those four have been responsible for Veronica's death?

Let's see if any or all are still alive today, Scott told himself, as a starting point. He went on the computer and accessed official and public databases. Going with Bennie Romero first, Scott learned that he had died of a drug overdose a decade ago. Still didn't mean he wasn't Veronica's killer, but he had found a way to escape justice.

Pulling up information on the other three suspects, as near as Scott could determine, all were alive and well and still living within the greater Bluegrass region of Kentucky. Good. Reinterrogating them, along with Oliver Dillman, could yield results. Or not.

His train of thought was interrupted by a video chat request on his computer from his sister Madison. Now Madison Lynley-Sneed, she was a law enforcement ranger in the Pisgah Ranger District, located in the Pisgah National Forest in North Carolina. She had recently wed National Park Service Investigative Services Branch Special Agent Garrett Sneed.

Scott accepted the chat and watched as Madison, two years his junior, appeared on the screen. "Hi."

"Hi, big brother." Bold aquamarine eyes beamed at him on an attractive face surrounded by long blond hair in a shaggy wolf cut with curly bangs. "Got a minute?"

He grinned. "I'm sure I can spare a couple," he joked. "What's up?"

"I need some advice," she told him with a catch to her voice.

"Okay." Scott braced himself for whatever was to come, while always happy to know that his younger siblings wanted his guidance.

Madison waited a beat then said, "I've been asked to conduct a seminar for the National Park Service Law Enforcement Training Center at Southwestern Community College."

"Sounds good," he said, sensing more to the story.

"Thing is, it conflicts with my working with kids on how to become a Blue Ridge Parkway junior ranger," she complained, her duties mostly within the Blue Ridge Mountains. "Sort of had my mind set on that. With Garrett away on assignment, well...what do you think?"

"I think you should go with your instincts on what works best for you at this time." Scott realized that was probably taking the easy way out, but he stood by it. "There will be other seminars, I'm sure. But it's always nice to encourage children to follow in your footsteps."

"Okay." She took a breath. "Thanks, as always, for being straight with me and a listening ear to your sister."

He grinned. "Happy to help, Madison."

She giggled. "So, what are you up to? Oh, wait," she uttered. "Russell mentioned a little about your latest cold case investigation. And a little girl left behind." Madison paused. "How's it going?"

"That little girl's not so little anymore," he couldn't help but point out, thinking about the kiss they'd shared. "But she's managed to move on with her life."

Madison nodded. "That's a good thing."

"Yeah." Scott leaned forward. "Regarding the case, as you might expect when we're talking about decades-old cases, the devil is in the details, which I'm still trying to piece together," he told her. He thought about the one sure bright spot in the investigation, getting to meet Abby, a definite breath of fresh air as far as he was concerned. "I'm getting there. Or trying to."

She smiled. "Well, I for one have the utmost confidence in you, Scott. We all know that when any of the Lynleys set his or her mind to something, there's no stopping us."

He laughed. "Spoken like a true Lynley." That, their parents would have approved of wholeheartedly.

They ended the conversation with plans to talk again soon.

Scott headed out for his first interview of the day. During the drive, he called Abby and put her on speakerphone. "Hey."

"Hi," she said cheerfully.

"I wanted to let you know that Zach Gilliard's story checked out," Scott told her. "He logged in to drop off items at the police station around the time he claimed to. No record of any serious offenses either."

"That's good to know." She sighed. "Guess it means Zach wasn't stalking me."

"Looks that way." Scott wasn't entirely convinced that the man's behavior in sending flowers anonymously and following her to the cemetery was on the up-and-up. But he wouldn't make a big deal out of it, frightening Abby unnecessarily. "Keep an eye out nevertheless for any indication to the contrary."

"I will," she promised.

"I'm on my way to speak with suspects in the original investigation into your aunt's murder," he told her.

"You really think one of them could have killed her and outfoxed the investigators at the time?" Abby questioned.

"Wouldn't be the first time a suspect had managed to delay justice for years." Scott switched lanes. "Whatever the case, I'll see what they have to say for themselves today and go from there."

"Good luck."

"I won't stop searching for answers, Abby. I hope you know that," he felt the need to say.

"I do, Scott," she assured him, "and thank you."

He paused. "It was a nice kiss."

"I agree." She took a long moment. "We should try it again sometime."

"I'd like that." He gazed out the windshield thoughtfully. "I'll see you later."

"All right."

After he ended the chat, Scott couldn't help but crack a grin as he envisioned what it would be like to make love to Abby. The fact that she seemed into him, too, made it all the more exciting. The most important thing to him was that he not allow past mistakes to define the future and its endless possibilities. Were they on the same trajectory?

THE KISS THAT was short and oh, so sweet had admittedly still been on Abby's mind even before Scott had brought it up as she disconnected her cell phone after chatting with him. She was sitting at her desk, wondering if this truly could be the start of something great. Or would it end up being another big disappointment when it came to romance in her life? She wasn't hedging her bets either way as yet, vowing to keep an open mind on Scott. Just as she was on his ability to solve a case that had grown ice-cold over two decades, where others before him had failed.

Her reverie came to a halt when Abby's boss, Darren Jordache, the supervisory senior resident agent in charge of the FBI's Owensboro satellite office, walked in. African American and in his late thirties, he was tall and good-looking, with short black hair in a line-up cut, a pencil mustache and brown eyes.

"Hi, Darren."

"Hi." He gave her a grim-faced look. "There's been a school bus incident on Highway 54."

"Oh, no," she uttered, fearing the worst. "What happened?"

"An armed murder suspect, Roy Lamb, hopped on the bus, filled with children, and killed the driver, a fifty-nine-year-old grandmother named Marissa Heigl. The Bureau's Hostage Rescue Team ended up killing Lamb after he threatened to start shooting students." Jordache grimaced. "Unfortunately, the bus crashed, flipping once. Dozens of students have been hospitalized," he told her. "Fortunately, none have life-threatening injuries."

"Thank goodness for that." Abby breathed a sigh of relief, though saddened about the bus driver's death. "What hospital?"

"You mean hospitals." Jordache mentioned the three local hospitals they'd been sent to. "Elise is already coordinating services for victims at two hospitals. I need you to head over to Kolton Lake General and see what they need in moving forward."

She got to her feet and told him, "I'm on my way."

He nodded. "This could've been a lot worse."

"I know," she said, having seen as much first-hand in her work.

Two hours later, Abby had provided resources to students, all of whom had been released from the hospital, and their parents, while reassuring them that the Bureau's victim services would continue to be available for as long as needed.

But when she was about to leave, Abby could have sworn that she saw Zach Gilliard at the end of the corridor. Had she imagined it? Had he followed her to the hospital? Probably against her better judgment, she moved toward him. Seemingly at the same time, the man began to head away from her, as if in a hurry to evade detection. By the time she reached the area, he was gone.

Had it really been Zach? Was he stalking her, in spite of Scott suggesting that he wasn't a threat?

Or have I allowed myself to get worked up over nothing? She decided that was probably the case. Even if Zach were there, he could have been visiting someone. And may not have even been aware of her presence.

She sucked in a deep breath and headed in the opposite direction. Impulsively, though, she looked over her shoulder. As if expecting Zach—or the man in question—to have resurfaced. But there was no one there.

SCOTT PULLED UP to the Dutch Colonial house on Wrightmoore Drive, where he'd learned that Oliver Dillman was doing a showing. Parked in the driveway was a silver Lexus UX 200 and a blue Acura Integra.

After a young couple left the two-story residence, and got into the Integra and drove off, with or without the sale being made, Scott left his SUV and went inside the house. He found the man he was looking for shutting things down in the roomy, staged home in the formal living room that had plenty of windows and a large, welcoming fireplace.

Recognizing Dillman from his website photograph, Scott studied him briefly. He was in his late fifties, over six feet tall, and sturdy enough in business casual attire and leather loafers. His salt-and-pepper short hair was wavy with a side part. Scott cleared his throat to gain the man's attention.

"Sorry, didn't hear you come in." Dillman, who had just closed the living room drapes, favored him with blue eyes. "You here for a showing?"

"Not exactly." Though Scott imagined it was a place he could live in were he in the market. "Oliver Dillman?" he asked knowingly, approaching across the oak hardwood flooring.

"Yeah, I'm Oliver Dillman." He met him halfway. "Who are you?"

Scott removed his identification, flashing it as he said, "FBI Special Agent Lynley."

Dillman cocked a thick brow. "What does an FBI agent want to see me about?"

"I've reopened the investigation into the murder of Veronica Liu," Scott told him levelly.

"Veronica Liu?" Dillman reacted to the name. "Haven't heard that name in years," he claimed. His brow furrowed. "Again, what does this have to do with me?"

Scott locked eyes with him. "Your name came up in the course of my reexamining the case, as one of the original persons questioned in relation to her death. I'd like to go over your statements and relationship to Ms. Liu."

"I'd be happy to tell you anything I can recall about Veronica, Agent Lynley, but I'm in a bit of a hurry," he argued. "I have another showing across town."

"I understand," Scott said succinctly. "I have no problem arranging a time for you to come down to the FBI field office to talk. Or we can do it now. Your call."

Dillman regarded him thoughtfully for a few moments and said, "Maybe it is best to get this over with now." He paused. "What would you like to know?"

Scott got right to it. "Did you have anything to do with Ms. Liu's murder?" he asked bluntly.

"Absolutely not!" Dillman insisted with a straight face. "I had an alibi for when Veronica was murdered."

"Which was?" Scott wanted to test his memory.

After a moment or two, he responded smoothly, "It was a long time ago, but as I recall, I was on the road in between showing houses and nowhere near Veronica's house."

"Had you ever been to her cabin?" Scott asked him.

"No," he replied flatly. "She never invited me over, so I had no reason to go there."

"Maybe your reason was that you didn't take rejection lightly and were more than willing to force the issue, if you didn't get what you wanted from her."

"Rejection? What?" Dillman's face tightened. "Who told you I was rejected by her?"

"Are you denying that you hit on Ms. Liu and she told you she wasn't interested?" Scott peered at him. "Or that you were fired from the real estate office because you went after another female agent who also rebuffed your ill-advised advances?"

Dillman did an about-face. "Okay, you got me. I did hit on Veronica and others at the agency who I was attracted to. I admit, I was a bit of a jerk back in those days. And it cost me my job. But I certainly wasn't so desperate as to murder someone simply because she wouldn't go out with me. To suggest otherwise, Agent Lynley, would be barking up the wrong tree."

"If you say so." Scott wasn't entirely convinced he was as innocent as he claimed to be. But there was simply no evidence at this time to indicate otherwise. "When you worked with

Ms. Liu, were you aware of anyone else who may have wished her harm?"

Dillman rubbed his jaw. "No one comes to mind," he answered. "Whoever killed Veronica, I doubt it had anything to do with her being a Realtor. She was a capable agent who knew how to close the deal, and was respected by her agents in the office and competitors alike, as far as I knew." He waited a beat and said, "I'd heard that she was seeing some guy who was two-timing her. Whether that had anything to do with Veronica's death, I have no idea."

Neither do I, Scott reflected, knowing that the person in question was her former boyfriend, Mathew Yang. *But I intend to find out.* "That should do it, for now," he told Dillman.

He nodded. "Hope you solve the case, Agent Lynley. Believe it or not, I feel just as bad as anyone that Veronica was murdered twenty years ago. She really was a damned good real estate agent and taught me a thing or two that I've carried with me to this day in the selling of houses."

"Nice to know." Scott gazed at him. "I can see myself out."

He left on that note, not believing Oliver Dillman should be moved up the list of suspects any more now than two decades ago. Unless circumstances should present themselves in rethinking that.

Chapter Eight

Scott stepped into the roomy office of Mathew Yang, who was the chief financial officer of the public relations firm Suehiro and Iwalani Communications, operating out of a high-rise on Fullerton Street in downtown Kolton Lake. Yang, who was in his midfifties and slender, with short black hair in a comb-over style, approached Scott.

"Special Agent Lynley, I take it," Yang said, regarding him with sable eyes behind wire-rimmed glasses.

Scott nodded. "Yes."

"Mathew Yang." He put out a hand. "Nice to meet you." After Scott shook his hand, Yang said, "I have to admit that it threw me for a loop when you said over the phone that you were re-opening the case into Veronica's death."

"It was something that needed to happen," Scott told him tersely. "Just happened to fall in my lap and I plan to see it through."

"I understand." Yang looked away. "Why don't we sit?"

He led him to a pair of leather wing chairs by a floor-to-ceiling window. After Scott sat, he said straightforwardly, "I'm reinterviewing everyone who was considered a suspect in the original investigation. Given the nature of your relationship at the time with Ms. Liu, while being married to another woman, you were obviously at the top of the list."

"I was also cleared of playing any role in Veronica's death," he pointed out.

Scott struck back. "That was then, this is now. You'll need to convince me that you're innocent of any wrongdoing in Ms. Liu's murder to take you off the front burners."

Yang ran a hand across his mouth uneasily. "Look, I'm not proud of the way I handled things with Veronica," he contended. "But I didn't kill her. I was in love with Veronica and planned to ask her to marry me, once I got a divorce."

"From what I understand, Ms. Liu never even knew you were already married." Scott eyed him sharply. "If this is incorrect, now's the time to say so."

"It's true." Yang drew a deep breath. "I never got the chance to confess this to Veronica before she was killed. But I had every intention of doing so. My marriage was in name only. We weren't even living together anymore. Once it became untenable, my then wife, Loretta, and I agreed to go our separate ways. When I met Veronica, she gave me a new lease on life as far as romance. We started making plans for a future together, which included her niece, Abby." He smoothed a brow musingly. "Never even met her till the funeral. Veronica said she wanted to wait on that till the time was right, so Abby wouldn't have another letdown in her life."

"But that ended up happening anyway," Scott said sadly, "when someone decided to murder Veronica Liu."

"It wasn't me," Yang insisted. "I was at work at the time, with witnesses. Believe me when I tell you, Agent Lynley, it tore me to pieces when I got the news that Veronica was dead."

So you say, Scott mused, knowing that the alibi had checked out. "What about your wife?" he pressed. "Was she as broken up about it?"

"As I said, we were estranged and Loretta no longer concerned herself about my love life," he argued. "Or vice versa."

Scott had heard all that before and found that, in many instances, one side or the other was reluctant to see the marriage end. To the contrary, more often than not, a spouse who was being cheated on wasn't very happy about the adultery. Jealous rage came to mind. Was that the case here? Could it have resulted in a revenge killing, in spite of the original investigation that concluded otherwise?

"I'd like to speak with your ex," Scott told him. "Get her side of this…"

"I'm afraid that won't be possible." Yang touched his glasses. "Loretta died of ovarian cancer eight years ago."

"I see." Scott wondered if she could have taken any relevant secrets with her to the grave.

"Neither of us had anything to do with what happened to Veronica," he asserted. "You have to believe that, Agent Lynley. Even after all these years, the idea that I could have harmed one hair on the head of someone I loved still pains me."

Scott sensed his sincerity, but continued to consider him a person of interest. "That should be all, for now." He rose.

"I suppose you've spoken with Abby?" Yang asked, standing.

"I have," Scott admitted.

"How's she doing?" His voice lowered an octave.

"As well as one could expect when having to relive a painful chapter in her life," he told him candidly.

"Many times, I've wanted to reach out to her, but just wasn't sure how."

"Maybe you'll figure it out," Scott said equably, knowing he would leave it up to Mathew and Abby as to if and when they'd want to get together.

Yang nodded. "Yeah, maybe."

Scott left the public relations firm with Veronica's ex-husband, Evan Liu, next up to be reinterviewed in trying to track down the killer of Abby's aunt.

AFTER WORK, Abby sat outside her cabin by the lake with her friend Phoebe Hoag on saucer chairs. She had known Phoebe since childhood and had kept in touch with her over the years, in spite of taking different paths in life, before both had resettled in Kolton Lake.

Phoebe, also thirty-two and a neurologist at Kolton Lake General, was gorgeous, with long chestnut hair in an A-line style and baby blue eyes. Just as slender as Abby and a little taller, Phoebe was fresh off a divorce from her college sweetheart and dating a cardiologist. While sipping beer, they talked about the recent school bus accident and fortunate passengers. Abby chose not to bring up the possible sighting of Zach Gilliard at the hospital, fearing Phoebe might think she was losing her mind. And Abby wondered if she might not agree, given what she had learned about him from Scott and having no further direct contact with Zach since seeing him at the cemetery.

Afterward, Abby told her friend about the reopening of the investigation into her aunt Veronica's murder.

"Seriously?" Phoebe fluttered her lashes in shock. "After all these years?"

"I know." Abby was still pinching herself to believe it was really happening. She remembered that she had sat beside Phoebe on the school bus that day, before Phoebe had been let off one stop earlier than she had. Abby could only imagine if it had been her friend who'd discovered her mother murdered in her own car in the driveway. "FBI Special Agent Scott Lynley decided it was a case worth pursuing." His pursuit of her or vice versa was something Abby had not expected either.

"Has he made any progress?"

"I suppose," Abby answered matter-of-factly. "He's talking to people who knew my aunt, original witnesses and suspects, looking at evidence, et cetera. But these things take time in such an old case." She understood, tempering her enthusiasm for good results, if not for the handsome agent himself.

Phoebe made a face. "I really hope this Agent

Lynley makes a breakthrough in finally solving the crime," she voiced.

"Me too." Abby lifted the beer bottle. "Aunt Veronica has waited long enough for the world to learn what she had to have known herself but was no longer able to communicate to anyone in the living world."

"I agree." Phoebe put the beer bottle to her glossy lips. "So, other than you and Jeanne Singletary, just how many people are still around who actually remember your aunt and can assist in the investigation?"

"Well, there's my aunt's ex, Evan Liu, and former lover, Mathew Yang," Abby told her, knowing they had continued to live in the area, though she didn't have a relationship with either. "Then there's Mayor Freda Myerson."

"Really?" Phoebe's sculpted brows shot up. "Mayor Myerson knew your aunt?"

"I guess not that well, but Aunt Veronica did sell the mayor her first home, when she was still just Freda Neville twenty-plus years ago."

"Who knew?" Phoebe chuckled. "I read once that Mayor Myerson had been married at least twice, had her fair share of wealthy boyfriends along the way, and was known to be a real reveler back in the day. That was before she settled down with her current husband, philanthropist Pierce Myerson, and turned her attention to becoming mayor of Kolton Lake, with an eye for higher political office."

"At least my aunt brushed shoulders with her way back when," Abby quipped while glancing at the lake. "In case Freda should someday decide to run for president."

"You never know." Phoebe giggled and drank beer. "In any event, let's keep our fingers crossed that the FBI agent knows what he's doing in taking on the case."

"Yeah, let's." Abby crossed her fingers for effect then said thoughtfully, "Speaking of Agent Lynley—Scott... I kind of have the hots for him and the feeling seems mutual."

"Oh, really?" Phoebe grinned. "Do tell."

Abby kept it short and sweet, knowing that she and Scott had barely scratched the surface, though enough to give her an itch as to the potential for a relationship with the special agent. She finished by revealing to her friend that they'd kissed.

"Hmm..." Phoebe's voice rose excitedly. "Can't wait to see if one thing will lead to another."

"Neither can I," Abby admitted while staying grounded should things not go that way.

"You deserve someone in your life who can actually prove to be more than the self-absorbed, undependable and otherwise bad-news types that have entered and exited your life over the years."

"Tell me something I don't already know." Abby chuckled and sipped the beer. "On second thought, don't tell me. I'll just have to live and learn whether there's something worth pursuing or not with Scott Lynley."

Phoebe smiled and clinked their beer bottles. "Fair enough."

In her head, Abby already believed it to be worthwhile. She just wouldn't put the cart ahead of the horse. But was more than ready to get in the saddle should she be invited to do so.

SCOTT RANG THE bell of the lodge-style house in the affluent town of Kolton Hills, adjacent to Kolton Lake, where Evan Liu resided on Benes Lane. A white BMW Alpina XB7 was parked in the driveway. The front door of the home opened and a dark-haired young woman wearing a housekeeping uniform stood there.

"Can I help you?" she asked.

"I'd like to see Evan Liu," he told her.

Her brown eyes regarded him curiously. "Is Mr. Liu expecting you?"

"Not exactly." Scott met her gaze. "I'm with the FBI. It's official business."

"Just a moment." She left him standing there for about a minute. When she came back, Scott was told, "Mr. Liu will see you. He's in his garden. You can go around the house and meet him there."

"Thanks," Scott said, and proceeded to follow a well-manicured path till he spotted a slender man in his early sixties, with short gray hair, wearing garden gloves while tending to some perennial plants. He stopped when Scott walked across the grass toward him.

"I'm Evan Liu," he said curiously, wiping his brow with the back of his hand.

"Special Agent Lynley," Scott told him, showing his identification.

Behind oval glasses, Liu trained black eyes on him. "What does an FBI agent need to see a retired pharmacist about?"

"Your ex-wife, Veronica Liu," Scott responded directly. "I've reopened the investigation into her murder."

"Really?" Liu's voice rang with surprise. "That happened so long ago."

"I'm a cold case investigator," Scott told him, wondering if he had been in touch with Abby. "No homicide is ever so long ago that we simply sweep it under the rug."

"I understand," he said lowly.

"Especially one that was inexplicable while shattering the life of your niece, Abby Zhang," Scott thought to add.

Liu stiffened. "How is she?"

"Abby is as well as could be expected when having to go through the ordeal again of her aunt's death." Scott met his stare. "She works for the FBI now as a victim specialist, in case you didn't know."

"I didn't," he confessed. "We stopped communicating after Veronica and I divorced. My mistake."

Scott agreed, but wasn't there to help Evan Liu make amends, though he was welcome to do so. Assuming he wasn't responsible for the tragedy she'd had to endure. "I'd like to ask you a few questions pertaining to Veronica Liu's death."

"Okay." Liu pursed his lips. "But just so you know, I had nothing to do with what happened to my ex-wife. We were divorced for two years when she was killed. The police at the time verified my alibi."

"So they did," Scott acknowledged. "It also came to light that your relationship with Veronica was strained and the divorce not entirely amicable. In my book, that leaves open the possibility that you might have wanted your ex-wife dead in an 'if I can't have you, no one can' kind of way. If true, it wouldn't have been unthinkable that you could have hired someone else to do your dirty work for you."

"Nonsense!" Liu shot back. "I'm sure you're just doing your job, Agent Lynley, but any suggestion that I could have used a hired killer to murder someone I had distanced myself from makes no sense."

"Murder rarely does make sense," Scott countered. "Particularly where it concerns matters of the heart. Being manipulative and vengeful can make people do crazy things."

"Not me," he snorted. "I admit that my marriage to Veronica was less than perfect. But it wasn't all my fault. We both made errors in judgment and it cost us the relationship. Was I happy that she kicked me out? No. But I got over it and learned from my mistakes. I fell in love with someone else and we're still going strong more than two decades later." Liu sighed. "As for Veronica, I'm sorry that someone murdered her. But it wasn't me. I knew how much she loved that little girl, Abby, after losing her own parents at such a young age. I would never have taken Veronica away from her, adding to Abby's sad childhood and beyond."

He struck Scott as legit enough in his tone. It was on that basis that he told Evan Liu he was off the hook as of now as a suspect in his ex-wife's death. But if he needed to work his way back around to Liu, Scott was more than prepared to do so. He allowed him to return to his gardening and Scott left the same way he came.

THAT EVENING, Scott walked into the Loren's Club, a nightclub on Dentry Avenue in Bowling Green where Katlyn Johansson worked as a bartender. He made his way through the crowd till he found the man he was looking for, Art Reilly, of the Bureau's Bowling Green resident agency.

"Hey," Scott said to him.

Reilly, who was nursing a drink at the bar, replied, "There you are. Was beginning to think I'd been stood up."

"Not a chance." Scott chuckled. "Sorry I'm late. I was delayed in the process of my investigation."

"Don't worry about it." He finished off the drink. "You're still buying, right?"

"Absolutely." Scott sat beside him. "The next one's on me."

Reilly nodded and regarded him with curiosity. "So, why am I here?"

"Well, as you know, I'm reinterviewing original suspects in the Veronica Liu homicide," Scott explained.

"Yeah?"

"One of them, Katlyn Johansson, happens to work in this very bar," he told him. "Since it's right in your neck of the woods, figured you might want to step into the ring with me in talking with her. Just in case it triggers something that I might miss."

"Okay, I'm game." Reilly rubbed his chin pensively. "Where is she?"

"Right there." Scott shifted his eyes toward the bartender who had presumably served Reilly his first drink. And was now headed their way.

Katlyn Johansson was in her midforties, medium size, and had a black bob with fuchsia highlights worn in a peekaboo hairstyle. She peered at Scott with blue eyes and said, "What can I get you?"

"A few minutes of your time." He fixed on her face. "Are you Katlyn Johansson?" he asked, though already knowing the answer from having done his homework.

"Who's asking?"

Scott flashed his ID. "FBI Special Agent Lynley."

She cocked a thin brow and favored Reilly. "Supervisory Senior Agent Reilly," he said tonelessly. "You may not remember me but—"

"I thought you looked familiar," Katlyn said. "We spoke years ago when you were investigating the murder of..."

"Veronica Liu," he told her.

"Yeah, that's right."

Scott leaned forward and said, "I've reopened the case."

"Really?" She cocked a brow. "And you want to question me again about it?"

"Just need to go over your original statement as part of the routine investigation," he claimed. "We can do it now or…"

"Go ahead." Katlyn rested her hands on the counter. "I have nothing to hide."

"If my memory serves me correctly," Reilly told her, scratching his pate, "you had words with Ms. Liu at the Tygers Club on Third Street, where you were working at the time, the night before she was killed. Do you recall what that was all about?"

Katlyn stared at him for an instant and replied thoughtfully, "Sure. It was just a misunderstanding. Back then, when I had a badass body as a dancer, men liked to ogle me while on stage. As I remember it, one of those was a guy Veronica Liu was with. She seemed to think I was hitting on him through the dancing, I guess. And let me know afterward to lay off her man. I didn't take too kindly to being accused of something I was innocent of and let her know this. That was about it."

"Actually, according to witnesses," Scott pointed out, "you followed Ms. Liu outside the establishment, seemingly itching for a fight.

So how far were you willing to take this?" he questioned.

"The witnesses got it wrong," she insisted. "I only went out to get some air. By then, Veronica was already gone. I never saw or spoke to her again, I swear." Katlyn took a breath. "Next thing I knew, I heard that she was shot to death and I was being interrogated about it by the cops…and you, Agent Reilly. And I'm no more guilty today of killing her than I was two decades ago."

"Sure about that?" Reilly asked, glaring at her, but with a tone that suggested he believed it to be true.

"Yeah. Committing cold-blooded murder to settle an imaginary romantic triangle is going overboard. Don't you think?"

Reilly tugged at his mustache and looked at Scott before saying, "She's still a weak link in the chain."

He was inclined to agree, but Scott had to ask the bartender, "Did you own a gun back then?"

"No." Katlyn shook her head. "I hate guns and would never own one."

"Okay." Scott realized that this was going nowhere with her. Then something that could only be called a long shot entered his head. "Do you happen to recall if there was anyone else at the bar that night who Veronica Liu may have had a beef with? Or otherwise got on the bad side of?" There was no record of such in the original report. Could it have been overlooked?

Katlyn pondered this. "It was so long ago..." She pressed her lips together. "I think Veronica may have exchanged words with another guy when her boyfriend was preoccupied with me. I can't be sure."

"Do you remember anything about this man?" Scott asked interestedly. "Age, race, size, hairstyle, et cetera."

"Definitely white, dark-haired and average size," she responded. "Can't remember any more than that, sorry." Just as swiftly, Katlyn uttered, "Now that I think about it, I had the feeling that they weren't strangers to one another. Don't ask me why. Anyway, I need to get back to work."

Scott nodded. He took out his wallet and put money on the counter, which included a nice tip, and said, "Why don't you give Agent Reilly here a refill?"

"All right." Katlyn looked at Scott. "What about you?"

He waved her off. "I'm good."

After briefly conferring with the supervisory senior special agent, who seemed to think this unsub was a nothing burger, Scott respectfully had to disagree. "All leads are worth pursuing, no matter how long the odds of hitting pay dirt."

Reilly didn't argue the point. "You're right. We obviously missed something in the equation. Check it out, see what you come up with. It's your case now, Lynley, and I'm pulling for you."

Scott accepted that from him for what it was worth, thanking Reilly for showing up, before leaving him at the bar as Scott headed home. During the drive, he couldn't help but wonder if, in fact, Veronica Liu had been targeted by someone she'd known at the club that night. If so, who? And what could have triggered such an act of violence?

It left Scott with more food for thought. And an even greater determination to get to the bottom of why Abby's aunt had been shot to death, for her to sadly discover.

Chapter Nine

On Saturday, Abby went for a morning swim.
Lake Kolton was gorgeous and the water warm.
Only a few boats were out. She wondered if
Scott was a swimmer. Or did he prefer riding
horses as a good substitute? She began with a
front crawl before moving into a backstroke
and finishing up with the butterfly as she made
her way to shore, feeling tired and energized
at the same time.

Out of the water, the blue one-piece swimsuit
clung to her like a second skin as she gazed back
at the lake and envisioned a time when she'd
gone swimming there with her aunt Veronica.
It was one of the ways in which they'd bonded
and Abby missed the most. At least the memories of the good times would stay with her, even
if the tragedy of her aunt's death would as well.

Inside the cabin, Abby dried off and changed
into shorts and a square-necked tank top, remaining barefoot as she did some house chores

and thought about Scott. She wondered how he was progressing in the investigation and whether or not one thing could truly lead to another in finding a killer who had eluded other investigators for two decades. Her thoughts wandered to the prospects for them beyond the cold case. Were the feelings she was starting to develop for him real? And were they reciprocated from his end beyond a nice kiss they'd shared?

When her cell phone rang, Abby saw that it was Scott calling, as though he had been reading her mind. She answered. "Hello."

"Hi." He paused. "If you're not busy this afternoon, I wanted to return the favor of your incredible meal by inviting you to dinner at my place."

Abby grinned. "I'd love to come to dinner and check out your place."

"Great." He gave her the address and said, "Should be easy to find."

"Okay." As she had GPS in her car, Abby was sure she would have no problem there. "Do you want me to bring anything?"

"Only yourself."

She laughed. "I think I can handle that."

"Actually, now that you mention it, if you're up for riding a horse, you might want to dress accordingly."

"I'm up for it," Abby told him. "Not very experienced in that department, but I did ride a few times when living in the Bay Area."

"Good to know," Scott said. "See you later."

"'Bye." Abby disconnected. She felt almost giddy at another opportunity to spend quality time with Scott. Whether it would lead to them taking things up a notch, if not beyond that, she wasn't sure. She would play it by ear and go with the flow, wherever it led.

A couple of hours later, Abby was driving east on US Route 60 toward Scott's house. She wondered if he was any more comfortable living alone than she was. Or had his divorce soured him on sharing his space with someone else?

She glanced into the rearview mirror nonchalantly and Abby thought she spotted a dark SUV that she had noticed pull onto the highway after she'd entered it from Kolton Lake. There was another car in between them. Yet she was almost certain that it was the same SUV. Was it following her?

She couldn't see the driver. Was it Zach Gilliard? Had she seen him at the hospital yesterday? Or was this whole stalking thing only her imagination probably going too far?

Get a grip, Abby ordered herself. Why would someone be following her the ninety or so miles from Kolton Lake to Louisville? But would distance truly matter to a crazy stalker bent on crowding or attacking, if not killing, her?

Abby changed lanes to see if the SUV did. Or if it would give her a better look at the driver. But the SUV made no attempt to follow her lead. When another car slid in front of the SUV, putting even more of a barrier between it and her, Abby considered that maybe she had once again allowed her imagination to run wild.

By the time she had exited the highway and watched the SUV continue on, Abby realized it had indeed all been in her head. She breathed a sigh of relief on that score. The last thing she needed was to visit Scott with shaky thoughts about a stalker and one who, had the driver been Zach Gilliard, Scott had already assured her, more or less, was no threat to her.

When she drove onto his property, Scott came out to greet her. Between wearing a cowboy hat, a button-down denim shirt, faded jeans and camel-colored leather boots, Abby was seeing him in a whole new, and just as pleasant as before, light. He was grinning broadly. She grinned back and got out of the car.

"Hey, cowboy."

"Hey." He touched the brim of his hat. "Have any trouble finding the place?"

"None whatsoever."

"Good. Dinner's been prepped and will be ready to chow down on in no time flat."

She nodded. "Great, because I'm starving."

"In that case, you've come to the right place." He laughed. "Come on in and I'll show you around."

The tour did not disappoint as Abby marveled at the place the FBI special agent called home. It was spacious, modernized, and seemed to suit him. "I love it," she uttered.

"Thanks." Scott gave a half grin. "I like being able to come back here to chill from the demands of the job."

Abby wondered if that included his current cold case. Not that she could blame him for needing a refuge when having to deal with the lives and deaths typically involved in a criminal investigation. She could say the same when at her log cabin.

"Let's go check out the barn now," he suggested.

"Okay." She smiled. "I'm looking forward to meeting the horses."

They made their way to the four-stall barn, where Scott introduced her to his Thoroughbred, Sammie, and two American Cream Draft horses, named Blaze and Lela. "Later, you can ride Lela, whom I suspect will warm up to you in a hurry."

"I think she already has," Abby said with a chuckle as she rubbed the horse's neck.

"I agree." Scott admired Abby and Lela as he rested a hand on the top of the stall door. "We should go wash up now and then we can eat."

"Sounds good," she told him as they headed back to the house.

To SAY HE wasn't totally turned on by Abby, with her long hair in a ponytail accentuating her attractive face, and dressed for the part on his ranch, would be a flat-out lie. On the contrary, Scott was taken by his guest in ways he had managed to suppress ever since his divorce. Maybe now he had a good reason to bring those emotions back to the surface.

Scott put those carnal thoughts on hold as he stood at the gas grill on his Ipe wood deck, where he was grilling some barbecued pork chops—and veggie burgers to make Abby feel right at home—to go with baked beans, coleslaw, whole wheat bread and freshly squeezed lemonade. This would be his first time trying the veggie burgers, but he was up for it.

"Dinner is served," Scott declared as he laid it out on the rectangular pine picnic table, where Abby was already seated on the bench.

"Looks delicious," she told him, flashing her teeth.

"Now it's time to see if the taste measures up," he said teasingly, sitting across from her.

Abby wasted little time in taking a bite of the veggie burger. "It's really good."

"Glad you like it." Scott grinned and tried his own burger. "That is tasty and something to add to my food group."

She laughed. "Thanks for being willing to step out of your comfort zone."

"I aim to please," he told her, and meant it where it concerned her.

"Same here." Abby went for a pork chop from the platter. "Mmm, excellent," she said a moment later after taking a bite.

Scott chuckled. "Maybe in my next life, I'll become a chef."

"Why not?" She laughed again and he enjoyed seeing it every time. "And who knows what I'd be? Perhaps a sculptress. Or maybe an engineer."

"I'm sure you would have been successful with any career you put your mind to." He spoke confidently.

"Likewise." She used a napkin to remove barbecue sauce from the corner of her mouth.

Scott spooned some baked beans and asked curiously, "How were things for you living with other relatives in the Bay Area?"

Abby pondered this before responding tranquilly, "Probably as good as could be expected, all things considered. A cousin on my mother's side, Kristin Shao, generously took me in when I had nowhere else to go. But she had her own family and so, while everyone tried their best to make it work out, I never quite felt as if I belonged. Do you know what I mean?"

"Yeah, I can understand that," he told her sincerely, counting his blessings that his family had never been broken while he was still a boy. The fact that Abby had survived her childhood experiences and come out stronger because of them was something to be admired. "What do you remember about your parents?"

"Not too much," she admitted, sipping her lemonade musingly. "I was only six when they passed, but I do recall them being touchy-feely and laughing a lot."

"Good memories to have," he said, even if unable to overcome the darker memories of what was to come in losing them the way she had.

"How about you?" Abby was holding coleslaw on a fork. "Must have been pretty hard losing your parents too?"

"Yeah, it was." Scott drank some lemonade. "I was much older than you when they died in a car accident, but it still took a while to wrap my head around. Both were so full of life, giving, and dedicated to their children and jobs."

"Sounds like they were great people," Abby said. "Wish I had been able to meet them."

"So do I. Mom and Dad would've liked you." He was certain. Just as Scott knew that his siblings would approve of him having Abby in his life.

Abby beamed and ate more of the veggie burgers. She grew more serious when asking, "Have you made any more headway on the investigation into Aunt Veronica's murder?"

Though part of Scott had wanted to avoid talking about the case in this get-together, so as not to dampen the mood, he knew that as long as this elephant was in the room or environment, there was no avoiding it. Moreover, he owed it to Abby to be as straight as he could without compromising the investigation in any way.

"I'm still waiting for the results on the retesting of forensic evidence," he told her, breaking off a piece of wheat bread. "I've been tracking down the original suspects to either eliminate them from further scrutiny or maintain as persons of interest."

She jutted her chin. "I hope there's a break in the case that can blow it wide open in terms of nailing my aunt's killer."

"I want that almost as much as you do, Abby." Scott regarded her across the table. "Every day

I feel as if it's moving in the right direction toward that end. You just have to be patient."

She gave a bob of her head. "Don't mean to rush you. I know you can't just wave a magic wand and solve something twenty years in the making."

"Believe me, I would if I could," he told her, feeling as though he did need to do more to push the envelope further. "That being said, no crime is unsolvable, apart from maybe Jack the Ripper's serial murders of prostitutes in Victorian England. We have a lot of forensic tools and investigative know-how in our favor. Just need to stay the course."

"That's all I can ask for," she offered, smiling at him.

Scott did consider one thing to that effect as he dabbed a napkin to his mouth. "Actually, I was wondering if you happen to remember any men whom your aunt may have been acquainted with at work or outside of, other than her ex-husband, Evan Liu, or boyfriend, Mathew Yang?"

"Hmm." Abby closed her eyes for reflection. "No one comes to mind. My aunt kept me at what she believed to be a safe distance from the men in her life. She was friendly enough with everyone I saw, including the mail carrier, a male neighbor and even one my teachers, Mr.

Pryce. But I wouldn't call any of them an acquaintance, per se. Why do you ask?"

Scott told her about reinterviewing Katlyn Johansson with the original FBI agent on the case, Art Reilly, on hand, and Katlyn's mention of a man whom Veronica was seen talking to in friendly terms possibly the night before she'd died.

Abby gazed at him. "You think this man could have killed Aunt Veronica?"

"Not necessarily," Scott contended, believing that it was a stretch to assume that this person could have been overlooked in the initial investigation as an unsub. But stranger things had happened. "Could have been a misinterpretation by Johansson and nothing more than an innocent exchange between your aunt and this man at the club. We'll see," he told her, leaving it at that.

"If I think of anyone else, I'll let you know," Abby promised.

"Good enough for me." Scott didn't want her to overthink this, any more than he wanted to himself. He'd been in this business long enough to know that the answers to the toughest questions were usually staring you right in the face. He only needed to see this for what it was. "Are you ready to go horseback riding?" he asked Abby.

"Ready as ever," she proclaimed. "Should be fun."

"It will be," he agreed, finishing off the glass of lemonade.

At the stables, Scott put on his Stetson and handed Abby a cowgirl straw hat, saying, "It belongs to my sister Annette, from her last visit. I'm sure she won't mind if you borrow it."

"Okay." Abby grinned and put it atop her head. "Fits perfectly."

He smiled, agreeing totally and liking how the hat looked on her as she posed with it.

They saddled up the horses and Scott helped Abby climb onto the American Cream Draft horse named Lela, and he got on Sammie, his Thoroughbred, before they went on the riding trail and he showed Abby more of the property while feeling that she fit right into his world, apart from both working for the Bureau.

WHEN THEY GOT back to his house forty-five minutes later, Scott poured them both a glass of red wine. Even after taking a few sips of the tasty drink, Abby was clearheaded enough to know that she found the FBI special agent incredibly handsome and sexy. And that she wanted him. Though she was not accustomed to initiating sexual advances, this time she felt like making an exception. Would Scott swallow the bait?

Before she could venture down that road, he kissed her and said desirously, "The wine tastes a lot better coming off your lips."

"Oh, really?" Abby felt even more turned on. "In that case, maybe we need to try that again."

"I'd like nothing better," Scott responded surely. He cupped her cheeks and kissed her again. Abby opened her mouth as the kiss intensified. She stood on her tiptoes and wrapped her hand around his head, taking in his manly scent, arousing her even more as she felt her heartbeat move erratically. "What do you say we take this up to my bedroom?" he asked huskily after pulling back and gazing into her eyes. "Or am I being premature in wanting to go to the next level of what we have going on here?"

"You're not being premature at all, Scott," Abby assured him. "I'm more than ready to move to that next level. Now!"

He beamed lustfully. "Say no more."

Hand in hand, they walked from the chef's kitchen and headed up the winding staircase to the second story. Stepping into the generous primary suite, Abby did a quick scan of the Old World style. It had a vaulted ceiling and interesting angles with an abundance of windows covered by honeycomb shades. The midcentury-modern furniture included a solid wood spindle bed, which she focused on, anticipating getting beneath the blue coverlet with Scott.

Abby turned to him and again fell into a passionate kiss before she broke it off and, with swollen lips, uttered unabashedly, "Let's get naked."

Scott grinned attentively. "The sooner the better."

They practically raced to disrobe and when both were completely in the nude, Abby regarded Scott's rock-hard body, making him even more desirable. She saw him appraising her, as well, making her slightly self-conscious till he said flatly, "You are so hot."

"So are you." Abby prided herself for staying in shape as she pulled her hair out of the ponytail and met his steady gaze. "Do you have protection?" she thought to ask, knowing that even in the face of wanting a man like never before, they still needed to be responsible.

"Yeah," he confirmed, and disappeared into the bathroom briefly. He returned with the condom in place on his erection, and said smoothly, "Now, where were we?"

"About to go to bed." She gulped. "Make love to me, Scott."

"With pleasure and more," he told her, scooping her into his muscular arms and carrying her to the bed, where he lay her down gently before joining her.

As they cuddled and resumed kissing, Scott first ran his fingers through her hair. Then he began caressing her breasts and nipples, driving Abby crazy with delight. "Mmm…" she cooed, nibbling on his lower lip.

"There's more where that came from," he stated, seemingly more than content to take his sweet time with foreplay. Then his hands went farther down and things reached a fever pitch before she could stand the pure torture no more. Through his mouth, she demanded, "I need you inside me!"

"I need that too." Scott kissed her again. "Just want to be sure you're ready. Don't want to rush this."

"I'm ready," Abby said fervently. "It's time!"

As though this triggered a signal in his brain, Scott obeyed her command and positioned himself between her legs, moving deep inside Abby. She was more than welcoming, arching her back and meeting him halfway and then some as her orgasm came almost instantly.

With the shuddering of her body and sounds of satisfaction that escaped Abby, she encouraged Scott, who had clearly been holding back, to join her on the other end. He picked up the pace and she clung to him as he trembled mightily with the powerful release that brought them even closer together.

When it was over, Abby had to say, "It was great." She could have even said "fantastic" or "mind-blowing," but had chosen to restrain herself. Now was probably not the time to get too carried away or emotional.

"More like amazing," Scott said, lying on his back while catching his breath.

She blushed. "You think?"

"I know." He kissed her shoulder. "Some things in life are simply meant to be."

Abby chuckled. "Having sex?"

"Having sex with someone you're in sync with."

"So we're in sync now, are we?"

"Yeah," he said without prelude. "I think you feel it too."

"Hmm…" Abby admittedly was beginning to feel this, as well, as a sense of belonging where it concerned Scott. Were the two one and the same? "I think you're right."

She could only wonder now where things were headed from here. And how far up the ladder they might climb.

Chapter Ten

"Stay the night," Scott requested when Abby indicated it was about time to drive back to Kolton Lake.

"Are you sure about that?" She gave him a tentative look as they lay in bed, where he was massaging her feet. "Wouldn't want to overstay my welcome."

"You wouldn't be doing that," he told her, surprised she would assume otherwise. "It's late and I want you around so I can make my famous cinnamon pancakes with maple syrup for you in the morning." He scrunched up his face. "Pretty please."

"Well, when you put it that way." She giggled, brushing up against him. "I do like pancakes and maple syrup."

"Then it's settled." Scott grinned and continued to massage her soft toes and heels. "How does that feel?"

"So good." Abby shut her eyes. "Mmm."

He kept it going, happy to pleasure her in any and every way he could. "I can think of a few other things that might feel even better," he teased her.

"Oh, really?" Her lashes fluttered coquettishly. "Let me guess…"

He chuckled. "Don't try too hard."

The natural banter between them left an impression on Scott, making him believe that what they had was more than just sexual chemistry and physical attraction. He could tell that she felt the same way, even if she was being as careful as he was for fear of having her heart broken. Giving in to their carnal instincts, though, led to them making love again.

Only, this time, it was slow and deliberate, with Scott wanting to explore every part of Abby, and allowing her the same courtesy toward him, as they made love well into the wee hours of the morning. Afterward, they cuddled and whispered a few sweet words to one another before falling asleep on a very good note.

IN THE MORNING, Scott allowed Abby to get some extra shut-eye, while he checked his messages on the laptop for any news pertaining to the investigation. He got word that the FBI Laboratory was still working diligently to see if any of the retesting of forensic evidence related to

Veronica Liu's murder yielded any positive results. He would follow up on it later.

Right now, he needed to prepare the breakfast he'd promised Abby before she awakened. Seeing her sleeping so peacefully like an angel stirred him, making Scott imagine it could become a regular thing after a night of making love. He, for one, wanted to experience again the sense of a real commitment in companionship and beyond. Whether or not Abby was of the same mind was something that would need to be determined, sooner or later.

Scott had just poured the pancake batter on the electric griddle, with the bacon already made, when Abby walked into the kitchen in her bare feet. She was wearing one of his oversize plaid shirts and it looked sexy on her. "Good morning, sleepyhead," he told her.

"Morning." She ran a hand through her hair haphazardly. "Smells good."

"It'll taste even better." He grinned. "Coffee's ready. Help yourself."

"Thanks." Abby grabbed a mug out of the cabinet and poured coffee into it. "So, is there anything you can't do well?"

Scott laughed, though he wasn't sure if she was referring to in bed or in the kitchen. Or even as a cold case detective. "I'm sure I can think of a few things," he voiced honestly. "But I'll take the compliment anyhow."

"You should." She colored. "What can I say, Mr. Lynley, you know how to treat a woman well, in more ways than one."

"Back at you, Ms. Zhang," Scott told her sincerely while reading between the lines and liking the progress of the book. He tossed pancakes on a platter with the bacon and said, "Breakfast is served."

She beamed. "Perfect."

An hour later, Scott gave Abby a kiss good-bye and watched as she got into her car and drove home. Though barely out of his grasp, he was already starting to miss her and wondered when they might get to do a repeat of the overnight stay. Hell, he was even willing to go further and admit that the feelings he was developing for the victim specialist were much stronger than seeing Abby whenever time allowed in their schedules. But this needed to be kept in check. At least while giving her the space she needed to make her own assessment of where they were and could be headed.

He went to the barn to tend to the horses and clean the stalls. When he got back to the house, Scott's eyes lit up when he received a call from his sister Annette. A few months younger than his brother, Russell, she had been adopted as an infant by their parents, completing the Lynley family.

He flopped onto the retro upholstered armchair in the great room and accepted the video request. "Hey, there," he said after her face appeared on the small screen.

"Hello, Scott." Annette was biracial and attractive with bold brown-green eyes and long, wavy brunette hair with a middle part and chin-length bangs. A detective with the Dabs County Sheriff's Department, based in Carol Creek, Indiana, Annette was married to Indiana State Police Organized Crime and Corruption Unit Investigator Hamilton McCade.

"Was just thinking about you," Scott had to admit, more or less, as the image of Abby wearing her cowgirl hat entered his head.

"Really?" Annette chuckled. "Hope the thoughts were pleasant."

"Always." He grinned. "Actually, your name came up yesterday when I lent someone the riding hat you left behind. I figured you wouldn't mind."

"Of course not. The bigger question is, who is the special lady you invited to the ranch to go riding?" She gave him the inquiring eye.

"Her name is Abby Zhang. She's a victim specialist for the Bureau." Scott decided he might as well give his sister more of what she wanted. "We've hit it off."

"Seriously?" Annette batted her eyes. "That's wonderful to hear, Scott." Her teeth shone. "I'm so glad you finally decided to let someone in again."

"Me too," he admitted. Maybe if things went his way, this time he could succeed where he had previously failed. "We're still in the early stages, but it looks promising right now."

"Promising is a good place to start." Annette smiled. "Like the rest of us Lynleys, you deserve to be happy and in love. I know you probably aren't quite ready to use the L-word, but it's something to think about."

"I'm doing just that." Scott didn't want to get ahead of himself, though it was hard not to fall in love with someone like Abby. But before he allowed himself to go quite that far, he needed to know that the feelings were reciprocated and go from there. Switching subjects, Scott said, in noting that it was Annette who'd phoned him, "So, what's happening with you?"

"Oh, just the usual small-town crime." She chuckled frivolously. "And missing my favorite oldest sibling."

"Back at you." He grinned. "You and Hamilton are welcome to visit anytime you like."

"I can say the same to you, Scott. Even feel free to bring Abby along."

"Thanks. I'll keep that in mind." Scott hoped

Abby could meet his sisters and brother one day, as they would surely bond, as he had with their significant others. But only when she was ready and willing.

He told Annette a little about the cold case connection between Abby and the homicide victim from twenty years ago, Veronica Liu.

"Wow." Annette's brow puckered. "Sorry to hear about Abby's aunt."

"It was a long time ago."

"Never long enough when something like that happens."

"You're right," he conceded. "Abby's dealing with it as best as possible."

"Hope you catch the killer, if they're still around."

"That's the objective."

Shortly after the call ended, Scott received an ominous text message on his phone.

Drop the Veronica Liu investigation. Otherwise, her niece Abby is next. Unless you want her death on your conscience, move on to another cold case.

The stark warning sent a chill up and down Scott's spine as he got to his feet. Who sent him the text? Had it come from Veronica Liu's killer? Or was someone else messing with him for some reason?

Scott sucked in a deep breath and peeked out the window, as though expecting to see someone surveilling his property. He saw no one. It didn't make him any less concerned. Was Abby in danger? Or only if he continued to pursue the case? Should he warn her that she could be in danger? Or would such a warning only cause Abby to worry needlessly?

Scott began pacing. *Would I be playing with fire by putting a possible killer to the test in continuing to dig into the case?* he asked himself after again reading the threatening text message. He had begun to care for Abby too much to want to see her hurt. Much less killed, as her aunt Veronica had been.

But as an FBI special agent who was dedicated to the job and obligated to perform as required to the best of his ability, backing off a case was not an option. The way Scott saw it, someone was beginning to feel the heat insofar as the investigation into Veronica Liu's murder. That meant he was getting close to nailing the culprit, indicating the unsub was still alive and desperate to evade detection and apprehension. Making them all the more dangerous.

It makes me even more determined to close the books on this investigation with an arrest, Scott mused, taking a breath. But he was equally committed to ensuring Abby's safety, whatever it took. In this case, it had to start with warning her. Just in case this was more than an idle threat. He would also have the Bureau see if the text could be traced and sender identified.

ABBY HAD JUST finished taking a shower and changing clothes, when she got a call from Scott, who wanted a video chat. Fresh thoughts of their night of passion rolled through her mind, and what it might portend for the future, before she accepted the request. His handsome face appeared on the screen. "Hey." She kept her tone neutral, though admittedly having butterflies in their first communication since she'd driven away from his ranch a few hours ago.

"Hi. I see you made it back."

"Of course." She looked at him, trying to read his eyes. "Did you think I wouldn't?"

"Just glad to see that you did." He paused thoughtfully. "After you left, I got a weird text message."

"How weird?"

"Someone warned me to stop the investigation into your aunt's murder…" Scott began, "or put your life at risk."

"Seriously?" Abby's eyes widened with shock. "I'm being threatened now?"

"I'm afraid so." Scott's brow creased. "Looks as if the unsub believes it's only a matter of time now before the cloak of hiding in plain view for years comes crashing down. The killer is sending a clear message that threatening to come after you unless I back off will somehow do the trick."

"I'd never want you to give up finding my aunt Veronica's killer—" Abby made it clear "—by allowing our personal relationship to interfere with your job as a cold case investigator." She would never put such pressure on him in what would be a major conflict of interest. No matter the strength of her feelings for him. Or vice versa.

"I know." Scott seemed to read her mind. "I feel the same way. Giving in to intimidation would be a big mistake," he stressed.

"I agree."

"Could be the unsub is just bluffing. Or not. Either way, you need to watch your back, Abby."

"I will," she promised, and thought about carrying pepper spray and being aware of her surroundings.

"I'll try to see if I can track down the sender of the text message," Scott said and took a breath. "In the meantime, I wouldn't want anything bad to happen to you."

"Neither would I." Abby felt the strong vibes between them. The last thing she could imagine was having her life cut short like her aunt's and, in the process, ending whatever she seemed to be building with Scott. A thought suddenly occurred to Abby that seemed worth mentioning. "This may or may not mean anything, but a couple of days ago when I was at the hospital for work, I thought I saw Zach Gilliard at the end of the corridor. Only, when I tried to verify this, he was gone. Then when driving to see you yesterday, I thought an SUV was following me."

Scott's brows knitted. "Why didn't you tell me?"

"Because when the SUV continued on after I exited the highway, I figured it was all in my head," she asserted. "Not worth bringing up. Probably still was nothing. Or maybe Zach is stalking me but trying to do so at a safe distance. I don't know."

"You're right. The SUV may not have been tailing you." He paused. "Or didn't want you to think so." Scott rested for a moment on that disturbing possibility. "As for Gilliard, as long as he stays away from you and hasn't threatened you verbally or physically in any identifiable way, there's not much we can do at the moment but stay alert."

"Okay." Abby sucked in a calming breath. "I'll be careful. But don't stop trying to find my aunt's killer. She deserves the chance to rest in peace."

"You're right, she does," Scott concurred. "And you deserve some closure and to get on with your life."

"True." She wondered how much of that life he would be a part of once the investigation had reached its conclusion.

After they disconnected, Abby went over in her mind everything they had talked about. Whatever happened from this point on, she was determined not to live her life in fear. Wasn't that something she tried to instill as a victim specialist in others? Besides, having Scott and the Bureau itself on her side made Abby feel that she had nothing to worry about. Or at least those worries shouldn't overwhelm her. Not when she suddenly had renewed optimism for what the future might hold.

Chapter Eleven

On Monday, Abby was at work when she got a call from the mayor's office, asking if she could meet with Mayor Myerson this afternoon. Of course, Abby jumped on this, figuring that the woman might have something useful to add to the ongoing investigation into the murder of Veronica Liu. In spite of the mayor's previous contention that their relationship had been limited.

With the possibility that her aunt's killer was now targeting Abby, she recognized that the sooner the unsub was exposed and brought to justice, the better.

At 1:00 p.m. sharp, Abby showed up as scheduled and was led into the office of Freda Myerson. The mayor was on the phone but got off swiftly and pasted a smile on her face. "Abby." She stood up and rounded her desk, putting out a hand. "Nice to see you again."

Abby smiled. "You too."

"Thanks for coming in."

"Thanks for inviting me," Abby said, restraining her curiosity.

"Have a seat," Freda told her, then asked, "Would you like some coffee or tea?"

Abby declined. "No thanks, I'm good."

"Okay." The mayor sat beside her in a fabric lounge chair near the window. "I ran into Jeanne Singletary over the weekend," she noted, a twinkle in her aquamarine eyes.

"You did?" Abby had come to believe they did not run in the same circles.

"Yes. We hadn't seen each other in a while, but given the reopening of the case into Veronica's death, it seemed like a good time to catch up." Freda sat back and regarded her thoughtfully. "How's the investigation progressing?"

Abby mused about this and Scott's efforts in cracking the case, before responding, "From what I understand, Agent Lynley is still reviewing old evidence and reinterviewing suspects. Not sure just how much progress has been made." Abby was certain, though, that Scott had managed to touch a nerve of quite possibly the unsub. That meant that Scott may have been closer to nailing the perp than met the eye.

"I see." Freda rested her hands in her lap. "Well, I want you to know that as mayor of Kolton Lake, I stand by my promise to offer assistance in any way I can to help the Bureau and Agent Lynley in their efforts to solve this twenty-year-old mystery."

"I appreciate that, Mayor Myerson," Abby said sincerely.

"Anyway, your name came up when chatting with Jeanne," she said casually.

"Did it?"

"Yes." Freda grinned. "We were talking about your work with the FBI as a victim specialist and how much you've given of your life to help others who have also been traumatized in one way or another." She paused. "Anyway, I thought that another way for you to honor Veronica's memory would be to join my Crime Victims Advisory Board."

Abby lifted a brow. "Really?"

"Yes, I think you'd make a great addition to the board, helping victims of violence and criminality in Kolton Lake transition to becoming survivors and pushing beyond their victimization in bettering their lives." Freda reached out and touched Abby's arm. "So, what do you say? Is this something you would be interested in?"

"Of course." Abby didn't need to take long to consider it, knowing that extending her ability to assist other victims of violent crime was a no-brainer. She was certain that the Bureau would approve of this additional role for her. "I'd be honored to become a member of your Crime Victims Advisory Board, Mayor Myerson."

"Terrific." Freda flashed her teeth. "And please call me Freda. We're all like family here, even if we could never replace your wonderful aunt Veronica."

Abby nodded gratefully. "Thank you."

"No, thank you, Abby." Freda patted her hand. "I'd say this position is long overdue for you, as I'm sure my predecessor as mayor would attest to."

After leaving the mayor's office, Abby rang Scott to share the exciting news. "You'll never guess who I just met with?"

"Hmm...don't keep me in suspense."

"Mayor Myerson," she told him, standing outside and zeroing in on a pair of northern cardinals flying by. "Or Freda, as she now insists that I call her."

"Did she remember something pertinent about your aunt?"

"Actually, the mayor wants me to join her Crime Victims Advisory Board."

"Is that so?"

Abby chuckled. "Yes, I was surprised too. Of course, I accepted."

"As you should have." Scott spoke supportively. "You can certainly do some good in spreading your reach as a victim advocate."

"My sentiments precisely." She switched the phone to her other ear. "Anything yet on who sent the text message?"

"Not yet." His voice dropped. "I'm working on it. I'll let you know what I come up with, if anything."

"All right."

"Be careful," Scott reiterated.

"I will," she promised and they said goodbye.

Heading to her car, Abby glanced over her shoulder, almost for effect. But more to see if there might have been a stalker or decades-old killer on the prowl. There was no one. She couldn't help but wonder if this was the calm before the storm. Or was the threat to her life being overblown?

Her thoughts moved in a more positive direction toward a new position with the mayor's Crime Victims Advisory Board and the good Abby believed she could do beyond her role with the Bureau in helping those most in need.

SCOTT CERTAINLY WELCOMED Abby having a role with Mayor Myerson's advisory board in assisting victims in getting over the hump. She had earned the right to be herself and spread her wings as Abby continued to use her skills with the Bureau. He was happy to have her in his life, as well, and could see nothing but good things ahead for them. But right now, his chief concern was tracking down whoever had sent him that text, while threatening Abby in the process.

Trying to interfere in an FBI cold case investigation wasn't the smartest thing. Yet the unsub had chosen to do just that, indicating to Scott the sense of urgency or panic felt for stopping the investigation cold before the truth emerged.

Well, that isn't going to happen, he vowed to himself, driving from his office to the Kentucky Regional Computer Forensics Laboratory on North Whittington Parkway. Not as long as he was on the case. He had promised Abby that he wouldn't stop until a killer had been identified. He owed it to her to see this through for more reasons than one. Not the least of which was that he cared for her and didn't want to come up short in giving Abby the peace of mind that was twenty years in the making.

After arriving at his destination, Scott headed inside and met with Margaret Kanoho, a digital evidence examiner. A native Hawaiian, Margaret was in her late thirties, slender, with black hair in a cropped pixie.

"Hello, Scott." She gazed at him with expectant brown eyes. "What do you need?"

"I need to track an anonymous text message I received," he responded, knowing this was a given the moment he received the disturbing text.

"Okay. Let's see what we can do." He handed her his cell phone and watched as she read the text out loud. "'Drop the Veronica Liu investigation. Otherwise, her niece Abby is next. Unless you want her death on your conscience, move on to another cold case.'"

"Someone is trying to put the brakes on my current investigation," Scott pointed out.

"I can see that." Margaret made a face. "Why don't we head over to the cell phone investigative kiosk, extract the data we can pull from the text, and put the info in a report and make a copy of it for your computer? Shouldn't take much more than thirty minutes or so."

"Okay." He gave a nod. "Let's do it."

Less than an hour later, Margaret said, "Not too surprisingly, it looks like the text came from a burner phone. We can trace the approximate location from where it was sent and see what other clues we can access. But my guess is, if the unsub was smart, he or she probably ditched the cell phone, making it that much harder to track down. Or the user."

"Figured as much." Scott's brow furrowed. "Still, why don't you dig deeper and maybe we'll get lucky."

"You've got it." She rubbed her nose. "I'll need some time, but will do some further forensic analysis of the data and let you know if I come up with anything more definitive."

"Thanks."

"If the anonymous texter is emboldened enough, the unsub will keep at it and make a mistake that can lead you right to the culprit's door," Margaret suggested.

"If that happens, I'll be ready to pounce," Scott clearly confirmed.

He left the RCFL and headed back to his office to further examine the data collected and cross-reference it with the info he had on earlier suspects to see if it triggered anything.

At 6:00 P.M., feeling the need to unwind, Abby got together with her friend Beverly Welch at Kolton Lake Park for a run. Sitting on the shores of Lake Kolton, the well-worn wide path was bordered by hickory and oak trees. Abby shared the news of her recent undertaking as they meandered their way along, passing other runners.

"Seriously?" Beverly widened her brown eyes. "It's wonderful that Mayor Myerson asked you to be part of her Crime Victims Advisory Board."

"I know, right?" Abby grinned in agreement. "Seems like the perfect complement to my duties with the FBI."

"Yeah, that's true. Just be sure you don't overwork yourself, so you don't have time to hang with your friends."

Abby laughed. "I'll always find time to hang with you, Bev," she promised.

"You better." Beverly gave her a warning look. "With a rambunctious ten-year-old running me ragged at times, I need my adult space with friends to maintain my sanity."

"I understand." Abby considered the possibility of becoming a mother herself someday, longing to have one or two children to run after day and night. She somehow found that to be much more inviting than a chore.

"Good. So, Ms. Advisory Board Member, what do you say we pick up some speed here and see who can reach the lake first?"

"You're on." Abby accepted the challenge, even as Beverly dashed ahead of her, momentarily leaving her in the dust.

Just as Abby started to pick up the pace, she heard another runner quickly approaching from behind. She felt herself being shoved to the ground, hitting it hard. Dazed, Abby heard a gruff male voice say, "Tell Agent Lynley to back off. Final warning!"

As she digested this ominous warning with the sounds of her attacker leaving, Abby saw a hooded, tall figure race off into the trees. Having had the wind knocked out of her, she struggled to get to her feet.

She was still wobbly when Beverly ran up to her and asked perceptively, while helping her to remain upright, "What happened?"

"I—I was attacked," Abby stammered.

"By who?"

Abby asked herself the same question. Was it Zach Gilliard? Or the unsub who'd sent Scott the text message? Could they have inexplicably been one and the same?

She pointed toward the woods in the direction the assailant had sprinted off, as though expecting him to still be within view.

Beverly peered. "I don't see anyone."

"Neither do I," Abby admitted. The person who had attacked her had vanished from sight completely.

As soon as he heard that Abby had been assaulted by someone in the park, Scott practically broke the speed limit driving to Kolton Lake. All kinds of thoughts raced through his head. Was this the work of the unsub who'd texted him? It appeared to be so, not just some random attack in the park.

Scott replayed the attacker's alarming words to Abby.

Tell Agent Lynley to back off. Final warning!

The unsub had clearly taken the threats to a whole new level after the text, as though Scott hadn't gotten the message. And that had turned into a direct physical threat to Abby's life. Or, at the very least, the unsub's way of demonstrating just what he was capable of, with Abby sure that she had been assaulted by a male attacker.

The one thing Scott knew for certain was that he couldn't bear the thought of losing Abby to violence. Not when they both suddenly had a lot more to live for in developing a bond that still needed to be explored over the course of time.

When he pulled into Abby's driveway, Scott saw her familiar vehicle and a gray Genesis G70 sedan. Exiting his SUV, he ran up to the log cabin, and the door was opened by Abby herself.

"Are you okay?" Scott asked her inside, disregarding her reassurances over the phone to that effect.

"I'm fine," she reiterated, forcing a smile. "Just a few minor aches and pains from being thrown to the ground."

Scott noted that she was still in her jogging

attire and looked a little ruffled, but otherwise was not the worse for wear. He gazed at the other person standing in the room.

"This is my friend Beverly Welch," Abby told him. "She was running just ahead of me when the attack occurred."

He acknowledged her. "Hey, Beverly."

"Hi."

"Scott's an FBI agent," Abby told her. "He's the one who reopened the cold case into my aunt Veronica's murder."

Beverly cocked a brow musingly. "Do you think this has something to do with that?" she asked him.

"Undoubtedly." Scott pondered the stark intimidation tactic sent to both of them and turned to Abby. "Did you get a good look at the attacker?"

"I'm afraid not." She sucked in a deep breath.

"What can you tell me about him?" he pressed.

"Only that he was tall, wore a hoodie and darkish clothing. It all happened so fast." Abby wrung her hands as she met Scott's steady gaze.

He angled his face. "Did the voice have any degree of familiarity?"

"Not really." She started at the question. "He seemed to be trying to disguise his voice by speaking in a raspy tone."

That didn't surprise Scott. All in all, the unsub was clearly going the extra mile to hide his identity. But this could only go so far. "Maybe surveillance video can help us identify him," he suggested.

"Maybe." Abby twisted her lips musingly. "Not sure if it makes any sense, with respect to Aunt Veronica's death and your investigation, but I think it could have been Zach Gilliard who attacked me."

Scott chewed on that unsettling thought as he got on his cell phone and asked that Gilliard be immediately brought in for questioning.

Chapter Twelve

Scott sat in an armless stacking chair, across a small metal table from Zach Gilliard, in an interrogation room at the FBI's Owensboro satellite office. He studied the unemployed warehouse worker, who Scott had previously decided was likely not a stalker in the true sense of the word for Abby to be concerned with. Had he misjudged Gilliard? Was he missing something about the man that could have linked him to the murder of Veronica Liu?

At forty-three, Zach Gilliard would have been twenty-three when Abby's aunt had been killed. That was certainly old enough for him to have targeted her. If so, why? And how had he managed to avoid a criminal record void of violence? Or other acts of aggression?

As though he hadn't a clue, Gilliard narrowed his eyes and asked, "Mind telling me what I'm doing here?"

Scott jutted his chin and snapped straightforwardly, "Two hours ago, Abby Zhang was attacked in Kolton Lake Park. Know anything about that?"

"Abby?" Gilliard wrinkled his forehead. "The victim specialist?"

"I think you know who she is," Scott said tartly. "Answer the question."

"I have no idea what you're talking about," he claimed. "I'm sorry someone attacked Abby. I hope she wasn't hurt badly, but I had nothing to do with it."

Scott peered at him. "Where were you at that time?"

"I was at work," the suspect said matter-of-factly.

Scott was dubious. "And where is work exactly?"

"Octalinn Industries, here in Owensboro, on East Second Street," he answered calmly. "I was hired two days ago as a forklift operator. Worked till 7:30 p.m. You can check with my supervisor, Genevieve Plunkett."

"I'll do that," Scott told him, making a note. He stared at him for a long moment, then asked curiously, "Did you live in the area twenty years ago?"

Gilliard leaned back, pensive. "Twenty years ago, I was living in New York City," he claimed. "Why do you ask?"

Scott ignored the question while thinking that should be easy enough to verify. "Does the name Veronica Liu mean anything to you?"

"No," Gilliard responded without preface. "Why should it?"

"No reason." Scott stood. "Hold tight for just a few minutes."

When he returned to the interrogation room, it was with the knowledge that Gilliard's alibi did check out. He wasn't the one who had attacked Abby. Scott could understand how she may have made that assumption, given Gilliard's penchant for apparently hanging around where he wasn't wanted. Not to mention the heat of the moment in not seeing the unsub's face, but in determining he was apparently of similar size. Hell, even the clothing Gilliard was wearing was not unlike what Abby had described of the attacker.

Yet Zach Gilliard clearly isn't our culprit. Scott eyed him at the table. "Your alibi held up."

Gilliard flashed a triumphant expression. "Am I free to go?"

"Just about." While he had the man's attention, Scott figured he may as well get some mileage out of this. Especially when considering that Gilliard may have still been stalking Abby after she'd thought she'd seen him lurking around at the hospital. Scott leaned forward and told him in no uncertain tone, "Stay away from Abby Zhang. I get that she helped you deal with an uncomfortable situation. That's her job. But now you need to leave Ms. Zhang alone. Am I making myself clear?"

"Yeah." Gilliard lowered his chin. "Don't worry. I won't be bothering Abby anymore."

"Good."

Scott sighed, sure he received the intended message, loud and clear. He gave Gilliard permission to leave, feeling that with the understanding between them where Abby was concerned, it was one less headache to deal with. But there was still the attack on Abby. With Gilliard no longer a suspect, it meant that the unsub was still on the loose and doing whatever he could to impede the cold case investigation. Meaning that Abby was still a target for as long as the case was active.

THAT NIGHT, Abby was still a little shaken at the thought of someone attacking her at Kolton Lake Park. All in a brazen attempt to dissuade Scott from getting to the bottom of her aunt Veronica's death. The fact that it wasn't Zach Gilliard was somewhat of a relief. Having someone you only wanted to help become dangerously fixated on you was nothing any victim spe-

cialist would wish for. But at least Zach was a
known entity that could have been dealt with
accordingly.

Not so much for an unsub she couldn't identify. *If only I'd been able to get a better look
at him*, Abby told herself, feeling restless lying
beside Scott, who was sound asleep. But then
again, the attacker's intent had obviously been
to rattle her while camouflaging his identity.
Meaning Scott would need more time to unravel the mystery, even while being quite understandably concerned for her safety. As she was.
This notwithstanding, though, she wouldn't be
bullied into asking him to back off the case and
leave her aunt Veronica in limbo for another
two decades.

No, if someone wished to come after her,
Abby intended to do her best to ward off an attacker. At least to slow him down enough for
the cavalry to come to the rescue. In this instance, very likely, in the form of Scott Lynley.
His interest in her had clearly moved beyond
an intimate connection. Or her being a gate-
way to the murder of her aunt Veronica. As had
Abby's interest in the FBI special agent risen
a few notches of late. Just how far they could
climb this mountain played on her mind. And,
if the truth be told, her heart, which was skip-

ping beats more and more as it related to her growing affections for Scott.

Abby fell asleep in his arms while wishing the aunt she had lost twenty years ago was still around to be there as Abby worked toward her own future.

"HAVE YOU EVER been hypnotized?" Scott asked Abby the next morning as they sat across from one another in a booth at the Kolton Lake Breakfast House on Larameer Lane. After the attack on her yesterday, he found himself wanting to stay by Abby's side 24/7. Yet he knew that was neither practical nor achievable, no matter his concern for her safety, given that they both had jobs that demanded their attention. Not to mention, he doubted that Abby would agree to his being her bodyguard, coming at the expense of the investigation into her aunt's murder. Right now, Scott believed that the best thing he could do for Abby was double down and solve the two-decades-old homicide. And not allow a current unsub, and presumably Veronica Liu's killer, to derail him. But to do that, Scott knew he would need Abby's help in a way neither had anticipated with, admittedly, an unpredictable outcome.

"Hypnotized?" Abby's eyes grew as she gripped her mug of coffee. "No. I'm not even sure I subscribe to the notion of hypnotizing, per se." She gazed at him inquiringly. "Why do you ask?"

Scott sat back. "Well, I was thinking that it might be a good idea if you were to see a forensic psychologist the Bureau works with. She specializes in hypnosis," he told her, glancing at his ham and cheese omelet. "And yes, it does work, when done by a qualified professional. In this instance, it could help you recall more details about the person—or animal—you saw moving quickly through the woods."

Abby pursed her lips. "You really think I could remember something that I never truly was able to home in on that day?" she questioned, and tasted the coffee.

"You'd be surprised what we can retain in our day-to-day encounters, observations, experiences and the like," he told her. "Most times, it's irrelevant. Other times, though, it could be critical to uncovering evidence of a crime, details on an unsub and more. Many skilled forensic psychologists have been successful over the years in pulling out such hidden memories from a subject's subconscious. I think it may be worth taking a shot here to see if it reveals anything useful to the investigation. No matter how small. Moreover, I'm sensing that whoever killed Veronica Liu is likely the same unsub who attacked you and is feeling very threatened by the investigation and being exposed. This could be a way to bridge the twenty-year gap and get the jump on the unsub before he can try to come after you again."

"You're right," Abby allowed, and bit into a piece of avocado toast. "I want this to be over. If you believe hypnosis might bring us closer to the truth, then I'm in."

Scott gave a pleased nod. "Good. I'll set it up." He sliced his fork into the omelet. "Whatever happens, I'll be there for support."

She smiled. "I was counting on that."

He grinned back and knew instinctively that, no matter what, he intended to be there for her beyond the case that had brought them together. As far as he was concerned, Abby was a keeper, and so was he for the right person, believing she was that for him.

ABBY WAS ADMITTEDLY a little nervous about the notion of being put under by a psychologist, hypnotist or whatever. Even if she was somewhat skeptical of the whole process, she had actually read about hypnotherapy and some people who were apparently successfully hypnotized for everything from weight loss to trying to stop smoking. And yes, for unlocking repressed memories from childhood traumas. But in her case, she wasn't holding on to things too painful to remember. In her mind, the memories of that tragic day were still pretty clear. Whatever she'd seen in the woods was not something she was hiding from, like a boogeyman. But rather something that had caught her eye at a cursory glance. She'd never pinned it to memory beyond the vague image that whizzed by.

Or had she locked away something that a forensic psychologist could indeed bring to the surface? And, in the process, help Scott nail a killer still on the prowl?

When they entered the Rutherford Building on East Main Street in downtown Louisville that afternoon, Abby had calmed her nerves, deciding she would be a big girl in continuing to do what she could to recall anything that could provide clues in the cruel murder of her aunt Veronica. If all else failed, it was surely another bonding experience of sorts with Scott.

On the fifth floor, they got off the elevator and stood outside the door of Dr. Rosalind Jimenez, a licensed clinical psychologist.

Scott took Abby's hands, steadying her as he said comfortingly, "You'll be fine."

She nodded and took a breath. "Let's do this."

Inside the office, they were greeted by a petite and slender Latina in her early forties, with brown eyes and blond hair in a shoulder-length cut and choppy bangs. She was stylishly dressed in an ivory skirt suit and designer sandals.

"I'm Dr. Jimenez," she introduced herself to Abby.

She shook the psychologist's hand. "Abby Zhang."

Rosalind faced Scott. "Nice to see you again, Agent Lynley."

"You too." He gave her a thin smile. "Thanks for seeing us on short notice."

"Happy to fit you in," she said, eyeing Abby. "I hope I can help you discover something long-buried that may be beneficial to Agent Lynley's investigation."

"Me too," Abby told her.

After Scott had settled in a separate viewing room to watch the session on a video screen, with Abby's permission, she went with Dr. Jimenez to the therapy room, noting that it looked more like a living room setting with its contemporary furnishings and native plants strategically placed to, Abby assumed, help patients feel relaxed.

After a brief explanation for how this worked, Abby lay on a quilted recliner chair, while the doctor took a seat nearby in an upholstered wingback chair.

It seemed to take only moments before Abby

was in a relaxed state and found herself in a trip back in time to when she was twelve years old.

"Tell me what happened when you first got off the school bus," Rosalind said.

Abby took a breath and uttered, "I waved goodbye to my friends and walked to my aunt Veronica's log cabin, a block away."

"Did you see anyone else at that point?"

"No."

"What happened then?" the psychologist asked.

"I saw Aunt Veronica's car in the driveway," Abby responded. "I could see that she was inside."

"What did you do then?"

"I walked over to the car and... I saw her sitting motionless behind the steering wheel." Abby sucked in a deep breath. "There was blood on my aunt's face," she cried. "Lots of it."

Rosalind said to her in a gentle tone, "I know that's difficult to see, Abby, so let's move on. Turn away from your aunt and look toward the woods." She paused. "Are you doing that?"

"Yes." Abby focused on the wooded area. "I see the trees."

"What else do you see in the woods, Abby?" she asked. "Is there someone out there? Take your time..."

Studying the woods, Abby sighed and replied, "There is something out there. Moving fast."

"It is a human or animal?" the psychologist asked.

"Human," she answered positively.

"Can you tell if the person is a man or woman?"

Abby peered through the deep recesses of her mind while zeroing in as best she could on the subject. "Looks like a man," she uttered, her voice lifted an octave.

"What can you tell me about him?" Rosalind pressed.

"Can't see much of him through the trees." Abby strained to gather more information. "Tall and... I think he might have glanced back at me..." Her voice shook. "I think he may have killed Aunt Veronica—"

"Try not to think about that part," the psychologist stressed evenly. "Concentrate again on this man and see if you can describe anything he's wearing."

"Dark pants," Abby said after a moment or two, then added, "He's got on a bright red windbreaker with the hood over his head." She made a strange sound. "He's gone now. Can't see him anymore."

"That's fine," Rosalind told her. "I'm going to bring you out of this and back to the present."

"Okay." Abby heard numbers being counted backward and it seemed as though she was passing through a time machine of sorts before suddenly opening her eyes. She was slightly disoriented, momentarily, as she sat up, while focusing on the forensic psychologist. "How did I do?"

Rosalind's eyes crinkled at the corners. "You did good, Abby. I think the memories we unlocked may prove useful to Agent Lynley."

"Really?" Abby could only vaguely recall what she'd seen and said.

"Yeah, you've given us more to work with in the investigation," Scott said matter-of-factly after walking into the room. He glanced at Rosalind. "Thanks for helping Abby to see some critical details of her experience that got lost in the corridors of time."

"It was my pleasure," she told him coolly. "Not to mention, my job as a clinical psychologist. Hope you're able to solve the case you're working on."

"And that's my job," he responded with confidence in his inflection. "We'll get it done."

Abby watched him as Scott met her eyes warmly and seemed to indicate that there was, indeed, light at the end of the tunnel that they both would soon be able to bask in.

Chapter Thirteen

"Call it a hunch," Scott told Abby as they headed back to Kolton Lake after the hypnosis session with Dr. Rosalind Jimenez. "The fact that while under hypnosis you felt you did see an adult male running through the woods and he appeared to have seen you, tells me that the unsub may see you as not simply a means to get me to drop the investigation by bloodline, but as a direct threat to identifying him."

"Seriously?" Abby shifted in the passenger seat. "But I didn't truly see his face in a way where I could point him out in a lineup or anything."

"But he doesn't know that," Scott surmised from behind the wheel. "Yes, the distance between you at the time would make such an identification highly unlikely. However, the unsub may feel he can't afford to take that chance. Hence the threats and attack on you, as we draw nearer to fingering him, one way or another."

"So, how will we go about doing that?" she queried. "The unsub still seems to be holding some of the key cards, at least in terms of getting to him and making an arrest."

"Well, I'm not much of a card player," Scott quipped, "but I'm more than capable of playing the hand I've been dealt. In this case, clothing you believe the unsub was wearing could provide some important clues about him."

"Such as?"

"Such as if the unsub did have on a bright red windbreaker, something that stands out, it's possible someone may remember a person with such a jacket."

Abby blinked. "I suppose."

Scott sat back. "Based on the nature of the attack, with robbery being ruled out more or less, my guess is that the unsub knew your aunt. Either on a personal level or work-related. In both cases, one person may be best positioned to speak to this, in terms of the red jacket he wore."

"Who?" Abby eyed him curiously.

"Your aunt's best friend and business partner," Scott said, ruminating. "Jeanne Singletary."

ABBY WAS ADMITTEDLY piqued as she and Scott drove to Singletary Realty. It seemed like a long shot at best that Jeanne would remember two decades later what she'd even worn back then on a given day. *Much less someone who knew my aunt Veronica*, Abby thought pessimistically. But there was always the possibility. She was open to anything that might assist Scott in breaking the case. As it was, Abby was still coming to grips with memories she'd never known were there being brought to the surface. She had seen someone, who had apparently seen her. And was willing to do whatever it took to silence her, while keeping her aunt's murder mystery just that.

When they entered the office, Jeanne was standing, holding a mug of coffee. She smiled. "Abby." And gazed through her glasses at Scott. "Agent Lynley."

Abby accepted her hug. "Hi, Jeanne."

After Scott acknowledged her, Jeanne eyed Abby and said, "I understand that you've accepted a role with Freda Myerson's Crime Victims Advisory Board."

"I have," she told her, remembering that the mayor had spoken with Jeanne before making the offer. "Seems like a good thing."

Jeanne grinned. "I couldn't agree more. You'll make a great asset to the board and I know that Veronica would approve."

"I think so too," Abby agreed maudlinly.

Jeanne shifted her eyes from one to the other

before landing solidly on Scott, and asked, "Do you have news on the investigation?"

"Yes," he responded equably. "Yesterday, someone attacked Abby at Kolton Lake Park."

"What?" Jeanne's brow wrinkled. She turned to Abby. "Were you hurt?"

"No," she told her. "Just a couple of bruises, and I had the wind knocked out of me."

"And you think this had something to do with your case?" Jeanne asked Scott.

"Yes. I was warned to close the case or Abby would be next." He spoke bluntly. "Then, in apparently following through on this, someone came after her in the park. Unfortunately, Abby didn't get a clear look at the attacker."

"I'm so glad you weren't seriously injured," Jeanne told her. "The fact that this person would go after your aunt and continue this pattern of violence against you twenty years later is sickening."

"Tell me about it." Abby wrinkled her nose. "We need to stop this."

Jeanne nodded. "I agree." Her cell phone rang but she ignored it. "Is there anything I can do to help?"

Scott lowered his chin and said, "As a matter of fact, there may be." He paused. "Abby went under hypnosis to see if she could remember anything relevant the day Veronica Liu was murdered."

"Really?" Jeanne put a hand on Abby's shoulder. "Did this trigger any memories?"

Abby waited a beat and answered unevenly, "I remembered there was a man running off into the woods, presumably away from the car where Aunt Veronica lay mortally wounded."

Jeanne's lower lip hung in shock. "Can you identify him?"

"No, he was too far away," Abby replied, disappointed that her twelve-year-old self had not been closer and more fixated on the man in the woods.

"What she did remember was that the unsub was wearing a bright red hooded windbreaker," Scott said. "I know it's been years, but do you happen to recall anyone in Veronica Liu's professional or social circles who may have worn such a jacket at that time?"

"Actually, I think I do." She pushed her glasses up pensively. "Oliver Dillman had a jacket matching that very description."

Scott glanced at Abby. "Your former employee?"

"Yes, that's the one," Jeanne stated. "I remember thinking that it stood out. I told him once, and he just brushed it off." She sighed. "Or maybe not. It seemed like, at one point, he did stop wearing the jacket. Come to think of it, it may have been after Veronica was killed."

Abby caught Scott's gaze, prompting her to say, "Maybe there was some symmetry there." She tried to picture if the shadowy male figure she'd seen in the woods that day two decades ago was, in fact, Oliver Dillman. Or, for that matter, the man who'd attacked her a day ago. She couldn't positively identify him for either crime. But the pieces did seem to fit. "If Oliver did kill Aunt Veronica while wearing that red jacket, it would stand to reason that he'd want to get rid of it as evidence in a crime, along with the murder weapon."

"I was thinking the same thing," Scott told her.

"That bastard." Jeanne squinted her eyes. "I sensed he was trouble way back when. But didn't have anything to go on that would hold up."

"It's not your fault." Abby made it clear, knowing that she had voiced her suspicions back then. If guilty, the man had pulled the wool over everyone's eyes, including law enforcement. "We can only speculate at this point."

"It may be a little more than speculation," Scott said contemplatively.

"So, are you going to arrest him?" Jeanne asked anxiously, hand firmly on her hip.

"Afraid it's not quite that simple," he responded, pursing his lips. "To make an arrest that sticks, we'll need more than a distant memory of a bright red hooded jacket that Dillman has long gotten rid of to nail him, if he's the unsub." Scott exhaled. "But it is an important step in the right direction."

In Abby's mind, that step would have to do till they were sure that Oliver Dillman was responsible for her aunt Veronica's murder. Until such time, she needed to be on guard and let the Bureau do its job with Scott in full pursuit of justice.

THE FOLLOWING DAY, Scott was in his office. He had just gotten off the phone with Elodie Zimbalist, the FBI agent he had assigned to Abby's protection while her life was being threatened in connection with the Veronica Liu cold case investigation. Believing that the two women could actually end up as friends, Scott was confident that Agent Zimbalist, a fifteen-year veteran of the Bureau and wife of a federal air marshal, would keep Abby safe with a killer at large.

Scott now believed the unsub could well be, after all, Oliver Dillman, the fifty-eight-year-old real estate agent who'd been spurned by Veronica twenty years ago and apparently hadn't taken it very well. It made Scott wonder how he'd misread the man previously, if true. At least the timing and circumstantial evidence seemed to fit. Not to mention, the vague description of the unsub who'd attacked Abby could have been Dillman. But the fact remained that he had an alibi for Veronica Liu's death and had been dismissed by the original investigators on the case as a strong suspect, if one at all.

Had they missed a crucial clue in the red windbreaker? Or in the nature and potential of stalker violence? Had Dillman been tested for gunshot residue? Could he have had the time to go to the cabin then successfully get far enough away from it to convince the authorities that he couldn't have been in two places at once?

Scott went to his laptop for an update on the forensic evidence in the Veronica Liu murder being retested by the FBI Laboratory. The hope was that their efforts might yield results that could tie the cold case to Oliver Dillman. Or provide a legal justification for compelling him to submit DNA and fingerprints as potential evidence in a homicide.

Appearing on the screen for a video chat was Madeline McAuliffe. The thirtysomething forensic firearms analyst had dark hair in a short shag and blue eyes. She gave him a nod. "Agent Lynley."

"Hello." He got right to it. "Have you come up with anything on the .38 Special used in the killing of Veronica Liu?" he asked succinctly.

"Yes and no," Madeline said, running a hand through her hair. "As you know, the cartridge removed from the victim and the casing found at the crime scene were a match. Regarding the ammo itself, further testing showed this was fired from a gun barrel with four lands and grooves and had a right-hand twist." She paused. "We reentered the evidence of the cartridge casing into the NIBIN's identification system but, thus far, haven't come back with a hit."

"Okay." Scott wasn't particularly surprised with this, given the length of time that had passed since the homicide. Still, he'd held out hope that the murder weapon was still around. "What about the Colt Python .357 Magnum revolver used to commit the crime?"

"Nothing there." Madeline frowned. "The database has drawn a blank on the firearm being used in any other shootings. But hey, it's not out of the realm of possibility that the murder weapon will eventually show up and we can use the ATF's National Tracing Center to get all the info we can in tracing it to the unsub."

"Yeah." Scott went with that, knowing that time wasn't on their side in terms of getting some solid evidence that could tie Oliver Dill-man to the heartless murder of Veronica Liu, before he got desperate enough to take another crack at Abby. Even in the capable hands of Agent Zimbalist, Scott did not wish to leave Dillman's possible deadly intentions to chance, if he could help it.

ELODIE ZIMBALIST WAS attractive and in her early thirties, like Abby. She regarded the slender, blue-eyed FBI agent, who had midlength sandy hair with a middle part, as they sat across the table from each other for lunch at Cheryl's Café on Frederica Street, near Smothers Park and Abby's office in Owensboro. When Scott had told her she would be given a bodyguard, Abby hadn't balked at the idea. If Oliver Dill-man truly was out to get her as someone who he thought could identify him as her aunt Ve-ronica's killer, Abby wasn't about to refuse pro-tection and unnecessarily place herself in the line of fire.

On the contrary, she welcomed having the FBI agent shadowing her every move, mak-ing sure Abby didn't fall prey to the worries of a man who may have felt he had nothing to lose and everything to gain in seeing her dead. Besides that, Elodie, who had insisted she be called by her first name, seemed affable enough to Abby. She'd learned, in fact, that she and the agent had both graduated from the University of Kentucky and were both lifelong fans of the Kentucky Wildcats football team.

Abby found herself envious that Elodie was happily married, knowing matrimony was something she had yet to experience. Maybe this would forever elude her. Or maybe Scott was the husband material she thought him to be. She was willing to wait him out, if this was truly the direction they were headed.

"So, what's it like to work for the Bureau as a victim specialist?" Elodie broke her reverie while holding a cheesesteak sandwich. "As an agent, I see cases more from a law enforcement perspective."

Abby suspected that this was more casual conversation than anything, but was happy to engage. "Oh, it's often challenging and puts me in various scenarios where victims need immediate assistance, to one degree or another." She nibbled on her tuna sandwich. "Definitely keeps me on my toes."

Elodie smiled. "I'll bet."

"What about you?" Abby asked, dabbing a napkin to her lips. "I take it that security detail isn't your usual assignment?"

"No, it isn't." She laughed. "It is required from time to time, such as now, when someone involved in a federal investigation is a potential target. Mostly, though, I'm involved with gathering intel, making arrests, executing search warrants and, of course, the dreaded paperwork."

"Oh, yes." Abby chuckled. "I can certainly relate to the paperwork drudgery."

Both laughed again and Abby found herself even more relaxed with Elodie Zimbalist, in spite of knowing they'd been brought together because of a cold case that was suddenly beginning to heat up in ways that threatened to blow it wide open.

With Abby caught directly in the center of it.

Chapter Fourteen

That afternoon, Scott turned his attention to the scientific reanalysis of the latent print and DNA evidence found at the crime scene, in and outside of Veronica's Liu's Mercedes-Benz the day she was murdered. With the advances in forensic technology over the past two decades, he hoped they might be able to shed new light on an old crime. He was on a Skype three-way video call with the FBI crime lab's Latent Print Unit's forensic examiner Matt D'Angelo and the Federal DNA Database Unit's laboratory scientist Kay Nakata.

Scott gazed at D'Angelo, who was in his thirties, with dark hair in a pompadour cut, a corporate beard and gray eyes, and said to him, "Anything on the partial print?"

"Yeah, got something for you," he responded. "Using our advanced chemical processing methods and state-of-the-art equipment, we were able to conduct friction ridge analysis on the latent print to determine that it belongs to the unidentified person's left index finger. An important clue when trying to nail the perp."

Scott concurred, which begged the next question. "Were you able to come up with anything from the Next Generation Identification system?" he asked, referring to the FBI's fingerprint database.

D'Angelo scratched his beard. "Well, we've compared the latent print to millions of known prints identifiable in the system's holdings. Unfortunately, we have yet to get a hit. Afraid your unsub may have managed to lay low in avoiding arrest and the taking of finger and palm prints that could be matched with the latent fingerprint."

"Yeah, appears that way." Scott made a face when pondering his current top person of interest. He turned his attention to lab tech Kay Nakata. She, too, was in her thirties, and narrow-faced, with long frizzy brunette hair and hazel eyes. "How are we looking with the unidentified DNA profile?"

Kay smiled when she replied, "We can now confirm that, when retested, the DNA submission is definitely that of an unidentified male DNA profile."

Scott nodded to that effect, which could mean that it belonged to the unsub. Or, in this instance, the one he did now suspect of having perpetrated the murder.

Oliver Dillman.

"I don't suppose you were able to get a hit on the DNA profile through the national DNA index system?" Scott asked her, regarding this arm of the Bureau's Combined DNA Index System.

Kay lost the smile and responded wanly, "Wish I had good news on that front. Thus far, there are no hits on CODIS's arrestee or convicted offender indices or forensic index. As Matt indicated, seems as though your unsub has kept his nose clean for years, or has gone underground. Thereby circumventing the system to his benefit."

Scott bristled at the notion. "Now that I've reopened the case, I have a strong suspicion that the unsub has resurfaced and may be targeting a witness, Abby Zhang." *Who has become so much more to me*, he thought honestly. "I just need to connect the dots and see if they can stick."

"We'll keep pushing to try and make this happen, Agent Lynley," Matt told him.

"Thanks, Matt." Scott sat back. "I'll take what I can get."

Kay leaned forward. "You know, it may or may not be a long shot, but in coming up empty with CODIS, you could try going the investigative genetic genealogy route in trying to track down the unsub behind the unidentified DNA profile."

"I'm way ahead of you there, Kay." Scott lifted his chin musingly. "I've already reached out to KentuckyFam, the nonprofit Lexington-based genetic genealogy database service, to try and see if they can assist in this investigation, even while you continue to find matches."

Kay smiled. "Smart thinking. If they can make a connection at all, KentuckyFam will provide some leads that may yield some positive results. In the meantime, as you say, we'll stick to what we're doing, and maybe hit the jackpot."

"Okay," Scott said and ended the three-way conversation. He sat back in his desk chair and contemplated working with the genetic genealogy firm in seeking answers. Having gone down this road before, the results had been mixed. But all things considered, using KentuckyFam, a take on the Kentucky ancestral family tree, was a worthwhile avenue to pin down a killer who was still on the prowl. And apparently going after Abby to keep his deadly secret.

Though Scott wanted nothing more than to haul in Oliver Dillman, if for no other reason than as a suspect in the attack on Abby, doing so prematurely might jeopardize the possible case against the man for the murder of Veronica Liu. The last thing Scott needed was to spook Dillman into skipping town. Or to have the case fall apart due to lack of evidence. Thereby risking it remaining a cold case forever.

What would that do to my growing relationship with Abby, if this was to hang over us like a cumulus cloud? Scott couldn't help but wonder as he rose. He wanted them to work. Maybe more than anything he'd wanted in recent memory. But he didn't want to see Abby left hanging, with her beloved aunt's murder investigation still unfinished business. Not if he could do something about it that would be good for both of them.

CYNTHIA SALAZAR, a forensic genetic genealogist with KentuckyFam, relished the opportunity to work with the FBI in tackling the cold case homicide involving the death of thirty-one-year-old Veronica Liu. She understood that two decades had gone by since the homicide and most other efforts to track down the perpetrator had fallen short. But this was what KentuckyFam excelled at. Having been fairly successful with investigative genetic genealogy in criminal forensic investigations over the years, Cynthia truly believed they could lend a helping hand to the case.

The twenty-nine-year-old single mother-to-be sat in a midback-padded chair with armrests at her ergonomic desk, pondering the opportunistic task before her. According to FBI Special Agent Scott Lynley, his chief suspect in the murder of Veronica Liu was a fifty-eight-year-old man named Oliver Dillman. Problem was, in spite of irrefutable and indirect evidence tying him to the victim in one manner or another, Dillman's DNA was not in the CODIS database. Meaning that it could not be matched with the unidentified male profile found at the crime scene.

This was where Cynthia and Kentucky-Fam came in. Through genome sequencing, they could develop a genealogical profile from the DNA of the unknown male by analyzing identity-by-descent, matching DNA segments to show shared ancestries. With millions of genetic profiles that were readily accessible through genealogy databases, in her way of thinking, in combing through the genetic branches of the family tree, she stood a good chance of finding distant relatives of the unsub. This could go a long way in helping Agent Lynley to zoom in on his person of interest in the murder, especially when combined with demographic identifiers related to the chief suspect.

Now was the time to put her skills to the test, Cynthia believed. If the unidentified crime scene male DNA profile belonged to Oliver Dillman, she would need to give the Bureau a major reason to pursue this angle in the investigation. The rest would be up to the handsome special agent working the case.

THAT EVENING, Abby agreed to an overnight stay at Scott's ranch, with the cold case investigator temporarily relieving Agent Zimbalist of her duties. Though Abby enjoyed Elodie's company and saw her as a new friend, she welcomed spending more time with Scott. In spite of the tension in the air now that they appeared to be closing in on her aunt Veronica's killer but had yet to make the case against Oliver Dillman official.

After ordering Chinese takeout of moo goo gai pan and egg drop soup, they ate in the dining room.

Sitting across the solid wood trestle dining table from Scott in a cross-back side chair, Abby gazed at him and asked curiously, "Do you really think that forensic genetic genealogy might be the key to solving the murder of my aunt Veronica?"

"Perhaps." He forked some food. "Not a perfect science, but it's worked in the past to solve a number of big cold cases. If we can tie the DNA evidence from the crime scene to Oliver Dillman's familial line of DNA, we can compel Dillman to submit his own DNA for comparison with the unidentified male DNA profile. Especially given the work connection between Dillman and your aunt and her rejecting his advances, to go along with his owning at the time a red jacket much like the one you saw a man wearing while under hypnosis. Dillman also fit the general physical description of the man who attacked you at the park."

"That does make for a compelling argument," Abby had to admit as she spooned her soup and pictured Oliver Dillman, whom she recalled seeing once or twice when accompanying her aunt Veronica to the real estate office. She had not seen him in the present day in which she could identify him conclusively. "Evidently, someone wants this investigation shut down. But what if it wasn't Dillman who came after me and threatened us both? After all, my initial belief was that the unsub may have been Zach Gilliard. That didn't exactly pan out. Maybe the hypnosis led to false memories."

"I doubt that." Scott regarded her intently.

"The fact that you were able to describe a bright red windbreaker with a hood that just happened to match one Dillman owned at the time, according to Jeanne Singletary, strikes me as much more than pure coincidence. Combine that with the other elements that lend themselves to Dillman being a serious suspect and the contentions here simply cannot be ignored."

"You're right." She met his gaze and put a fork to the moo goo gai pan. Coincidences and criminality did not typically go hand in hand. "Seems like Oliver Dillman has some major explaining to do, if totally innocent, past and present. But would he really shoot my aunt to death merely because she rejected him?"

"Wouldn't be the first time that's happened," Scott replied matter-of-factly, sitting back. "Some people refuse to take no for an answer and turn rejection into a personal affront that could lead to deadly consequences. Beyond that, Dillman and Veronica worked together and there could have been some animosity there on Dillman's part that caused him to lose it in targeting her. And then you, two decades later, for fear of recognizing him when the investigation got too close. We won't know for sure till we see if the pieces fit into place and can bring him in."

"Okay." Abby drank water thoughtfully. "I'd just like it over, one way or the other."

"It will be soon, I promise," Scott said in a way that made her believe him.

"And what about us?" She threw it out there, feeling the need to. "Where do you see things going?" *I may as well lay it on the line*, Abby told herself, wanting to know if there was a future between them. Or was it all in her head?

He looked her right in the eye and answered without prelude. "I see them going as far as we can take what we've been given." Scott tilted his face. "I'm into you, Abby, and want nothing more than to let things play out between us, with no holding back."

She swallowed thickly. "I feel the same way."

He grinned, leaned over, kissed her as though to prove a point and uttered smoothly, "Good."

Abby flashed her teeth, feeling a tingle of excitement. She believed that no matter the outcome in the cold case investigation, things between them gave her real reason for optimism. Something that had eluded her when it came to relationships in the past. Scott had proved to be cut from an entirely different cloth. She was seeing that more and more with each passing day.

And found herself giving back as much, accordingly.

THE FOLLOWING MORNING, Scott saddled up the horses and they went riding. Abby seemed almost as much a natural on the American Cream Draft horse as he was on his Thoroughbred. He saw that as another sign they truly were on the same wavelength. As last night would attest to when they'd made love like there was no tomorrow. Of course, he believed there would be many more days ahead for them to cultivate what they had started. He wasn't about to allow Oliver Dillman or any other unsub to come between him and Abby, preventing them from giving themselves the opportunity to find the lasting love they both so richly deserved.

"It's breathtaking out here," Abby commented as they rode across rolling hills.

"I agree." Scott smiled, thinking of how cute she looked wearing Annette's cowgirl hat. If he had his way, one day she would be riding with a hat of her very own. "But if the truth be told, you take my breath away even more."

She giggled, blushing. "Ever the charmer."

"Is it working?" he teased her.

"I'll let you figure that one out all on your own."

Scott laughed. "I'll take that as a yes."

"Smart man." She beamed. "Race you back to the barn."

"You're on." He loved this playful side of her,

probably as much as the other qualities that made Abby the woman she was. "But don't take it too personally if I win."

"I won't, if you don't," she quipped, and took off.

Scott gave her a generous head start before directing his horse, Sammie, to go after Abby, while pushing away for the moment the cold case that continued to be a thorn in their sides.

Chapter Fifteen

Two days later, Scott was in his office when he received a video call from Cynthia Salazar.

He accepted and gazed on the laptop at the KentuckyFam forensic genetic genealogist whose short dark brown hair had light blond balayage ombré highlights. "Hey," he said.

"Hi, Agent Lynley." Cynthia fixed him with green eyes behind geometric gold glasses. "I have news for you."

He sat back. "I'm listening."

"Okay." She took a breath. "Utilizing information you gave me, I was able to construct a genealogical profile of the crime scene unknown male DNA profile," she said evenly. "Turns out there was a rather large family tree with DNA submitted to genealogy databases that corresponded with the unknown suspect's DNA. It resulted in a very close DNA match with a man named Walter Dillman, who gave his saliva to a genealogy project. I did some digging and learned that, though Mr. Dillman died twelve years ago, he did have a son…"

"Oliver Dillman," Scott guessed.

"Bingo!" Cynthia's face lit up. "Though your murder suspect has never used a genealogy service, he might as well have," she argued. "Given the other correlates you have on him, I'm betting that once you get his DNA, it will be a match with the unknown male DNA profile from the car at the crime scene."

Scott grinned. "I have a feeling you're right," he stated instinctively. "Send me everything you have and more!"

"Will do."

"Good work, Cynthia."

She blushed. "I love my job and being able to assist in cold case criminal investigations. Hopefully, this can lead to an arrest and conviction of Veronica Liu's murderer, Agent Lynley."

"I'll let you know how it works out," he told her and said goodbye.

When Scott presented his case half an hour later to Diane Huggett, the assistant special agent in charge in the Louisville field office, he was practically bursting at the seams in his desire to compel Oliver Dillman to submit a DNA sample. And, in the process, almost certainly linking it to the DNA an unsub left behind at the crime scene, before or after Veronica Liu was shot to death.

"All the signs point toward this guy," Scott insisted, standing on the opposite side of his boss's credenza desk. "Dillman's got guilt written all over him. Including a strong likelihood that he is the unsub who attacked my chief witness in the investigation of Veronica Liu's murder, her niece, Abby Zhang."

Diane leaned forward in her blue task chair and said, "You present a convincing argument, Lynley."

"I was hoping I would." He maintained a serious look.

"I'd love to see this case solved. Especially for that little girl who is now a great asset for the Bureau's Victim Assistance Program."

"Couldn't agree more." Scott could almost taste the joy this would give Abby to close the case with an arrest and conviction. She deserved at least that much, if not much more. "I'll need that search warrant to get Dillman's DNA, for starters."

"You've got it." Diane's eyes twinkled. "I'll get on the phone with Judge Helen Urich."

Scott nodded and was now tasked with going after Oliver Dillman and possibly encountering resistance from the murder suspect.

"I HAVE A search warrant to get Dillman's DNA on record," Scott told Abby over the phone. "It's the first major step in learning once and for all if the unidentified male DNA profile belongs to him."

"Really?" She was in her office when taking the call and elated with the news.

"Yeah. KentuckyFam and the forensic genetic genealogist came through in finding a very near match of Dillman in his late father."

"Wow." Abby had always been curious about her own family tree, wondering how far back she could go to get a genetic roadmap that led to herself. Her parents and grandparents had given her snippets of their genealogy. But that had only left her wanting to know more. Maybe when this cold case investigation was over, she would pursue that in earnest. And perhaps, even talk Scott into seeing who'd come before him and his more immediate family. "I have a good feeling about this, Scott." To feel otherwise would be like practically giving up on identifying her aunt Veronica's killer. Abby would never do that, so long as the case remained open.

"Same here. Of course, the proof is in the pudding, as they say. Or, in this instance, the DNA."

"Very true." She chuckled. "At least you aren't

giving Oliver Dillman a choice in turning over the DNA."

"Not a chance!" Scott made clear. "I'd say that the man has run long enough from his past. It's high time it caught up with him."

"Amen to that," Abby said, her voice betraying the need to have closure in this dark place in her life.

"I'll keep you informed on how things turn out."

"I wouldn't expect any less."

"Catch you later."

"Definitely," she told him, going beyond the common phrase and thinking in literal terms about spending time together and what it could signify beyond that.

Afterward, Abby briefed Elodie Zimbalist and then, with the accompaniment of the FBI agent, rendezvoused with Victim Services Coordinator Elise Martinez for a crisis intervention in Hancock County. Only, the agents had averted the crisis at the last moment. So instead, Abby took Elodie and Elise out for lunch, happy to have connected with two women in the Bureau she could call friends.

WITH HIS GLOCK 17 GEN5 MOS placed firmly inside the shoulder gun holster, and in possession of a search warrant, Scott left Murlock

Realty Group, where Oliver Dillman worked, having been told that he hadn't come in that day.

Hope he hasn't skipped town, Scott ruminated as he hustled back to his Ford Explorer. He wouldn't put it past Dillman to make a run for it. Especially if he felt the walls were beginning to close in on him.

Scott decided that it was more likely that Dillman had simply chosen to take the day off. Perhaps dealing with a hangover. Or maybe he was stalking another woman, believing he was out of the woods as a murder suspect, fresh off his latest warning to back off the investigation. Whatever the case, Scott took solace in the fact that Agent Zimbalist was keeping an eye on Abby, and would be ready to go into action should any trouble arise.

Putting his cell phone on speaker and placing it in a dashboard holder, Scott made arrangements for agents from the Owensboro FBI office to meet him at Dillman's house on Circle Court. In the meantime, Scott barreled toward the location, believing there was not a moment to waste here. Desperate people were prone to desperate acts. Before he was onto them, Scott wanted to get Dillman's DNA on record and act accordingly should it prove to be a match with the unknown crime scene profile.

When he arrived at the ranch home on a cul-de-sac, Scott waited for backup while noting that there was no sign of Dillman's silver Lexus UX 200. He considered that the car could be parked in the garage. Or, his number one suspect in the murder of Veronica Liu could be anywhere right now.

When the agents showed up, ready and willing to do their part for a colleague in Abby by taking down Dillman, if necessary, Scott made his move. He identified himself and banged on the door, calling out to Dillman while demanding that anyone inside open up. Just as it appeared that there may be no one home, the door opened.

A slender thirtysomething African American woman, with an Afro that had a shaved undercut, stood there glaring at them with big sable eyes.

Flashing his badge, Scott told her, "FBI Special Agent Lynley. I'm looking for Oliver Dillman."

"He's not here," she claimed, full lips pursed. "Who are you?"

"Shannon Emmanuel. I'm Oliver's girlfriend."

Scott cocked a brow with the age difference. "Where can I find Dillman?"

"I have no idea." Shannon hunched her shoulders. "He didn't come home last night."

"Mind if we come inside?" Scott asked. "We need to make sure you're being on the level with us."

"Be my guest." She parted the way and the FBI agents went in and fanned out.

Scott remained standing with Shannon in the open-concept living area with traditional furnishings. "Does Dillman often stay out all night?" he questioned.

"Sometimes," she confessed. "He likes his own space. And I respect that, since I feel the same way. It's what makes this work."

"I see."

"Clear," an agent shouted, indicating that no one else was present. Least of all, Oliver Dillman.

So where is he? Scott asked himself, fearful that Dillman had taken off upon sensing that they were onto him. "Why don't we have a seat?" he told Shannon. She complied, sitting on a track armchair, while he sat on the leather sofa. "When did you last speak to Dillman?"

"Last night about eight," she replied.

"Did he say where he was?"

"A bar. He didn't tell me which one. I didn't ask."

Scott brushed the tip of his nose. "Did he indicate that he didn't intend to come home last night?"

"No. But Oliver doesn't always let me in on his plans." She sighed. "So, what's this all about anyway? Why does the FBI want to talk to my boyfriend?"

"Dillman's a person of interest in a cold case investigation," he told her straightforwardly.

Her eyes widened. "You mean murder?"

"Yeah, I'm afraid so, which is why we need to find him. Do you have any clue as to where Dillman might be?"

Shannon started at the question and answered, "I wish I did." She paused. "He could be with another woman. Oliver is prone to stray every now and then, but since we aren't exactly exclusive, that's his choice."

Scott decided this was as good a time as any to get to the real root of the visit. "I have a search warrant to collect Dillman's DNA." He presented it to her. "As the man is absent, I'll have to get his DNA in another way." Scott stood, inviting her to as well. "I need you to show me his razor or toothbrush."

Shannon rose and led him to the bathroom, pointing to the objects in question. Scott donned a pair of nitrile gloves and gathered the suspect's toothbrush and a razor that had a few hairs stuck to it. He placed them in an evidence bag.

Now we need to get this to the crime lab in

a hurry to see what they come up with, Scott told himself anxiously.

At the front door, he handed Shannon his card with his cell phone number and said, "If Dillman shows up, tell him the FBI needs to reinterview him as soon as we can arrange it."

She glanced at the card. "Okay."

Outside, Scott got on the phone and issued a BOLO for Oliver Dillman and his silver Lexus.

WHEN KOLTON LAKE PD Homicide Detective Selena Nunez got word that a man had been found shot to death in a Lexus UX 200 in an isolated section of Kolton Lake Park, she headed straight to the crime scene. Another day in the life of someone who had spent the last two decades dealing with death. It was never easy to lose people. Even those you didn't know. But, at least, if within her power, she would try to get to the bottom of it for the loved ones left behind.

Arriving in her duty vehicle, Selena parked behind a squad car with its lights flashing. She got out of the car, showed her identification to the tall, bald-headed male officer at the scene, and said to him routinely, as if clueless, "What do we have?"

"A deceased male," he told her. "Apparently

died by a self-inflicted single gunshot to the head, with the weapon on his lap."

"Hmm…" Selena frowned. Too many people chose to check out that way these days. Never giving themselves a chance to see if there just might be a better tomorrow. Next week. Or next year.

She approached the vehicle and, after putting on latex gloves, opened the driver's-side front door and took a look inside. The decedent was slumped against the steering wheel. From what she could make out, she guessed him to be in his late fifties. A gunshot wound was in his left temple. Blood had spilled out onto his yellow shirt and khaki pants. Selena noted the firearm, resting precariously on one leg. She leaned forward, studying the gun. It looked to be a Colt Python .357 Magnum revolver. "Do we have a name for the deceased?" she asked the officer.

"I ran the license plate," he answered characteristically. "The car is registered to an Oliver Dillman."

Oliver Dillman. Where had she heard that name? Selena contemplated this for a long moment before it clicked.

As she recalled, Dillman had been one of the suspects in the murder of Veronica Liu twenty years ago, but had been given a pass when circumstances suggested he wasn't the killer. Now he had apparently offed himself. Coincidence?

Or could there be some symmetry here between the past and present? She called in the Crime Scene Investigation Unit to come collect and preserve evidence of a potential crime.

Just then, Selena got a message over her radio, indicating that a BOLO had been issued for Oliver Dillman as a person of interest in a cold case homicide.

Chapter Sixteen

Scott received word that Oliver Dillman had been found dead in his car in Kolton Lake Park, with preliminary indications that it was suicide. This was troubling in the sense that Scott would have preferred to interrogate the murder suspect and, if found guilty, see to it that Dillman spent the rest of his miserable life behind bars. Instead, the death short-circuited that plan and all was now within the jurisdiction of the Kolton Lake Police Department.

When he arrived at the death scene, Scott took a moment to study the decedent, who was still in his car, and mused about the irony of how he died in relation to Veronica Liu's murder in her vehicle. Was this justice served? Or more like justice denied?

Detective Selena Nunez approached and said to him bleakly, "Looks like our cases have intersected, Agent Lynley."

Scott grimaced. "Yeah, seems that way, Detective. Or maybe it's more that this thing has come full circle for you," he remarked thoughtfully.

"I admit, it does give me the déjà vu heebie-jeebies," Selena uttered. "Having Dillman reenter my orbit again two decades later does catch my attention."

"Any chance that someone could have offed him and made it look like a suicide?" Scott had no reason to believe this, given that Dillman had emerged as his prime suspect in the cold case murder. But all bases needed to be covered.

"Always a chance, though not very likely by all appearances," she told him. "The firearm apparently used, a Colt Python .357 Magnum revolver, was on Dillman's lap prior to being bagged by the CSI Unit for evidence. No indication as yet that anyone else was at the scene when it happened. We're checking out surveillance video in the park to see the comings and goings in this area."

Scott looked at her with reaction to the gun make and model, in particular. "Did you say it was a Colt Python .357 Magnum revolver?"

Selena met his regard with a perceptive nod. "I know what you're thinking. Same thing entered my head. It's the same type of firearm as the gun used to shoot to death Veronica Liu," she recalled. Her brow wrinkled. "Hard to conceive that this is, in fact, the murder weapon, still in service. But as we were able to recover a shell casing at the scene that we think came from the Colt Python .357 Magnum, ballistics will make a clear determination on whether that's true and if it was the same handgun in both shootings, along with the ammo comparisons between the two shootings."

"Good." Ideally, Scott would've preferred that the evidence be turned over to the FBI Laboratory, but he had no real authority to take over her current case, which was well within the Kolton PD's jurisdiction to investigate. Still, he hadn't counted on Dillman keeping the murder weapon around two decades later. What were the chances of that? And, if true, actually using it to shoot himself to death? *Maybe*, Scott considered, *Dillman's suicide was his way of redemption or giving them what they needed to close the case*. He asked the detective curiously, "Did Dillman happen to leave a suicide note?"

"Not that we've been able to determine thus far," she said. "But then, as you know, that isn't always the case. Sometimes, a despondent person decides on the spur of the moment to end it all, and leave everyone to question why."

"Yeah," Scott allowed. But was that actually what had happened here? Or was it possibly made to look like the man had taken his own life? "Having Oliver Dillman check out like this complicates my investigation somewhat," he confessed, not comfortable with some still-unanswered questions.

"I can imagine." Selena ran a hand through her hair. "Heard that you put the BOLO out on Dillman. Obviously, you had good reason to believe he was the unsub or had crucial information in Veronica Liu's murder?"

"You could say that, on both fronts." Scott glanced again at Dillman's dead body, knowing he would remain that way till the medical examiner arrived. "Pending verification, I think it was Dillman's DNA that was left on Veronica Liu's vehicle. Other factors also lead me to believe he was the culprit in her death. I'm guessing that he knew we were onto him and, when faced with a long stint behind bars, chose to take the easy way out."

"Appears that way." Selena angled her face. "If so, we'll be able to close the books on two cases at once, making both of our lives a little easier."

"Yeah, we'll see if it works out that way." Scott had been around long enough in law enforcement to know not to get too far ahead of himself in any investigation. Least of all, one that had been anything but cut-and-dried for the past two decades. Yet he clung to the notion that Dillman's death could put this to rest and give Abby the closure she needed, once a couple of other things fell into place.

"OLIVER DILLMAN'S DEAD?" Abby gasped as she gazed at Scott's solemn face in her log cabin.

"The early indications are that Dillman killed himself as we were closing in." Scott was holding a glass of wine while standing near the living room windows overlooking the lake. "We'll know just how true that is once the autopsy is completed."

She batted her lashes musingly. "What about my aunt Veronica's murder?" Abby could only hope that Dillman's death wouldn't put that into a deep freeze all over again.

"We'll get the answers we need there, too, soon," Scott stressed. "We have Dillman's DNA and fingerprints to compare with the unidentified ones found at your aunt's crime scene. Beyond that, the firearm we believe Dillman used to take his life was a Colt Python .357 Magnum revolver, the same type of weapon used in Veronica Liu's murder. It's a good chance that this is the very same gun that, against all odds, Dillman chose to hang on to. It's being examined by the Kolton Lake PD's Ballistics Laboratory, even as we speak."

"Okay." Abby sipped her wine. "So, we hold our breath till then?"

Scott touched her cheek. "We trust the system to do its job," he said steadfastly. "The rest will take care of itself."

She nodded thoughtfully, even as Abby wondered about the rest, as it pertained to their lives after the case was officially closed. Having Scott so near, she had practically forgotten what it was like to not have him around. She was sure that whatever else happened, they would continue to be a part of each other's lives. All that remained was to what extent. She looked at him now, trying to read his thoughts and wondering if they synchronized with hers on where this was going between them when all was said and done.

THE BRECKINRIDGE COUNTY Medical Examiner and Coroner's Office was located in Hardinsburg, Kentucky, seventeen miles from Kolton Lake. Scott met Selena Nunez there the following morning once news came that the autopsy on Oliver Dillman had been done, with both seeking definitive answers.

Greeting them in the examination suite was Chief Medical Examiner Daryl Fujimoto, MD. In his midforties and thickset, he had black hair in a buzz cut, a thin goatee, deeply lined brown eyes, and was wearing surgical garb. He gave nods and said, "Agent Lynley. Detective Nunez."

"Hey, Doc," Selena said.

Scott acknowledged him and asked without delay, "So, what can you tell us about the cause and manner of Oliver Dillman's death?"

Fujimoto sighed then answered in an even tone of voice, "You can check out the full report when it's ready, but I can tell you that Mr. Dillman's death was caused by a direct-contact single gunshot to the left-side temple. With no obvious signs of foul play—and none pointed out to me, along with the decedent confirmed to be left-handed—in my opinion, his death was almost certainly self-inflicted."

"Had Dillman been drinking?" the detective asked curiously. "Or otherwise under the influence of something?"

"The decedent's blood alcohol level was almost three times the legal limit," Fujimoto responded matter-of-factly. "I've ordered toxicology tests to further determine if, and to what extent, there were any drugs in his system that may have played a role in the death. If only the decedent's state of mind."

Scott listened intently as Fujimoto spoke, seeing little reason to doubt the findings, in light of the police investigation. But there was still more he needed from the pathologist, for further clarification. "What was the estimated time of death?"

"I'd say sometime between nine and midnight the night before last," he responded candidly.

Scott mused about his questioning of Dillman's girlfriend, Shannon Emmanuel, who'd claimed she had last spoken to him around 8:00 p.m. Had his plans been in place then? Or had this been an impromptu act? Or neither?

Scott asked Fujimoto, "Did you happen to test Dillman's hands for gunshot residue?"

The medical examiner rubbed his goatee and replied, "I did at that, given that Mr. Dillman was under criminal investigation, making GSR testing mandatory."

"And...?" Scott gazed at him anxiously.

"Using a scanning electron microscope, along with energy-dispersive X-ray analysis, the tests came back positive for some traces of gunshot residue on the decedent's hands. Though this could have technically come from putting them up in a defensive manner or residual GSR, when coupled with the other factors, it makes the conclusion that this was self-inflicted that much more likely."

"Works for me," Selena stated. "Seems like Dillman's violent past finally caught up to him in what, honestly, was a long time coming, if I'm reading the tea leaves correctly."

Scott, too, had to go along with this, considering. At least, at face value. But he was keeping an open mind on Dillman's untimely demise, till being able to effectively link it with the remaining pieces of the puzzle as they pertained to the murder of Veronica Liu.

DETECTIVE NUNEZ'S ASSUMPTIONS about Oliver Dillman's history picked up steam in Scott's mind, validating his own discernment as he accompanied her to the Kolton Lake PD's Ballistics Laboratory. There, Gregg Borelli, a firearms examiner, had tested the weapon and ammo connected to Dillman's death and compared it with the .38 Special cartridge and casing used in Veronica Liu's murder.

Borelli—who was in his thirties, lean and around six feet tall, with long and slicked-back brown hair in a man bun—gazed at them with blue eyes, as he told them at his workstation, "I think I have what you're looking for..."

Scott regarded him. "Go on."

"Okay. After test-firing the Colt Python .357 Magnum revolver found at the scene of Oliver Dillman's death, I compared it with the .38 Special cartridge Dillman was shot with and the casing recovered. The ammo was both fired from the same gun barrel with four lands and grooves with a right-hand twist, and the ballistic markings on the casings were a perfect match with the cartridge removed from Dillman's head."

"Suspected as much," Selena told him. "Now, what about the .38 Special round used to kill Veronica Liu?"

Borelli's face lit up. "We're talking about the same weapon used," he said confidently. "I compared the .38 Special cartridge and casing used in the Liu murder to the ammo in the Dillman shooting, and the two were totally in sync and shot from the Colt Python .357 Magnum revolver recovered from Dillman's vehicle."

"You're sure about that?" Scott asked, if only to hear him say it for the record, given the implications.

"Yeah, I'm sure." Borelli's face hardened. "This is what the Kolton Lake PD pays me for. You can have the FBI crime lab verify my findings, but they won't be any different. The same firearm was used in separate shootings spanning two decades."

And presumably with the same shooter, Scott realized, assessing the forensic ballistics info as measured with the autopsy results on Oliver Dillman. This still left the results of the DNA testing and unidentified partial print found at the crime scene to nail down Dillman as the shooter in Veronica Liu's cold-blooded execution.

ABBY MAY HAVE jumped the gun a bit, but she couldn't resist meeting with Jeanne Singletary for lunch at the Twenty-Second Street Bistro in Kolton Lake to share the news about the cold case that they both had been burdened by for two decades. Though Abby had invited Elodie Zimbalist to join them, her soon-to-be ex-FBI bodyguard had chosen to give them their space and was sitting at a nearby table, on her cell phone for presumably her next assignment.

"The investigation into Aunt Veronica's murder may finally be coming to a head," Abby said as they sat in a booth with mugs of hot coffee and lunch menus between them.

Jeanne's brow lifted. "Really?"

"Yep. Looks like your read on Oliver Dillman and his bright red hooded windbreaker has yielded positive results," she told her. "Well, maybe not so much the jacket, per se, but the man who was wearing it." Abby sighed. "Dillman's dead."

"Dead?" Jeanne regarded her with shock, nearly spitting out her coffee.

"Yes. Apparently, he took his own life the night before last," Abby said, knowing it was public knowledge by now. "There was a BOLO out by the authorities to bring him in for questioning and to collect his DNA in connection to Aunt Veronica's death."

"And rather than man up, he chose to escape being held accountable for a despicable act of murder by killing himself?" Jeanne's mouth hung open in anger.

"Sure looks that way." Abby was outraged as well. She would have much preferred that Dillman face her and Jeanne in court for his heinous actions before having to pay for his crime by imprisonment.

"The Bureau still needs to tie up a few loose ends, but Scott and Kolton Lake PD Detective Selena Nunez, the original investigator on the case, seem to believe he's the culprit. Including recovering the murder weapon and linking it to Dillman." It was still astounding to Abby that he had not bothered to get rid of the gun before deciding to turn it on himself. But then, she couldn't exactly get into the head of a killer and the choices he made.

"Well, if this can finally give Veronica the long overdue resting in peace that she deserves, so be it," Jeanne declared, glancing at her menu.

"That's true, I suppose." Abby was not about to look a gift horse in the mouth. But she wasn't quite ready to pronounce victory either. Not until Scott felt he had enough to close the case for good.

Jeanne smiled at her. "Why don't we order?" she suggested. "I, for one, am starved and the food will go down much better with your news of the day. And maybe I'll order something a little stronger than coffee to help wash it down."

She smiled back at her aunt's best friend and business partner. "Yes, let's have lunch." Abby lifted her menu and looked to see what was best, having regained her own appetite as she contemplated what may lie ahead.

Chapter Seventeen

Scott was in his car on the laptop when Federal DNA Database Unit Laboratory Scientist Kay Nakata and the Bureau's crime lab's Latent Print Unit forensic examiner Matt D'Angelo appeared on the screen.

After updating them on where things stood in the investigation, Scott favored Kay with a direct look and watched her face brighten as she said, "Yay to KentuckyFam. Had a feeling they might be able to help in this cold case."

Scott grinned. "They did come through," he reiterated, wondering if she would do so, as well, when asking the lab tech in earnest, "What do you have for me on the DNA comparison?"

"I have great news, Agent Lynley." Her white teeth shone. "In comparing the DNA samples you provided from the suspect, Oliver Dillman, to the unidentified male DNA profile taken from the Mercedes-Benz belonging to murdered victim Veronica Liu, I'm happy to say it's a match!"

"Really?" Scott asked routinely, but had no trouble believing her.

"Absolutely," Kay asserted. "The DNA belongs to the very same person."

"Oliver Dillman?"

"Yes," she stressed. "Of course, I'm not the one to say that he murdered Ms. Liu, but he did definitely leave his DNA on her car, for one reason or another."

I can think of only one solid reason, Scott told himself, piecing this with the other solid and circumstantial evidence that correlated with Dillman's involvement in the homicide twenty years ago and his own death. "That's good enough for me," he affirmed. "The fact that Oliver Dillman was at the crime scene when he wasn't supposed to be, and has now suddenly taken himself out of the equation, tells me pretty much all I need to know."

"Makes sense," Kay uttered.

Scott gave Matt the benefit of his attention, wondering if he had been able to match the latent print from the car with Dillman's left index finger, on the off chance that it would somehow be a hit, in spite of Dillman's prints being on file as a licensed real estate agent. "What did you come up with on the print comparison, out of curiosity?"

D'Angelo pulled on his beard and said levelly, "I examined the print from Oliver Dillman's left index finger and put it under the microscope to see if it miraculously lined up with the unidentified person's left index finger latent print. As expected, they were not a match."

Scott nodded accordingly. "Had to try."

"My guess is the partial print left on the car was unrelated to the homicide," D'Angelo suggested. "It most likely was put there at some other time by someone else who knew Veronica Liu. Or who came into contact with her vehicle by happenstance."

Kay agreed, arguing, "Frankly, I'm surprised there weren't even more unidentified latent prints left on the car. Between family, friends, coworkers, auto repair personnel, vehicles are like a magnet for finger and palm prints."

Scott did not disagree. Only in this instance, they were able to account for all prints on Veronica Liu's car other than this one. If it didn't belong to Dillman, could there have been someone else involved in the murder? There was no evidence to support this angle, Scott realized, but more than enough to believe that Oliver Dillman acted alone in shooting to death Abby's aunt.

D'Angelo broke into his thoughts when he said, "Since I had Dillman's prints, I ran them through the Next Generation Identification system just for the hell of it, to see if anything came up."

"Did anything?" Scott asked, wondering if Dillman could have previously run afoul of the law and it had been missed.

D'Angelo shook his head. "Not a thing. Looks like, apart from the homicide in question, Dillman managed to keep his nose clean through the years."

There was the attack on Abby. Scott believed that Dillman was most likely the unsub, having the most to lose with her possibly identifying him, were the investigation to continue. The fact that he had chosen to take his own life wouldn't let him off the hook. "I think I have what I need to pin the murder of Veronica Liu squarely on Oliver Dillman's shoulders," Scott told them assuredly. Now he needed to convey this to Abby, the person with the most vested interest in having the right conclusion necessary to put the case to rest.

LATE THAT AFTERNOON, Abby was walking with Scott along the sandy shoreline of Lake Kolton. Both were barefoot and glancing periodically at the lake, mesmerized by the sun's rays reflecting off the smooth surface of the water. She was being briefed about the state of things in the investigation into her aunt Veronica's murder.

Abby listened attentively as Scott told her fluidly, "Oliver Dillman's DNA matched the unidentified male DNA profile left on your aunt's car. When you add this to the fact that the Colt Python .357 Magnum revolver and ammo Dillman used to kill himself was forensically matched with the murder weapon and .38 Special cartridge used in Veronica Liu's death, we have our killer."

Abby was almost speechless trying to put into words the elation she felt now that her aunt's murderer had been officially identified for the whole world to see. "So, it's over then?" she dared to ask, gazing up at him with expectation.

A grin played on Scott's lips when answering coolly, "Other than a little paperwork and a sign-off by the assistant special agent in charge in the Bureau's Louisville field office, Diane Huggett, and the Kolton Lake PD, the original law enforcement agency investigating the homicide? Yeah, I'd say this case can finally be closed with a satisfactory outcome."

Abby showed her teeth. "Thank you, Scott, for all your hard work in taking this seriously." She felt as though a tremendous weight had been lifted off her shoulders. "I once feared it would forever go unresolved."

"I couldn't have done much of it without your help, Abby," he told her, voice lowered in expressing his sincerity. "Without your dedication to your aunt and holding on to some crucial details inside your head, waiting to be released under the right circumstances, Dillman might have forever remained under the radar."

She thought about the bright red windbreaker he'd been wearing the day of the murder and how it had somehow stood out within her subconscious mind for two decades. Had Dillman not seen her as a real threat, which may never have actually been the case, in attacking her at the park that day, the truth could well have stayed hidden for all time.

"I'm glad I was able to contribute in a small way," she uttered modestly. "I only knew that Aunt Veronica was there for me when no one else was. I needed to return the favor."

"And you did," he promised her. "On some other plane, I think she knows that."

Abby nodded and suddenly realized that Scott's long arm was territorially across her shoulders as they continued to walk on the shoreline. She liked the feel of this and wondered if it was a sign of things to come now that they had crossed one major bridge on their journey.

THE NEXT DAY, Scott was at work, finishing up what was needed in the Veronica Liu cold case, eager to put it behind him and move on to new cases sitting on his desk. He admittedly hated leaving Abby's log cabin after staying the night. Moreover, he hated having to be away from the gorgeous victim specialist at all. But if he had his way, that wouldn't be a problem for too much longer as he looked ahead. He intended to ask Abby to marry him. Yes, they hadn't known each other a superlong time by conventional standards. So what? Knowing someone for a longer period of time hadn't exactly worked in his favor previously.

Scott sat back, dismissing the short span of their romance. *When you know, you just know that someone's right for you and you're right for them*, he told himself. Waiting wouldn't change that. It would only make it more frustrating living their lives apart. If Abby accepted his proposal, they could work out the logistics later.

His cell phone rang and Scott saw that the caller was his brother, Russell. Answering, he said easily, "Russ."

"Hi. Just checking in to see how your latest cold case is coming along."

"Funny you should mention that." Scott smiled out of a corner of his lips. "As a matter of fact, I was just able to solve the case."

"Why am I not surprised?" Russell laughed. "Guess that's why the Louisville Kentucky FBI field office doesn't want to let you go. They damned well know a great cold case agent when they have one in their midst."

Scott chuckled while eating it up. "Back at you, little brother, in holding down the fort in the Bureau's Houston field office."

"So, give me the short story on who the unsub was and how you cracked the case."

"Okay." Scott did just that, sparing him the tedious details about going after Oliver Dillman, while playing up the involvement of Abby Zhang.

Russell remarked, "Sounds like you two made a great team."

"More like make a great team," Scott corrected him, knowing his brother would demand more. And he was happy to oblige.

"Hmm…am I missing something here?" Russell's voice lowered an octave. "Have you been holding back on us?"

"Not exactly." Scott thought about having confided in Annette that he was interested in Abby romantically. His sister had apparently kept it under wraps, allowing him to spill the beans in his own good time. Now was as good a time as any to get started on that score. He finished with, "I'll let you know how she responds when I pop the question."

"You're full of surprises, Scott," Russell told him wryly. "And that's why I love you, big bro. Never a dull chat."

"Works both ways." Scott chuckled. "Later."

No sooner had he disconnected when his phone rang again. Scott didn't recognize the caller as he answered in his professional voice, "Agent Lynley."

"Agent Lynley," the man said unevenly, "my name's Elliot McGowan. I'm an attorney based in Kolton Lake, representing the recently deceased Oliver Dillman."

Scott reacted, wondering why Dillman's lawyer would be contacting him. "I'm listening."

"We need to talk," McGowan said in vague terms. "Can we meet?"

If only out of curiosity alone, although his interest was piqued by more than that, Scott felt he had no real choice but to accept meeting with the dead man's attorney.

IN THE MORNING, Abby revisited some crime victims as part of her duties and to make additional referrals, where needed. Afterward, she headed over to Kolton Lake General to meet her friend Dr. Phoebe Hoag for lunch in the cafeteria.

Abby got off on the third floor in search of

Phoebe and, after heading down the hall, instead found herself nearly running into Zach Gilliard. Though he seemed almost as shocked to see her, Abby had to ask him suspiciously, "Are you following me?"

"No." Zach's thick brows knitted. "Absolutely not!"

She remained wary. "So, why are you here?"

"I was visiting a friend," he claimed, stuffing his hands in the pockets of his cargo pants.

She rolled her eyes. "Yeah, right."

"It's true. I'm not stalking you, Abby. I swear." Zach made a face. "After that FBI Agent... Lynley...warned me in less than a subtle tone to stay away from you, I got the message and have tried my best to do so. Even if I never felt I did anything wrong by simply sending you thank-you roses and having a brief chat at the cemetery."

"Okay, I get it." In spite of wondering if she may have overreacted where it concerned him, Abby was happy that Scott had applied pressure in getting Zach to back off, in spite of his not having made any overt threats. Or having been guilty of shoving her to the ground at Kolton Lake Park, with Oliver Dillman proving to be the perp. Her instincts told her that Zach could still have been a problem, had he been given an opportunity for his interest in her to escalate.

He took a breath. "Anyway, sorry we almost ran into one another. My bad."

"It's no one's fault," she told him, and meant it.

Zach nodded, stepping aside. "I'll let you go wherever you were headed."

"Same." Abby met his eyes briefly, unsure what to make of him, but eager to be on her way. "Goodbye, Zach."

"'Bye, Abby." After a moment, he walked away.

She watched him for a few seconds before heading in the opposite direction, where she spotted Phoebe.

Her friend, wearing a white lab coat, approached her. "Sorry I'm a little late."

Abby smiled. "No problem."

Phoebe glanced over her shoulder. "Who was that man you were talking to?"

Without bothering to look his way again, Abby replied with a sigh, "It's a long story."

Phoebe cupped her arm. "You can tell me all about it over lunch."

"SOUNDS LIKE A creep to me," Phoebe remarked fifteen minutes later as they sat by the wall in the cafeteria.

"Maybe Zach's just misunderstood or lonely," Abby suggested, trying to give him the benefit of the doubt that she may have misread his gratitude toward her.

Phoebe wasn't buying it. "Isn't that how all stalkers get started in the wrong direction, by just *seeming* lonely and misunderstood?"

Abby gave a little chuckle while lifting her turkey grinder. "Believe me, I'm not trying to cover for him," she insisted. "But as a victim specialist, I can't let those I help get to me, any more than some unruly or unsettled patients who might become fixated on you."

Phoebe smiled. "Point taken." She bit into her club sandwich. "Guess some things come with the territory, like it or not."

Abby concurred. "In any event, Scott has warned Zach to stay away and he seems to be abiding by that."

"That's good," Phoebe said and ate more of the sandwich. A moment later, she looked across the table at Abby and asked curiously, "So, what's happening with you and the FBI agent these days?"

Abby put her sandwich back on the plate and dabbed a paper napkin to her mouth. "As a matter of fact, that's what I wanted to talk to you about, in a manner of speaking..." she began, and then sprang the news on her about the case of her aunt Veronica's murder being solved at last.

"Seriously?" Phoebe tilted her head to one side. "Tell me more."

"A guy named Oliver Dillman, who used to work with Aunt Veronica, who rejected his advances, apparently shot her to death in a jealous rage, I suppose," Abby told her, and sipped iced tea.

"Oliver Dillman?" Phoebe's mouth gaped. "Isn't that the real estate agent who took his own life the other night at Kolton Lake Park?"

"That's him," she told her.

"I read about it." Phoebe paused. "So, he killed himself because the FBI had figured out what he did to your aunt twenty years ago?"

"Sure looks that way." Abby tasted the tea. "The gun Dillman used to kill himself was the same weapon that was used to murder Aunt Veronica. The ammo between the shootings matched up as well."

"Wow." Phoebe drank her black coffee. "This is so unreal."

"I know." Abby sighed. "As it turns out, I actually saw Oliver Dillman right after it happened as he ran off into the woods."

"What?" Phoebe's jaw dropped. "Why am I just hearing about this?"

"I never realized it till undergoing hypnosis recently," she admitted to her. "You knew I saw something out in the woods as I got to

Aunt Veronica's car. Though I never got a good look at a face, the hypnosis revealed that it was a man wearing a bright red windbreaker with a hood. According to my aunt's business partner, Jeanne Singletary, one matching that description was worn by Oliver Dillman. Scott was about to connect the various dots before pinning the murder on him."

Phoebe shook her head in astonishment. "How did he get away with it for so long?"

Abby lifted her hands in equal disbelief. "Same way others have gotten away with terrible crimes over the decades, even centuries," she reasoned. "By being clever enough to conceal their identities, keep the authorities guessing, and by refraining from committing similar crimes."

"I suppose you're right." Phoebe took a breath. "Thank goodness it's over."

"Yeah, it's a big relief." Abby couldn't begin to express just how much. Never knowing why someone went after her aunt Veronica had been a big drag on her own life. Now she could finally move on. Hopefully, with Scott.

As though reading her mind, Phoebe leaned forward and said, "You never did say where things are with you and Scott on the personal side."

"I didn't, did I?" Abby giggled.

"Well...?"

It took her a moment or two of contemplation before Abby looked her friend since childhood in the eye and told her, "I think I'm in love."

Phoebe's face lit up. "Seriously?"

"Yes." She couldn't deny what she was feeling, even to herself. "There's just something about Scott Lynley that has tapped into my emotions on a level I've not experienced before." *Not to mention he's a great lover.* Abby colored at the thought. "While he's been married before," she pointed out, "it wasn't the right fit for him or her, so I can't hold that against him in moving on. Any more than my own previous relationships that went nowhere."

"That's fair enough," Phoebe allowed, picking at the remains of her sandwich. "Most of us fail to get it right the first time," she conceded. "You think he feels the same way about you?"

Abby twisted her lips contemplatively. Did he? Or had she somehow read his expressions, tender words and body language all wrong? "Yes," she uttered. "But so I don't jinx things, I won't speak for him. We'll just have to see what happens." Or doesn't, she had to prepare herself for, whether Abby wanted to think in those terms or not.

Chapter Eighteen

Scott stepped inside the McGowan and Ku-suda Law Offices in the Rellington Building on Ninth Street in downtown Kolton Lake. He wondered just what Dillman's attorney would be contacting him for, after the man was dead. *Guess I'm about to find out*, Scott mused as a young and thin, blond-haired female office assistant ushered him into a large, carpeted office with window walls and modern furnishings.

After she left, he was approached by a tall, navy-suited, medium-sized man in his late fifties with short, wavy reddish hair. Regarding Scott with deep gray eyes, he stuck out a hand and said casually, "I'm Elliot McGowan."

"Special Agent Lynley." Scott flashed his identification as such and met the attorney's gaze squarely while they shook hands.

"Thanks for coming."

"I admit being surprised to hear from a lawyer on behalf of Oliver Dillman," Scott said forthrightly.

"I understand where you're coming from, Agent Lynley." McGowan rubbed his crooked nose. "Why don't we sit down and I'll explain?" He pointed toward a guest lounge chair for Scott, while taking a seat in his own leather executive chair, behind a U-desk suite. McGowan sighed. "Mr. Dillman—Oliver—and I go back a long way."

"How long is that?" Scott asked, as though he needed to, while seated.

"Since we were teenagers. We both attended Kolton Lake High School back in the day and stayed in touch infrequently. I've been Oliver's attorney for probably ten years now, just normal dealings pertaining to legal advice on real estate transactions, investments, liabilities, that type of thing." McGowan leaned back in his chair before saying, "I was saddened to hear about Oliver's passing."

So was I, though likely for entirely different reasons, Scott told himself. He straightened his shoulders impatiently and asked the lawyer bluntly, "Mind telling me why I'm here?"

"Of course." McGowan leaned forward and pressed his hands against the wooden desktop. "Not long ago, Mr. Dillman handed me an envelope and requested that, in the event of his death, I was to give it to you, Agent Lynley…"

"Is that so?" Scott narrowed his eyes, mystified.

"Yep." McGowan opened a top drawer and removed a padded envelope. He slid it across the desk. "I'm fulfilling that obligation."

"Do you know what's in it?" Scott asked curiously before picking up the envelope.

"Have no idea," he claimed. "Oliver never told me and I never asked, out of respect for him as a client."

"I see." Scott lifted the yellow envelope and, feeling it, could tell that there was what seemed to be a smallish box inside. Whatever was within, he preferred to see what Dillman was up to alone. "Is there anything else you want to tell me about your client?" he asked the lawyer, wondering if any attorney-client privilege would be waived under the circumstances.

"Nothing I can think of," McGowan said. "Apart from my legal responsibilities regarding his estate, whatever Oliver felt he wanted to say to you is likely in that envelope."

"In that case, I think we're finished here," Scott said, getting to his feet before being told the same by the lawyer.

"Right," McGowan agreed, standing.

Scott accepted another handshake and was out the door. He waited until he was inside his SUV before grabbing latex gloves from the glove compartment. After putting them on, he tore open the envelope and removed the small box. Opening it, he saw that it contained a flash drive.

Is this Dillman's confession to murdering Veronica Liu? Scott asked himself. A virtual suicide note? Or both?

He lifted his laptop from the passenger seat and slid in the flash drive, watching as Oliver Dillman's face appeared and he began to speak.

ABBY FELT A bit nervous returning to the cemetery to visit her aunt Veronica's gravesite, recalling that Zach Gilliard had followed her there previously. But as she scanned the well-manicured grounds, there was no sign of the mass shooting survivor who had seemed infatuated with her. Or maybe she had been spooked by him for no good or bad reason. Whatever.

He shouldn't be a problem anymore, she thought, with Scott running interference for her. For which Abby was most grateful. Along with other reasons to be glad he was in her life.

She focused on her aunt's headstone and spoke to her aloud in a sentimental tone of voice. "It's finally over, Aunt Veronica. The man who took you from me has been identified and can no longer pose a threat to anyone else, ever again. You can now rest in peace eternally, and I'll do my best to forever keep you in my memory."

Abby took another cursory glance around the cemetery and spotted only an elderly couple, who seemed oblivious to her presence. She turned back to her aunt Veronica's grave and said a silent prayer, one that included being able to find the happiness that had eluded her aunt. Particularly when it came to romance and making the wrong choices in her life. In Abby's way of thinking, she had turned the corner in that respect and could see only promise and possibilities for what may lie ahead.

SITTING BACK IN his SUV's front seat, Scott was fully attentive as he watched Oliver Dillman speak to him from the grave.

"Hello, Agent Lynley. There's no sugarcoating it. If you're watching this now, it means I'm no longer alive. Since I'm sure you're a busy man, as I used to be, I won't take up too much of your time."

Dillman sucked in a deep breath and continued. "I made the mistake of first getting romantically involved with Freda Neville twenty-plus years ago. That was way before she would go on to become Kolton Lake Mayor Freda Myerson. Anyway, what was only playing the field for me was something altogether different for her. With a jealous streak a mile long, Freda mistakenly saw my coming on to my work colleague Veronica Liu as one competitor too many.

"Truthfully, I actually thought that Freda was pulling my leg when she swore she'd kill Veronica if she tried to come between us. The night before her death, I made the mistake of talking shop with Veronica when we ran into each other at the Tygers Club. It really set off Freda, who was there with me, in a way I hadn't seen before."

He drew a breath and Scott recalled the bartender and former exotic dancer Katlyn Johansson remembering the exchange between Veronica and an unidentified man. Scott had had no way of knowing at the time that this was Oliver Dillman. Much less that he'd been in the company of Freda Neville.

"Convinced that I was two-timing her with Veronica, Freda just lost it," Dillman stated. "She wanted to kill the person Freda thought was standing in the way of what we had. Next day, with Freda wearing my red jacket, I followed her to Veronica's cabin, still not believing she would actually commit murder."

Dillman sucked in another deep breath. Scott was jarred as he considered the bright red windbreaker that Abby had revealed under hypnosis had been worn by her aunt's ostensive killer.

Scott peered at the laptop screen as Dillman uttered in a shaky voice, "I watched as Freda shot Veronica while she was in her car. Then Freda took off for the woods. I went to check on Veronica, but could tell that she was already gone. That's when I saw her niece, Abby Zhang, walking down the street, heading toward the cabin.

"I hid behind the cabin and waited for her to see what she saw and go inside, before I took off running into the woods myself." Dillman grabbed a can of beer, drank a generous amount and then continued. "When I caught up to Freda, I tried to get her to turn herself in. But she threatened to implicate me in the murder—say we'd both planned it—if I didn't keep my mouth shut. What could I do?"

He threw his hands up, as if in surrender, and said, "Things were never the same for us after that. A little while later, we went our separate ways, with the secret still intact." Dillman drank more beer. "Stayed that way till you reopened the case, Agent Lynley. Freda was spooked that you would find out the truth and arrest her for murder, causing her carefully structured world to come crashing down around her. She warned me to keep a lid on it. Or else."

Scott contemplated all he had heard with incredulity as Dillman tasted more beer, burped and said, "Anyway, I got to thinking… I'd run into some money issues, bad debts, that sort of thing, and decided that Freda owed me. She agreed to the tune of one hundred grand and we could keep this thing buried forever. But first, I needed to get you to back off. Hence the text message warning on a burner phone. When that didn't seem to work, I came after Abby Zhang. I was never going to hurt her. Just scare her, so you'd drop the case and I'd get what I needed from Freda."

Dillman sat back and stared into the camera. "To be clear, I don't trust Freda. Not one bit, after what she did to Veronica. But being in real estate, I understand that everything's worth the risk for the rewards that come from it." He finished off the beer. "If you're watching this, it means my lawyer handed it over as requested, in the event of my death. And it would only come if Freda chose not to hold up her end of the bargain and I ended up paying for it with my life. If that's the case, it tells you all you need to know, Agent Lynley, about just what Freda is capable of and willing to do to Abby Zhang. Next time you talk to Abby, give her my apologies about what happened at the park. And, of course, the death of my former colleague Veronica Liu."

The video ended, leaving Scott visibly shaken. Especially when it came to fear for Abby's safety. No matter how this played in sorting out the facts of presumably fingering the wrong unsub in Oliver Dillman, in spite of the direct and indirect evidence to support the contention, Scott knew that, if everything Dillman confessed to was true, Abby's life could be in grave danger. With her enemy, Mayor Freda Myerson, hidden in public view. And Abby's new role with the Crime Victims Advisory Board only a smoke screen for the mayor to keep an eye on her, hoping Abby didn't remember it was Freda she'd seen running in the woods the day Veronica Liu was murdered, and not Oliver Dillman.

Scott doubted it would take much for Freda to want to eliminate the last threat to her cushy life and political aspirations, even with Dillman now out of the picture.

I can't let the mayor add Abby to her list of killings, Scott asserted determinedly, closing the laptop and setting it back on the seat. The love of his life would not become another victim of homicide. He took out the cell phone from his pocket and called Abby, needing to warn her about Freda.

There was no answer. Scott typed Abby a text message.

Abby. Oliver Dillman may not have killed your aunt. His ex-girlfriend Mayor Freda Myerson appears to be the guilty party. Stay away from her. Call me ASAP.

He sent it off and then headed over to Abby's log cabin, sensing that she needed him now as much as he needed her. Before Freda Myerson could end what he and Abby had ahead and what they were building upon in the special way they both deserved.

AFTER ARRIVING HOME, Abby turned off the security system and took her cell phone upstairs to charge. Back downstairs, she went into the kitchen to pour herself a glass of wine. She took a sip and thought about where things would go from here, now that her aunt Veronica's murder had been solved. Abby believed that there was a future to be had with Scott and that both would pursue this, even if their past relationships had soured them as far as happy endings. The past was certainly not always a barometer of the future. Nor should it be, other than using it as a learning experience for a better outcome down the line.

Abby kept that thought in mind as she thought she heard a sound. Then there was a knock on the door. She hadn't been expecting any guests, but considered that her friends Phoebe and Beverly were prone to dropping by uninvited. Putting her wineglass on the counter, Abby walked to the door. She looked out the peephole and was surprised to see that it was Freda Myerson. The mayor was wearing casual clothing, which included a dark hoodie.

Without giving it another thought, albeit curious, Abby opened the door. "Mayor... Freda..."

"Hello, Abby." She showed her teeth. "Did I catch you at a bad time?"

"No, not at all." Abby smiled back. "Come in."

Inside, Freda faced her and said, "I was in the neighborhood and thought I'd take a chance you were home to discuss more about the Crime Victims Advisory Board."

"I'm here," Abby quipped. "And I'd be happy to talk about my role with the board. Can I pour you a glass of wine? I have coffee and tea as well."

"No thanks." Freda stared at her. "So, I understand that Agent Lynley was able to close the case on Veronica's death by identifying Oliver Dillman as the killer?"

"Yes, that's true." Abby was thoughtful. "All the evidence, such as Dillman's red windbreaker, which I saw him wearing the day Aunt Veronica was killed, pointed to Oliver. Including the murder weapon, which he also used to take his own life. How weird is that after holding on to the gun for two decades?"

"Pretty weird," the mayor agreed. She paused for a long moment before saying distantly, "Problem is, Abby, Oliver wasn't the one you saw wearing the hooded red jacket. It was me."

"What?" Abby met Freda's suddenly cold eyes with confusion. "I don't understand."

"Oliver and I were dating at the time," she stated coolly. "I wore his jacket as a show of affection. Or, at least, it began that way. I thought he was the love of my life. Or wanted him to be, if only Oliver didn't have such a wandering eye. One that paid far too much attention to Veronica Liu, who seemed just as infatuated with him as I was. At the time, I was very much the jealous type and took it personally when someone tried to steal what was mine. Very personally."

Abby gulped in asking, ill at ease, "So what are you saying?"

"You're smart, Abby. Figure it out." Freda waited a beat. "It was me who shot and killed your aunt. Not Oliver."

"You—" Abby's voice broke as she weighed this stunning admission.

"That's right." Freda's face tightened. "He was much too weak to do anything like that.

Honestly, I wonder now what I ever saw in the man. At the time, though, I felt Oliver Dillman was someone I wanted to spend the rest of my life with. Silly me. Anyway, I intended to be in and out after waiting in the woods for your aunt to arrive home. I made sure she knew it was me who was about to take her life before I pulled the trigger. I left her there to die and thought I'd made a clean getaway. Then I looked back and saw you had come home from school a little sooner than anticipated. I was sure we'd made eye contact and actually thought about coming out of the woods and killing you too. But it was too risky at that point and I took off.

"When you never mentioned this to anyone and were sent away to be with relatives in San Francisco, I thought I was in the clear." Freda snorted. "But in the back of my mind was the fear that you just might remember seeing me and my house of sand would come crumbling down around me."

"I never did remember seeing you, Freda," Abby admitted, her heart beating wildly while trying to come to terms with the fact that Mayor Myerson had just confessed to murdering her aunt Veronica. How had she come to believe the person she'd seen that day under hypnosis was a male? Why couldn't she have gotten a close look at the killer to see her for who she really was?

"And maybe you never would have, Abby. Problem is, even with Oliver dead and identified as the shooter—giving me the cover I needed to get away with it forever—I simply cannot afford to take that chance." On that note, Freda removed a handgun from the pocket of her dark-colored hoodie. She pointed it at Abby and said tersely, "It's loaded."

Abby stared at the firearm. She recognized it as a Taurus G2C 9 mm Luger. "You're going to kill me?" she blurted out.

"I'm afraid I don't really have much choice, Abby." Freda's voice fell an octave. "I've come too far to see my life as mayor of Kolton Lake and wife of a brilliant man in Pierce Myerson, who actually gets me and accepts me for who I am, be potentially ruined by something that happened two decades ago."

I need to somehow buy time, Abby told herself as she stood there. She had no way of knowing if Scott had possibly figured this out or not. Even if he had decided that Oliver Dillman wasn't the culprit after all in her aunt's death, Abby doubted Scott would be able to ride in on his Thoroughbred horse, Sammie, to save her from the mayor. *I have to find a way to come out of this alive*, Abby thought, knowing that any future she might have with Scott had suddenly been put in serious jeopardy.

She regarded the mayor hotly. "Oliver Dillman didn't take his own life, did he?" Abby had a feeling, in spite of the conclusions drawn by the medical examiner and authorities.

"Not exactly." Freda gave a derisive chuckle. "Seriously, I thought that Oliver and I were through twenty years ago. But then, just like that, he came waltzing back into my life when the cold case was reopened. When he should have simply left well enough alone, instead, Oliver tried to hit me up for one hundred grand." Her nostrils flared. "Or, in other words, the man was blackmailing me in order to keep his mouth shut for something he caused to happen way back when by two-timing me with the likes of Veronica. And who knows how many other women?

"Well, I would have none of it then," she hissed, keeping the gun aimed at Abby, "and I certainly wouldn't allow Oliver to control my life now!" Freda sighed. "So, yes, I killed him with the very gun I used to shoot your aunt. Wisely, I thought it was a good move to hold on to it as an insurance policy, in case I needed it again. I agreed to meet Oliver at Kolton Lake Park in an area that I knew was remote and had an escape route. He foolishly agreed to this, believing he would pocket the hundred grand and maybe use me as a forever piggy bank to fuel his excesses. That was his fatal error in judgment."

Stunned by all this, Abby's mouth became a straight line as she voiced, "So you set him up to make it look like a suicide, while planting the revolver that you knew would implicate Oliver Dillman in my aunt Veronica's death?"

"Brilliant, wasn't it, if I say so myself." Freda laughed humorlessly. "Why not kill two birds with one stone, so to speak. I allowed Oliver to think he'd succeeded in getting the payoff, then followed him back to his car, where I shot him at point-blank range with the very same Colt Python .357 Magnum revolver I shot your aunt with, and strategically placed it on Oliver's lap. With him being seen as Veronica's killer, it let me off the hook. Except for the fact that you present a final loose end that could someday come back to haunt me for past sins. I can't allow that to happen, Abby."

She cringed in horror. "You'll never get away with this, Freda."

"I've heard that before." The mayor chuckled nastily. "Something tells me I will get away with it—again." She pointed the gun's muzzle at Abby's face. "Why don't we take a little walk?"

"To where?" Abby's eyes narrowed with suspicion.

"Not far," she claimed. "Out in the woods, where you'll have a fighting chance to escape unharmed. If you do, then I'm toast." She laughed, waving the gun threateningly. "But I must warn you, Abby, I've become a pretty good markswoman with enough target practice over the years to know how to make it count when my mind is made up."

With her arms folded defiantly across her chest, as if to stop incoming bullets, Abby challenged her. "And what if I refuse to leave the cabin?"

"Then I'll simply shoot you in the face right here and now!" Freda asserted. "Don't test me." She tightened her grip on the firearm. "What's it going to be, Abby?"

As if she needed to think about it, Abby took only a moment before responding firmly, "I'll take my chances out in the woods."

"Thought you might." The mayor grinned crookedly. "Let's go."

Abby glanced around the cabin, looking for anything she might grab to hit her with. Though she spotted an item or two that might do the trick, with Freda laser-focused on her and brandishing a gun, Abby saw no benefit in making a courageous last-second stand. Only to come up short.

And in the process, lose any chance of surviving her aunt Veronica's killer in Freda Myerson, and having a life with Scott Lynley. Those were odds that Abby wasn't willing to take as she headed out of the cabin, with her whole world on the line.

Just as was the case with the mayor, who was once again playing this game of cold-blooded murder for keeps.

Chapter Nineteen

Scott was still trying to wrap his head around Oliver Dillman's long-winded but telling confession after his own death to being a party to Veronica Liu's murder, albeit after the fact. While pointing the finger squarely at his ex-lover Freda Neville, now Mayor Freda Myerson, as the real culprit in the death of Abby's aunt. Including being the one who was wearing the hooded bright red jacket instead of Dillman. Presumably, the unidentified left index fingerprint found on Veronica's Mercedes-Benz had no bearing on the case, per se, beyond clearing others along the way.

All things being equal, Scott had no reason not to believe the pre-deathbed confession of a man who chose to lay it all out on the line in the name of a blackmail payday. Only to pay the ultimate price with his life. If so, that was on him, as greed and opportunity often made for a bad combination. Especially when pitted against a cunning killer who was more than willing to take out anyone who stood in her way.

That included Abby, much to Scott's chagrin.

When he arrived at her cabin, having already called for backup, he spotted Abby's Subaru parked in the driveway. No sign of another vehicle that may have been driven by Freda Myerson. Not that he would have expected the mayor to show up with her own car. Much less an official vehicle with a driver. Still, Scott wondered if his instincts that she might have come after Abby were way off base. Especially since Myerson could not have known that Dillman had left a recorded video message in the event of his untimely death.

Once out of his SUV, Scott headed toward the cabin, when out of the corner of his eye, he spotted movement in the wooded area. Peering in that direction, he saw two figures. One was definitely Abby. The other was someone wearing a hoodie. That person appeared to be holding a gun and directing Abby to walk. Then, suddenly, Abby began to run, as if told to do so.

It didn't take putting two and two together for Scott to realize that the one holding the gun, presumably Freda Myerson, fully intended to shoot Abby in the back. Head. Or wherever. And then probably make an escape to a car waiting for her on the other side of the clearing. Whereupon she would resume her mayoral duties and get on with the life she had carved out for herself with her past buried for good.

Not happening, Scott determined at the thought of such an unwanted scenario. He whipped out his Glock pistol from the holster and took off. Then he heard a shot ring out. And another. His heart skipped a beat as he raced into the woods, praying that he wasn't too late to save the woman of his dreams and, hopefully, future wife and mother of their children.

Abby did not believe for a moment that she was capable of outrunning a bullet. Much less two, three or four fired by a maniacal mayor intent on covering her murderous tracks. But desperate times called for desperate measures. Or, in this instance, called upon her skills as a jogger and her awareness of the wooded area outside her log cabin to try to evade a sure destiny with death, were she to give in to it.

Before the first shot could even be fired, even with barely a head start, Abby had put into motion a plan to zigzag to the point of near exhaustion in confusing the shooter, while strategically using the dense black walnut and yellowwood trees as cover. It was apparently working as she heard one shot and then another, neither hitting the mark as Abby measured her breathing while managing to avoid becoming the fatal victim of a killer's target practice.

Then Abby heard the sound of a familiar voice say in a demanding tone, "FBI! Mayor Myerson, drop the weapon. Now! Or so help me, you won't make it out of the woods alive!" A moment later, a shot was fired away from Abby, followed by another shot, before she heard Scott say concisely, "I won't allow you to escape justice through suicide by cop."

Abby knew that this was in reference to those who try to compel law enforcement to use deadly force against them while shying away from self-inflicted death. Turning around, she could see Freda Myerson lying on the ground and Scott standing over her, kicking away the gun from the mayor's outstretched hand.

With it all seemingly happening in a blur, Abby found herself pivoting and racing back to the man she loved and her would-be killer. When she got there, she saw that Freda had been shot in the shoulder and was moaning in pain, but didn't appear as if she was at death's door.

Scott put away his gun and wrapped his arms around Abby, and asked her tenderly, "Are you hurt?"

"No. Guess today was my lucky day, sort of,"

she told him shakily. "The trees acted as great cover for flying bullets."

"Yeah, I can see that." He separated them and took out his cell phone, where he called 9-1-1 and reported the crime and Mayor Myerson's being shot.

Afterward, Abby gazed up at him curiously. "How did you know about Freda…and what she had planned for me?"

Scott sighed and answered, "Oliver Dillman left me a video message to be delivered by his attorney, should Dillman meet with foul play. In it, he incriminated the mayor as the one who actually shot your aunt in a jealous rage and roped him into helping to cover it up. Or be accused as participating in the murder. I texted you to warn you about her."

"I had my phone charging upstairs when Freda unexpectedly showed up at the cabin," Abby explained.

"Oh. Myerson was the one you saw wearing the red windbreaker that day," Scott informed her.

"I know," Abby uttered sadly, glaring at the mayor, who seemed to be drifting in and out of consciousness, no longer a threat. "Freda admitted it while practically gloating about coming after my aunt in her misguided vindictiveness over something that was never true.

The mayor also confessed to seeing me at the same time I saw her in the woods and had actually thought about finishing me off, as well, but chickened out. Thank goodness for that."

Scott gazed at her, asking in earnest, "What else did the mayor have to say?"

"That after Oliver Dillman tried to blackmail her, she tricked him into meeting her at Kolton Lake Park, where the mayor fatally shot him with the same Colt Python .357 Magnum revolver Freda shot Aunt Veronica with, and then planted the firearm on him to make it seem as though he had killed himself." Abby took a breath and wrung her hands as they trembled. "The entire thing is almost too much to believe."

"Yeah, it is." Scott pulled her to him. "But it's over now, Abby. Neither Freda Myerson nor Oliver Dillman, who also confessed to attacking you at the park to get me to shut down the investigation so he could sponge the mayor for money unabated, can ever hurt you again. And at least for the mayor, she will pay for what she did to your aunt Veronica Liu."

"I'm happy to know that," Abby stated, her voice breaking. "It's all I ever wanted." Or, at least, she'd thought it was. Up until Scott had entered her life. She stood on her toes and kissed him. "Now I want something more."

"So do I." He grinned charmingly. "So much more."

"How much is that?" she challenged him.

"Enough to make you my wife," Scott said boldly.

She raised her brows playfully. "Oh, really?"

"Yeah, if you'll have me," he reiterated. "I know the timing sucks, with us fresh off the cold case and still needing to deal with the mayor over there, but I'm in love with you, Abby, and for that, there's no time like the present to ask you to marry me and have a great life, including bringing children into the world as an extension of us." He drew a breath. "So, what do you say?"

Between rapid beats of her heart, Abby replied affectionately, "I say that if you hadn't asked me to marry you, I would have asked you to marry me. I've fallen in love with you, too, Scott, and yes, I'd love to become your wife and mother of our future children."

"Then consider both a done deal," he declared, "with a few steps along the way to bring it to fruition. Starting with this…" He planted a solid kiss on her mouth.

Abby parted her lips ever so slightly as she was all in with the kiss. She managed to put aside for the moment that they were standing in a forested crime scene, with her aunt Veronica's killer probably taking it all in with envy while facing a bleak future of her own making.

Unlocking their lips, Abby tasted the sweet kiss and told Scott devotedly, "That is a good start to a lifetime of happiness."

The huge grin on his handsome face told her he didn't disagree one bit.

Epilogue

Six months later, Scott sat in a Louisville federal courthouse, where the trial was underway for Freda Myerson. The former Kolton Lake mayor had been charged with the murders of Veronica Liu and Oliver Dillman, and the attempted murder of Abby Zhang Lynley, a witness aiding an FBI cold case investigation. Having recovered from a bullet wound to the shoulder and recently served with divorce papers by her husband, Pierce Myerson, the defendant looked less than confident in her chances of acquittal.

With good reason, Scott believed as he contemplated the strong case against Myerson on all charges. In the murder of Veronica Liu, there was Dillman's taped indictment of his former lover. The Colt Python .357 Magnum revolver she'd used in the homicide was traced through the ATF's NIBIN to an imprisoned drug dealer named Pablo Rodrigues, who was prepared to testify to selling the handgun to Freda Neville more than twenty years ago. Moreover, the former exotic dancer Katlyn Johansson was also a scheduled prosecution witness in claiming to have seen Neville with Oliver Dillman at the Tygers Club the night before Veronica Liu had been gunned down, establishing a link between the couple.

Scott glanced at US District Judge Craig Redcorn. In his early sixties, the Shawnee husband, father and grandfather had fine silver hair and sable eyes behind round glasses. The no-nonsense judge was always in control of his courtroom. Musing about the brazen murder of Oliver Dillman that Myerson was accused of, Scott considered the smoking gun, so to speak, or murder weapon that could be traced back to her. Then, there was the Kolton Lake Park surveillance video that showed a blue Nissan Murano, registered to the former mayor as her private vehicle, leaving the park near the remote area where Dillman had been found shot to death in his car. A reasonable inference could be made that the two former lovers had met one final time before only one walked away, according to Myerson's confession to Abby.

Scott's thoughts were interrupted by a text message on his cell phone. It came from his cousin Gavin Lynley, who was a special agent for the Mississippi Department of Corrections

Investigation Division's Special Operations and Major Crimes Units. Gavin wanted to pass along some good vibes in the successful prosecution of the object of Scott's cold case investigation, Freda Myerson.

Scott grinned in appreciation, knowing that his cousin, close to all the Lynley siblings, always had his back. And vice versa. He thought about Abby's impending testimony, as well as his own, against Myerson, who'd tried to shoot Abby to death in broad daylight. And might have succeeded, had Abby not been so quick and clever enough to zigzag just enough to throw her would-be killer off balance, while also using the trees themselves to Abby's advantage. This clear case of attempted murder was, to Scott, perhaps the strongest of the pretty persuasive cases against the former mayor. But no matter what happened, he intended to always be there in support of his wife and mother of their unborn child.

As if on cue, Scott turned as the prosecution called its star witness to take the stand. Abby Zhang Lynley. He watched as she entered the courtroom. She was as gorgeous as ever in a stylish chambray shawl-collar skirt suit and black pumps. Her long hair was worn in a cute twisted updo. They made eye contact and he mouthed silently to her to get up there and do what she needed to help put her aunt Veronica's killer away.

Scott sat back and took a breath while awaiting Abby's chance to finally exorcise the demons that Freda Myerson had brought upon her life.

ABBY GLANCED AT Scott and smiled as she sat in the witness box, representing them both as a witness for the prosecution. Not just as professional colleagues for the FBI. But as husband and wife. And, now two months pregnant, a mother-to-be to their first child, for which she couldn't be more elated. Being with the man she loved, and about to start a family, was all Abby could have asked for. Well, if all had been right with the world, she would have also asked that her parents and Aunt Veronica, as well as Scott's parents, could have been there to see them tie the knot. Since that hadn't been possible, Abby intended to count her blessings as they were.

That included the forces that fell into place to bring her to this moment in time in which she was being called upon to make sure that the former Freda Neville paid dearly for the bad things she had chosen to do against anyone who got in her way.

Abby had the expected butterflies in testifying against a woman who had pretended to be contrite in the death of her aunt Veronica Liu but in fact felt gleeful that her aunt was dead by Freda's own hand. Turned out that the invitation to become part of the ex-mayor's Crime Victims Advisory Board had been nothing more than a smoke screen for Freda to hide behind while keeping a close eye on Abby, should she get too close to the truth.

You won't get away with what you've done, a voice in Abby's head told Freda in earnest as she gazed at the defendant, who shot her back a cold stare. *There's nowhere else for you to hide from your terrible choices as a human being, Freda*, she thought candidly.

Abby regarded Naomi Bloom, the assistant US attorney, who was just a few years older than her, tall and slender, with long straight hair in a blunt cut and parted neatly in the middle. Naomi flashed her small blue eyes at Abby and said softly, "You'll do fine."

Abby nodded with that show of confidence, and took a breath before being asked a few identification-related and lead-up questions. Then she was asked about her memories of the day her aunt Veronica was murdered. Almost feeling as though she was under hypnosis again, Abby was drawn back to when she was twelve years old in recounting the moment she'd stepped off the school bus and headed the block away to her aunt's cabin. Seeing her inside the car, Abby confessed that her first thought had been that her aunt Veronica had simply fallen asleep, with her often working long hours.

It was only when she'd seen her up close, Abby testified, that she'd realized something was very wrong. Her aunt had not been moving and was bloodied. Abby had sensed that she was no longer alive.

Sighing deeply, Abby took a moment when Naomi readdressed her to talk about the person Abby had seen running off in the woods. Though she admitted to never getting a clear look at the killer's face, it was the bright red hooded windbreaker the suspect was wearing that stood out, seared into Abby's memory. She knew that Jeanne Singletary would testify later about a jacket matching this description that belonged to Oliver Dillman, Freda Myerson's ex-boyfriend, which Abby testified that Freda admitted to wearing the day she'd shot to death Veronica Liu.

By the time the testimony moved forward to the present and Freda's attempt to murder her as an unaware witness to a violent crime more than two decades ago, Abby had warmed up and was more than ready to take it to the disgraced former mayor of Kolton Lake.

Naomi Bloom positioned herself strategically on one side of the witness box as she asked Abby coolly, "Mrs. Lynley, why don't you walk us through that day six months ago, when you received a most unexpected visit from Mayor Freda Myerson…"

Abby looked Freda squarely in the eye and said succinctly, "I can do that." She proceeded to describe every moment of the encounter, in which Abby had seen her life flash before her eyes, as Freda had confessed to perpetrating two murders and her full intention to commit a third, with Abby the victim.

"With my life on the line," Abby recalled, "I honestly feared that Freda Myerson would succeed in her deadly plans for me, with the former mayor bragging about her marksmanship. At that point, all I could do was run for my life in the woods and hope for the best." She drew a breath and gazed first at her diamond contour wedding ring in 14k rose gold with round diamonds, then at her husband, Scott, who favored her with his handsome crooked grin. "Had Agent Scott Lynley not arrived when he did and stopped Freda in her tracks, I'm certain I wouldn't be sitting in this courtroom now. And the ex-mayor might still have her old job. But things found a way to work out when they least seemed possible."

The assistant US attorney seemed more than satisfied with the testimony and finished up with a few more pointed questions and follow-ups. Abby then had to endure a withering cross-examination from the defense, for which she didn't falter, before she was excused. She left the witness box, feeling confident that she had given it her all in making the case against the defendant, before Abby was joined by Scott and they walked out of the courtroom, hand in hand.

"You knocked it out of the park," he told her cheerfully.

"Really?" Abby met his penetrating eyes. "You think so?"

"Of course." Scott smiled. "You were ready for this and delivered. Freda Myerson is toast and will pay for it."

"I'm glad to hear you say that." She stood on her tiptoes, cupped his cheeks and kissed him on the mouth. "Let's go home, darling," Abby said of their ranch, with her having sold the log cabin and, with it, finally putting to rest many unsettling memories.

He kissed her this time and, wrapping his arm around her waist, agreed endearingly. "Yeah, let's, sweetheart."

Two weeks later, the trial ended with closing arguments. After less than three hours of deliberation, the jury came back with a guilty verdict on all counts. US District Judge Craig Redcorn imposed the maximum sentence of life in federal prison for Freda Myerson.

Overjoyed with the news, Abby felt at peace that the long arm of the law had finally caught up with Freda Myerson in meting out overdue justice for the killing of her aunt Veronica Liu.

Abby knew that she would have welcomed Scott with open arms as part of the family had her aunt lived, and took solace in this as she rode leisurely alongside her husband on their horses along the trail, while wearing her own cowgirl hat and feeling like she truly belonged there.

* * * * *

INTRIGUE

Seek thrills. Solve crimes. Justice served.

Available Next Month

Conard County: Murderous Intent Rachel Lee
Peril In Piney Woods Debra Webb

....

Smoky Mountains Graveyard Lena Diaz
K-9 Missing Person Cassie Miles

....

Innocent Witness Julie Anne Lindsey
Shadow Survivors Julie Miller

Larger Print

Keep reading for an excerpt of a new title
from the Intrigue series,
BIG SKY DECEPTION by B.J. Daniels

Chapter One

Clay Wheaton flinched as he heard the heavy tread of footfalls ascending the fire escape stairs of the old Fortune Creek Hotel. His visitor moved slowly, purposefully, the climb to the fourth and top floor sounding like a death march.

His killer was coming.

He had no idea who he would come face-to-face with when he opened the door in a few minutes. But this had been a long time coming. Though it wasn't something a man looked forward to even at his advanced age.

He glanced over at Rowdy lying lifeless on the bed where he'd left him earlier. The sight of his lifelong companion nearly broke his heart. He rose and went to him, his hand moving almost of its own accord to slip into the back under the Western outfit for the controls.

Instantly, Rowdy came to life. His animated eyes flew open, his head turned, his mouth gaping as he looked around. "We could make a run for it," Rowdy said in the cowboy voice it had taken years to perfect. "It wouldn't be the first time we've had to vamoose. You do the running part. I'll do the singing part."

The dummy broke into an old Western classic and quickly stopped. "Or maybe not," Clay said as the lumbering footfalls ended at the top of the stairs and the exit door creaked open.

"Sorry, my old friend," Clay said in his own voice. "You need to go into your case. You don't want to see this."

"No," Rowdy cried. "We go down together like an old horse who can't quite make it home in a blizzard with his faithful rider. This can't be the end of the trail for us."

The footsteps stopped outside his hotel room door, followed swiftly by a single knock. "Sorry," Clay whispered, his voice breaking as he removed his hand, folded the dummy in half and lowered him gently into the special case with Rowdy's name and brand on it.

Rowdy the Rodeo Cowboy. The two of them had traveled the world, singing and joking, and sharing years and years together. Rowdy had become his best friend, his entire life after leaving too many burning bridges behind them. "Sorry, old friend," he whispered unable to look into Rowdy's carved wooden face, the paint faded, but the eyes still bright and lifelike. He closed the case with trembling fingers.

This knock was much louder. He heard the door handle rattle. He'd been running for years, but now his reckoning was at hand. He pushed the case under the bed, straightened the bed cover over it and went to open the door.

Behind him he would have sworn he heard Rowdy moving in his case as if trying to get out, as if trying to save him. Old hotels and the noises they made? Or just his imagination?

Too late for regrets, he opened the door to his killer.

"MOLLY LOCKHART?" The voice on the phone was male, ringing with authority.

"Yes?" she said distractedly as she pulled her keyboard toward her, unconsciously lining it up with the edge of her desk as she continued to type. She had a report due before the meeting today at Henson and Powers, the financial institution where she worked as an analyst. She wouldn't have taken the call, but her assistant had said the caller was a lawman, the matter urgent, and had put it through.

"My name's Sheriff Brandt Parker from Fortune Creek, Montana. I found your name as the person to call. Do you know Clay Wheaton?"

Her fingers froze over the keys. "I'm sorry, what did you say? Just the last part please." She really didn't have time for this—whatever it was.

"Your name was found in the man's hotel room as the person to call."

"The person to call about what?"

The sheriff cleared his throat. "Do you know Clay Wheaton?"

"Yes." She said it with just enough vacillation that she heard the lawman cough. "He's my...father."

"Oh, I'm so sorry. I'm afraid I have bad news. Mr. Wheaton is dead." Another pause, then, "He's been murdered."

"Murdered?" she repeated. She'd known that she'd be getting a call one day that he had died. Given her father's age it was inevitable. He was close to sixty-five. But *murdered*? She couldn't imagine why anyone would want to murder him unless they'd seen his act.

"I hate to give you this kind of news over the phone," the sheriff said. "Is there someone there with you?"

"I'm fine, Sheriff," she said, realizing it was true. Her father had made his choice years ago when he'd left her and her mother to travel the world with—quite literally— a dummy. There was only one thing she wanted to know. "Where is Rowdy?"

The lawman sounded taken aback. "I beg your pardon?"

"My father's dummy. You do know Clay Wheaton is... was a ventriloquist, right?"

"Yes, his dummy. It wasn't found in his hotel room. I'm afraid it's missing."

"Missing?" She sighed heavily. "What did you say your name was again?"

"Sheriff Brandt Parker."

"And you are where?"

"Fortune Creek, Montana. I'm going to need to know who else I should notify."

"There is no one else. Just find Rowdy. I'm on my way there."

BRANDT HUNG UP and looked at the dispatcher. The sixty-something Helen Graves was looking at him, one eyebrow tilted at the ceiling in question. "Okay," he said. "That was the strangest reaction I've ever had when telling someone that their father's been murdered."

"Maybe she's in shock."

"I don't think so. She wants me to find the dummy—not the killer—but the *dummy*."

"Why?"

"I have no idea, but she's on her way here. I'll try the other number Clay Wheaton left." The deceased had left only two names and numbers on hotel stationery atop the bureau next to his bed with a note that said, *In case of emergency.* He put through the call, which turned out to be an insurance agency. "I'm calling for Georgia Eden."

"I'll connect you to the claims department."

"Georgia Eden," a young woman answered cheerfully with a slight southern accent.

Brandt introduced himself. "I'm calling on behalf of Clay Wheaton."

"What does he want now?" she asked impatiently.

"Are you a relative of his?"

"Good heavens, no. He's my client. What is this about? You said you're a sheriff? Is he in some kind of trouble?"

"He was murdered."

"Murdered?" He heard her sit up in her squeaky chair, her tone suddenly worried. "Where's Rowdy?"

What was it with this dummy? "I…don't know."

"Rowdy would have been with him. Clay never let him out of his sight. He took Rowdy everywhere with him. I doubt he went to the toilet without him. Are you telling me Rowdy is missing?"

Brandt ran a hand down over his face. He had to ask. "What is it with this dummy?"

"I beg your pardon?"

"I thought you might be more interested in your client's murder than his…doll."

Her words came out like thrown bricks. "That…*doll* as you call it, is insured for a very large amount of money."

"You're kidding."

"I would not kid about something like that since I'm the one who wrote the policy," Georgia said. "Where are you calling from?" He told her. "This could cost me more than my job if Rowdy isn't found. I'll be on the next plane."

"We don't have an airport," he said quickly.

She groaned. "Where is Fortune Creek, Montana?"

"In the middle of nowhere, actually at the end of a road in the mountains at the most northwest corner of the state," he said. "The closest airport is Kalispell. You'd have to rent a car from there."

"Great."

"If there is anything else I can do—"

"Just find that dummy."

"You mean that doll."

"Yes," she said sarcastically. "Find Rowdy, *please.* Otherwise…I'm dead."

Brandt hung up, shaking his head as he stood and reached for his Stetson. "Helen, if anyone comes looking for me, I'll be over at the hotel looking for a ventriloquist's dummy." She frowned in confusion. "Apparently, that's all anyone cares about. Meanwhile, I have a murder to solve."

As he headed out the door for the walk across the street to the hotel, he couldn't help being disturbed by the reactions he'd gotten to Clay Wheaton's death. He thought about the note the dead man had left and the only two numbers on it.

Had he suspected he might be murdered? Or traveling alone—except for his dummy—had he always left such a note just in case? After all, at sixty-two, he was no spring chicken, his grandmother would have said.

Whatever the victim's thinking, how was it that both women had cared more about the dummy than the man behind it?

Maybe worse, both women were headed this way.